Also by Mercedes Ron

My Fault
Your Fault
Our Fault

MY FAULT

MERCEDES RON

Bloom *books*

Originally published as *Culpables: Culpa mía*, © Mercedes Ron,
2017. Translated from Spanish by Adrian Nathan West.

Published by Bloom Books, an imprint of Sourcebooks
P.O. Box 4410, Naperville, Illinois 60567-4410
(630) 961-3900
sourcebooks.com

Originally published as *Culpables: Culpa mía* in 2017 in Spain by Montena Random
House Mondadori, an imprint of Penguin Random House Grupo Editorial.

Cataloging-in-Publication data is on file with the Library of Congress.

Printed and bound in the United States of America.
KP 10 9 8 7 6 5 4 3 2

To my mother, thank you for being my friend,
my confidante, everything I've ever needed
and more. Thank you for making sure
I always had a book in my hands.

PROLOGUE

"Leave me alone!" she said, trying to get around me and through the door. I grabbed her by the arms and forced her to look at me.

"You want to tell me what the hell's going on with you?" I asked, furious.

She looked back, and I could see her eyes were hiding something dark, yet she smiled at me joylessly.

"This is your world, Nicholas," she replied calmly. "I'm living your life, hanging out with your friends, and feeling like I don't have a care in the world. That's how you are, and that's how I'm supposed to be, too," she said and stepped back, pulling away from me.

I couldn't believe what I was hearing.

"You're out of control," I hissed at her. I didn't like who the girl I was in love with was turning into. But when I thought about it, what she was doing and *how* she was doing it were the same things I had done before I met her. I was the one who got her into all this. It was my fault. It was my fault she was destroying herself.

In a way, we'd switched roles. She had shown up and dragged me out of the black hole I'd fallen into, but in doing so, she'd wound up taking my place.

1

Noah

WHILE I ROLLED THE WINDOW OF MY MOTHER'S CAR UP AND down, I couldn't stop thinking what the next hellish year had in store for me. I couldn't stop asking myself how we'd ended up like this, leaving our home to cross the country on our way to California. Three months had passed since I'd gotten the terrible news that would change my life forever, the same news that would make me want to cry at night, that would make me rant and rave like I was eleven instead of seventeen.

But what could I do? I wasn't an adult. I had eleven months, three weeks, and two days to go before I turned eighteen and could go away to college, far away from a mother who only thought about herself, far from these strangers I'd end up living with, because from now on I would have to share my life with two people I knew nothing about—two men, to make matters worse.

"Can you stop doing that? You're getting on my nerves," my mother said as she put the keys in the ignition and started the car.

"Lots of things you do get on my nerves, and I have to put up and shut up," I hissed back. The loud sigh I heard in reply was so routine, it didn't even surprise me.

How could she make me do this? Didn't she even care about my feelings? *Of course I do*, she'd told me as we were leaving my beloved hometown. Six years had passed since my parents split—and nothing about their divorce had been conventional, let alone amicable. It had been incredibly traumatic, but in the end, I'd gotten over it…or, at least, I was trying to.

It was hard for me to adapt to change; I was terrified of strangers. I'm not timid, but I'm reserved about my private life, and having to share twenty-four hours of every day with two people I barely knew made me so anxious, I wanted to get out of the car and throw up.

"I still can't understand why you won't let me stay," I said, trying to convince her one last time. "I'm not a little girl. I know how to take care of myself. Plus, I'll be in college next year, and I'll be living on my own in another country then. It's basically the same thing," I argued, trying to get her to see the light and knowing that everything I was saying was true.

"I'm not going to miss out on your last year in high school. I want to enjoy my daughter before she goes away to study. I told you a thousand times, Noah—you're my child, I want you to be part of this new family. For God's sake! You really think I'm going to let you go that far away from me without a single adult?" she answered, keeping her eyes on the road and gesturing with her right hand.

My mother didn't understand how hard this was for me. She was starting a new life with a new husband she supposedly loved. But what about me?

"You don't get it, Mom. Did you never stop to think that this is my last year of high school? That all my friends are here, my boyfriend, my job, my team? My whole life!" I shouted, trying to hold back tears. The situation was getting the best of me, that much was clear. I never, and I mean *never,* cried in front of anyone.

Crying was for weaklings, people who can't control their feelings. I was someone who'd cried so much in the course of my life that I'd decided never to shed another tear.

Those thoughts reminded me of when all the madness began. I still regretted not going with my mother on that damn cruise to Fiji. Because it was there, on a boat in the middle of the South Pacific, that she'd met the incredible, enigmatic William Leister.

If I could go back in time, I wouldn't hesitate a second to tell my mother yes when she showed up in the middle of April with two tickets so we could go on vacation together. They'd been a present from her best friend, Alicia. The poor thing had broken her right leg, an arm, and two ribs in a car accident. Obviously, she and her husband couldn't go off to the islands, so she gave the trip to my mom. But come on now—mid-April? I was in the middle of exams, and the volleyball team had back-to-back games. My team had just climbed from second place to first, and that hadn't happened as long as I could remember. It was one of the greatest joys of my life. Now, though, seeing the consequences of staying home, I'd happily give back my trophy, leave the team, and fail English Lit and Spanish just to keep that wedding from ever happening.

Getting married on a ship? My mother was out of her mind! And going and doing it without telling me a single word! I found out when she got back, and she said it all blithely, like marrying a millionaire in the middle of the ocean was the most normal thing in the world. The whole situation was surreal, and now she wanted to move to a mansion in California, in the United States. It wasn't even my country! I had been born in Canada, even if my mom was from Texas and my dad from Colorado. I didn't want to leave. It was everything I knew.

"Now, you have to realize I want what's best for you," my mother said, bringing me back to reality. "You know what I've been through, what *we've* been through. And I've finally found a good man who loves and respects me. I haven't felt this happy in a long time. I need him, and I know you'll come to love him. And he can offer you a future we could never have dreamed of before. You can go to any college you like, Noah."

"But I don't want to go to some fancy college, Mom, and I don't want a stranger paying for it," I replied, feeling a shiver as I thought how, at the end of the month, I'd be starting at a new fancy high school full of little rich kids.

"He's not a stranger, he's my husband, and you better get used to the idea," she added cuttingly.

"I'm never going to get used to the idea," I said, looking away from her face to the road.

My mother sighed again, and I wished the conversation would just end—I didn't want to go on talking.

"I get that you're going to miss Dan and all your friends, Noah, but look on the bright side—you're going to have a brother!" she exclaimed.

I turned to her with a weary look.

"Please don't try to sell this like something it's not."

"You're going to love him, though. Nick is a sweetheart," she told me, smiling as she gazed down the highway. "He's mature, responsible, and he's probably dying to introduce you to all his pals. Every time I've been there and he's around, he's stayed in his room studying or reading a book. You might even have the same tastes."

"Yeah, right. I'm sure he's crazy about Jane Austen." I rolled my eyes. "How old is he again?" I knew, of course; all my mother had talked about for months was him and Will. It was ironic that for some reason Nick had never managed to find a hole in his schedule to introduce himself to me. Moving in with a new family before I'd even met all the members of it just kind of summed up how crazy this all was.

"He's a little older than you, but you're more mature than most girls your age. You'll get along great."

Now she was kissing up to me. *Mature.* I still wasn't sure whether that word defined me, and I doubted a guy who was nearly twenty-two would really feel like showing me the city or letting me meet his friends. If I even wanted to, which was a whole different question.

"We're here," my mother announced.

I looked at the tall palm trees and the streets between the monumental mansions. Each house took up at least half a block. Some were English or Victorian style; lots of others were modern with glass walls and huge yards. I started to get scared as we continued up the road and the houses got bigger and bigger.

At last we reached a set of immense gates, ten feet high, and when my mother pulled a small device out of the glove box and pushed the button, they started to open. She put the car back in gear, and we went down a hill surrounded by gardens and tall pines that smelled pleasantly of summer and sea.

"The house isn't as high up as the others in the development, which means we have the best views of the beach," she remarked with a big smile. I looked over at her, and it was as if I didn't even know her. Did she not realize what was surrounding us? Could she not see that it was all just too much?

I didn't have time to formulate the other questions I had aloud because we reached the house and the only thing I could think to say was "Oh my God!"

It was white with a sand-colored roof way up high. It had three stories at least, but it was hard to tell with all those balconies, windows, and everything else. In front of us was an impressive porch with the lights on—it was after seven—and that gave the place a fairy-tale aspect. The sun would go down soon, and the sky was filled with colors that marked a sharp contrast to the immaculate appearance of the place.

My mother turned off her motor after pulling around the fountain and parking in front of the steps that led to the main entrance. My first impression on getting out was that we'd come to the most luxurious hotel in all of California. But it wasn't a hotel, it was a house—a home, supposedly, or at least that's what my mother wanted me to believe.

William Leister appeared in the doorway just as I shut the door behind me. Behind him were three men in penguin suits.

My mother's new husband wasn't dressed as he had been on the few occasions when I'd agreed to be in the same room with him. Instead of a suit or a name-brand vest, he was wearing white shorts, a lightblue polo shirt, and sandals. His dark hair was tousled instead of combed back. I had to admit, I got what my mother saw in him—he was very handsome. He was tall, a good deal taller than my mother, and had maintained himself well. His face was harmonious, though the signs of age were evident on it—the crow's feet, the lines across his forehead—and a few gray hairs among the black gave him an alluring, mature air.

My mother ran over to him like a schoolgirl and hugged him. I took my time, walking around to the trunk to get my things.

Gloved hands appeared from nowhere, and I leapt back.

"I will take your things, Miss," one of the men in the penguin suits said.

"I can do it on my own, thanks," I responded, feeling very uncomfortable.

The man looked at me as if I were out of my mind.

"Let Martin help you, Noah," I heard William Leister say behind my back.

Grudgingly, I released my suitcase.

"I'm so happy to see you," my mother's husband continued, smiling affectionately. Next to him, my mother motioned for me to behave, smile, do something.

"I can't say the same," I responded, stretching out a hand for him to shake. I knew what I'd just done was terrible manners, but in that moment, I felt like telling the truth.

I wanted to make completely clear what my position was concerning this change in our lives.

William didn't seem offended. He held my hand longer than necessary, and I felt strange.

"I know this is a very abrupt change in your life, Noah, but I want you to feel at home, to enjoy what I have to offer you, and especially for you to accept me as part of your family...eventually." He added this last part when he noticed my incredulity. From his side, my mother's blue eyes shot arrows at me.

All I could do was nod and step back so he'd let go of my hand. I didn't feel comfortable with those shows of intimacy, especially from someone I hardly knew. My mother had gotten married—great for her. That didn't make that man anyone to me—not a father, not a stepfather, not anything like that. I already had a dad, and he'd been enough for one lifetime.

"How about I show you around the house?" he proposed with a big smile, as far as possible from my coldness and bad mood.

"Come on, Noah," my mother said, taking my arm and giving me no choice but to walk beside her.

All the lights were on inside, so I didn't miss a single detail of this mansion that would have been too big for a family of twenty, let alone four. The ceilings were high, with exposed wood beams and big windows opening to the outside. A huge stairway in the middle of an immense room split in two on the upper floor. My mother and her husband took me all through the mansion, from the living room and the kitchen with its oversize island—which I knew my mother would be crazy about—to the gym, the heated pool, party rooms, and a big library that made an impression on me.

"Your mother told me you love to read and write," William said, awakening me from my stupor.

"Same as tons of other people," I replied bitterly. I didn't like him being so friendly with me. I didn't like him talking to me at all, to tell the truth.

"Noah," my mother said, and looked me dead in the eyes. I knew she was having a tough time, but she'd deal. I was going to have a whole bad year, and there was nothing I could do about it.

William didn't seem to notice our silent exchange and went on smiling as if nothing was happening.

I was frustrated and uncomfortable. This was too much—too different, too extravagant. I didn't know if I could ever get used to living in a place like this.

All at once, I needed to be alone; I needed time to assimilate everything.

"I'm tired. Can I see my room?" I asked in a less strident tone.

"Of course. On the left wing of the second floor is where you and Nicholas have your rooms. You can have anyone you want over, Nick won't mind. Plus you two will be sharing the game room from now on."

The game room? Seriously? I smiled as best I could to keep from thinking about how from now on I was going to have to live with William's son. All I knew about him was what my mother had told me—that he was twenty-one, was studying at the University of California, and was an appalling prep. I mean, I made up that last part, but it had to be true.

As we climbed the stairs, all I could think about was how from now on, I'd have two men I didn't know under the same roof. It had been six years since a man—my father—was in my house. I'd gotten used to just women, just the two of us. My life had never been a bed of roses, especially during my first eleven years of life. The problems with my father had scarred me as well as my mother.

Once Dad was gone, Mom and I got by as best we could, managing to live like two regular everyday people, and as I grew older, my mother turned into one of my best friends. She gave me the freedom I wanted, and that was because she trusted me and I trusted her...or at least I did until she decided to throw our lives overboard.

"Here's your room," my mother said, standing in front of a dark door.

I looked at her and then at William. They seemed to be expecting something.

"Can I go in?" I asked sarcastically when they didn't step aside.

"This room is my special present to you, Noah," my mother said, her eyes shining with anticipation.

I looked at her warily, and when she stood back, I opened the door carefully, afraid of what I might find.

The first thing I noticed was the delicate scent of daisies and the sea. Then my eyes landed on the wall across from the door. It was made entirely of glass. The views were so spectacular, I was speechless. The whole ocean was visible from where I stood; the house must have been on top of a cliff because I could only see water from where I stood. Water, and the picture-perfect sun, which was in the middle of setting. It was incredible.

"Oh my God!" I repeated. That was my new favorite phrase. My eyes now roved the rest of the room—it was huge. On the left-hand wall was a canopy bed with a big pile of white cushions that coordinated with the soft blue of the walls. The furniture was white and blue, too, and included a desk with a gigantic Mac, a beautiful sofa, a changing table with a mirror, and a big shelf with all my books. Those colors and that stunning view were the most beautiful things I'd ever seen.

I was overwhelmed. Was all this for me?

"You like?" my mother said from behind me.

"It's incredible. Thank you," I answered, feeling grateful but at the same time uncomfortable. I didn't want them buying me things like these. I didn't need them.

"I spent two weeks working with a professional decorator. I wanted you to have everything you've ever wanted and I've never been able to give you." I could tell she was moved. As I looked at her, I knew I couldn't complain. A room like this is every teenager's dream and every mother's too.

I walked over and hugged her. It had been three months since I'd done that or even touched her at all, and I was sure she needed it.

"Thanks, Noah," she said in my ear, so only I could hear. "I swear I'll do everything in my power to make both of us happy."

"We will be, Mom," I told her, but I knew it wasn't in my hands.

My mother let me go, wiped off one of the tears that had slipped down her cheek, and walked back to her new husband.

"We'll leave you to settle in," William said kindly.

I nodded without thanking him. Nothing in that room represented any effort whatsoever from him. It was money, nothing else.

I closed the door and noticed there wasn't a lock. The floor was wood, covered with a white rug so thick you could use it as a mattress. The bathroom was as big as my old bedroom and had a massaging shower, a bathtub, and two sinks. I walked over to the window and looked outside. Below me I could see the backyard, the humongous pool, and the gardens with their flowers and palm trees.

I left the bathroom and noticed the empty doorframe in the bathroom wall. My God...

Crossing the room, I walked into what supposedly was the

dream of any woman, girl, or teenager: the walk-in closet. Not an empty walk-in closet, but one full of clothing waiting to be worn. I exhaled a breath I'd been holding in for a long time and began to look through all the unbelievable outfits. Everything was name-brand with the tags still on, and just a quick glance was enough to get a sense of how much they'd spent. My mother—or whoever had convinced her to blow all that money—was crazy.

I couldn't shake that uneasy feeling that nothing was real, that soon I would wake up and I'd be back in my old room with my single bed and the same clothes as always. And worst of all, that was what I wanted with all my heart because this wasn't my life, it wasn't what I wanted. I wanted to go back home. I felt queasy, anxious. I fell to the floor, resting my head between my knees and inhaling and exhaling as many times as I needed until the urge to cry finally passed.

As if she were reading my mind, my friend Beth sent me a text just then.

You make it in OK? I already miss you.

I smiled at the screen and sent her a photo from my dressing table. Right away I got back five emojis with their mouths gaping open.

I hate you. You know that, right?

I laughed and replied:

If it was up to me, I'd give it all to you. Honestly I'd give anything to be home with everyone, at Dan's place watching a movie or just hanging out on that gross couch in your bedroom.

Don't be so negative. You're rich now! Fucking enjoy it!

But I wasn't rich. William was.

I left my phone on the floor and opened my suitcases, taking out some shorts and a T-shirt. I didn't want to change how I was, and there was no way I was going to start wearing name-brand polos.

I got into the shower to wash off all the grime and discomfort from that long trip. I was happy not to be one of those girls who had to do much for her hair to look good. Fortunately, I'd inherited my mother's wavy hair, and as soon as I dried it, I was good to go. I dressed in the clothes I'd picked out and decided to walk around the house and find something to eat.

It was weird, doing it by myself. I felt like an intruder. It would take me a long time to get used to living here, to the luxury, the immensity of the place. In my old apartment, you just had to speak a little louder than normal to get someone to hear you, no matter what room they were in. Here, you could forget that.

I walked toward the kitchen, praying I wouldn't get lost. I was dying of hunger. My body desperately needed junk food.

Unfortunately, when I turned the corner, I realized I wasn't alone.

Someone was digging through the fridge. All I could see of him was his dark hair. Just as I was about to say something, a deafening bark made me shriek like a little girl.

I turned just as the head of black hair emerged from behind the refrigerator door to see who was causing such a racket.

But he wasn't what had frightened me. Next to the island in the kitchen was a black dog. Beautiful, but with a look in its eyes as if it wanted to eat me one morsel at a time. It was a Labrador, I thought, but I couldn't say. My eyes went from the dog to the boy standing beside it.

I looked with curiosity but also with surprise at who could only be William's son, Nicholas Leister. The first thing that came into my head when I saw him was *Look at those eyes!* They were sky-blue, bright as the walls of my room, a complete contrast to his raven hair, which was unkempt and damp with sweat. He must have just worked out because he had on leggings and a baggy muscle shirt. My God, he was handsome, I had to admit that, but I didn't let what I was thinking distract me from who was in front of me: my new brother, the person I'd have to live with for a year, a year that I sensed would be outright torture. And his dog went on growling at me as if it could guess at my thoughts.

"You're Nicholas, right?" I asked, trying to control my fear of that vicious animal that wouldn't stop growling. I was surprised and angry at the way he looked over at his pet and smiled.

"The one and only," he said and then looked back at me. "You must be the daughter of my father's new wife." I couldn't believe he would say it so coldly.

He rolled his eyes. "So your name was…?" I couldn't help feeling shocked as he asked that question.

He didn't know my name? Our parents were married, my mother and I had moved, and he didn't even know what to call me?

2

Nick

"NOAH," SHE REPLIED CONTEMPTUOUSLY. "MY NAME'S NOAH."

It was funny how she scowled at me. My new stepsister seemed offended I didn't give a shit what her and her mother's names were, but I had to admit that at least I remembered her mother's. How couldn't I? The last three weeks, she'd spent more time in my house than I had. Raffaella Morgan was now a part of my life, and to make matters worse, she'd brought company.

"Isn't that a dude's name?" I asked, knowing it would bother her. "No offense, obviously," I added when I saw her honey-colored eyes open with surprise.

"It's a girl's name, too," she answered a second later. I watched her look at me and then at Thor, my dog, and I couldn't help laughing. "Probably your limited vocabulary doesn't include the word *unisex*." Thor kept growling and baring his teeth. It wasn't his fault; we'd trained him not to trust strangers. With one word from me, he'd turn back into the sweet dog he always was...but it was too fun seeing the look of fear on my new stepsister's face.

"Don't worry about my vocabulary, it's pretty extensive," I replied, closing the fridge and turning to face her, for real this time. "There's one word I know that my dog loves. Starts with an A, then two Ts, then A-C-K." She looked scared, and I couldn't help but laugh.

She was thin and tall—probably close to five eight, but I wasn't sure—well put together, I had to admit. But her face was so girlish it was impossible to have any lustful thoughts about her. Unless I'd heard wrong, she hadn't even finished high school, but you could guess that after one glance at her shorts, her T-shirt, and her black Converse. All she needed was to pull her hair back in a ponytail to look like the typical teenager waiting impatiently for someone to open the doors of some big box store so she could buy the latest TikTok trend all the fifteen-year-olds were freaking out about. Still, I couldn't take my eyes off her hair; its color was strange, somewhere between dirty blond and red.

"Very funny," she said sarcastically but obviously terrified. "Get him out of here. He looks ready to kill me." She took a step back. As she did, Thor took a step forward.

Good boy, I thought. Maybe she could use a scare, a special reception to let her know whom this house really belonged to and how unwelcome she was.

"Thor, forward," I ordered him sternly. Noah looked back and forth from him to me and stepped farther back until she hit the wall.

Thor walked slowly toward her, growling and showing his teeth. He was scary, but I knew he wouldn't do anything. Not unless I ordered him to.

"What are you doing?" she asked. "This isn't funny."

But it was.

"My dog usually gets along great with everyone. It's weird that he's on the verge of attacking you," I remarked, amused as she tried to control her fear.

"Are you going to do anything?" she whined.

Do anything? How about I tell you to go back where you came from?

"You've been here, what? Five minutes? And you're already bossing people around?" I said, walking over to the tap and pouring a glass of water. "Maybe I should leave you here for a while to get to know the place on your own."

"Were you dropped on your head often as a child? Get that dog away from me!"

I turned, a little surprised at her audacity. Had she just insulted me?

I think even my dog got it because he walked closer to her. She hardly had space to move. Then, before I could stop her, Noah turned in fright and grabbed the first thing in reach on the counter, a frying pan. Before she could hit Thor, I grabbed his collar with one hand and stopped her with the other.

"What the fuck are you doing?" I shouted, grabbing the pan and putting it back on the counter. My dog was furious, and Noah shrank into my chest, stifling a scream.

I was surprised she'd turn to me for protection when I was the one threatening her.

"Thor, sit!" He relaxed, sat down, and started wagging his tail cheerfully.

I looked down at Noah, who was clutching my T-shirt with both hands. I smiled, but then she seemed to realize what was happening. She raised her hands and shoved me away.

"Are you an idiot or what?"

"First, this better be the last time you try to attack my dog. Second…" As I looked at her, I noticed the freckles on her nose and cheeks. "Don't ever insult me again or we're going to have problems."

Her expression was strange. Her eyes were glued to my face, but then they moved down to my chest, incapable of holding my stare.

I stepped back. My breathing had sped up, but I had no idea why. I'd had enough of her for one day, and I'd only known her for five minutes.

"It would be best if we got along, little sister," I said, turning my back, grabbing my sandwich off the counter, and heading for the door.

"Don't call me that. I'm not your sister, not even close," she replied. She said it with so much hate, so much sincerity, that I stopped to look at her again. Her eyes were shining with determination, and I knew she was no happier than I was about our parents being together.

"Well, we agree about one thing then...little sister," I repeated, rolling my eyes and enjoying watching her little hands clench into fists.

Just then, I heard laughter behind me. I turned and found myself face-to-face with my father...and his wife.

"I see you've met," my father said, entering the kitchen and smiling from ear to ear. It had been a long time since I'd seen him smile in that way, and honestly, I was happy to see it and happy to know he was rebuilding his life. Even if he'd left something behind on the way: me.

Raffaella smiled at me gently from the door, and I forced myself to make the closest expression to a smile that I could. That was all that woman would get. It wasn't her fault, I just couldn't manage anything more.

My father and I didn't have an affectionate relationship, or much of a relationship at all, but I had been completely in agreement with his building that wall that separated us from the outside world. What had happened with my mother had left its mark on both of us, especially me. I was her son, and I had to watch her leave without looking back.

Since then, I didn't trust women, I didn't care about them, and all that mattered to me was sex or maybe having a good time with them at parties. What else should I want?

"Noah, have you met Thor?" Raffaella asked her daughter, who was still standing by the counter not trying to conceal her bad mood.

Then Noah did something I didn't expect. She walked forward, crouched down, and started calling Thor.

"Thor, come here, boy." She seemed gentle, friendly. And brave—you had to give her that. Just a second ago she was trembling before the same animal in fear.

I'd expected her to go rat me out to her mom.

Thor walked over wagging his tail. He turned to me and then to her and must have realized something wasn't right. My attitude was so serious even he couldn't overlook it.

Tail between his legs, he came back and sat down beside me. My stepsister was flustered.

"Good boy," I congratulated him with a big smile.

Noah stood up. There was hatred in those long-lashed eyes. Then she turned back to her mother.

"I'm going to bed," she announced.

I decided to do the opposite because there was a party on the beach that night and I was supposed to be there.

"I'm going out tonight. Don't wait up for me," I said, feeling strange saying this to several people instead of just Dad.

Just as I made it past the doorframe, Dad stopped me—me and my *little sister*.

"The four of us are going out to dinner tonight," he said, focusing his attention on me.

Bullshit!

"Dad, I'm sorry, but I need to go…"

"I'm so tired from the trip…"

"This is going to be our first dinner as a family, and I want you both to be there," my father said, interrupting both of us. Standing next to me, Noah blew out all the air in her lungs.

"Can't we make it tomorrow?" she said.

"Sorry, honey, but we have a business party tomorrow," my father responded.

It was strange how he addressed her. I mean, he didn't even know her! I was already in college; I could do what I wanted. I was an adult, in other words. But Noah! Having to deal with a teenager would have to be any newly married couple's nightmare.

"Noah, we're going out to dinner together, period, no more discussion," Raffaella said, bringing the conversation to a close.

I decided it would be best to give in this time. I'd have dinner with them, and then I'd go to my friend Anna's... my *special friend* Anna's. Then the two of us would go to the party.

"Give me half an hour to shower," I said, pointing to my sweaty clothes.

My father nodded with satisfaction, his wife smiled, and I realized I was being the responsible child that night...or so I was making them believe.

3

Noah

WHAT A DAMN *IDIOT*!

As I climbed the stairs, stomping as loud as I could, I couldn't stop thinking about the ten minutes I'd spent with my new idiot stepbrother. How could he be such a dickhead, a stuck-up psycho? God, I couldn't stand him, and there was no way I could deal with living with him. It was bad enough that he was my mother's new husband's son, but after what had happened, my annoyance had reached stratospheric levels.

This was supposed to be the perfect adorable little boy my mother had told me about?

I hated how he talked to me, how he looked at me. As if he were better than me just because he had money. He had looked me up and down and then laughed…laughed right in my face.

I slammed the door behind me as I walked into my room, but the place was so big no one would hear me. It was night out, and barely any light entered my window. In the darkness, the sea was black, and I couldn't see the dividing line between it and the sky.

Nervous, I hurriedly turned on the light.

I went straight to the bed and jumped on it, staring up at the beams in the ceiling. To top it off, I was supposed to have dinner with them. Did my mother not realize that the last thing I felt like doing right now was being surrounded by people? I needed to be alone, to rest, to take stock of all the changes happening in my life, to accept them and learn to live with them, even if deep down I knew that was impossible.

I grabbed my phone, not sure whether to call my boyfriend, Dan. I didn't want him to worry when he heard the bitterness in my voice. I'd only been in California an hour, and already his absence stung.

Ten minutes after I went up, my mother came in. At least she bothered knocking, but then she walked right in when I didn't answer.

"Noah, in fifteen minutes we need to be downstairs," she said patiently.

"You say that like it takes an hour and a half just to walk down the steps," I responded, sitting up in bed. My mother had let her blond hair down and combed it. She looked elegant. We hadn't even been here two hours, and already she looked like a different person.

"I'm saying this because you need to change clothes first." She ignored my tone.

Not understanding, I looked down at my outfit.

"What's wrong with how I'm dressed?" I asked defensively.

"You're wearing sneakers, Noah. We have to dress up tonight. You don't think you're going to go out in shorts and a T-shirt, do you?" she asked, exasperated.

I stood up and faced her. My patience with this day was at an end.

"Let's see if you can get this through your head, Mom. I don't want to go to dinner with you and your husband, I have no interest in getting to know his spoiled demon of a son, and I'm certainly not getting dressed up for it." I tried to control my overwhelming urge to take her car and drive off into town.

"Stop acting like a five-year-old, put on your clothes, and come to dinner with me and your new family." Her tone was harsh. But when she saw my expression, her face relaxed, and she said, "I'm not asking you to do this every day. Just tonight. Please. For me."

I took a few deep breaths, swallowed down all the things I wanted to say, and nodded.

"Just tonight."

When my mother left, I walked into the closet. Disgusted with everything and everyone, I looked for an outfit that would be comfortable and that I wouldn't hate. I wanted to show them I could be an adult, too. Nicholas's amused, unbelieving expression as he gawked at me with his bright eyes was still stuck in my mind. He had looked at me like I was just a little girl he was having fun scaring with his horrible dog.

My suitcase was open on the floor. I kneeled down and started going through my clothes. My mother was probably expecting me to go down in something she'd bought me, but that was the last thing I was considering. If I gave in, I'd be setting a bad precedent. Accepting that clothing was like accepting this new life; it would mean losing my dignity.

In a rage, I picked my black Ramones dress. Who could say it wasn't elegant? I looked around for some shoes. I wasn't a shoe girl, but if I went downstairs in my Chucks, my mother would definitely lose her cool and tell me to change. Finally I chose some decent-looking sandals with a little bit of a heel—nothing I couldn't manage.

I walked over to the giant mirror on one of the walls and looked at myself slowly. My friend Beth would certainly approve. And I think Dan had always found that dress sexy.

I let down my hair and smoothed it out, and I put a little gloss on my lips. Satisfied with the result, I grabbed a small purse and headed for the door.

Just as I opened it, I found Nicholas, who stopped to look me over while that wicked Thor stood beside him. I couldn't help taking a step back.

For some inexplicable reason, my new brother smiled, and his eyes shone with some obscure, indecipherable emotion.

"Didn't anyone teach you how to dress out there in the boonies?" he said.

I gave him my most angelic smile.

"Yeah...but whoever tried was a dickhead, kind of like you, so I guess I never paid attention."

He didn't expect that answer, and I certainly didn't expect to see a smile spread across those sensuous lips. I suddenly noticed again how tall and virile he was. He was wearing slacks and a button-down with the top two buttons undone. No tie. I didn't let the cool blue of those eyes intimidate me. Instead, I looked over at his dog. Instead of stalking me like a killer, he was now wagging his tail with interest.

"Your dog seems completely different. Are you going to tell him to attack me now, or will you wait till after dinner?" I grinned, feigning friendliness.

"I don't know, Freckles. Depends on how you behave." With that, he turned his back to me and walked downstairs.

I stood still for a few seconds, trying to control my emotions. Freckles! He'd called me Freckles! He was looking for trouble... real trouble.

I walked behind him, trying to convince myself that it wasn't worth it to get angry over his remarks or the way he looked at me or just the fact of his being there. He was one of many people who were destined to get on my nerves in this city, so I might as well get used to it.

Once I was downstairs, I found myself surprised again at the magnificence of the house. It felt somehow old but at the same time sophisticated and modern. Waiting for my mother, ignoring the person next to me, I looked at the crystal lamp hanging between the beams in the ceiling. It must have been made of thousands of pieces of glass that seemed to fall like frozen raindrops, as though wanting to reach the ground but forced to linger in the air for who knew how long.

Our eyes met briefly, but instead of looking away myself, I decided to try to make him do it instead. I didn't want him to think he was getting to me, that he could just treat me as he liked.

But his eyes didn't budge. He was observing me with unbelievable determination. Right when I thought I couldn't take it anymore, my mother appeared with William.

"Well, the gang's all here," he said, looking at us and smirking. For me, the occasion was utterly joyless. "I've reserved a table at the club. I hope you all are hungry." He headed for the door with my mother hanging off his arm.

Mom's eyes turned to saucers when she saw my dress.

"What are you wearing?" she whispered in my ear.

I pretended not to listen and walked outside. The air was warm and refreshing, and I could hear the waves in the distance breaking against the shore.

"You want to ride with us, Nick?" William asked his son.

But he had already turned his back and was walking toward an immaculate black 4x4 that stood high off the ground. It must have just come from the dealership. I rolled my eyes. Typical!

"I'll take mine," he said, turning around as he opened the door. "I'm hanging out with Miles after dinner. We're going to finish the report on the Refford case."

"Excellent," his father said. I had no idea what they were talking about. "Maybe you want to ride with him to the club,

Noah? That way you can get to know each other a little better?" William seemed to think he'd just had the most brilliant idea ever.

I looked over at Nick, who had raised an eyebrow waiting for my response. He seemed to think the whole situation was funny.

"I don't want to ride with someone if I don't know how they drive," I said to my new stepfather, hoping that would hit his son where it hurt. Most guys don't appreciate the implication that they can't drive. Turning away from the SUV, I got into Will's black Mercedes, enjoying the solitude of the back seat as we crisscrossed streets on our way to some rich guys' club.

All I wanted was for the night to end as soon as possible, to finish this happy family act that my mother and her husband were trying to create, and to go back to my room to try to rest.

Fifteen minutes later, we entered a kind of suburb with big, well-groomed yards. It was night, but I could read the brightly lit sign by the road welcoming us to the Mary Read Yacht Club. Before letting us through, a guard in a fancy cabin next to a gate peeked out to see who was in the car. It was evident he recognized the driver.

"Mr. Leister, good evening. Miss," he added, turning to my mother.

My new stepfather said hello to the guard, and we entered the club.

"Noah, your member's card will be here next week, but if you need in before then, just say my name or Ella's," he said, looking over at my mother.

It felt like a jab in the heart when I heard him call her that. That had been my father's name for her, and I was sure my mother didn't care for it at all—too many bad memories. But how was she going to tell her wonderful new husband that?

My mother was a pro at forgetting things that were sad or difficult. Whereas I kept them inside, deep inside, until they all finally exploded and came out.

We stopped the car right at the door to the luxurious establishment. A valet let my mother and me out, took a tip from William, and drove the car off to who knows where.

The restaurant was amazing. Everything seemed made of glass. I could see a couple of tables from where I stood, along with huge aquariums full of crabs, fish, and squid waiting to be killed and served. I felt someone behind me, a breath on my ear that gave me the shivers. When I turned, I saw Nicholas. Even with my heels on, he was half a head taller than me. He barely even looked at me.

"I've got a reservation under the name William Leister," William said to the hostess. For some strange reason, her expression changed, and she hurried to led us through the dining room, which was at once packed, calm, and cozy.

Our table was in one of the best spots, with the same warm candlelight that prevailed all over the restaurant. The glass wall gave an impressive view of the ocean. I wondered if those kinds of transparent walls were common in California.

I was freaking out, to tell the truth.

We sat down, and right away my mother and William started chatting and smiling like infatuated fools. In the meantime, I noticed the astonished, incredulous look the waitress gave Nick.

He didn't seem to realize it. He just toyed with the tiny salt shaker. His hands were very well cared for, tan, and big. I looked from them to his arms until I reached his face, and I noticed that his eyes were looking at me with interest. I held my breath.

"What are you going to order?" my mother asked, breaking the spell.

I let them pick for me, since I didn't know what half the dishes on the menu were anyway. While we waited and I stirred my iced tea, distracted, William tried to drag his son and me into a conversation.

"I was telling Noah earlier about all the sports you can

practice here in the club, Nick. Nicholas plays basketball, and he's one heck of a surfer, too."

A *surfer*. How cliché. I'd thought Nicholas was sitting there bored, but he clearly noticed my disdain. He bent over the table, rested both his elbows on it, and put me on the spot. "Something amusing, Noah?" He did all he could to sound friendly, but I knew deep down I'd gotten to him. "Do you think surfing is silly or something?"

Before my mother could answer—I knew she was about to—I copied him, bending over.

"You said it, not me." And I gave him an innocent smile.

I liked team sports, sports with strategy that required a good leader and consistency and hard work. I'd found all that in volleyball, and I was sure that surfing couldn't compare.

Before he could respond—and I could tell he wanted to—the waitress arrived, and he looked at her as if he knew her.

My mother and William got into an animated conversation when a couple stopped to say hi to them.

The waitress was young with dark brown hair and was wearing a black apron. She laid the plates on the table and, while doing so, bumped Nick's elbow unintentionally.

"Sorry, Nick," she said, then turned to me as if she'd made a mistake. From Nick's expression, I could see that something weird was going on with them.

Since our parents were distracted, I bent over and asked, to clear up my doubts, "You know her?"

"Who?" he asked, playing dumb.

"The waitress," I replied, observing his reactions. He didn't give away anything. He was serious but relaxed. I realized then that Nicholas Leister was very good at hiding his thoughts.

"Yeah, she's taken care of me before," he answered, seeming to dare me to contradict him. *Well, well, well, Nick's a little liar.* Why didn't that surprise me?

"Yeah, I'll bet she's *taken care* of you lots of times."

"What are you getting at, little sister?" This time, the term made me smile.

"How you rich people are all the same—you think that having money makes you the kings of the world. That girl hasn't taken her eyes off you since you walked in the door. It's obvious she knows you." Somewhat angrily, though I didn't know why, I continued, "And you won't even look at her. It's *disgusting.*"

"You've got some very interesting theories about *rich people,* as you call them. I can tell you don't like them. Of course, that's not stopping you and your mother from living under our roof and enjoying all the comforts money can buy. If you hate us so much, what are you doing sitting at this table?"

I tried to control my temper. He knew how to get under my skin.

"Seems to me you and your mother are even worse off than that waitress," he confessed, being sure I alone could hear him. "You pretend to be something you're not, when both of you have sold yourselves for money."

That was too much. I was blind with rage.

I grabbed the glass in front of me and tried to throw its contents in his face.

Too bad it was empty.

4

Nick

THE LOOK ON HER FACE WHEN SHE SAW HER GLASS WAS EMPTY dissolved any trace of anger or irritation I might have been holding in since we sat down.

That girl was anything but predictable. I was surprised by how easily she lost her cool and how just a few words could throw her off.

Her cheeks with their little freckles turned pink when she realized how ridiculous she looked. She stared at me, then at the glass, and then to both sides of her, as if hoping to reassure herself that no one had seen what an idiot she was.

Leaving aside how funny the situation was—and it was funny as hell—I couldn't let her act like that with me. What if the glass had been full? I couldn't let some snot-nosed seventeen-year-old even think about trying some stunt like that with me. She was going to find out what kind of big brother she'd lucked into. I'd let her know how much trouble she'd be in if she tried to play with me again.

I gave her a winning smile, and she looked back at me warily. I enjoyed seeing the fear hidden in her eyes between those long lashes.

"Don't do that again," I said calmly.

After a few seconds' pause, she turned to her mother, and the evening went on without any more incidents. Noah didn't speak to me again, she didn't pay me any attention at all, and that bothered me and pleased me at the same time. While she answered my father's questions and talked unenthusiastically with her mother, I made my observations.

She was a simple girl. But I could tell she was going to cause me problems. She made funny faces when she tried the shellfish they'd served for the table. She barely tasted a bite of it. No wonder she looked so thin in that black dress. She'd made me pause when I saw her come out of her bedroom, lingering over her long legs, her narrow waist, and her breasts. She was pretty hot considering she hadn't gone under the knife like most chicks in California.

I had to admit it—she was good-looking, even more so than I'd thought at first, and that and other thoughts clouded my mood. I couldn't let a person like her distract me, especially not if we were living under the same roof.

I looked at her face again. She didn't have on a jot of makeup. Strange… All the girls I knew spent at least an hour in their rooms on their makeup alone, and this included girls ten times hotter than Noah, but there she was, not worried in the least about going to a luxury restaurant without even putting on lipstick. Not that she needed it—she was lucky to have taut, almost perfect skin. And those freckles gave her a girly look, reminding me she wasn't even out of high school.

Before I knew it, Noah was turning to me with an irritated expression. She'd caught me staring.

"You want a photo?" she asked with that acidic humor I was starting to realize was a trademark.

"Yeah. Nude, obviously," I said, enjoying the slight redness in her cheeks. Her eyes shone angrily, and she turned back to our parents, who hadn't even noticed the little dustup that was taking place a foot away from them.

When I brought my soda to my lips, I could see the waitress looking at me from behind the bar. I checked to see if my father noticed and then excused myself, saying I was going to the bathroom. Noah seemed to follow me with her eyes, but I ignored her. I had something more important to deal with.

I walked to the bar and sat on a stool in front of Claudia, the waitress I slept with once in a while. I had dealings with her cousin, too—more complicated but beneficial nonetheless.

Claudia looked at me with a tense smile, leaned on the bar, and offered a partial view of her breasts. As much as she could manage with the uniform she had on.

"I see you've found another girl to spend time with," she said. Funny.

"She's my stepsister," I said, and then looked down at my wristwatch. I would be seeing Anna in forty-five minutes. I looked back at the brunette in front of me, gawking. "I don't know why you care," I added, standing up. "Tell Ronnie I'll be waiting for him tonight on the docks at Kyle's party."

Claudia clenched her jaw, probably pissed at how little attention I was paying to her. I couldn't get why girls expected a relationship with a guy like me. Didn't I warn them I didn't want a commitment? Wasn't it clear that I'd sleep with whomever I felt like? Why did they think they could change me?

I'd stopped sleeping with Claudia for that very reason, and she still hadn't forgiven me for it.

"You're going to the party?" she asked, sounding slightly hopeful.

"Obvs," I responded, ignoring her irritation before I headed back to the table. "Me and Anna. By the way, try to do a better job of pretending you don't know me. My stepsister's already figured out we've slept together, and I'd prefer my father not do the same."

Claudia pressed her lips together and turned around without a word.

I got back just as dessert was being dropped off. After ten minutes, with my father and his new wife hogging the conversation, I decided I'd played the role of good son enough for one day.

"Sorry, but I need to go," I said, looking at Dad, whose brow furrowed briefly.

"To Miles's place?"

I nodded and tapped my watch.

"What's going on with the case?"

I struggled not to sigh with resignation and lied as best I could. "His parents have left us in charge of all the paperwork. I guess that means we've got a real case, and with just us working on it, it'll take years," I replied, aware that Noah was observing me with interest.

"A real case? What are you studying?" she asked. She looked surprised, even a little disconcerted.

"Law," I said. She seemed impressed. "Does that surprise you?" I was putting her in a corner with that question, and I enjoyed it.

Her attitude changed, and she looked down her nose at me.

"It does, honestly. I thought that was a major that required having a brain."

"Noah!" her mother shouted.

That little snotnose was trying to taunt me.

Before I could say anything, my father butted in.

"You've both started off on the wrong foot." His expression was icy.

It was all I could do not to stand up and walk out with no explanation. I'd had enough of the happy family for one day; I needed to bounce and stop trying to fake interest in all that bullshit.

"Sorry, I've got to go," I declared, getting up and dropping my napkin on the table. No way I was going to lose my cool in front of Dad.

Noah got up, too, without an ounce of elegance, and threw her own napkin down, not even trying to appear polite.

"If he's going, I'm going, too," she affirmed, glaring at her mother, who started looking from side to side, overwhelmed and upset.

"Sit down," her mother ordered between clenched teeth.

I couldn't waste time on this nonsense. I had places to be.

"I'll take her with me," I said to everyone's surprise, Noah's included.

She looked at me with suspicion, not believing me, as if she thought I were concealing my true intentions. Honestly I couldn't wait to lose her, and if taking her home would make that happen faster, then so be it. Especially if it meant I could get away from my father as well.

"I wouldn't walk five feet with you," she said proudly, enunciating each word.

Before anyone could respond, I grabbed my jacket, and as I slipped it on, I said to everyone in general, "I'm not in the mood for these grade school games. I'll see you tomorrow."

"Nicholas, wait," my father commanded. "Noah, go with him and get some rest. We'll be back in a while."

My new sister seemed to be wavering. Then she sighed, scowled, and said, "Fine, I'll go with you."

5

Noah

THE LAST THING I WANTED AT THAT MOMENT WAS TO OWE something to that bastard, but I was even less inclined to stay behind with my mother and her husband and watch her drool over him while he waved around his bucks and showed off how much pull he had.

Nicholas turned his back to me and walked out.

I said an unenthusiastic goodbye to Mom and hurried after him. When I reached the door, I stopped, crossed my arms, and waited for the valet to pull his car around.

Big surprise—he pulled a pack of cigarettes out of his jacket and lit one up, bringing it slowly to his lips and then expelling the smoke in long plumes.

I'd never smoked; I'd never even tried tobacco when all my friends were into it and would sneak cigarettes in the girls' bathroom at school. I didn't understand what pleasure a person could take in inhaling carcinogenic smoke that left a nasty scent on your hair and clothes and was also bad for like a thousand organs.

As if he was reading my mind, Nicholas smiled mirthfully and held out his pack.

"You want one, little sister?" he asked, and then took another drag off his.

"I don't smoke. And if I were you, I wouldn't, either. You don't want to endanger the only neuron you've got." I stepped forward so I didn't have to see him.

I could feel he was close to me, but I didn't move, even when the smoke coming out of his mouth snaked creepily around my neck.

"Be careful. I might just leave you here stranded so you can walk home," he warned me just as his car was pulling up.

I ignored him as much as I could during the drive. His SUV was so high off the ground he could see everything if I wasn't careful getting in, and as I did, I regretted putting on those dumb shoes. All the frustration, anger, and sorrow had grown worse as the night went on, and the five or more arguments I'd had with this idiot had turned it into the absolute worst night of my life.

I struggled to put on my seat belt while Nicholas stuck the key in the ignition, pressed his hand against my headrest, hit reverse, and then turned onto the road leading out. I wasn't surprised that he didn't follow the roundabout—a roundabout that was placed there precisely in order to keep people from driving the way Nicholas was.

I couldn't help but groan when we got back on the main road. Outside the club, my stepbrother sped up, hitting seventy, deliberately ignoring the traffic signs that said the speed limit was forty-five.

"What's your problem, anyway?" Nicholas asked in a weary tone, as if he couldn't put up with me a minute more. *That makes two of us,* I thought.

"Well, I don't want to die on the road with some maniac who doesn't know how to read a road sign. That's one problem," I shouted. I was at my limit. Anything else and I'd start screaming like a banshee. I knew I was short-fused. One of the things I hated most about myself was my lack of self-control when I got angry, the way I could so easily raise my voice and turn to insults.

"What the fuck's up with you? You haven't stopped complaining ever since I had the misfortune of meeting you, and honestly, I don't give a shit what your problems are. This is my home, my city, and my car, so shut your mouth until we get back," he said, shouting just as I had.

An intense heat filled my body from head to toe when I heard those words. Nobody told me what to do...least of all him.

"Who the hell are you to tell me to shut up?!" I was beside myself.

Nicholas jerked the wheel and braked so hard, if I hadn't put on my seat belt, I'd have shot right through the windshield.

When I got over the shock, I looked back and was scared to see two cars turning quickly right to avoid hitting us. Horns honked, and drivers shouted insults, and for a moment, I was stunned. Then I reacted.

"What the hell are you doing?" I shrieked, terrified someone might run us over.

Utterly unperturbed, Nicholas said, "Get out."

It must have looked comical the way my mouth fell open.

"You can't be serious," I said.

"I'm not going to say it twice," he warned me, his voice so composed it was chilling.

This was getting grim.

"Well, you're going to have to because there's no way I'm moving from here." I tried to stare at him as coldly as he was at me.

He pulled out his keys, got out, and left his door open. My eyes bugged out as I watched him walk around the back and reappear next to my door.

I've got to admit, he was a scary bastard when he got pissed off, and at that moment, he couldn't have been any angrier. My heart started pounding when I felt that sensation I knew so well: fear. Terror.

He opened my door and repeated the same phrase from before. "Get out."

My mind was clicking at a thousand miles an hour. He was nuts; he couldn't just leave me there in the middle of the road in the dark, surrounded by trees.

"I won't." I refused, and I cursed myself as I noticed the tremor in my voice. An irrational fear was gathering in the pit of my stomach. If that idiot left me here, I thought, looking out into the black night, some fool would run me down.

He'd surprised me again, and once again, it was not a good surprise.

He crawled up on my seat, unclicked my seat belt, and pulled me out of the car so fast I couldn't protest.

"Are you out of your mind?" I shouted as he walked back to the driver's seat.

"Get this straight," he told me over his shoulder. He looked like a statue of ice. "You're not going to talk to me like that. I've got enough problems of my own without putting up with your shit. Get an Uber, call your mom, I don't care. I'm out."

He got back in and put his car in gear. I could feel my hands shaking.

"Nicholas, you can't leave me here!" I roared as the car started to roll and the tires squealed. "Nicholas!"

That scream was followed by a deep silence that made me worry my heart would stop.

The sky was just short of black, and the moon was far from full. I tried to control my fear and my irrational desire to kill that son of a bitch who had left me stranded here my first day in the city.

I held on to the hope that Nicholas would come back, but as the minutes passed, I was more and more worried. I took out my phone, but the battery was dead, and the damned thing had shut off. Fuck! All I could do—and this was as awful and as dangerous as just standing here—was try to thumb a ride and pray that a civilized adult would take pity on me and take me home. And if that happened, I'd take care of that bastard stepbrother and enjoy it. Things wouldn't go on like this. That dickhead didn't know whom or what he was playing with.

I saw a car coming from the direction of the yacht club, and I prayed it was Will's Mercedes.

I came as close to it as I could without risking getting hit and stuck out my thumb the way I'd seen people do in movies. I knew that half the time a girl tried to do it she ended up murdered and thrown in a ditch. But I forced myself to push those little details out of my mind.

The first car drove past, the second shouted a series of insults, the third made a bunch of nasty sexual comments, and the fourth… The fourth stopped on the roadside five feet from where I'd been standing.

I approached it with a feeling of alarm, wondering who the insane but very opportune individual was who had decided to help out a girl who could easily pass as a prostitute.

I felt relieved when I saw that the person getting out of the car was a boy, more or less my age. The lights gave me a glimpse of his dark hair, his stature, and his evident (but just then extremely welcome) air of a pampered rich kid.

"Are you okay?" he asked, walking toward me just as I walked toward him.

When we were in front of each other, we each did the same thing: his eyes looked my dress up and down, and I checked out his expensive jeans, his name-brand polo, and his gentle, worried eyes.

"Yeah. Thanks for stopping. This idiot just left me here hanging." I felt embarrassed, stupid, for letting something like that happen.

The young man seemed surprised.

"He just left you here…here? In the middle of nowhere at eleven at night?"

So it would be okay if he'd left me in the middle of a park at lunchtime? I asked myself, feeling a sudden hatred toward any and all beings endowed with a Y chromosome. But still, the kid seemed like he wanted to help. It was no time to pick fights.

"Any chance you'd mind taking me home?" I asked, not bothering to answer his question. "As you can tell, I really just want this night to end."

The kid smiled. He wasn't ugly. He was easy on the eyes, in fact, with a kindly face, probably the type to help anyone out of a jam. Either that, or my mind was trying to sell me a parallel reality in which everything was the color of roses and boys treated women with the respect they deserved instead of throwing them out on the roadside in high heels in the middle of the night.

"You sure you don't want to go to a wild party at a mansion on the beach? That way you can have all night to thank me for the way this little misfortune allowed you and me to meet each other," he said, tickled.

I don't know if it was hysteria, suppressed rage, or the fact that I just wanted to kill someone, but I laughed right in his face.

"Sorry, but…all I want to do is get home and put today behind me. I've had enough of this city for now." I uttered these words more calmly, not wanting to appear crazy for laughing before.

"No worries. But at least you can tell me your name, right?" He seemed awfully amused in this situation that had nothing amusing about it. But since he was my savior, I felt I should be nice to him if I didn't want to end up sleeping with the squirrels.

"My name's Noah. Noah Morgan." I put out my hand, and he immediately squeezed it.

"I'm Zack," he said with a radiant smile. "Shall we?" He pointed at his gleaming black Porsche.

"Thanks, Zack. Seriously."

I was surprised that he walked me to the passenger side and helped me get in, just like in an old-fashioned movie. It was strange. Strange and refreshing. Despite what all the statistics seemed to say, chivalry was apparently still not dead, even if people like Nicholas Leister might make you think so.

As soon as Zack got in the driver's seat, I knew he wouldn't be like Nicholas. He was evidently a good guy, educated, reasonable, the typical boy a mother would die for her daughter to go out with. I put on my seat belt and sighed with relief, knowing that the worst had been avoided.

"Where to?" he asked, putting the car in gear and taking off in the same direction Nicholas had more than an hour before.

"You know William Leister's house?" I asked, assuming everyone in that neighborhood of rich people knew each other.

"Yeah, of course. But what do you want to go there for?"

"That's where I live," I responded, feeling a jab in my chest as I realized that however painful that was, it was true.

Zack laughed, unbelieving.

"You live at Nicholas Leister's place?" I ground my teeth as I heard that name.

"Worse—I'm his stepsister." How disgusting to have to admit I was related to that dimwit.

Zack looked away from the road a second to turn his surprised eyes toward me. I guess he wasn't the responsible driver I'd imagined.

"You're not serious…or are you?"

"Oh, I'm serious. He's the one who left me stranded here." It was humiliating to admit.

Zack laughed sardonically.

"Honestly, I feel for you," he said, and that made me feel

even worse. "Nicholas Leister is the absolute worst." He shifted gears and slowed down as we pulled into a residential area.

"So you know him?" I tried to bring together in my mind the gentleman to my left and the delinquent in the 4x4.

"Unfortunately, I do," he replied. "His father saved my father's ass in a pretty nasty case with the IRS just over a year ago. He's a good attorney, and his little bastard son can't help rubbing it in my face every time he gets the chance. We went to high school together. I can assure you he's the most egotistical, rude son of a bitch you'll ever meet."

Damn! Apparently I wasn't the only member of the Anti-Nicholas Leister Club. That made me feel a bit better.

"I'd like to say something nice about him," Zack went on, "but he's got more dirty laundry than anyone I've ever met. Take my advice and stay away from him."

"Easy for you to say. We live under the same roof." I guess I wasn't feeling better after all.

"He's at the party I mentioned, in case you want to give him a kick in the ass," he said with a grin. That information was a complete surprise.

"He's going to the party?" I felt hot shame burning all over my body.

"You're not really thinking..." he started to ask apprehensively.

"I'm going," I told him, as sure of it as I'd ever been of anything in my entire life. "And I will give him that kick in the ass."

Twenty minutes later, we were on the beach in front of an enormous house. But the size wasn't what caught the eye so much as the quantity of people gathered around it, on the entrance stairs, anywhere you turned.

The music was audible from a mile away, so loud I thought I could feel my brain bouncing around in my skull.

"Are you sure about this?" my new best friend asked. Since I'd told Zack my plan, he'd been trying to convince me to abandon ship. It seemed my new stepbrother, apart from being a hardhead and a moron, was prone to scrapping. "Noah, you have no idea what you're getting into. You already saw how it didn't even bother him to leave you back there. What makes you think he's going to care what you have to say to him?"

Gripping the door handle, I responded, "Trust me. He'll never do anything like that to me again."

We got out of the car and walked toward the immense entry-way of the house. It was like going to one of those parties you see in movies, like in *Never Back Down* or *The Fast and the Furious.* Just crazy. Beer kegs were laid out all over the front yard, and a bunch of guys were shouting and encouraging each other to drink more. The girls were wearing bikinis, some of them just bras and panties.

"Are all the parties he goes to like this?" I asked, looking grossed out as a couple hooked up against one of the walls of the house, not even caring that everyone was watching them. It was repugnant.

"Not all of them," he responded, chuckling. "This one is mixed." That threw me off. Mixed? What did he mean?

"Are you saying because there are guys and girls at the same party?" I returned to memories of my past, when I was twelve and my mother had organized my first party with boys. A total disaster, so far as I recalled: the boys had thrown me and my friends in the pool, and we'd ended up founding the Anti-Boys Chapter of the Best Friends Forever Club. I knew it was stupid, but I had been twelve, not seventeen.

Zack grabbed my arm and dragged me forward. His fingers were warm, and I felt calmer knowing he was there. This party could intimidate anyone, let alone an outsider like myself.

"What I mean is anyone can come," he said, pushing through the crowd and going inside. The music was wild and repetitive and drilled into your eardrums so deep it hurt just to be there.

"I don't get it." He pushed me into one of the rooms where the music killed you slowly rather than instantly and where I could talk without shredding my vocal cords.

"Anyone who pays can come," he told me, waving at some of the guys there. I didn't like him having the kind of friends I saw there. "They use the money to buy all kinds of liquor and…" He looked at me a few moments, maybe wondering whether I was old enough to hear this. "And all the stuff you need for a party to get lit."

Drugs. Great. And he thought that was funny. What the hell had I gotten into?

There were couples lying on the sofa and others standing up dancing to the rhythm of the music, and I realized that among the rich kids in expensive clothes, there were people who could have been from the worst neighborhoods. It was an explosive mix.

"I'm starting to think this was a bad idea," I told my companion, but by now he was sitting on one of the couches with a bottle of beer in his hand.

"Come here, Noah," he said, tugging my arm till I fell in his lap. "Let's have fun tonight. Don't waste your time on that asshole." His fingers stroked my hair and my shoulders, and I tensed up and then stood as fast as I could.

"I'm here for one reason." I glared at him. I'd been wrong about Zack, it was obvious. "Thanks for bringing me." I turned around and walked away.

I didn't really know what to do here after giving the cold shoulder to the one guy who wasn't so drunk he'd smash his car into a tree if I asked him to take me home. But I couldn't stop imagining the confused look on Nicholas's face when he saw me. Had Zack lied to me, though? Maybe he was just a crazy drunk trying to drag me to the worst place ever. Well, I was going to look, and if I found Nicholas, I was going to do what I came there for.

I went toward the kitchen, where there were fewer people,

thinking I'd get a glass of cold water. I didn't know whether to drink it or dump it over my head to try to wake up from this nightmare. This day seemed like it would never end.

When I turned down the little hallway leading there, I stopped.

There he was—no shirt on, just jeans, surrounded by girls and four muscular friends a little shorter than him.

I watched him for a few moments.

Was this the same guy I'd been having dinner with at a luxury restaurant just a little while ago?

He was, and so it surprised me to see him now. He looked like he'd just stepped out of a mafia movie. They were playing beer pong, but with shots of tequila. My dear stepbrother was killing it. He hadn't missed once. That meant he wasn't as drunk as the others.

Nicholas shot and missed on purpose. It was so obvious I couldn't see how the others didn't realize it, but they all jeered at him and cracked up laughing. He grabbed his shot and downed it fast.

When it was his friend's turn, Nicholas went over to a hot brunette girl who was sitting on the black-marble countertop. She was wearing a sky-blue bikini top and shorts that showed off her sun-bronzed legs.

I was too dressed up—too covered up—for a party like this.

Nicholas buried his hand in the hair on the back of her neck, pulled her head back, and French kissed her in the most disgusting way I could imagine, especially with all those people there.

That was my chance. I'd catch him by surprise and quell my burning desire to tear his goddamn head off.

He hadn't even bothered to see if I was okay. I could have still been stuck there, and he wouldn't have lifted a finger for me. I was furious I'd let myself be treated that way, even more so for finding myself here in this madhouse thanks to him, so I walked across the kitchen, grabbed his arm to turn him around, and, shocking even myself, instead of slapping him as I'd planned, I punched him in the jaw, nearly breaking one or more of my knuckles. It was worth it, though, and he deserved it.

He was briefly disconcerted, as if he didn't understand what had happened, who I was, or why I'd hit him. But that just lasted a few seconds, and then his face changed, his posture changed, and I found myself pinned where I was standing.

Everyone gathered around us. It was silent as a grave. All eyes were on us.

"What the fuck are you doing here?" he asked, so furious I feared for my life.

If looks could kill, I was already dead, boxed up, and buried.

"You're surprised I could walk here?" I asked, trying not to be intimidated by his stance, his height, and those terrifying muscles. "You're a piece of shit, you know that?"

A dry, measured laugh erupted from his esophagus.

"Noah, you have no idea what you're getting into." He took a step forward, and I could feel the heat radiating off his body. "At home, you may be my stepsister, but outside those four walls," he continued, so soft only I could hear it, "this is my world, and I won't put up with any of your bullshit."

I didn't let him intimidate me. There was no way I'd ever allow him to see how much his words and his behavior scared me. I'd lived a life of violence. I wasn't going to put up with it anymore.

"Fuck you," I said, and turned around, ready to get out of there. A hand grabbed my arm and pulled, not letting me take another step.

"Let me go," I ordered him, turning around so he could see I was serious.

He smiled and looked at everyone gawking and then back at me.

"Who'd you come here with?" he asked.

I gulped. No way I was answering.

"Who brought you here?" he screamed so loud I flinched. That was the last straw.

"Let me go, you son of a…" I started howling, but it was pointless. He was holding onto me so tight it hurt.

Then someone else spoke up.

"I know who it was," said a fat guy with not a free inch of skin left for more tattoos. "Zack Rogers showed up with her."

"Bring him to me."

My stepbrother was acting like a delinquent, and I was really getting scared. I regretted hitting him, not because he didn't deserve it but because I was afraid I'd provoked the devil himself.

Two minutes later, Zack appeared in the kitchen, and the circle opened to let him through. He looked at me as if I'd betrayed him.

What the hell was the deal with these people?

"You brought her here?" my stepbrother asked him calmly.

Zack hesitated and then nodded. He didn't break eye contact with Nicholas, but I could tell he was scared.

Before I knew it, Nicholas had punched Zack in the stomach so hard he bent over in pain.

I shouted, afraid for him, with that same pain in my chest I always felt whenever I witnessed any type of violence.

"Don't you dare do that again," I said to Nicholas.

He turned around, grabbed by arm, and started dragging me toward the door.

I didn't have the strength to protest. When we got there, he stopped. He took his cell phone out of his pocket, cursed under his breath, and waited for whomever he was calling to answer.

"Wait for me here," he said, looking for a place where the noise from the people and the music wouldn't bother him. He ended up just past the stairs leading up to the porch. He could see me perfectly, so there was no point in running.

"You okay?" some guy asked me.

"Honestly, no." I was a wreck. I leaned against the window, unable to avoid certain memories that I'd kept buried in the depths of my mind and that were now resurfacing to torment me just then. "I feel faint."

"Here, have a drink," he said, handing me a cup.

I took it without even looking. My throat was so dry, it didn't matter what it was. I closed my eyes and opened them once the cup was empty, only to see Nicholas flying up the stairs.

"What the hell are you doing?" he said, tearing the cup out of my hands.

I was going to respond, but he was already looking away from me toward the guy who'd given it to me. He grabbed him by his shirt and nearly lifted him off the ground.

"What the fuck did you give her?" he asked, shaking him around.

I looked with horror at the cup.

"Shit!"

6

Nick

"SHIT!"

"What the hell did you give her?" I asked the dickhead I was holding by the collar.

I could see the terror in his eyes.

"Answer me!" I shouted, cursing the day I'd ever met my stepsister, cursing that moron Zack Rogers for bringing her to a party like this.

"Jesus, dude!" The guy's eyes were like saucers. "Burundanga, okay!" he admitted when I slammed him into the wall.

Jesus. A date rape drug. It was colorless and odorless and easy to slip into a drink without a person realizing it.

Just thinking about what could have happened clouded my mind, and I couldn't control myself. What kind of dirtbag would do that to a girl? When I finished with him, you wouldn't be able to identify him from his license photo. My hands were going to look like hamburger by the time the night was over.

I lost count of how many times I hit him.

"Nicholas, stop!" a voice behind me shouted. I stopped my hand before it slammed back into that bastard's face.

"Bring that shit to another one of my parties and this is going to look compassionate compared to what happens next time," I threatened him, making sure he'd heard every word. "Understand?"

He stumbled off, bleeding, trying to get as far from me as possible, and I turned back around to find Noah terrified.

Something shifted inside me when I saw her expression. I couldn't stand her, I could happily have wrung her neck, but, dammit, no one deserved to be drugged without their consent. By the look on her face, I could tell this night had taken Noah past her limits.

I tried to talk myself down, observing her as I walked over slowly. When I was close, she started walking backward, mouth ajar, frighted and trembling.

"Jesus, Noah, I'm not going to hurt you, okay?" I said. I felt like a criminal, and I hadn't even done anything.

When I left her, I just assumed she'd call her mom and she and my dad would pick her up and take her back home. I never thought she'd climb into the car of the first idiot who came along and show up at a party absolutely unsuited to a girl her age.

"What did he give me?" she asked, looking at me like I was a demon.

I sighed and looked up, trying to put my thoughts in order. My father had just called to ask where the hell Noah was. Her mother was worried, so I said I'd call her right back. I told him Noah was with me, at Miles's house, and we were watching a movie with his sister.

It was a lie, made up on the spot, but my father could never know what had happened tonight or where. I'd gotten out of too many bad situations for him to learn that nothing had actually changed. It had been hard for me to keep my private life under wraps, and I sure wasn't going to let someone like Noah spoil it.

It hadn't even been a day, and she'd managed to be a bigger pain in my ass than any woman I'd ever had the pleasure of meeting.

"You all right?" I asked, ignoring her question.

"I want to kill you," she answered. I could see her eyelids were drooping. I needed to get her on the phone with her mom ASAP before the situation got worse.

"Yeah, let's take a rain check on that," I said, grabbing her arm. "You'll be all right. Try to relax."

When we reached my car, I opened the passenger-side door and waited for her to sit down. Then I took out my phone.

"You need to tell your mother you're fine and not to stay up for you," I said, looking for Dad's number in my contacts. "Tell her we're watching a movie at some friend's place."

"Up yours," she said, head lolling back, shutting her eyes.

I grabbed her face and opened her eyes. She looked me with such hatred I wanted to find something I could kick, break, and shatter into a million pieces.

"Call her or this is going to get ugly for real," I said, imagining what might happen if my father found out what had happened tonight. Not to mention Noah's mother.

"What are you going to do to me?" she said, her pupils getting more dilated. "Leave me behind so someone can rape me? Wait... you already did that once."

I get it—I deserved that—but there was no time for sarcasm.

"I'm dialing her now. If you're smart, you'll tell her what I said."

A few seconds later, I heard Raffaella's voice on the other line.

"Noah, are you okay?"

She looked at me before responding.

"Yeah," she answered, to my relief, "we're watching a movie. We'll be home a little late." Her eyes turned up toward the roof of the car.

"I'm so glad you went, sweetie. You'll love Nick's friends, just wait…"

I looked aside when I heard that.

"For sure," Noah said.

"See you tomorrow, babe. I love you."

"You too. Bye."

I took the phone and slipped it into my pocket.

I walked around to the driver's side. We'd have to wait there and see how good Noah's tolerance for drugs was.

"I'm hot," she said, eyes closed, and I could tell—sweat covered her forehead and neck.

"It'll pass. Don't let it worry you," I told her, hoping my words wouldn't betray me.

"What are the effects of this stuff?" Her voice was groggy.

"Sweating, fever and chills. It makes you tired," I said, hoping that was it.

If she started vomiting or her heart beat too fast, I'd have to take her to the hospital, and that wouldn't end well.

Her cheeks were red, and her hair was sticking to her forehead. I noticed she had a hair band around one of her wrists. I leaned over her and took it off. The least I could do was help her be as comfortable as possible.

"What are you doing?" she asked, very clearly scared.

I breathed deep, trying to keep my emotions in check. I'd never done anything out of line with a woman, and seeing how terrified Noah was that I would was like a kick in the balls.

I'd only known the girl for a few hours, and she was already wearing me out.

"I'm helping you," I said, pulling her long, colorful hair back into a sloppy ponytail on top of her head.

"To do that, you'd have to disappear," she slurred.

I couldn't help but chuckle. She had guts, more than any other girl I'd ever met. She didn't know whom she was playing with, didn't know who I was or what I was capable of, but that was refreshing somehow.

I thought of the look she had just after punching me. It had been completely unexpected—the first time anyone had punched me in forever.

Instinctively, I grabbed her right hand and looked at her swollen knuckles. It must have taken all the strength she had to leave her hand looking like that. I felt bad for her. I had a vision of myself teaching Noah to throw a punch the right way.

She was worrying me. Now that her hair wasn't covering her face, I noticed certain traits that had escaped me before. Her neck was pretty, her cheekbones high with their irresistible dusting of freckles. That made me grin for some reason. Her eyelashes were long and cast shadows on her cheeks, but the thing that really caught my eye was that little tattoo just under her left ear.

It was a knot, a figure eight.

I looked at my own arm, where I'd gotten that same tattoo three and a half years before. It was a perfect knot, one that wouldn't give out easily, and that's why I'd chosen it. It meant that if things came together right, if you used your head, the result could be indestructible. I didn't understand how she could have that tattoo or anything else actually—it clashed with the image I'd created of her in my mind.

I ran a finger carefully over that tattoo, so tiny compared to mine, and felt how both of us got goose bumps. Noah twitched unconsciously, and I felt something strange, uncomfortable, in the pit of my stomach.

I threw on my seat belt, grabbed the wheel, put the car in gear, and looked back at her tattoo before focusing on the road. Luckily I'd only had time for one beer and one shot, so I was able to drive home with peace of mind.

The outside lights were on as always. It was incredibly late, and I prayed our parents were in bed. Noah was out of commission, and I couldn't let Dad catch us.

I parked in my space and got out, trying not to make noise. I carefully unbuckled Noah's seat belt and took her in my arms. She was burning up. I was worried her fever might turn dangerous.

"Where are we?" she asked in a voice I could barely hear.

"Home," I said to calm her down, turning so I could open the door without disturbing her.

Inside it was totally dark except for the faint light of a table lamp in the living room. No sooner had Raffaella moved there than she'd gotten obsessed with leaving a light or two on at night.

It was strange to me that Noah was still conscious, and I rushed her to her bed so I could leave her there more comfortable.

"No," she said, frightened.

"Easy now," I said, astonished at how tightly she was holding me.

"Don't leave me alone. I'm scared." There was panic in her voice. It was weird because I was sure I was the one who had scared her and I couldn't imagine why she'd want to stay with me.

"Noah, this is your room," I said, sitting on her bed and holding her in my lap.

She opened her eyes, and I saw terror in them.

"The light," she muttered as if she were hardly capable of pronouncing the words.

It was weird. There wasn't any light on.

"Turn it on," she almost begged.

I observed her a few seconds before realizing that what scared her wasn't that I was in her room or the drugs or the fact that she could barely move; it was the darkness.

"You're scared of the dark?" I asked, leaning over her and turning on the lamp on her nightstand.

Her body instantly relaxed.

I raised an eyebrow, asking myself how this chick could be so complicated. I got up, arranged her against the pillows, and then stood there a moment, making sure her breathing was normal. It was. Noah was a strong girl.

"Get out of my room," she commanded me, and I did.

I think it was the sanest thing I did all night.

1

Noah

WHEN I OPENED MY EYES THAT MORNING, I FELT AWFUL. FOR THE first time in my life, the light bothered me. My head hurt like crazy, and I felt weird all over. It was hard to explain, but I was aware of every movement, every sensation taking place in my body, and it was uncomfortable, irritating, upsetting. My throat was dry, as if I hadn't drunk anything in a week.

I stumbled over to the bathroom and looked at myself in the mirror.

Jesus Lord, how horrible!

Then I remembered.

And my body trembled from head to toe.

My eyes were swollen, my hair messy and pulled back in a ratty ponytail. I didn't remember pulling it back, though. I took off my dress, brushed my teeth to clean that bitter taste from my mouth, and put on my pajama shorts and my favorite T-shirt with the holes in it.

Memories flashed through my head like stop-motion photographs. Drugs. That was all I could think. Someone had drugged me. I'd taken drugs, I'd gotten in a stranger's car, I'd gone to a party full of goons...and it was all one person's fault.

I walked out of my bedroom, slammed the door, and went to Nicholas's room.

I didn't bother knocking before opening the door to what looked like a bear cave with a person under a dark blanket in a huge bed.

I walked over and shook the person sleeping there like a log, as if nothing had happened, as if it wasn't his fault someone had drugged me.

"Dammit," he muttered without opening his eyes.

His disheveled hair was camouflaged against the dark-satin sheets. I pulled hard on the cover until he was exposed. I didn't care.

Fortunately he wasn't naked, but his white boxers did throw me off for a second. He was sleeping facedown, giving me the perfect panorama of his broad back, his long legs, and—forgive me for saying so—his splendid ass.

But I forced myself to focus on what was really important.

"What happened last night?" I nearly shouted, shaking his arm so he'd wake up.

He grunted and grabbed hold of my hand, still with his eyes closed, and with one jerk, he pulled me into his bed.

I fell down next to him and tried to struggle away, but it was futile.

"Even when you're high you can't shut the fuck up," he said before finally opening his eyes.

Two blue irises focused on mine.

"What do you want?" he asked, letting go of my wrist and sitting up.

I got out of the bed immediately.

"What did you do to me last night while I was out of it?" I asked, fearing the worst.

If that bastard had done something to me...

"Oh, I did it all," he said contemptuously and then laughed. I struck him on the chest.

"Moron!" I shouted, feeling the blood rise to my cheeks.

He ignored me and stood up.

Then someone or something entered the room: a creature covered in hair dark like his owner's, dark like that damned room.

"Hey, Thor, you hungry, boy? Have I got a tasty treat for you." He grinned at me as he said this.

"I'm going." I walked toward the door. I never wanted to see that idiot again, and knowing that I'd have to made my mood even worse than it already was.

Nicholas intercepted me in the middle of the room, and I almost ran into his bare chest.

"I'm sorry about what happened last night." For a few miraculous seconds, I thought he was sincerely apologizing. How wrong I was: "But you can't say a fucking word, or I'm screwed." Now I knew all he wanted was to save his ass. As for me, he couldn't care less.

I laughed bitterly. "So says the future lawyer."

"Keep your trap shut." He ignored my comment.

"Or what?"

He eyed me up and then jabbed a finger under my right ear, in a place that meant something special to me. "Or else that knot might not be strong enough to hold you." What did he know about my tattoo or about how strong I was?

"How about you ignore me and I'll ignore you. We'll deal with the brief moments when we have to be together. Sound good?" I walked around him and left.

Thor wagged his tail, watching me go.

At least the dog didn't hate me anymore, I told myself by way of consolation.

I went straight back to my room. I didn't like not remembering what had happened—not at all. Nicholas could have seen something in me that I never wanted to show him, and that was what made me hate him in that moment. I'd struggled to understand how I could manage to reject him so forcefully in so little time, but it was normal if I considered that Nicholas Leister represented absolutely everything I hated in a person: he was violent, dangerous, an abuser, a liar, threatening...everything that made me take off running in the opposite direction.

I saw my purse had been slung down on the bed. I grabbed my phone and plugged it in. Dammit, Dan was going to kill me. I'd promised him I'd call him last night. He must have been climbing the walls. Fucking Nicholas Leister! Everything was his fault!

When I turned on my phone and opened my messages, I saw that there were no new ones—no missed calls, either. That was strange.

It was beautiful out, a perfect day for the beach or to take a swim for the first time in that amazing pool. If I'd been in a better mood, I'd have gone outside to sunbathe, read a good book, and try to forget what had happened or, even worse, what might have happened. With those thoughts in my head, I walked into my big fancy closet. In a drawer, I saw a ton of swimsuits, but I didn't stop looking until I found a one-piece.

I looked at my naked body in the mirror, with special attention on that part I felt mortified about. But I decided to put it out of my mind. After all, I was at home.

In a sundress and with a violet towel, I walked out of my bedroom to face my first breakfast in that house.

It was unsettling walking around here. I felt the same as I had when I was a little girl and would sleep over at a friend's house and at night I'd want to go to the restroom but wouldn't because I was scared I'd run into someone from their family.

Downstairs, I found my mother in her white-silk robe and sandals with Will, who was wearing a suit, ready for work.

"Good morning, Noah," she said. "How'd you sleep?"

Fabulously, considering I was unconscious and with a fiendish headache.

"It wasn't the best night I've ever had," I answered.

She came over to kiss me on the cheek.

"Did you have fun with Nick and his friends?" she asked hopefully.

Oh, Mom, you can't even imagine. You have no idea who your new stepson is.

"Speak of the devil," William said behind my back, getting up from the table just as Nick entered.

"What's up, guys?" he said on his way to the fridge.

"Did you have fun last night?" my mother asked him. "How was the movie?"

Movie?

I started to ask, "What?," but Nick slammed the refrigerator shut and turned around with an icy stare.

"It was great, right, Noah?"

I realized there I had him. If I told the truth, who knew what his father would say. I could even go to the police and turn him in for offering alcohol to a minor—me—for letting someone drug me, and obviously for leaving me out in the middle of the road.

I couldn't have enjoyed it more as I let him know with my gaze that I had no idea what we were talking about.

"I can't really remember," I answered my mother, watching him turn tense. "Was it *Sleeping with the Enemy* or *Traffic*?" I was going to enjoy seeing him in that situation, but he just laughed it off, wiping the smile off my face.

"I think you mean *Cruel Intentions*," he responded, surprising me by naming one of my favorite movies. Ironic, when you considered that the two main characters were a stepbrother and stepsister who hated each other...

Sensing something was up, my mother asked, "What are you two talking about?"

"Nothing," we said in unison, and that bothered me even more.

For a moment, we were in a standoff: I was trying to intimidate him; he was trying to let me know he was having fun.

"You gonna move or what?" I asked, trying to get to the refrigerator.

"Look, Freckles, you and I need to work some things out if we're going to live under the same roof."

"I've got an idea," I said. "How about when you come in, I'll go out, and when I see you, I'll ignore you, and when you talk, I'll pretend I can't hear you?" I cursed the moment I'd met him.

"Sorry, I got hung up on the in-and-out part," he said—the pervert—grinning and making me blush.

Dammit.

"You're gross," I said and tried to push him aside until he finally yielded and I could grab the orange juice.

My mother had walked off with a cup of coffee in one hand and a newspaper in the other. I knew what she wanted: she wanted for me to get along with Nicholas, for us to become friends and for a miracle to happen so I'd love him like the brother I'd never had.

Ridiculous.

I sat down on one of the benches next to the island and poured the juice into a crystal glass. Nicholas was wearing track pants and a tank top. His arms were shapely, and after seeing him punch two guys in ten minutes, I knew I should stay away from him. Who knew what he was capable of?

When he turned around with his coffee, I saw it: the tattoo. He had the same one I had on my neck. The same knot, that symbol that meant so much to me. That monster had an identical knot on his arm.

I felt a sharp pain in my chest as he came over and sat down in front of me, watching me until he noticed what I was looking at. Then he took a sip of his coffee, put his cup on the table, and leaned over.

"I was surprised, too," he said.

I felt uncomfortable, exposed.

"So it looks like we've got something in common," he continued. He didn't seem overjoyed that we had the same tattoo, either.

I stood up, pulling off my hair band and letting my hair fall until the tattoo was no longer visible. Then I walked out. That last thing he'd said had shifted something inside me, as if he knew the meaning behind that tattoo, as if he understood…

I went to the backyard. There was a beautiful view of the sea, and the salt breeze was warm and fragrant. I couldn't deny it: I loved the view and having the water so close now that I lived here.

I walked over to the wooden deck chairs next to the pool, which was rectangular with a fountain in the corner by the garden that gave it an exotic but elegant touch. Next to the cliff, to the left of the garden, was a jacuzzi located strategically between two enormous rocks to provide a beautiful view of the property.

Deciding I would try to enjoy it, I took off my dress, making sure there was nobody around, and lay back thinking I would soak up some rays and try to get a nice tan in the next week. I had to take advantage of what was left of the summer vacation because in a month, I'd be starting classes at my new and extremely expensive school. I grabbed my phone and looked to see if I had any missed calls from my friends or, more importantly, from my boyfriend Dan.

Nothing.

That stung, but I didn't let it get to me. He'd call, I was sure of it. When I told him I had to leave, he flipped out. We'd been going out for nine months, and he was my first real boyfriend. I loved him, I knew I loved him because he had never judged me, he'd been there when I needed him…and plus, he was hot. When we started, I could hardly contain myself, I was the happiest teenager on the planet. And then I had to run off to another country.

I texted him:

> I'm here and I miss you, I wish I was with you, call me when you get this.

I looked at the message. He had last been online thirty minutes before. I sighed, laid my phone on the chair, and went to the pool.

The water was the perfect temperature, so I stretched out, raised my hands, and dove in. It was liberating and refreshing at the same time. I swam, enjoying just letting the tension go and getting some exercise.

Fifteen minutes later, I got out and lay back in the deck chair, letting the sun work its magic. I grabbed the phone to see if anyone had answered and saw that Dan was connected but he hadn't written. That made me frown.

Just then, Beth wrote, gossipy as ever.

> Hey, babe, what's up? Talk to me.

I smiled and responded, a little nostalgic:

> Well, my stepbrother is worse than I could imagine but I'm trying to get used to the idea that I'll have to live with him. You can't imagine how bad I want to be with you all. I miss you!

I had a knot in my throat as I wrote her. Beth and I were on the same volleyball team. I had been captain the past two years. Now that I was gone, she'd taken over. She was happy, and that made me happy, too. At least she could get something good out of my leaving...even if she'd never told me she'd wanted to be team captain.

> You're probably exaggerating! Enjoy your new life as a millionaire. Like I always said: your mom knows how to pick them! Hahaha.

I hated that remark. She had told me that more than once. I couldn't stand people thinking my mom had married for money. She wasn't like that, she was anything but—she liked simple stuff, the same way I did. She'd married William because she really was in love with him.

I decided not to say anything about it. I didn't want to argue, especially when she was thousands of miles away.

Then she sent me a photo.

It was her and Dan with flushed faces and their arms crossed. Dan was blond with brown eyes—a spectacle to behold. It hurt me to see him so happy. It hadn't even been forty-eight hours since I left. He could be a little sadder, no? I couldn't help but ask her:

> Are you with him right now?

Her response took a while to come, and that alarmed me.

> Yeah, we're at Rose's house. I'll tell him to get in touch with you soon.

Since when did I need Beth to tell my boyfriend to answer my texts?

A minute later, a message with a smiley emoji came in from Dan:

Hey, babe, miss me yet?

Hell yes, I did! I wanted to shout, but I restrained myself and answered, mood worsening:

Why, you don't?

It took him a few seconds to respond. I hated him dillydallying.

Of course I do. It's not the same without you. But I've got to go. I'll call later, OK? I love you.

A thousand butterflies flicked around in my stomach when I read that. I texted him goodbye and set my phone aside.

I couldn't wait to talk to him, hear his voice. I couldn't figure out what on earth to do to keep from missing him every second of the day.

I heard voices coming over to the garden. I turned quickly, grabbed my dress, and threw it over my head.

It was Nick with three other guys.

Shit.

I'd seen them all the day before at the party. One was tan, almost as tall as Nick, with golden-blond hair and blue eyes. One was shorter in comparison with a black eye. That didn't surprise me. I'd seen Nick in action and could assume his friends were just as violent and reckless. The last one really caught my eye, probably because he was the first one to walk straight toward me. His hair was dark brown and his eyes black as night. He was very, very intimidating, especially with the tattoos covering his arms.

"Hey, good-looking...did you just climb out of my fantasies and show up here?" he asked, lying in the deck chair next to me.

Nick flopped down on the other, grinning.

"Excuse me?" I asked, sitting up.

He laughed and looked at Nick.

"You were right, she's a live one," he said, making me uncomfortable.

He was disgusting. The other two guys jumped in the pool and splashed water everywhere. The water made my dress cling to my body.

"Careful, assholes!" Nick shouted, grabbing my towel and using it to dry off.

"You guys can keep splashing in this direction," goon number three said, gawking at my breasts, now clearly visible through my soaked dress. "You're one hell of a catch for a fifteen-year-old."

"I'm seventeen, and if you keep looking at me like that, I'll take a certain part of your anatomy and do serious damage to it," I said, pulling the dress away from my torso.

Nicholas thew the towel back to me, and I covered up.

"Drop it, dude," he said. "Otherwise I'm gonna have to throw her in the water to get her to shut up, and I'd rather just stay here where I am."

"Excuse me?" I said, chuckling. Nick was in his bathing suit, and I had a spectacular view of his bare chest and his tattoos.

He took off his Ray-Bans and stared at me with his blue eyes. They looked remarkable under the sun, and for a few moments, I was thrown off.

"You don't think I forgot you hitting me last night, do you?" I looked down at my knuckles, which still ached. His jaw wasn't even slightly bruised.

"Are you threatening me?" I asked. He was getting the better of me.

"Nick, I love this chick. She needs to come out with us more often," the tattooed guy said before he got up and dove into the pool.

"Listen, Freckles, you can't just talk to me however you like," he warned me. "See those guys? They respect me, you know why? Because they know I could put them on their ass at the drop of a hat. So be careful how you talk to me, give me my distance, and everything will be fine."

As he spoke, I thought to myself how I could best respond.

"Funny how you think you're the one who can threaten me when I could rat you out to your dad whenever I felt like it," I said.

He clenched his teeth. I smiled. Noah one, Nick zero.

"You don't want to play this game with me, Noah, believe me."

Needing to do something with my hands, I bent over to grab some suntan lotion. "Then you'd better stop hoping I treat you with a respect you're light-years away from deserving. You don't want me to spill the beans about last night? Then drop the little remarks and tell your boyfriends to leave me alone."

Before he could respond, one of the goons got out of the pool and sat down beside me. Water from his body dripped all over me, and I jerked away, irritated.

"You want some help with that, babe? I could rub it on your back."

"Beat it, Hugo. My little sister and I are having an important conversation," Nick ordered him.

Hugo got back up without a need to hear it twice. Good.

"Are we hanging out tonight?" Hugo asked. Nick nodded. "Stakes are high, bro, we need to win these races no matter what."

Nick's eyes shot arrows at him. Interesting.

Did I just hear the word *races*?

"I said leave."

Hugo looked bewildered for a moment before glancing at me and seeming to realize he'd said too much.

When he and the rest of his friends left, I turned around and looked at my stepbrother.

"Races?"

Nick put his glasses back on and stretched out in the direction of the sun.

"Don't ask questions if you don't want answers."

I bit my lip, intrigued, but still, I wasn't going to press him. Whatever Nicholas Leister was wrapped up in couldn't interest me less.

Or so I thought.

That afternoon, I decided to spend some time with my mom. William's company was having a gala that night, and she'd told me we needed to go as a family. I wasn't particularly excited about it, but I knew there was no getting out of it: William had been working on the event for months, and we were expected to be there.

I found myself sitting on a sofa in my mother's dressing room. Her bedroom was even more lavish than mine. Decorated in cream tones with a California king bed, it looked like a luxury hotel room and had two walk-in closets. I'd never thought a person needed even one, but when I saw the hundreds of shirts, ties, and suits William had, I understood.

That night would be important for my mother. Obviously, many close friends and important industry heads and law people would be there, not all of whom had had the honor of meeting my mother in person. She was so nervous that it was funny.

"Mom, you're going to look gorgeous no matter what you wear. Why don't you just relax?"

She looked at me with a radiant smile. It was wonderful, seeing her so happy.

"Thanks, Noah," she said, holding up a white-and-green dress for me to see. "So this one?"

I nodded, thinking about what the evening had in store. If

Nicholas was going to take off again to get in trouble, then I would be free to do the same—or so I told myself, by way of consolation.

"Your dress is marvelous, too," my mother said, and in my mind, I saw it again. "Honey, don't make faces, you're not going to die just because you dress up a little for one day."

"Sorry," I said. My mood had been like a roller coaster lately. "It's just that going to dinner and a gala isn't exactly what I'm in the mood for."

"It'll be fun, I promise," she said, trying to cheer me up.

I thought of Dan, of how much he would have liked to see me in the dress I had on that night. What was the point of getting all pretty if no one I cared about was going to notice me?

"I'm sure," I said, trying to put a happy face. "I guess I should go get ready."

My mother dropped what she was doing and came over.

"Thanks for doing this for me, dear. It means a lot."

I nodded, trying to smile.

"No worries," I replied, letting her wrap her arms around me. I realized how much I needed that contact, especially after what had happened the night before. I held her tight, and for a few moments, everything felt just as it had when I was little.

8

Nick

I WAS GOING TO NEED TO KEEP MY EYE ON NOAH. THINGS COULD have gone bad the night before if my dad had found out what we were up to. I was worried about how to keep my private life hidden now that there were more than two people in the house. I didn't let my two worlds mix. I was careful about that—I needed to be.

Same as every year, we were having races in the desert, and that day, I'd need to be there. They were crazy: rock music, drugs, expensive cars, and races until the sun came up or the cops came, but they almost never bothered us, since it all happened in the middle of nowhere. The girls were wild, everyone drank, and adrenaline was the perfect extra ingredient to make it the best night of your life—as long as you weren't the loser.

Ronnie's gang always competed against us. Whoever won got to keep the loser's car, plus all the cash from the bets. It was dangerous, I knew that firsthand, and for that reason, everyone trusted me when it got down to the wire. Ronnie and I had a friendly deal, but it could be broken as easily as tearing up a sheet of paper, and that night I had to be on guard, not to mention win.

Noah would need to keep her mouth shut, so I stopped at her door before it was time to head to the hotel where the gala was happening.

I knocked three times and waited almost a minute before she came out.

"What do you want?" she grunted.

I walked past her into her room. Before my father had married her mother, it had been mine.

"You know this used to be my gym?" I said, walking over to her bed.

"Oh no, the poor little rich boy had to give up his machines," she joked.

I stared at her, meaning to intimidate her, but as my eyes traced out the lines of her body, I couldn't help but admire it. My friends were right, she was hot, and I didn't know if that was good or bad, given my situation.

Her hair was done up elaborately, pulled back in a bun with curls framing her face. It looked elegant and easygoing at the same time. What surprised me the most, apart from the light-blue dress that hung to her feet and left little to the imagination, was her makeup: her skin looked like alabaster and her eyes like two bottomless wells. I didn't usually like chicks with a bunch of makeup on, but I had to admit, those long eyelashes made me want to reach out and touch them, and those lips—that carmine color could make any man lose his mind.

I tried to restrain the unexpected desire that overtook me and made the first nasty remark that came into my head.

"Who did the paint job?" I asked. I could tell it had gotten under her skin when I saw the blood rise in her cheeks.

"I did it so you'd keep your eyes off me," she said, turning around and grabbing a necklace off her nightstand. I could see her bare back and the silk of the dress like a waterfall.

Without even realizing it, I walked over. My fingers were aching to feel that skin that looked so soft...

"What are you doing?" she asked.

Seeing her up close, I noticed that not a single freckle was visible.

I took the necklace out of her hands and lifted it up as if I were going to help her. But she clearly didn't trust me.

"Come on, little sister, am I that bad a guy?" I asked her, asking myself at the same time what the hell I was doing.

"You're the worst," she said, snatching it back. When I felt her skin graze mine, my hair stood up on end.

Dammit!

I stepped back, frustrated at the feelings she was causing. My desire was taking over, and it was killing me to think that not only could I not touch her, I could barely even look at her.

"I came to make sure you won't mouth off tonight," I said as she put on her necklace deftly.

"Mouth off about what?"

I was close enough to smell her perfume, which was almost intoxicating.

"You know I've got things to do after the gala, and I don't want you making any smart comments when I tell my father I've got to go."

"Oh, because you'll have to *work on the case,* am I right?"

I grinned.

"You got it. Perfect. See you around, sister."

"Not so fast, Nicholas." I stopped a few feet from the door and froze as I noticed that tickle in my stomach when she said my name aloud. "What do I get out of all this?"

When I turned back, she had a smug, almost heart-shaped smile on her face.

"What you get is I won't waste my time trying to make your life a living hell."

Noah raised an eyebrow.

"I don't see how you could do that."

"Trust me, you don't want to find out, either."

"If you leave the gala, you're taking me with you. There's nothing that appeals to me less than being surrounded by people I don't know at someone else's party."

"Sorry, Freckles, but as you might have realized, taxi driver's not a job I aspire to." As I said this, I pointed at my designer outfit.

"Well, find an excuse that includes both of us because I'm not going to play the perfect daughter while you take off for your secret illegal races."

Shit. Just hearing her say it made me nervous.

"Fine, I guess I can make something up," I said, just to put her off. When the time came for me to leave, she wouldn't even notice.

"It's amazing how you've managed to dupe everyone," she said. "You know my mother thinks you're the perfect son?"

"I am perfect in lots of ways, babe." I couldn't help it—I was enjoying the conversation. Arguing with this girl was highly stimulating. "Whenever you feel like it, I'll show you."

She looked at me self-righteously. Normally I couldn't beat the girls off with a stick. Just one look and they were all up on me doing whatever they could to please me. I had a rep: women respected me and adored me at the same time. I gave them pleasure, and they gave me my space. It had always been like that since I was fourteen and learned what a handsome face and a good body could make a woman do. But there was Noah, staring me down at every second, completely unperturbed by my presence.

"Is that what you tell girls to get them into bed?" she asked. "Well, with me, it's not going to work, so save your strength." When I absorbed her words, I could feel an uncomfortable pressure in my pants.

I imagined tearing off her dress and doing all the things to her that I knew drove women wild. It would be fun, driving Noah wild until she couldn't stop shouting my name.

Dammit.

"Don't worry about that. I like women, not girls with pigtails and freckles."

"I never wear pigtails, dumbass."

I laughed and tried to relax. Now I did want to see her in pigtails!

"Well, I guess we've got a deal," I said, thinking it was time for me to go.

"I guess you think coming in here and telling me what to do is a deal?"

"You got it, little sister. Bye now."

Her eyes were ice-cold. I walked off, not bothering to look back, but once outside, I leaned against the wall. I'd never let myself get that out of control. Shit. I felt...exposed, like a thirteen-year-old boy.

I took out my phone and tried to clear my head.

I'll come by your place before the party.

I walked down the hall to the steps.

I needed to blow off some steam before the night arrived, and with Anna was the best way to do it.

Twenty minutes later, I was at her door. Anna was the perfect cover-up for what would be happening that night. She was the daughter of one of the most important bankers in Los Angeles, and our fathers had known each other since college. Anna had grown up torturing me as she matured, and I had thrown myself at her feet when I was a kid and had no idea how to treat a woman.

We'd learned together, and we both knew what the other liked. Plus, she never got out of line and never asked for explanations.

When she came and opened the door, I dragged her off to her room.

"What are you doing?" she asked when I locked the door and wrapped my arms around her.

"It's called fucking. You might have heard of it," I responded as I threw her on the bed.

She smiled and pulled her dress up provocatively. Unlike Noah, she wore her hair down, and her dress was so short I didn't have to work hard to get to what I was interested in.

"We'll be late," she complained, bringing her face close to mine and kissing me on the mouth.

"You know I don't give a shit," I said, taking her to ecstasy just as I found the calm I'd needed ever since that witch with freckles had first come into my life.

———————

Fifteen minutes later, I was adjusting my tie and lighting a cigarette on Anna's balcony.

She walked up beside me, her dress now back in place, hair combed, lips swollen from kissing.

"How do I look?" she said, pressing her body into mine.

I examined her. She was hot. Her body was hot. Her hair was dark brown, just like her eyes. I'd never gotten why Anna didn't have a real boyfriend—she could have had anyone she wanted, and yet there she was, wasting time with a guy like me.

"Great," I said, stepping away. I needed a few seconds to relax, finish my smoke, and visualize how this night was going to go.

"Are you nervous about Ronnie?" she asked, leaning against the railing. She knew I needed my space, my alone time. That was why I kept going back to her.

I took a drag and expelled the smoke slowly.

"Nah, I'm not nervous." *Irritated* was more like it.

"Is it your stepmother?" She knew about my father's new marriage and how much the situation bothered me despite my attempts to cover it up.

"Her daughter," I said, stubbing the cigarette out on the sole of my shoe. "She doesn't know who I am or what I'm capable of," I continued.

"You want me to make it clear to her?" she asked, and just imagining Noah and Anna facing off was both hilarious and upsetting.

"No. I just need her to keep her mouth closed and stay out of my business."

"You don't want to take her down the road to perdition?" Anna asked. For a second, I thought, *Yes, I do.*

"Better to keep her away from it. I don't want her giving me more problems like she did last night."

The wind shook Anna's hair away from her neck. I walked over to her and pushed it behind her ear. And then my brain looked for something that wasn't there—that tattoo, the knot, wasn't there, and just then, that tattoo was the only thing I wanted to kiss.

I let her go, even though she clearly wanted more.

"Let's go," I said. "We're going to be late."

"Thought you didn't care." Anna's irritation was evident.

"Right you are," I said, a little confused myself.

9

Noah

As soon as Nick left, I sat on my bed to catch my breath. *Races...* That was my weak spot all right. It was one of the few things I'd inherited from my father, one of the few things I had enjoyed doing with him. I remembered sitting on the floor at his feet watching NASCAR on TV. My father had been one of the best drivers of his generation, until everything went bad.

I could see my mother's face when she forbid me from ever returning to that world—fast cars, races. At just ten years old, I'd known everything there was to know about driving, and when my legs were long enough to reach the pedals, my father had let me drive with him. It was one of the most incredible experiences of my life. I could still remember the euphoria of pure speed, the sand clinging to the windshield, getting in the car, the squeal of the tires—above all, the peace of mind it gave me. Racing meant nothing else mattered. We were alone, the car and me. No one else.

But that was then. My mother had since told me in no uncertain terms to stay away from racing, and I had to accept that, regardless of how much I missed it.

I sighed, got up, and grabbed my phone, which wouldn't stop vibrating. My friends didn't seem to miss me. They were going to another party that night, and they didn't seem to realize I was still in the group chat, able to read all the details about who and where and how much everybody was planning to drink.

I was sad but also irritated. Dan still hadn't called me. I was longing to hear his voice, to talk the way we'd talked before I left, for hours and hours. Why wouldn't he call me? Had he forgotten about me?

With these thoughts, I left my room and found my mother and Will in the vestibule. He was wearing a tux and looked like a Hollywood actor with his elegant bearing, which, sadly, his son had inherited. I had to admit that when I'd seen Nick in his black suit and white shirt, it had been hard not to stare or snap a photo. He was beyond handsome, but that was the only positive thing about him. The race, though, that had surprised me. So we had more in common than just a tattoo.

My mother was dazzling. All eyes would be on her that night and rightly so.

"Noah, you're gorgeous," she said, beaming, but whatever, she was my mom, I would always be pretty to her.

Will looked me over and furrowed his brow, making me immediately uncomfortable.

"Is something up?" I asked, surprised and annoyed. Surely he wasn't going to tell me to cover up. One thing would be if it was me thinking it, but him? I didn't know what I'd say back. But then his face relaxed.

"Au contraire, you look stunning!"

"Just one little touch-up," my mother said, digging through her bag, pulling out a small bottle, and spraying my bare shoulders and neckline. "Now you'll make an even better impression."

Whatever. My mother thought I was still a little girl in pigtails, as Nicholas put it.

We went outside, where a sparkling limousine was waiting for us. I was surprised but at the same time fed up. I don't know why it surprised me—what else should I expect?—but still, I couldn't get used to this fancy lifestyle.

Will and my mom poured themselves glasses of champagne and, to my surprise, offered me one, which I accepted with pleasure, drank in one gulp, and refilled before they could realize it. If I wanted to get through the night, those wouldn't be the last ones I had.

Nicholas had already left. I envied his freedom to come and go and do as he pleased. I would have to get a job soon if I expected to have a car. No way I was going to depend on anyone else to get where I needed to go.

I took my phone out of my clutch and saw that Dan hadn't called me and there were no messages for me in our group chat. I took a few deep breaths and told myself he'd call. He'd probably lost his phone or something else had kept him from just hitting the damn button and talking to me.

That clouded my mood as we reached the hotel. To my surprise, a bunch of photographers were there waiting to immortalize the moment when William Leister would expand his company and with it his fortune. I felt so out of place that I would have taken off running if I wasn't wearing those damned high heels.

"Nicholas should be here already," William said. His attitude was serious. "He knows the family photos come at the beginning of the dinner." This was the first time since I'd met Will that I'd seen him actually angry.

We waited for ten minutes in the limo while people shouted for us to come out so they could get a picture. It was ridiculous to stay huddled in there, but I guessed millionaires didn't mind making dozens of photographers wait for their damned snapshot.

Then there was a commotion, and the photographers turned away and started shouting my stepbrother's name.

"He's here!" William shouted, irritated but also relieved. "Come on, honey," he told my mother and opened the door.

As soon as I got out, I could see the photographers' flashes practically blinding Nick and his date. They looked like real movie stars, and they were being treated like they were, too.

How could so many people know his name?

Our eyes met. I looked at him with indifference despite how handsome he was, and he scowled at me before turning back to his girlfriend or friend with benefits or whatever the hell she was. He kissed her on the lips, and the photographers went wild.

When they separated, the people shouted for more.

"Anna, how are you?" Will greeted Nicholas's date. He was clearly livid. "If you don't mind, we need to take some family photos, but we'll be back with you in a few minutes." What a gentle way of getting someone off your back!

Anna eyed me up. I could tell she hated me, probably for all the trash Nicholas had talked. And I hadn't even had the pleasure of getting to know her. I ignored her and went over to my mother so we could take the damned photos and get them over with. We stood in front of a backdrop with ads for God knows what, and the flashes blinded me for a second.

When my mother had married one of the most important lawyers and businessmen in the United States, I hadn't been surprised to hear she'd sometimes popped up in the papers or magazines, but this was totally crazy. Leister Enterprises: that was the logo you saw everywhere. I even saw actual stars. I freaked out when I spied Johana Mavis in one corner in a dress that was out of this world.

"Tell me that isn't my favorite writer," I said, grabbing the person next to me, whom I thought was my mother. But when my fingers touched that forearm, I realized it was too hard to be hers.

"You want me to introduce you?" he asked, and I looked up at him, immediately retracting my hand.

"You know her?" I couldn't believe it.

"Yeah," he said like it was no big deal. "My father's firm handles a lot of Hollywood bigshots' cases. From the time I was a kid, I've known more stars than probably anyone else in LA. Famous people like lawyers—they need them to stay out of jail. You'd be surprised how much it happens."

I took a glass of champagne from a passing waiter with a nervous feeling in my stomach.

"What about your girlfriend?" I asked to distract myself. "You didn't just leave her alone after that public display of affection, did you?"

"Do you want the intro or not?" he asked.

"You don't need to ask. It's obvious that I do. I've been a fan of Johana for as long as I can remember. She wrote the best books of all time," I said. His attitude amused me. Some way he had of doing someone a favor!

"Come on, then, and don't start shrieking like a baby, please."

Oh God... Johana smiled wide when she saw Nick coming over to say hi.

"Nick, you look amazing!" she said, giving him a hug. I was freaking out before. Now I was completely gaga.

"Thanks. You're stunning as always. Have you seen Dad?" he asked. I analyzed each of Johana's movements and engraved them in my memory. What I wouldn't have given to have a camera just then.

"Yeah, I congratulated him," she laughed. "We need more lawyers like him."

When the chitchat was over, Nicholas turned to me.

"Johana, I'd like to introduce you to your number one fan: my stepsister Noah. I call her Freckles, though," he said. He was laughing, but in that moment, I couldn't care less.

"You're the greatest. I absolutely love your books," I said, my voice cracking. Amazing. All those years practicing these phrases in my mind to wind up saying the most cliché thing ever.

Nicholas tried not to smirk, but I could see the sarcasm in his eyes.

"Thanks," she said and then hugged me. *She hugged me!*

"You want a photo?" she asked, grabbing me and pulling me over next to her.

"Man, I don't have a camera," I said.

"Jesus, Noah. Why do you think God invented cell phones?" said Nicholas.

I smiled, realizing how flummoxed I must be.

Johana put her arm over my shoulders, Nick aimed his iPhone, and the greatest moment of my life was thus immortalized.

"Thank you so much," I said, still amazed I was actually looking at her.

"No problem, sweetie," she said before smiling and walking off with a friend.

"You owe me one, little sister," Nick said, slipping his phone in his pocket before leaning in and continuing in a whisper, "and that means keeping your mouth shut."

I felt a shiver go up my spine when his hot breath touched my neck. I didn't care what I was getting myself into anymore. I couldn't stop smiling.

That was, until my phone buzzed. I opened my messages, expecting to see my photo with Johana. And that was when everything came crashing down. My heart stopped, my hands started to shake, and I felt hot all over. It couldn't be.

It was a photo all right—a photo of Dan making out with a girl. A girl I knew better than I knew myself.

"I can't believe it," I said under my breath. I had a knot in my throat, and if I'd wanted to, I could have shed several years' worth of tears I'd kept bottled up inside.

"What's up?" I heard. I realized Nick was there, and he must have seen the photo flash across my screen.

My breathing sped up; I felt betrayed, hurt, deceived. I had to get out of there.

I pressed my phone into his chest and exited through a door to the left. I needed fresh air. I needed to be alone.

I went into the bathroom and walked over to the mirror, leaning on the counter, looking at my feet.

Take it easy…take it easy…don't break down, not now, don't cry, they don't deserve it…

I looked up at my reflection. What was it that hurt more? That the first guy I'd ever loved had cheated on me or that he had done so with my best friend?

Beth… Beth!

I wanted to shout, to hit someone; I needed to do something with all that built-up rage; I needed to do something to keep from breaking into a million pieces. Right when my whole life had been turned upside down, when I was totally alone in a new city with no friends, with no one at all, where no one even cared who I was.

Son of a… I took a few deep breaths to calm down. They'd soon learn what I was capable of.

Once I had myself under control, I returned to the hall, where everyone was eating canapés and blabbing pleasantly about nonsense. No one knew how much pain I was feeling just then, how bad I wanted to shout at all those superficial people that they had no idea what it meant to actually suffer, and I wanted to shove all those glasses of champagne onto the ground and watch them break.

Champagne…good idea. I went straight to the bar.

A guy, Mexican maybe, was serving cocktails, and he turned to me as he wiped his hands with a damp towel.

"What can I offer you, ma'am?" he asked.

I laughed and said, "I'm seventeen years old, and you can't be much older, so don't talk to me like I'm one of these bougie bitches with a face-lift," I said. To my surprise, he started cracking up.

"You wouldn't say that if you didn't know your way around here," he said, looking at all the multimillionaires laughing it up behind me.

"Please, don't even insinuate that I've got anything in common with these people. I'm here because my dumbass crazy mother decided to marry William Leister, not because this is paradise for me," I said, draining the glass of champagne and handing it back to the bartender to refill it.

"Wait a second," he said, looking behind him and then back at me. "You're Nick Leister's stepsister?"

Dear God, not another of that dickhead's friends, please.

"I am," I said, impatient to get served again and drown my miseries.

"I feel sorry for you," he confessed, finally pouring the champagne. My mood was getting a little better. Anyone who hated Nick automatically had a place on the list of my favorite people in the world.

"What do you know him from, apart from his unquestioned reputation as a stuck-up asshole?"

"I don't think you want to know," he said, refilling my glass a second time without needing to be asked.

At that rate, I'd be drunk before midnight.

"If you're talking about the races, I already know," I said, realizing how much I wanted to get out of here. Was I really going to sit in that room full of people I didn't know but hated with all my soul? Was I going to stay away from the thing I loved the most just because my mom had asked me to? Had she asked me when she'd decided to turn our lives upside down? If I hadn't left, I'd still have a boyfriend and a best friend—or maybe I'd had to leave to find out the truth.

"I'm going to the races, and you're taking me," I said, and I felt that tingle in my body I got when I was doing something bad—something risky, something liberating, something that told me I wasn't going to be the good little girl everyone expected me to be.

That night I would do whatever the hell I wanted, and if I got my revenge, too, then all the better.

10

Nick

I watched her walk off and understood nothing. Then I looked at the message under the photo.

> This is what happens when you leave town. Did you re-
> ally think Dan would wait forever for you?

Who the hell was Dan? And who was this bitch Kay to send a message like that?

I didn't hesitate to open the photos on her phone. There were tons of pictures of her with some brunette chick, the same one in the other photo, I thought, and then some more with friends. And one in what looked like her old school. There I saw what I was looking for.

This so-called Dan had Noah's face in his hands and was kissing her and she couldn't stop laughing. I guessed she had known someone was taking their picture. So he'd cheated on her.

I turned off the screen and put her phone in my pocket. I had no idea why, but I wanted to toss it in the bottom of the ocean. Something got to me when I saw that picture of Noah kissing another guy. I suddenly wanted to punch anybody who decided to get in my way that night.

I went to the table with a card with my name on it. Noah was supposed to sit on one side of me and Anna on the other. Across from me would be my father and his wife. There were two other couples whose names I couldn't remember, but Dad had said I needed to show them the most charming and perfect version possible of William Leister's offspring.

Not two seconds after I sat down, Anna appeared next to me. I could smell her perfume as soon as she did, and I leaned over to take a sip of the bloodred wine that had been poured into all the glasses.

"Where's your sister?" she asked insolently.

"She's upset because some guy cheated on her."

Anna laughed. It pissed me off, honestly.

"It's to be expected. She's a little girl," Anna said, and I could sense the contempt in her voice.

I observed her for a moment as I analyzed her response. She sure seemed to dislike Noah even though she barely knew her. It was true she must not have appreciated Noah punching me in the face the night before.

"Talk to me about something else. It's enough having her in my house," I said, setting my glass back on the table.

Without realizing it, though, my eyes were already scanning the room for Noah. Most of the guests had already sat down, but she was at the bar on the other side of the room waiting for the bartender to come over.

I stood up when I saw who it was and walked over firmly. I was absolutely not going to let Mario get to know my new stepsister. But I got there too late, hearing the words "See you at the door in five minutes."

"In five minutes, you'll be sitting in a limousine waiting to go back home," I interrupted them.

"Hello to you, too, Nick," she said.

"Don't be an idiot," I said. "What the hell do you think you're doing?"

Mario was part of my past, and he absolutely couldn't get acquainted with Noah. It was too risky. He clearly knew what I was thinking, and that was why he hadn't hesitated one second to suck up to her.

"Not everything concerns you, Nicholas," Noah said, and I had the urge to shut her up. "Can I have my phone back?" she asked, stretching out the palm of her hand. There wasn't a trace of the tears I'd seen in her eyes before. Nothing. She was cold as ice. "Today, not next year please."

She was pushing it that night. Mario laughed and raised his hands as if to say he was giving up.

"I wouldn't mess with her," he said, as though he'd known her his whole life.

"Noah, stop playing. You don't even know him," I told her, trying to reason with her, while I took the phone out of my pocket and slapped it down on her hand.

"I guess you do? Anyway, for your information, I'm going to those races you're trying so hard to keep secret."

I stepped in close.

"What have you been smoking, little girl? You better stay as far as you can from where I'm going, hear me?"

But Noah wasn't daunted.

"I can go and not say a word about where *we're* going tonight, or I can stay here and tell your father everything. Your call."

Goddammit!

I didn't get the attitude. Most girls, if their boyfriend cheated on them, would break down and run off to cry in a corner for days, and her reaction was to try to get under my skin?

I was tired of all this. I couldn't waste my life dealing with her.

I turned around and went back to my table. My biggest worry was that my father would find out what I was up to when I was out of the house. I'd always tried to keep my private and family lives apart, and now I had this miserable little snotnose here who not only didn't care what I said, she had even decided to get mixed up in my business.

After about twenty minutes, I stood up and went to the bar, where my father and his new wife were drinking and chatting with a couple of friends. When he saw me coming over, he smiled, and when I got there, he clapped me on the back. I hated that. I needed my space, and the fact that he was the one invading it only made matters worse.

"Are you headed out already?" he asked. There was no reproach in his tone. Good. That meant I could leave without any problems.

"Yeah," I said, leaving my drink on a bar table. "I've got to get up early tomorrow to keep working on the case."

My father nodded.

"Noah already went home, so don't worry about it. You look tired. Go on home."

I nodded, satisfied, and walked out with Anna at my side.

11

Noah

My mind was cloudy. The only thing that mattered to me was payback. Major payback. I kept thinking over and over about Dan's and Beth's lips touching. It was disgusting. Just imagining it made me want to throw up. I saw everything in red. I was blinded by hatred, pain, and a profound need for revenge.

I was in my closet taking off my clothes, and on the other side of the wall was a boy I'd just met two hours ago who was patiently waiting on my bed for me to finish. I couldn't show up at the races in a ball gown, let alone in stiletto heels. I put on a pair of jean shorts, a blue tank top, and some ordinary sandals. You couldn't look like a Goody Two-shoes in a place like that, so I was happy to have on all that makeup, even if it wasn't my usual thing. I pulled the goddamn bobby pins out of my hair—I must have had a hundred in—let my long hair down, and then pulled it back in a ponytail.

I had exactly one thought in my head: hooking up with the hottest and baddest guy there. That would make me feel satisfied, less used, less deceived, and like less of an idiot, even if deep down I knew none of that could erase reality: I was destroyed and struggling to hold my heart together.

Had Beth told Dan everything I'd confessed to her? Had they laughed at me while I was still trying to give it my all in my first and only relationship? Had they planned this?

I took a deep breath and tried to swallow the pain.

When I stepped out, Mario, the bartender I'd just met, stared at me admiringly, and I knew I'd achieved the effect I was going for.

"You look good," he said. He smiled, and I responded in kind but unenthusiastically. I wasn't in the mood for stupid compliments.

"Thanks," I said, grabbing my bag off the bed and heading for the door. "Shall we?"

Mario stood up and followed me, and soon, we were climbing into his car.

Half an hour later, Mario turned off onto a secondary road surrounded by dry fields and red-and-orange dust. As we drove on, I could no longer hear the cars on the freeway. Instead it was just repetitive music getting louder and louder.

"You ever done something like this before?" Mario asked, one hand on the wheel and the other resting on the back of my seat.

"I've been in quite a few races, yeah," I said in a surly tone.

He looked over and then back at the road. Then I saw tons of people in the distance and neon lights around a deserted area full of badly parked cars.

The music was deafening. The people there were between twenty and thirty. Everyone was drinking, dancing, and partying like this was the last day of their lives. Mario stopped close to where most of them were and got out, waiting for me to do the same.

"What is this place?" I asked him, and he chuckled.

"Don't worry, these are the spectators. The important people are the ones over there," he said, pointing to the left, where a big group of guys and girls were lying on the hoods of fancy souped-up cars with god-awful music blasting from their trunks.

I saw fluorescent fabrics all around, and beneath the headlights—which were the main source of light out there—they glowed brightly. Many of the girls had painted their bodies and even their faces in fluorescent paint.

"I see you pay attention to the details," Mario said. I had no idea what he was talking about. But then he pointed at my chest, and I saw that whatever my mother had sprayed all over me was now shining on my pale skin like a thousand little fluorescent dots. Ridiculous.

"Honestly, I had no idea," I said.

"Still and all, it's for the best," he said, looking at my shorts and my shirt. "Not just anyone can come here, and no offense, but you're dressed a little more modestly than most people here."

Modest! The girls there could have been strippers if they'd just taken off their micro-minis and bikini tops.

"I don't know if you know the deal here, but there are gangs or groups. Your brother is the leader of one, and it's important he beats Ronnie," Mario said when we were close to the cars that would be racing.

Nick was a gang leader? That was unexpected, but I shouldn't have been surprised. From what little I knew of him, it made sense he'd be involved in something like that. He was violent, frightening, and a hard-ass, and he hid it with amazing aplomb whenever he was hanging out with the people he'd grown up around. But he was a rich kid! This kind of thing didn't happen in his world. What was a dude whose father was one of the most important lawyers in the country doing running a gang like the one I was looking at right now?

Mario stopped next to a couple of guys who could have given

me nightmares for a month straight. They had tattoos on their arms and were wearing baggy clothes and cross pendants and all kinds of silver and gold chains. The girls beside them were dressed provocatively, but that was nothing compared to the ones near where we'd parked.

Mario fist-bumped the guys like they'd been friends all their lives, and they started jostling each other and laughing. It was strange to see such warm camaraderie. If you just looked at them, they were terrifying. All the guys had fluorescent-yellow bands around their forearms or wrists or in their hair. I realized all of them were members of the same gang. Nick's gang.

"Who's the hot chick?" one asked, and they all laughed as they looked over at me. People kept showing up and walking back and forth. But not them. They stayed where they were. I didn't like the comment, but my only reaction was a scowl. Mario came to my aid.

"Y'all aren't going to believe it, but she's Nick's stepsister," he said. I was disappointed; I didn't want anyone to know. I wanted to go unnoticed that night or at least have a good time without getting labeled as the goody-goody gold-digger stepsister-of-Nick.

If it was even possible, they laughed harder, and the girls looked at me with renewed interest.

"Bring our new friend something to drink!" a black guy said. He was holding a red cup and had his arm around the waist of a hot girl. She turned around, poured something into a cup, and passed it to me while the others went on talking and listening to their shrill music.

"So you're our friend's new girl?" she asked, eyeing me up. I did the same. If she wasn't going to respect me, why should I respect her? She was black, tall, and very thin. Her hair was in thin braids that descended to her waist. She was wearing white shorts and a dark-blue T-shirt.

"Stepsister," I corrected her, grabbing my cup and looking at it with suspicion. "You didn't put anything in it, did you?" I asked. I didn't trust these people. I'd already been drugged once. I didn't need it to happen again.

"What kind of person do you think I am?" she asked, offended. "It's beer, and if you want anything weaker, you're in the wrong place." She turned so fast her braids almost hit me and walked away swaying her hips sexily, causing many men there to stop and stare.

"You've only been here half an hour, and people are already placing bets on you," Mario said.

"What kind of bets?" I asked, flustered.

"How soon you're going to need to throw away your beer and take off running back home." His face was expectant.

So that was how it was?

I glared at him and all the guys looking at me like I was a joke and drank the entire contents of that oversize cup. As I did, they started shouting louder and louder, and when I finished, a little woozy and with an urge to cough, all present clapped and whistled.

I lifted the cup with a smile.

"Who's going to get me a refill?" For a moment, I felt free and happy.

The girl from before came back, this time with a smile on her lips.

"My name's Jenna," she said, handing me another cup. "If you really want to win these boys over, let your hair down, drink this, and hook up with the best-looking one. In that order."

I burst out laughing. Was she serious? And if she was, did I care? I'd gone there with one goal in mind: get vengeance somehow on my disgusting ex-boyfriend and my ex-best friend, so letting my hair down and having fun…what was the harm in that?

"I think I'll listen to you," I told her, throwing away my hair band away and letting my hair fall over my shoulders as I took a swig of something much stronger than beer.

Jenna started dancing, amused. There was hardly any light there apart from the fluorescent-yellow bands and the headlights farther off.

"I'm Noah, by the way," I said, realizing I'd failed to introduce myself.

She smiled. She seemed nice. All of a sudden, I heard a commotion. The guys who were sitting on the hoods of the cars got up and walked toward someone who was pulling up. Right away, I recognized Noah's SUV.

"Here comes the dream and nightmare of any girl with eyes," Jenna announced.

Whatever, I thought. Nick was hot, but as soon as he opened his mouth, you wanted to take off running or start banging your head against the wall.

I took another drink to keep from looking at him, counting the minutes until he'd come over and say something to me. It was fine. I expected it, and it would give me the chance to vent some of my frustration.

But he didn't do it. Actually, he deliberately ignored me for half an hour. That surprised me at first, but I was grateful afterward because I was having fun with Jenna, enjoying her energetic way of talking and dancing to the hardcore music that was playing.

"I should introduce you to my guy," she said as I watched her, thinking to myself that she could swing her hips better than Beyonce herself. I followed her to where all the people were standing. The other girls were drinking or talking, and two or three were flirting with guys, trying to get them to dance along.

Jenna's boyfriend was the guy I'd seen her with when I had gotten there, I thought. Just then, he was in the middle of a discussion with Nick.

I tensed as I approached them, standing at some distance from everyone else.

"Lion!" Jenna shouted, pulling on his shoulders and giving him a kiss on the cheek. Lion and Nick both turned toward us. Nicholas didn't look excited to see me.

"This is Noah," she said, spinning him all the way around so I could get a good look at him. Lion was the same height as Nick and very striking with his green eyes—green like the mint in a mojito—and his perfectly sculpted, muscular body.

Jenna was a lucky woman!

"What's up, Noah?" he said with a friendly smile but keeping an eye on my stepbrother.

"Nice to meet you," I said, smiling back. I was really starting to like Jenna, and I didn't want her boyfriend to believe all the stuff Nick had certainly told him about me.

"Wow, you can be nice and everything," Nicholas said cynically. I geared up, ready to attack for the third, maybe the fourth time.

I wasn't in the mood for another fight, though, so I resorted to a universal gesture: raising my middle finger and walking off in search of something better to do.

That was when I felt his arm loop through mine, pulling me toward a dark corner between two expensive cars. Jenna and her boyfriend watched us for a moment, but then she kissed him hard. It stung to see a couple that looked so good together, so happy. Not even four hours ago, I too thought I had the best guy in the world by my side, and now...

"What do you want?" I asked Nick, expelling all my rage. He'd pushed me into the car, so I was trapped between him and the door of a gray BMW.

He'd changed clothes. Now he was wearing jeans that left his Calvin Klein underwear exposed and a tight black T-shirt that showed off his muscular arms.

He didn't answer, just looked at me briefly before grabbing my phone from my hand and showing me the screen with the photo that had broken my heart two inches from my face.

"Who is this?" he asked me. Was he pretending to be interested in my private life?

I reached out to grab my phone, but he pulled it away, observing my reaction.

"What do you care?" I hissed with as much contempt as I could muster.

"Me? I couldn't give less of a shit. But I'm guessing it must be your boyfriend, or ex-boyfriend if you've got any self-respect. And since women are all basically the same, I'd imagine that your main goal tonight, besides pestering me, is getting your revenge on this dickhead."

How could he know that? Was it so obvious that payback was the one thing on my mind? He continued, "So let me offer my assistance. I'll kiss you and we'll take a bunch of photos of it, and in exchange you'll take your ass back home. I don't want you here, Noah."

I was shocked and needed some time to absorb what he'd said. As I lingered there, he stared at whatever was happening behind me. Kiss this idiot? Never! And yet, if I thought about it, he really was hot, and maybe I wasn't into it exactly, but I knew perfectly well how that bastard Dan would take it. He had a big head and thought he was the best-looking guy at the school, and nothing would bother him like seeing me with a guy who was obviously his physical superior.

"Fine," I said. From Nick's expression, I could see he'd assumed I wouldn't go along with it. "I want that fucker to feel like the biggest piece of shit in the world, and if I've got to kiss you to make that happen?" I shrugged. "Then so be it. But I don't want to go anywhere else tonight. I'm having fun, so here's the deal. You offer me your body to help me get revenge on my stupid ex-boyfriend, and I promise I won't crash any more of your parties."

He smiled, and I looked back at him confused. What was so funny?

"You're honestly fucked up in the head, you know that, right?" He shook his own head in disbelief.

"I'm in a bad, bad place right now, and all I care about is seeing that bastard suffer as much as I'm suffering right now." I could hear the pain in my voice. That photo kept flashing over and over in my mind, tormenting me. I didn't care that Nick was my stepbrother or that he was a grade-A imbecile. I wanted vengeance, that was it. I knew the drinks I'd had that night were affecting my judgment, but I didn't care.

"So are you going to kiss me or not?" I dared him.

Nick laughed.

That pissed me off, so I did something I'd been wanting to do ever since I met him: I raised one foot and kicked him straight in the shin. He shouted, more from surprise than pain.

"Stop laughing, jerkoff! There are plenty of dudes here. If you're not going to do it, someone else will." As soon as I'd spoken, I got ready to walk off and show him I was serious.

"That's not gonna happen," he said brusquely. "I want you out of here, so get over here." He pulled me over to the hood of the car, where no one else at the party could see us, thankfully. I hopped up on the hood, and Nicholas looked at my legs, my waist, my chest, my eyes.

"You must really be pissed to do this," he said, pulling out the iPhone and turning on the camera.

"You must be really desperate not to see me anymore," I counterattacked, pretending I wasn't nervous at all. I could barely stand him; I hated him actually, and for the same reason, it made me happy to know I was using him for my benefit.

He didn't say anything back. He just opened my knees with his hands and got between them. While he held the phone with one hand, the other stroked the bare flesh of my thighs. Despite what I'd thought or what I wished I'd thought, that contact didn't leave my body indifferent.

"Just get it over with," I said, and he looked irate, but his left hand grabbed the nape of my neck, and he slammed his lips into mine.

I couldn't suppress a tickle in my stomach. His lips were soft, his chin prickly with a slight growth of beard. He kissed me angrily, as if he were making me pay for all the arguments we'd had since we met. I realized then that I hadn't heard the camera click.

I shoved him as hard as I could but only managed to move him a few inches.

"Why don't you take the photo already?" This was the closest he'd ever been to me and the best view I'd ever had of those bright eyes with their long lashes. He wasn't hard to look at. My god! The son of a bitch was making my legs tremble, it didn't matter how much I hated him.

"How about you open your mouth without making some stupid-ass comment and we can finally get this over with?" he replied.

He lifted the phone to the height of our heads. As I watched him, my lips grew involuntarily moist. Then he pulled me into him. He kissed me; I heard the click. He put his tongue in my mouth, and when he started to move it, I felt suddenly weightless. Our lips were moving in unison, and it wasn't just because of the photo.

I liked feeling what I felt just then. My entire body was burning with passion for the moment, and deep down in my soul, I knew I had my revenge. I was enjoying that kiss, and I couldn't wait for my ex-boyfriend to find out!

His hands were back on my legs. This was lust, pure, undiluted lust. And hate. We hated each other, we couldn't stand each other, and that made it okay for us to use each other in this way.

I reached up and ran my hands through his dark hair. Screw being prudent!

His hands were on my lower thighs, squeezing them, making me shiver, making parts of my body I'd prefer not to name catch fire. He bit my lower lip, and I wanted to scream.

"Don't stop," I said when he reached my waist. I wanted him to keep going, wanted him to make me forget all I was feeling at that instant, to make all my sorrow vanish, all my demons. I wanted to use him for that, use him the way so many boys use girls, I wanted...

He pulled away.

I opened my eyes. What was he doing?

"You've got your photo," he said, and dropped the phone into my hand.

I was panting. I was angry that he'd stopped; I was angry that the one time he did something right, he had to mess it up; I was angry because he was incorrigible and I hated everything he, his father, and his godforsaken life had done to mine.

"That's it?" I asked. My cheeks were on fire. My body was yearning for him to touch me again.

"Try to stay out of my way tonight," he warned me.

What had happened? What had we just done?

I watched him as he walked away, feeling a strange, indescribable sensation.

12

Nick

I THOUGHT I WAS GOING TO EXPLODE JUST THEN. EACH OF MY nerve endings had awakened with a burning, unsettling intensity. My anger grew as I walked over to my friends.

Why the hell had I kissed her? Why had I entered her game? Since when did I let a girl get me so hot without me taking the reins? The answer to all these questions had four letters: *Noah*.

Since I'd seen her tonight, I hadn't been able to get her out of my head. I didn't know if it was the attraction of the forbidden, since she was my stepsister, or if I needed somehow to feel I could control her, put out that fire that kept shooting out of her mouth and make her act like all the other women I'd known and managed to control.

But Noah was completely different from all of them. She didn't throw herself at my feet, she didn't get weak in the knees when she looked at me, she didn't back down when I challenged her, no—she'd answer back, and her reactions were fiercer than mine. It was exasperating…and exciting at the same time. Mentally, I couldn't stop telling myself that she was an unbearable, whiny little bitch, that I should ignore her, but my body was betraying me, and I didn't know what the hell to do. I'd kissed her. I'd offered to do it not because I gave a damn about her getting revenge on her ex-boyfriend or wanted her out of the party; it was just pure desire. I wanted to taste her, to feel her. As soon as I saw her that night, I wanted to get between her legs and make her mine. It was uncomfortable, hellishly uncomfortable, and frustrating, especially since I couldn't stand her. Why did she have to be so goddamn attractive?

Her shorts left most of her long legs free to excite me. She was daring any man to reach out and touch them, to kiss her. Her hair drove me wild, especially when she let it down to frame her face, which was flushed from the alcohol. But more exciting still were her lips: soft as velvet and sharp as steel when she wanted to say something wounding. She'd driven me crazy when she'd opened her mouth, when her tongue had interwoven with mine without shame, without hesitation. It was nothing like any other girl I'd kissed before. She'd followed my rhythm, let me take control, and I'd bitten her lip from pure carnal desire because I'd wanted to consume her but also let her know who was in charge.

"That's it?" she'd asked me, cheeks flushed, eyes bright with longing. What the fuck did she want me to do, though? If she wasn't who she was, I'd have taken her straight to the back seat of my car. If she wasn't so damn hard to put up with, I'd have given her the best night of her life. If she wasn't...if she wasn't turning my whole world upside down...

"Dude, where were you? The first race is about to begin!" Lion shouted from the place where he'd parked my black Ferrari next to my enemy's souped-up Audi.

That was exactly what I needed. Discharging all that built-up tension at 170 miles per hour down a sand track in the middle of the night and leaving one of the losers from Ronnie's gang in the dust. I needed to blow off steam, feel the adrenaline—adrenaline was better than desire, better than knowing that I wouldn't have the one thing I really wanted that night…

"Tell Kyle I've got this one," I said, walking over to the car. My friends were waiting for me, having fun before the flag came down, drinking, dancing, in a good mood because they assumed we'd take the night's prize money. That was the deal. Fifteen thousand dollars was on the line, plus the loser's car in the final. I'd been putting off a race against Ronnie too long. Not because I feared losing—anything but. The problem was that he was a thug and a bad sport. Every year, the pot got bigger, and every year, there was more tension between our two gangs. He'd made it evident what would happen if things got out of hand. Everyone here knew the rules.

There were four gangs competing that night, and each had brought in its best drivers. Eight different cars were racing in total. We drew to find out which gang would compete against which, and we had two separate brackets. There would be three races per bracket until one was left, and that person would race the winner from the other bracket. That made six races in total, not counting the final.

And I was going to be in that final.

Since I'd started racing five years before, my team had always won. Ronnie respected me, but I knew he'd fuck me over if he ever got the chance. I was from a good family, I wasn't in it for the money, and that got to him. He needed the cash—needed it to buy drugs and keep the guys in his gang in line. It was one thing to throw money around, another to play with the one thing that seemed to matter to him. If he lost his car, I'd need to be ready for trouble.

I ran a hand along the roof of my Ferrari. I loved that damn car; it was perfect, the fastest, the best purchase I'd ever made. I only let people I trusted drive it. My car. My rules. That was the deal. Driving it was a privilege. Everyone in my gang knew that.

"Kyle's gonna be mad, bro," Lion said with an awkward expression. After the drawing, we'd decided how to divvy up our guys. The four gangs were equally represented in both brackets. I knew Kyle had been gunning for Greg, the guy I'd be going against, but sorry—I was driving in this race myself.

I looked over at Lion. I was glad he was there that night. He was one of my best friends. I'd met him in one of the worst periods of my life, and we'd been inseparable ever since. I was the one who'd introduced him to his girl Jenna. She was the daughter of oil execs and had grown up in the same development as me, and we'd known each other since we were kids. She was still in high school. She wasn't like the other daughters of millionaires—she was special, and I cared about her a lot. Lion had been hung up on her from the first moment he saw her.

"Fuck Kyle," I said. Lion probably thought that was over the line, but he didn't say anything. He knew when I wasn't in the mood for bullshit. And just then, I definitely was not in the mood.

"The second curve is tighter than the first, so brake early or you'll skid off the road," he told me as I got in the car and put it in gear. From fifteen feet away, people were already shouting euphorically, anxious for the race to begin. Two girls were holding the fluorescent flags, ready to motion for us to take off.

"Got it," I said. And I couldn't help but add, "Keep an eye on Noah." I squeezed the wheel tightly as I realized she was still stuck in my head. I couldn't help it; I needed to know someone was taking care of her. This kind of party was dangerous for a girl like her, and Lion knew that better than anyone.

"Don't worry, Jenna's all over it." That eased my mind. But then I looked where he was looking. There, with a fluorescent bandana tied around her head, as though she were a member of my gang, was Noah, arms locked with Jenna, smiling radiantly. She was euphoric. Drunk and euphoric.

Dammit.

"See you at the finish line," I said, the way we always did when we raced.

The flags came down, the engine roared, and the wind in my face made me forget those honey-colored eyes and that scandalous body.

———————

We'd won all the races so far. Elsewhere, on the other sand tracks, all the competition had been eliminated. Just Ronnie was left. No surprise. My guy Kyle was good, but Ronnie was one of the best.

The final was going to be tough, and I was nervous about the outcome.

I still had twenty minutes to go, and I was leaning on my car drinking a beer and smoking a cigarette. Noah was with Jenna. They were living it up, as far as I could tell, dancing, drinking, just having fun. I got it—Noah probably thought she could drink away the memories of her boyfriend. I kept an eye on her every movement.

"You're being weird tonight," a familiar voice said from behind my back. I turned to Anna when I felt her warm breath on my neck. Just like me, she had changed. She was wearing a skimpy dress that revealed her huge boobs and thin legs. She was gazing at me with desire. We always looked at each other that way.

"It's not the best night," I said, trying to get her to understand she shouldn't expect any sweet nothings from me.

"I could make it a lot better," she said, sidling up to me and giving me a view of her cleavage. "All you've got to do is come with me," she added seductively.

I had fifteen minutes left till the last race. And the truth was, I could use a little release with Anna in the back of my ride.

"Make it quick," I said, dragging her to my car.

Fifteen minutes later, we went back to where everyone was standing, waiting on the finale. Sex with Anna had helped me clear my head. I could have whoever I wanted—there was no need to get all hung up on some seventeen-year-old.

And then I saw her.

Everyone had moved from the starting line to the finish. Normally Lion and Jenna always stayed behind. But there wasn't a trace of them.

I saw just one thing before my black Ferrari took off without me: the reddish-blond hair of my stepsister in the rearview mirror.

13

Noah

AFTER WHAT HAD HAPPENED WITH NICK, I DECIDED TO STAY AWAY from him tonight. That was what he'd asked for, after all. What had happened between us was weird, but it was pleasant. Then he'd opened his mouth and I'd remembered who I was dealing with.

Still, I'd gotten what I wanted. I'd gotten my revenge on Dan, even if deep down I realized that nothing could make me feel better after the two people who mattered most to me had betrayed me behind my back.

The photo Nick had taken had shaken me. I'd never taken photos of Dan and me kissing. For that matter, Dan had never kissed me like that. When I looked at the picture, I got goose bumps. You could see us in it in profile, his lips half-open and pressed into mine, our eyes closed, enjoying the moment. My cheeks were bright red, Nick's face was hard, cold, irresistible. He really was attractive. Dan would be climbing the walls. I knew it. He was just that egotistical, even if normally he saved his self-centered attitude for other people and didn't make me a victim of it. I sent him the picture of him cheating, so he'd know I had it.

Then I wrote a text under the photo of Nick and me before sending it.

All I needed was four hours to find a bigger man than you. Thanks for opening my eyes. By the way, in your picture you look like a fish sucking air. Learn to kiss, douchebag!

I looked at the photo of him and Beth kissing.

His face still drew me in, but I knew that with that message, our relationship was over. I would never see him again, and for the first time, I was happy there was a border between us. As for Beth, I just wrote her a two-word message that I sent along with the photo of her and Dan kissing:

We're done.

I exhaled all the air I'd been holding in. That was it. With that, nine months of romance and seven years of friendship were finished. I felt my eyes grow damp, but I didn't spill a single tear. To hell with them. They didn't deserve it.

I put my phone in my back pocket and tried to find Nick. Last I saw him, he was leaning against his black Ferrari and drinking a beer. I turned around and walked straight over to Jenna.

We danced, laughed, entertained ourselves. My new friend was crazy. Now and then she'd run off to make out with her boyfriend, and I'd remember what had happened and feel depressed. I tried to distract myself watching the races; I loved the sport, and it brought back some of my favorite memories from back when going to the races was an everyday thing for me. I noted the techniques of all the different drivers. Nick's friend was pretty good, but Nick was better. His first race impressed me.

As the night went on, I found myself analyzing the different strategies and asking myself what was missing, how to increase our side's advantage. The problem was the second curve. If you hit it too slow, you fell behind; if you took it too fast, you risked spinning out.

I was dying to get on the track. I felt like I could do it better. I wanted to feel the wind in my face, the adrenaline in my body that speed always brought with it, feel that control over the car, knowing I was the one telling it where to go.

These thoughts were swirling in my head when I realized the last race was about to begin. This guy Ronnie was racing against Nicholas. If I had the chance, I thought, I could smoke him with my eyes closed.

Everyone had gotten in their cars and driven over to the finish line. Jenna, Lion, and I had to stay behind, but they left for a second to get her car. Nicholas had vanished, too, taking off toward his SUV with that dark-haired bimbo. So there I was, alone, with a rocket ship just waiting for someone to get behind the wheel.

I saw Ronnie walk over to his tuner and glance over at me. He was a scary dude. He was ripped like a gladiator and had hundreds of tattoos all over his arms and back.

"Yo, bae," he said, leaning his forearms on the hood. "Who are you?"

I was intimidated, but I thought it was smart to answer him.

"Noah," I said.

"I've been watching you," he admitted. "I know how to tell a chick who knows this game from one who's just standing around. And you know this game," he said, slapping the hood.

"I might have raced a time or two," I said, wondering where everyone else was. I didn't like the way that dude was looking at me; he gave me the creeps.

"I can imagine," he replied. "Why don't you race me then?"

Was he really proposing what I thought he was proposing?

"You're supposed to race Nicholas," I said doubtfully.

"Yeah, but Nicholas ain't here, is he?"

I felt the adrenaline coursing through my veins. Racing again. That was what I wanted. What I needed. And it was true— Nicholas wasn't there to tell me no.

"I don't think it's a good idea," I said, biting my lip but seeing the keys of the Ferrari in the ignition.

Ronnie clicked his tongue and walked over slowly.

It's actually a great idea, I thought. But I kept that to myself.

"Nick already got behind the wheel tonight. And it's about time he lets a woman try, no?"

Guys like Nick were the reason nobody took girls like me seriously.

"Or are you scared?" Ronnie added. He knew how to hit me where it hurt.

That infuriated me, and I was sure he could see my answer on my face before I opened my mouth.

"You're on," I said with a smirk. He grinned back at me.

"Good job, Precious. See you at the starting line."

I knew what he was thinking: that he could beat me like a cheap rug. *Well, I hate to tell you, Ronnie, but I forgot to mention that you're racing against the daughter of a NASCAR champ.*

The car was dope. Leather seats, impeccable body, and the roar of that motor...what a pleasure, what memories. I slid it into gear and rolled slowly to the starting line. No one knew who was inside. No one but my adversary.

I smiled like a little kid. I didn't want to think about the consequences, didn't want to think of how Nick would probably kill me; I just wanted to have fun.

Come on, Ronnie, you hard-ass.

When the flags gave the signal, I stomped the accelerator, and in under a second, I was off. It was moving, liberating, relaxing, scary... Nothing could have been better. I hadn't done anything like that in years. I couldn't remember the last time I'd done something for me, something I liked, something that didn't have to do with my mom or her husband or my ex-boyfriend or ex-best friend. I was free, free as a bird, and in a state of pure ecstasy.

Ronnie was gunning it next to me. I stepped down harder and shouted like crazy as I glided past the first curve, leaving him behind.

"Hell yes!" I shouted.

But the second curve was fast approaching, and that was the tough one. So I asked myself the million-dollar question: slow down and avoid danger or push it to the limit and risk running off the track?

Needless to say, I chose the second.

I accelerated while calculating the absolute minimum I could slow down at the key moment to round the curve in safety.

When I saw it up close, I realized it was tighter than I'd thought at first. Shit. I was going to start spinning out. I braked and jerked the wheel with all my strength, heard the sand hitting the car, the tires squealing under the abuse.

I clenched my jaw and shouted when I made it through without killing myself. The motor growled, telling me to go faster, and who was I to say no?

"Yes!" I shrieked, seeing Ronnie behind me, almost on my bumper. In his reflection in the mirror, his face was enraged. He knew he was losing.

"Suck it!" I shouted in bliss. "All you big-shot macho dickheads can suck it!"

I'd made it through the hard part. The rest was a cakewalk. I sped up toward the finish line. Another mile or two and I had him. My heart was racing, I was thrilled... =and then Ronnie hit me from behind. I lurched forward, and the seat belt dug into my chest.

"You fucker!" I said and gripped the wheel tighter. Ronnie was a maniac; he kept slowing down and speeding up, trying to ram me again. I rocked to one side to avoid a third attempt, but he followed me, this time striking me to the right. That son of a bitch was destroying my car!

I pulled right quickly and gave him a taste of his own medicine, almost breaking off his side mirror, and when I saw he was distracted and more pissed off than ever, I put the pedal to the floor, ready to reach my destination.

Just a few feet more, three, two...then it was over. I'd crossed the finished line.

The screams were deafening; people were waving their hands and their fluorescent bandanas in the air. It was wild, the feeling of winning, knowing I'd left that thug in the dust.

I braked next to the mass of spectators, looked in the rearview, and saw Ronnie getting out of the car in fury. He kicked the door of my car. I just laughed.

Then someone appeared in my window, opened the door, and pulled me out of the interior, almost lifting me in the air.

"Are you out of your fucking mind?!" Nicholas said. He looked rabid.

"Jesus, Nicholas!"

I'd never seen him so mad. Not even when we'd fought at the party the night before and he'd been handing out beatings like they were candy. His hair was messy, it looked like he'd been pulling on it, and his gaze told me he wished I was dead and buried and he'd never have to lay eyes on me again.

I was so scared, I blurted out the first thing that came into my head: "I won, though."

Face almost touching mine, he asked, "Do you have any idea what you've done?!" I was terrified, but I wasn't going to let him cow me, so I shook and shook until he had to let me go.

"Don't you dare yell at me."

That rich fucker. It wasn't like I'd wrecked his car; I'd taken perfect care of it. Whatever damage it had received was the fault of that dumbass, Ronnie. Plus, I'd won the race! I'd won!

That was when Jenna and Lion came over, leaving behind the chaos. As I pricked up my ears, I heard screaming and whistling coming from all around.

"Cheater! Cheater!"

That meant the public was on my side. They'd seen Ronnie playing dirty; he'd broken the rules and rear-ended me; that was strictly illegal, especially in a car like that, which wasn't made for harsh impact.

"Let her go, Nicholas," Lion said, but his face was no friendlier than Nick's.

Jenna's expression was nasty, too, and that surprised as well as hurt me.

"Here comes Ronnie," she said, and Nicholas released me so abruptly that I hit my back against the car.

What the hell was going on? Why was everyone so pissed off?

Nicholas turned around with his fists clenched.

"You broke the rules, Leister, and you know exactly what that means," Ronnie said, clearly furious, but with a grin across that face full of piercings and tattoos.

"Bullshit," Nicholas said. Lion was next to him, and the other guys in his gang approached to give him support. Ronnie's crew did the same. Less than a minute had passed, and I still had no idea what was going on. "It's not my fault if someone else gets in my car and drives on the track. There's no way you're pinning that on me."

Now I started to see what was going on.

"She's a member of your gang, Leister. That makes her your responsibility."

"No, she's not," Nicholas said, but then he turned and looked at me. I saw surprise in his eyes and anger again, or, rather, a new anger, three times as fierce as the old one.

"She's got the bandana on. That means she's in the gang," Ronnie blustered.

Now I got it. The bandana made me a member. But if I was, then what was the problem with me racing in Nicholas's place?

"You broke the rules, Leister. The final was between you and me. So that makes me the winner." All those behind him howled in agreement, and his eyes seemed to dare us to say otherwise.

"This is bullshit," Nicholas said, stepping forward. Lion did the same, his fists pressed into his hips.

With that dumbass smile of his, Ronnie started shaking his head even as Nicholas was speaking.

"You can go ahead and hand over the fifteen thousand and that baby right there," he said, looking at Nick's black Ferrari.

What the...?

I stepped forward; I didn't care who was standing across from me. I could feel Nick getting tenser, but before he could push me back, I spoke:

"You were the one who told me to race you," I shouted. "And I beat you. A seventeen-year-old girl beat you." Ronnie's face twisted into an expression of wrath. I thought he'd kill me. But that wouldn't stop me from saying what I had to say. "I wounded your puny little masculine ego, and now you want to try to make everyone think you've got some right to the money and the car." I would have continued, but Nicholas got in front of me.

"Shut your mouth and get in my car," he said through clenched teeth. "Now!"

"Fuck that!" I shouted, looking past him to Ronnie. I wasn't going to let that fuckhead manipulate the situation to his benefit, and there was no way in hell I was letting him take the car. I won the race; he never even took the lead. "You should learn to race, dumbass!"

Nick's gang shouted their agreement. That made me feel better.

Someone pulled me back as Nick turned to Ronnie with the veins in his neck ready to explode. I saw Ronnie's face and thought they might beat each other to death.

"Shut up, Noah, now," Jenna said in my ear. "You're going to make this way worse than you can imagine."

I didn't respond. Nick and Ronnie were staring each other down. A fight seemed inevitable. But then Nick grabbed the keys from me and handed them over.

No!

"I'll send you the cash tomorrow," he said, feigning calm.

All around us was silence. Ronnie smiled, took the keys, and started spinning them around his finger. Nicholas was struggling to breathe, and I could tell he was seething, ready to explode.

"Yo, try to keep that bitch at home," Ronnie said. That was when Nicholas lost it.

It happened so quickly, no one saw it coming. His fist struck Ronnie's jaw with such force, he laid him out over the hood of his car.

Fists started flying all around me. The two gangs were going at it, and now I was in the middle of that inferno. Someone hit me from behind, and I fell face-first on the ground, scratching my knees and hands.

"Noah!" Jenna shouted, kneeling to help me get up.

They were fighting like their lives depended on it. I was in a panic. There were more than fifty muscular, scary guys there throwing blows.

Someone grabbed my arm and pulled Jenna and me away at the same time. It was Lion. His face looked stony and determined. His lip was bleeding. He spit on the ground as he struggled to get us out.

"Get in there and lock your doors," he said, pointing at Nick's SUV.

Lion hopped in the driver's seat and pulled out, coming to a stop where Nick was beating on a now-disoriented Ronnie.

"Nick!" he shouted as loudly as possible, making himself heard over the group of men fighting and falling.

Nick punched Ronnie one more time in the stomach and ran toward us. His lip was busted, his cheek bruised. He'd barely hit the passenger door when Lion turned the wheel and hit the gas.

That was when I turned around.

My heart froze. Ronnie was lifting up a handgun and pointing it at the back of the car.

"Get down!" I shouted as the rear windshield shattered into a million pieces, and then we started racing away, and I thought I'd lose my mind.

"Fuck!" Nicholas and Lion screamed. Jenna and I were shouting as well.

"Son of a," Nicholas said while Lion pulled out onto the highway. At this hour of the night, there wasn't a single car on the road, and I was grateful to see Lion wasn't worried about the speed limit. I turned back and saw several other cars doing the same, but as long as I didn't see Ronnie, I could breathe easy.

"Are you okay?" Nicholas asked, looking first at me, then at Jenna.

"Jenna, talk to me," Lion said, looking into the rearview, face heavy with worry.

"That goddamn son of a bitch!" she shouted hysterically. I was trembling from head to toe.

"I see you're good as ever," Lion said, laughing despite his nerves.

"Find a gas station," Nick said.

I was petrified, scared to even breathe too loudly. No one had ever pointed a gun at me in my life. Ronnie had looked me in the eyes before shooting. I'd have that image of his face in my head for a long time.

I couldn't take it all in. How had things gotten so out of control?

I was on the verge of a breakdown. First there had been Dan and Beth, then the adrenaline that had run through me for the first time in years, the good and bad memories it had awakened, the weakness and guilt I'd felt when Nick had to give his car to that asshole, the pain in my knees and hands, which were bleeding from the fall. As the rush faded away, I started to grasp all that had happened.

Ten minutes later, in uncomfortable silence, we arrived at a gas station that was open all night.

Lion cut the engine and got out to open the door for Jenna and give her a long, passionate hug. Nick got out at the same time and walked inside. I didn't move. I couldn't watch him. I didn't want to.

I felt guilty; everything that had happened had been my fault, and that fight could have been a thousand times worse. I had no idea what Ronnie was doing with a gun, but I'd at least figured out that those races were nothing like the ones I'd seen as a girl, and the people here were nothing like the people back there. This was dangerous, there was a lot of money on the line, and the drivers were all criminals. I'd left a gang member looking ridiculous and forced my newly acquired stepbrother into a fight.

The situation had been bad to start with, but now it was worse than I could imagine.

Nicholas emerged from the gas station with a full bag and

handed bandages, alcohol, and a bottle of pain reliever to Jenna and Lion. One of the guys fighting had split open her forehead. Lion cleaned her up and made sure she was all right.

Nicholas came around to the other side of the car. He took out alcohol and a bandage without bothering to look at me. He emptied a bottle of water on his head, shook out his hair, and then opened my door. I tried to get out. I could take care of my own wounds. But he wouldn't let me.

"Give me your hands," he said in an inexpressive tone. His lip was destroyed, the bruise on his cheek awful. And all of it had been my fault. I felt a knot in my stomach.

"I'm sorry," I whispered so softly I didn't even know whether he'd heard.

He took one of my hands and delicately cleansed the wound, which was full of blood and dirt.

I didn't know what to say. I'd have preferred he yell at me or tell me how stupid and terrible I was, but instead, he just tended to my injuries. Behind us, Jenna and Lion were talking softly, sweetly. She was now looking after him. Nicholas looked at me only once before walking around to the driver's seat. Minutes later, we were back on the road. No one said a word, not even Jenna or Lion.

It was then that I realized I had fucked up bad.

14

Nick

FOUR DAYS LATER, AND I STILL HADN'T SHOWN UP AT HOME. After what happened at the races, I didn't want to even stick my head in. I wasn't sure how I'd react when I came face-to-face with Noah again. A small part of me wanted to strangle her and make her pay for what her stupid little game had cost me. My car, my black Ferrari, which had cost more than two hundred thousand dollars, and the definitive end of my truce with Ronnie's gang. That fucker had tried to shoot us in the back. I still remembered the feeling in my chest as I heard the shot and Noah screaming in the back seat. I hadn't wanted to look back. I had been scared at what I'd find; I'd never known that kind of fear before. And all that because some dumb girl had been incapable even once of paying attention to what she was told.

When I had seen her race, I had felt completely powerless. I had no idea where she'd learned to drive like that, but she had sure beaten Ronnie's ass. I had to admire the way she'd taken that second curve—not even I would have had the balls to hit it at that speed—but all that told me was how little survival instinct she had.

And then I couldn't get out of my head that kiss I'd given her or how much I wanted to do it again. I couldn't forget those full, savory lips, that body... They drove me wild.

Dammit.

I couldn't go home; I didn't know how I'd act. One part of me, the perverted one, the one that clearly didn't need my head to think, wanted to grab that girl with her blond hair and honey-colored eyes and do it all to her, make her pay for losing my most treasured possession; the other wanted to make her afraid to even be near me, to even breathe too loudly when I was in the room. The first option was the more attractive, and admitting it made me hate myself.

I'd been partying for four days straight, staying up till the early morning and always waking up with a different girl. Ronnie and I were done forever after what had happened, and I was worried about how he'd act the next time we saw each other, which would happen sooner rather than later, since we moved in the same circles.

Amazing. That girl had screwed up everything in no time whatsoever, and to make it worse, I still had to see her every damn morning once I returned home.

I went home once I'd fixed the back windshield of my car. I was in a bad mood, and it was about to get worse. I parked in my spot, put on my sunglasses—my hangover was killing me—and walked to the door, thinking I'd just disappear into my room for the rest of the day, but no dice. As soon as I walked in, I heard a shout coming from the kitchen that made me curse under my breath and pray for the patience I'd need to put up with that moment.

I walked slowly to the kitchen, where my stepmother, her daughter, and Jenna were having breakfast at the island. Noah— my personal blond hell. She seemed thrown off when she saw me walk in. Her skin was tan, her hair blonder and more colorful than the last time I'd seen her. She was wearing a swimsuit, but a towel wrapped under her armpits covered up most of it. She was dripping water onto the counter over her bowl of cereal. Jenna was doing basically the same, but with no towel and with that welcoming smile she reserved for friends and family.

So they were friends now?

"Nick, you're finally back. You dad was calling you all day yesterday," Raffaella said gently, but her face seemed to tell me she'd been up all night. Unlike Noah, who seemed happy to just throw on whatever, she took good care of her appearance and had pulled her platinum hair back and was wearing a suit of neatly ironed white linen.

She was taking her new role as Mrs. William Leister seriously.

"I've been busy," I said, cutting her off as I walked to the fridge and took out a beer.

"What's the deal, Nick? You aren't going to say hi?" Jenna said, turning around in her chair to face me.

I gave her a nasty look. Jenna knew perfectly well that I wasn't in the mood. Why didn't she act like Noah and just shut up and eat her cereal?

I grunted, brought the beer to my lips, and noticed how Noah was trying to act completely unaffected by my presence.

"Nicholas, your father was calling because we're going to New York tonight," Raffaella said, getting my attention. "He's got a conference, and he wants me to go. I'd like it if you could stay here with Noah. I don't want her all alone in such a big house, and—"

"Mom, I told you I'm fine," my stepsister said with a scowl. "I can stay here by myself. Anyway, Jenna will stay here and keep me company, right, Jenna?"

Jenna nodded, shrugging, looking first at me and then at Noah. So she was trying to ignore me *and* she wanted me to leave. Interesting.

"I'll stay," I said, not really knowing what I was getting into.

By the face she made in response, I could tell Noah would have rather been anywhere but there just then.

"Thank you, Nick. That really makes me feel better," Raffaella said, getting up and taking one last sip of coffee. "I'm going to go pack my bags. I'll see you all before I go." And with that, she left.

"You don't need to worry about me. I know how to take care of myself," Noah said.

I walked over and sat down next to her.

"I very much doubt that, but that's not why I'm staying," I said, staring her straight in the eye. "I think it's that I missed you, Freckles. You going to make me lose another two hundred thousand dollars today?"

Noah took a few deep breaths and started babbling a response, and I decided to bring her torture to an end.

"Relax. I wasn't being serious anyway. You couldn't pay me back in your wildest dreams." As I spoke, I realized my anger and my desire for her were growing in concert. I looked down involuntarily at her cleavage, wet from the pool, and at her tattoo, which drove me completely wild.

"Are you telling me you're going to forget it?" she asked incredulously.

"Let's say I'll find another way for you to pay me back." Right away, I realized I was flirting with her again. *Dammit.*

"Look, how about we go back to the beginning? I'll ignore you, you can ignore me, and everyone will be happy."

I glanced over at Jenna, who had an expression of intrigue, with a little smile flowering across her fleshy lips.

I turned around and walked out to the yard.

15

Noah

SEEING HIM HIT ME LIKE A TON OF BRICKS AFTER THOSE FOUR DAYS when I'd managed to more or less forget what had happened at the races and had tried to avoid thinking about him—and when I did think of him, I felt a strange, unpleasant sensation in my stomach. I knew I'd made him lose his prize possession and that they could have killed us that night, but it wasn't all my fault. If it hadn't been for Dan cheating on me, I'd never have gone; plus, that thug Ronnie had tricked me, had made me think I was allowed to compete, and it was only once he saw me win that he'd taken advantage of the stupid rules to keep the fifteen thousand dollars and Nick's car.

I thought it would take days, months, years until that little rich kid would forgive me and forget what I had done, but it turned out that despite all the things I'd imagined Nick would say to me, he was there and the slate seemed to be wiped clean.

But making me pay some other way—that had to be a joke, right?

I didn't know what to think anymore, and I also didn't want to spend too long trying to figure out what Nicholas Leister would ask me to do to make up for this. Jesus—two hundred thousand dollars. I was sure I'd never see that much money in my life. Only someone as rich as him could blow something like that off, and even if I knew that car was just a toy for him, one of many he could buy, I felt relieved and thankful that he was willing to forgive me.

I'd spent the past few days trying to get used to life in that house, full of remorse and all kinds of other mixed-up feelings. The worst part, the source of my sorrow, was knowing that my boyfriend had decided to cheat on me. And now he was calling me and sending me thousands of messages trying to get me to forgive him and even get back together with him.

Every time my phone rang, my heart stopped, and when it started again, the beats hurt like a hammer blow. All that time I spent sunbathing reminded me of the things that tied me to my city, my home, and how that was all gone forever. That was what pained me most. My best friend had decided to cast aside our friendship for a guy, *my guy,* and he had the gall to ask me to forgive him. Was he crazy?

There was no way I'd ever speak with either of them again, no way I'd ever be so stupid to throw myself at some guy's feet. Men had given me enough problems, and here I was, living with an attractive, dangerous guy with a parallel life that no one with half a brain would bother getting close to.

"You must be Nick's worst nightmare," Jenna said. She took a pack of cigarettes out from between her breasts and lit one. I couldn't help but look around to see if Mom was nearby.

Jenna was the one good thing I'd gotten out of that disastrous night. Her joy, her sense of humor, had made the past few days easier. She told me that she'd known Nicholas since he was a boy. In fact, she was the person who knew him best.

According to her, my new stepbrother was an incorrigible man-whore who thought about nothing but parties, drinking, having fun, sex, and beating Ronnie as many times as he had to for people to realize he was the real king of the night around here.

None of that surprised me, but there was one thing that did, even if she couldn't tell me much about it. When Nicholas was eighteen, he left his father's home for a while and was living at Lion's place in a rough part of town and getting into all kinds of trouble. That was where he'd met all those delinquents who lived a life of crime. Lion was one of the friends he held on to from that period.

I was shocked. My mother must have had no idea. If she did, she'd have told me. Now I understood how a guy from a rich family like Nick had wound up in the kind of shady business I'd seen the two nights I'd hung out with him.

"Why do you say that?" I asked Jenna, distracted, looking down into my bowl of cereal.

"Have you seen yourself?" she asked, and I felt slightly offended. "You're the typical good girl who's never even broken a dish, and all of the sudden you hop in a car, win a race, and get us all into a shitload of trouble. You're not exactly what I'd call predictable, Noah, I'd bet you anything right now Nick is thinking of giving it to you every which way right on top of this counter to try to get over his frustration at losing his car. That's how he usually solves his problems. He's not the type to just *forget it*." She made air quotes as she said these last words and laughed as she looked at my stunned expression.

"Come on!" she said. "Don't tell me it never even crossed your mind. If I hadn't known him since I was in diapers, I'd be throwing myself at him, too, just like every other girl in this town."

In my mind, I started re-creating that kiss we had given each other on the hood of the car. It wasn't the first time I'd remembered it, and my body always reacted by shivering and wishing his hands would caress me again...but that just meant I had eyes!

"Believe me when I say this—I'm not letting him *give it to me* anywhere. I've known enough pretty faces to last a lifetime. Guys like that will screw you over the first chance they get. Just look at my boyfriend Dan."

"Ex-boyfriend Dan," she corrected me, taking a drag from her cigarette. "You're right, guys like him are dangerous, but that doesn't mean you shouldn't enjoy what they can offer you to get over your old guy. Who says a woman can't sleep with a guy for the simple pleasure of doing it? You're single, you're pretty, it's summer. Enjoy it and don't think too much."

I laughed out loud. Jenna was crazy! I wasn't that kind of girl.

"How about we drop the subject of the Leisters and you promise to stay over tonight," I said. If I had to spend three days alone with Nicholas in that gigantic house, I'd die before Monday arrived.

Jenna thought it over.

"Nick will almost certainly invite the guys, which means Lion will be here, and if you add in the alcohol and music..." Her fingers drummed her cheek. "Then I'm in!" She smiled.

That put me in a good mood. With Jenna next to me, the days would pass quicker, and that was what I needed just then: for the days to fly by without having to think about where they were taking me.

———

Just as Jenna had said, a few hours later the house was pure madness. It wasn't even 9:00 p.m. when the doorbell started ringing. A bunch of guys and girls with beer kegs soon rolled in. When he heard the racket, Nicholas peeked out over the top of the stairs to invite everyone in, telling them to put on the music.

Drinks flowed like water, and the music boomed from speakers I couldn't even see. I felt out of place in my athletic shorts with my hair pulled back. Jenna had gone home to change and still wasn't back, so I went to my room to try to freshen up a little, looking through my closet to see if there was something that would be comfortable and still nice to wear.

I found a pair of black shorts that fit me like a second skin and an orange top that looked great with the tan I was starting to get. Satisfied, I let my hair down, threw on some flats—to hell with wearing heels in my own home—and ran off when I heard another doorbell ring over the music.

Before I got there, Jenna had already come in along with her boyfriend, Lion. The two of them were a spectacle. She hadn't skimped on the high heels, but she was a little shorter than her boyfriend in his jeans and baggy black T-shirt.

Jenna hurried over with a smile.

"Girl, you are fine," she said. "You already got your eye on someone? It'd be a shame to let that body go to waste!" she shouted, making me blush and giggle at the same time.

"Let's get a drink. I'm parched," Lion said. He'd already waved to several guys who came over to bump fists with him.

In the kitchen, Jenna went straight for the beer keg, and when she handed me a foamy cup, I took it happily. It was good, crisp, refreshing, and I was happy for a distraction to help me forget my ex.

As I drank, my mind washed away the bad feelings and the image of Dan, so blond, so handsome, how his hands used to caress me when we were alone or how he'd kiss me on the nose in the wintertime and laugh, saying I looked like a reindeer. It was stupid to keep dwelling on those things, but that had been nine months of my life. Not so many, maybe, but they'd been intense. I'd loved him. He'd been my first real boyfriend, and him cheating on me with someone who mattered so much to me...the mere fact that he'd cheated on me...

Now I was pissed. I went back for another beer. Just then, an email popped up on my phone. I assumed it would be Dan, but when I looked, I saw it was the same person who had sent me the photo of Dan and Beth kissing. Whoever that was, they obviously wanted to torment me because the subject line read:

MORE EVIDENCE OF DECEPTION FOR YOU.

I clicked on the file, my heart racing, but before I could see anything, my phone died. Shit. No battery. I should have figured; all day I'd been getting messages and calls from Dan that I'd tried to ignore. With my nerves frayed, prey to some masochistic instinct— because if it wasn't that, why in the hell would I want to see more pictures of my boyfriend cheating on me?—I saw Nick's iPhone on the table in the living room. There were tons of people around, so no one noticed when I grabbed it and walked off to a corner close to Will's office. My hands were shaking so much I could hardly hit the keys, and I had to rewrite my email address like five times. When I finally entered it and my password correctly, I opened the file, and there, along with the photo I'd already seen, were tons of snapshots of Dan and Beth hooking up at the same party. I'd assumed that was where he'd cheated on me for the first time...but no. There were more of them in other places, even selfies, with their arms stretched out, their lips swollen, their eyes gleaming. I got so mad looking at them that the fury and pain almost made me drop the phone on the floor.

That was when someone came up behind me.

"What the hell are you doing with my phone?"

I jumped, and before I could close out the screen, Nicholas grabbed the phone out of my hands and started looking at the pictures with a scowl.

"Give it!" I said, feeling myself starting to drown in my misfortunes.

He smiled mischievously.

"Did you forget it's mine?" he replied, engrossed in the screen.

I turned around to walk off. I knew I was close to losing it; I could feel it in the tremor in my hands and the sting in my eyes that I felt every time I wanted to cry.

A hand grabbed my arm.

I turned around to see Nick's eyes boring into me.

"Why are you looking at this shit? Are you a masochist or what?" he asked, disgusted, putting his phone in his back pocket and grabbing my arm. I guess I wasn't the only one asking that question.

"Maybe. But either way, you're the last person I want to see right now," I said, thinking he was the perfect person to take my bad mood out on.

He gave me a strange look, almost as if he actually wanted to understand what was going on in my head.

"What's up with that, Freckles?"

I rolled my eyes at that damned nickname he'd given me.

"Let's see," I said sarcastically. "Since I got here, all you've done is talk bad about me, threaten me, leave me stranded in the middle of nowhere, act like a horndog, and...oh, I forgot! Let someone drug me!" I counted these episodes off on my fingers.

"So now it's my fault that your asshole boyfriend cheated on you," he said, letting me go and observing me as if he found the whole thing funny.

"I'm just pissed off at life in general, so leave me alone, okay?" I said, ready to walk past him and go to my room. He stood in my way and grabbed me around the waist with one arm. Before I knew what was happening, he pushed me into Will's office, closed the door, and looked me in the eye. The room was dark except for the light of the moon coming in through the windows behind the desk and chairs.

I exhaled all the air I had in my lungs when he stepped forward and trapped me against the door. When I looked closely at him, I saw how drunk he was.

"Stop thinking about that asshole," he said, pushing my hair back and kissing the skin of my shoulder.

It was as unexpected as it was intense. It reminded me of the kiss at the races. What had started as simple vengeance had turned into a pleasurable, exciting kiss...and now the same thing was happening again.

"What are you doing?" I asked when his lips started to slowly climb my neck, leaving a trail of little hot pecks until he reached my ear. I had to close my eyes when I felt his teeth digging into me.

"I'm showing you how good life can be," he responded, his breathing accelerating as he reached a hand under my shirt and started stroking my back, softly at first and then pressing me into his firm body.

He couldn't know what he was doing. Had he forgotten whom he was kissing? We hated each other, even more now that I had lost his favorite toy and his archenemy had fired a gun at his back. It was my fault...but if all that was true, why couldn't I stop enjoying these hot, unexpected caresses?

"I've been holding back with you... Dammit, you're stuck in my head, and I can't stop thinking of you," he said, picking me up easily and forcing me to wrap my legs around his back.

I didn't even have time to assimilate his words because all at once, his lips were over mine, ardent, possessive, kissing me in a way no one ever had.

It was strange, feeling him this way, especially after how he'd acted just a few hours before, but my thoughts, my feelings, my problems, anything that had affected me in the past, all that was in the background now because—my God!—that boy knew exactly what he was doing.

His tongue jutted against mine passionately, and his breath was intoxicating. Without realizing it, I responded in kind. My hands wrapped around his neck and pulled him into me, as if he were my oxygen...a contradiction, since the way he was kissing me made it almost impossible to breathe.

I pulled his hair, making him lean his head back so I could catch my breath. He grunted from the pain when I had to pull harder because he refused to take his mouth away from mine.

We were panting, and his blue eyes looked straight into mine while I tried to control the waves of burning pleasure flowing through my body from head to toe. My legs were still around him, and he pulled me into him tightly as if he couldn't bear for any space to exist between our two bodies.

"You're rough," I gasped, unable to contain myself. Not that I cared—we'd only been in there for five minutes, and he already had me in the palm of his hand.

"And you're unbearable."

I couldn't say anything back—his lips were too quick to attack.

All that was too intense. I felt him all over. One of his hands started unbuttoning my top while the other gripped my thighs. He started walking to the right, probably intending to lay me out on the desk there, but I pulled him toward me, and my back struck the wall. I heard a click, and the lights came on, illuminating everything around us and ourselves with painful clarity.

It was as if someone had dumped cold water on our heads. Nicholas stopped, looked at me surprised, breathing hard like me, and reality imposed itself on the physical attraction of our bodies. Nicholas leaned his forehead into mine and closed his eyes for a few seconds that seemed interminable.

"Shit!" he exclaimed, dropping me. He turned around and walked out the door without looking back.

Reality hit me so hard that my legs gave out from under me

and I fell to the floor, leaned back against the wall, and hugged my knees. Only then did I start to grasp what we'd done.

Hooking up with Nicholas wouldn't solve anything. It wouldn't undo Dan's cheating on me, it wouldn't fill up the solitude of living in that place without family or friends, and it certainly wouldn't help the two of us get along any better. That episode with Nick could only mean one thing: *problems*.

16

Nick

INSIDE, I WAS BURNING. IN EVERY POSSIBLE SENSE OF THE WORD. For days, I hadn't been able to stop thinking of that kiss at the races, and it was ruining my mood. Seeing her in my own home, rubbing something I couldn't have in my face, was more than I could bear. She looked incredible tonight; I couldn't take my eyes off her body. Her legs, her breasts, her long, shimmering hair... I couldn't take her dancing in front of me with my friends while every guy had his eye on her. I'd heard more than a few of them utter obscenities about her, and I was surprised by how much it affected me. I was usually the first one to say stuff like that when a hot chick was around, but people talking about Noah that way drove me mad.

When I'd seen her with my phone and realized what photos she was looking at, I'd felt pity for her and rage at the people hurting her, especially her ex-boyfriend, but that didn't mean I'd planned to take her into my dad's office and make out with her. Obviously, I'd had a few too many drinks and didn't realize what I was doing until the lights came on and I saw it all clearly. Her cheeks were pink, her lips swollen from my kisses... Jesus, just thinking about it made me want to go back for more. But I couldn't, not with her. She was my stepsister, dammit, the same stepsister who was screwing up my entire life and had made me lose my car.

I tried to clear my head by going outside. I wanted to stay away from her. I couldn't sleep with someone who was living in my home, someone I'd see every day and who just happened to be the daughter of the woman who had taken my mother's place, a place I'd learned to forget about a long time ago.

I stayed outside until everyone started to leave. The house was a wreck, with plastic cups all over the lawn, beer bottles everywhere—a complete disaster. Frustrated, I walked to the kitchen door, where I could see the last few stragglers, among them Jenna and Lion. She was sitting on his lap, and he was kissing her neck, making her giggle.

I almost threw up in my mouth. Who'd have ever thought those two would end up that way? Lion was the same as me; he liked women, parties, races, drugs...but now he'd turned into a little girl's lapdog.

Women were only good for one thing. If you let it go past that, you'd have problems. I knew what I was talking about from experience.

"Hey, bro!" Lion shouted, and I turned around. "Tomorrow there's a barbecue at Joe's. See you there?"

Barbecue at Joe's. That could only mean one thing: a party till dawn, hot chicks, and good music...but I had plans for the next day, plans six hours away that excited and depressed me in equal measure.

"I'm going to Vegas tomorrow," I told him, making an ambivalent face he instantly understood.

"All right, man. Have fun and say hi to Maddie," he replied.

"I'll see you both when I get back," I said, and then crossed the house and walked upstairs to my room. There was a soft light coming from under Noah's door, and I wondered if she was awake, but then I remembered she was afraid of the dark.

Someday when things calmed down, I'd ask her about that. But for now, I just wanted to sleep. The next day would be long.

My phone alarm went off at 6:30 in the morning. I groaned and turned it off, telling myself I'd need to get the lead out if I wanted to be in Vegas by noon. I hoped a long drive would help dispel the bad mood that was lingering from the night before. I got out of bed and took a quick shower before putting on jeans and a T-shirt, remembering the hellish heat in Nevada, which I'd hated since the first time I ever went there. Vegas was amazing as long as you stayed in the air-conditioned hotels, but outside, no one could stand more than an hour in that dry desert heat before it got to them.

As soon as I walked past Noah's door again, the memory of the night before assailed me. As if I hadn't had enough after dreaming of her all night long!

I walked downstairs to the kitchen for a cup of coffee. Prett, our cook, wouldn't get there until ten, so I had to figure out how to make a halfway decent breakfast on my own. At seven, I was in the car and ready to take off.

With the music distracting me, I tried to ignore the feeling that always overcame me when I had to see Madison. I still remembered the day I found out she was born. It horrified me to think that if it hadn't been for a simple coincidence, my sister and I never would have met. My life had been pretty fucked-up at the time: I hadn't lived with my father, Lion and I had been roommates, and we'd been getting into hella trouble. One weekend we'd gone with some friends to Vegas. I'd always hated Vegas because it was where my mother lived with her new husband, Robert Grason.

It had been painful to see my mother after seven years, especially with a baby in her arms. I had frozen—so had she—and we'd looked at each other for a few seconds as if seeing ghosts from our past. My mother had abandoned me when I was twelve. One day I'd come out of school, and she hadn't been there to pick me up. Since then it had just been the two of us, me and Dad, no one else.

I'd always had a good relationship with my mom, and even if, when I'd grown up, Dad had hardly ever been home, it had been fine because she'd been enough. I could still remember the hole in my heart when I realized I'd never see her there again.

But that sorrow had soon turned to hatred toward my mother and women in general. The only person who was supposed to love me above all else had traded me for a millionaire hotel mogul in Vegas whose name my father had cleared after he'd been accused of fraud to the tune of tens of millions of dollars.

Dad had told me the whole story when I was old enough. My mother had never been happy with him. She'd loved me, but with every day that had passed, she'd become more and more obsessed with money. It hadn't been enough to be married to one of the most prestigious lawyers and businessmen in America—no, she'd wanted to get in the bed of that fraudster Grason. The man who'd forbidden her to see me or have any contact with my father. And when she'd agreed, that had been the end of any relationship between us.

That meant my father had gotten full custody and my mother had renounced all parental rights. When things had gotten weird was when we'd seen each other again. I had known that girl with the blond hair and blue eyes was my sister, and even if I'd wanted to pretend I didn't care, at a certain point, I'd realized it meant something to me.

I had told my father, and he had been even more surprised

than me. He'd asked me what I wanted to do. If I'd wanted to get to know her or have some kind of relationship with her, he'd promised to help.

Dad and I hadn't been getting along great at the time. He'd gotten me out of jail twice, and I had been totally out of pocket. The pretext of helping me with Madison had gotten him what he wanted: to keep me on a short leash.

After months struggling with the lawyers, the judge had gotten me permission to see my sister twice a week, as long as I had her home by seven. Mom and I had no contact whatsoever—it was a social worker who brought Madison to me so I could pick her up and spend time with her. Because of the distance, I didn't get to see her often, but at least twice a month, I'd take her out and enjoy the company of the only girl I'd decided to open my heart to.

That meant I had to give up the life I'd known before then. I had to go back home, return to college, and promise not to get wrapped up in any more problems. My father was unequivocal: if I screwed up, no more visits with Madison.

Mom and I didn't see each other after the trial, but it was impossible to act like she didn't exist. My sister talked about her all the time and told her things about me. That was the worst thing because it meant I could never really break off the relationship. The pain would always be there, hidden deep in my soul. In the end, she'd always be my mom.

Four and a half hours later, I stopped at the park where my sister always waited for me with the social worker. I made sure the present I had for her was visible in the passenger seat, and I got out, walking toward the fountain in the middle of the park, where there were kids running around and playing. I'd never been a fan of little kids, and I still hated how they were so whiny and needy, but one of those whiny, needy little kids had captured my heart.

I couldn't help smiling when I saw her little blond head from behind. Just then she was bending over the fountain, not in the least afraid of falling in.

"Hey, Maddie!" I shouted, getting her attention and watching her eyes swell as she saw me there, ten feet away. "You thinking of taking a dip?" I asked. A huge grin crossed her angel face, and she ran over toward me.

"Nick!" she shrieked as she reached me. I bent over and lifted her in the air. Her golden curls flew out, and her blue eyes, just like mine, gazed at me full of excitement. "You came!" She wrapped her little arms around my neck.

I hugged her tight. That little girl had my whole heart in her hands.

"Of course I came, it's not every day a girl turns five years old. What do you expect?" I set her on the ground and placed a palm on top of her head. "You're huge! How much have you grown? At least thirty or forty feet!" I said, seeing the pride on her face.

"More than that, more like a *hundwed twenty*!" she said, hopping up and down.

"Wow! Soon you'll even be taller than me," I said as the tall, tubby woman with the folder under her arm came over.

"What's up, Anne?" I asked the woman overseeing my visits with my little sister.

"Getting by," she said in her usual expressionless tone. "I've got tons of work today, so I'd be appreciative if you'd bring your sister back on time, not a minute earlier or later, okay, Nicholas? We don't want a repeat of last time, do we?"

Last time, my sister had cried so much when I'd told her I had to go that I'd ended up an hour and a half late to my appointment with Anne. All hell had broken loose: she'd called the cops, Social Services...and I'd almost lost my right to even see Madison.

"Relax, I'll be here at seven," I said to calm her down, picking Maddie up and taking her to my car.

"You know what, Nick?" she said, running her fingers through my hair. Since she'd been old enough to do it, her favorite pastime had been messing up my hair.

"What?" I asked. Despite our joking earlier, my sister was smaller than normal for her age. She suffered from type 1 diabetes. Her pancreas didn't produce any insulin. For two years, she'd had to take shots three times a day, and we'd had to be very careful about what she ate. It was a common disease, but that didn't mean it wasn't dangerous. Madison had to keep a blood sugar monitor on her at all times, and if her glucose levels got out of whack, we had to give her shots or food.

"Mom said I can eat a hamburger today," she replied with a radiant smile.

I frowned at her. My sister didn't lie, but I didn't want to take the risk of letting her eat something that would make her feel bad. And I definitely wasn't going to call her mom to find out if she was telling the truth. Contacts like that had to go through Anne, and she hadn't said anything to me.

"Maddie, Anne didn't tell me anything about that," I said as I put her in the driver's side. She opened her eyes wide and stared at me.

"But Mama said I could," she insisted. "She said it's my birthday and I can go to McDonald's."

I sighed. I didn't want to force my sister to miss out on something all little kids like. I hated that she couldn't just enjoy a normal life. I'd had to give her injections in the stomach, and I hated the bruises that the continual injections left on her pale skin.

"Fine, I'll call Anne and see what she says," I told her, opening the trunk of the car and taking out the car seat.

"Nick, will you play with me today?" she asked. It was evident to me that the caretakers who were raising my sister didn't like to play the games she liked. My mother was never home; she was always off traveling with her dickhead husband, and my sister spent too much time with people who didn't love her as she deserved.

"Speaking of playing, I've got a present for you, Princess," I said as I adjusted the seat. I stretched out to grab the round package wrapped in shiny paper with a big bow that the sales attendant at the store had wrapped for me.

"Yay!" she shouted, jumping up and down.

With a smile, I handed the gift to her. Its contents couldn't have been more obvious.

She scratched off the paper like an animal, revealing the fuchsia-colored soccer ball.

"Ooh, pretty," she said. "I love it, Nick! It's pink, but it's a really pretty pink, it's not that little baby pink Mom likes so much. Plus Mom never lets me play soccer, but I can play with you, right?" she shouted, almost bursting my ear drums.

What could I say? My sister loved soccer, way more than any of those cheesy dolls her parents wouldn't stop buying her.

I looked at her blue dress, her patent-leather shoes, and her lace leggings.

"Who dressed you?" I asked, picking her up again. She was light as a feather; she probably weighed less than the ball I'd just given her. She was like my mother in that way, and just looking at Madison always gave me an ache in my chest. She was a consolation in a way for losing my mother when I was so young. The only ways she resembled me were her bright blue eyes and her dark lashes. She even had my mother's dimples!

Maddie gave me a sour look—a look she'd clearly learned from me.

"Miss Lillian wouldn't let me put on my soccer uniform. I told her you and me played together, and she chewed me out and said I shouldn't be doing exercise because I'll get sick, but it's not true, I can play with you as long as I've had my shot. You know that. We can play, right, Nick, can't we?"

"Easy, kiddo, of course we can play, and you can tell Lillian that when I'm here, we'll play whatever we want, got it? I'll get you some clothes so we can do it without messing up your dress." I kissed her on the cheek and strapped her into the seat. She wouldn't stay still; she kept toying with the ball, and it was several seconds before I finally had her snug and could return to the driver's seat.

I called Anne along the way and asked about the hamburger, and she said yes, McDonald's was fine. Once that problem was resolved, I talked to Madison while I drove to my favorite McDonald's in Las Vegas. Before I got her out, I grabbed her backpack with the injection she had to take every day at the same hour before lunch.

"Ready?" I asked her, and lifted her dress, pinching a bit of skin under her belly button and bringing the needle close to her translucent skin.

Her eyes always watered, but she never complained. My sister was brave, and I hated her having that disease. If I could have, I would have had it in her place without a second's hesitation, but life was like that: unfair.

"Yeah," she whispered.

———

Ten minutes later, we were eating, surrounded by lots of laughter and people with screaming children.

"Is it good?" I asked, watching her get ketchup all over her face.

She nodded. It was nice to see her eating.

"You know what, Nick? Soon I'll be going to school," she said, stuffing her mouth with fries. "Mom said it'll be lots of fun and I'll meet tons of new kids. Mom says when you started school you used to get in fights with girls like me because they wanted to be your girlfriend and you didn't want to because you said they were dumb."

I tried to conceal my anger at knowing my mother was talking about me as if she'd been there for me, a good mother and not one who had left me when I'd needed her most.

"That's true, but that won't happen to you because you're way more fun than other girls," I said, taking a sip of my Coke.

"I'm never going to have a boyfriend," she affirmed, and I couldn't help but chuckle. "Do you have a girlfriend, Nick?"

For no apparent reason, Noah's face appeared in my mind. I didn't have a girlfriend, but I would have liked to do with her the things you did with a girlfriend. Jesus—what the hell was I thinking?

"No, I don't have a girlfriend," I said. "You're the only girl for me." I bent over and tugged one of her curls.

Maddie smiled, and we went on talking. It was fun to chat with her. I felt relaxed—felt like myself. Strangely, being with a five-year-old girl brought me more inner peace than being with a woman. After lunch, I took her for a drive around Vegas, I bought her a complete pink-and-white soccer uniform, cleats included, and we accidentally forgot her little doll's outfit in the changing room. The rest of the day flew by, and before I knew it, I had ten minutes until Anne would come pick her up. We were already at the park, where we'd been kicking the ball for half an hour. I knew this next part would be hard.

My sister wasn't good at goodbyes. She didn't understand why I had to go or why I couldn't live with her the way her friends' brothers and sisters did. She was a mess, and anytime we separated, I was left with horrible sorrow and an unbearable urge to take her with me.

"Listen, Maddie, soon Anne's going to be here," I said, sitting her on my lap. We were stretched out on the grass, and she was running her hands through my hair again. But when I said that, she stopped, and her lower lip started to tremble, just as I had feared.

"Why do you have to go?" she asked with glassy eyes, and the pain struck to the depths of my heart.

"Hey, why are you crying?" I said. "We always have such fun when I come here. If I lived here all the time, you'd get bored of me." I wiped her tears away with a finger.

"I wouldn't get bored," she said, heaving slightly. "You love me, you play with me, and you let me do fun stuff. Mom won't let me do almost anything."

"Mom's just worried about you. Anyway, I promise you I'll come more often." As I told her this, I swore to myself I really would. "How about I try to be here when you start school?"

Her eyes lit up.

"But Mom will be there."

"Don't you worry about that," I said, calming her down, just as I saw Anne walking up the cobblestone trail.

I got up with Maddie in my arms, and she turned and saw the social worker.

"Don't go!" she screamed, crying like mad and hiding her head against my neck.

"Come on, Madison, don't cry," I said, trying to keep my own feelings under control as well. "It's okay." I hated seeing her like that. I rubbed her back, trying to console her.

"No! Stay with me! We can keep playing!" she begged. My T-shirt was wet with her tears. By then we had reached Anne, who stretched out her arms to take Maddie away from me. But I stepped back. I wasn't ready to let her go.

"If you stop crying, I'll bring you a very special present next time. What do you say?" I proposed, but she just went on howling with her arms wrapped tightly around my neck. I struggled to get free of her; she was clinging with all her might.

"Time to hand her over," Anne said impatiently.

I hated that woman.

"Maddie, you've got to go," I said, trying to calm her down. Only after a minute did I pull hard enough to get her off me, and I saw her face streaked with tears. Her curls were glued to her forehead.

Anna took her in her arms, and she reached out, shouting my name.

"You should go, Nicholas," Anne said, carrying her away. I wanted to grab Maddie from her and take her far away, where I could care for her and give her the love I knew she needed.

"I love you, Princess, see you soon," I said, walking over to kiss her on the head and then turning around and not looking back. My sister's wails were the only thing I could think of during the six hours it took me to drive back to Los Angeles.

17

Noah

AT ELEVEN THIRTY, I FINALLY ADMITTED TO MYSELF THERE WAS no way I was getting any sleep. Since the night before and what had happened with Nicholas, the memory of his kisses and his hands all over me wouldn't leave me in peace. My mind could think of nothing but him and his lips pressed against mine. I guessed I was glad for the distraction. It was better than wallowing around in my sorrows and my memory of my life from before.

What I didn't like was being all alone in this huge house. I had no idea where Nicholas was, but I hadn't seen him leave, even though I'd gotten up at eight.

Why the hell should I care? I didn't know. Since when did his location matter to me? Probably he was sleeping with one of the easy girls on his list, not even remembering what had happened between us. Was I alone in thinking it was crazy? We were brother and sister or something like it! We lived under the same roof, we couldn't stand each other, and any memory that wasn't those kisses and caresses made my blood pressure rise...

But I needed attention. My mother was on the other end of the country, and my friends and the people I'd known all my life were far away. Everything here was new to me; I didn't even know how to get around this gigantic city. Jenna was inseparable from her boyfriend, so I could forget about having her around too often. And I needed someone just then, someone to talk to or at least be there so I wouldn't feel so alone.

At least I'd managed to get Nick's dog to like me. Just then, Thor and I were both lying on the sofa. His dark, hairy head was resting on my lap, and I was scratching his ears at a steady rhythm. That dog was nothing like the way Nick had portrayed him: he was a sweetie, easy to win over as long as you had a handful of dog biscuits at the ready. That was how sad my life was: the one person I could lean on in this house wasn't even a person, just a four-legged creature that loved to have his ears scratched and whose favorite pastime was chasing a ball over and over.

I was watching a movie on TV when I heard the front door open. Thor was so sleepy he just lifted his ears a bit when a tall figure appeared over the threshold. I saw who it was and felt almost sick.

Nick turned toward the living room and walked over, observing me.

Under the faint light of the TV and the lamp in the entryway, I couldn't see much, but he was obviously exhausted. He leaned against the doorway and looked at me apathetically.

"What are you doing up?" he asked a few seconds later. I was briefly hypnotized and couldn't answer. He looked older. Weary. But no less handsome. I tried to focus on the question.

"I couldn't sleep," I said warily. It must have been the first time since we met that we'd talked to each other in a remotely normal fashion.

He nodded and looked at Thor.

"I see you've got him on your side. My dog's a traitor."

I smiled involuntarily when I saw that Nick really seemed irritated.

"You know," I joked, "it's not easy to resist my charms."

Shit.

We paused and looked each other in the eye. Then he turned to the TV.

"Are you seriously watching cartoons?" I was happy for this change of subject.

"*Mulan* is one of my favorites," I confessed.

He grinned, and I felt the butterflies in my stomach again.

"Chill, Freckles, it used to be my favorite, too. When I was four years old." Despite his sarcasm, he came over and flopped down beside me on the sofa, resting his feet next to mine on the coffee table. For a moment, we watched the film in silence.

This was too weird. And just when I thought it couldn't get more uncomfortable, I noticed Nick was staring at me. I froze, knowing how close together we were. This new Nick had nothing to do with the one I'd met when I arrived. He was so relaxed, with not a trace of that disdainful attitude from before...and in his eyes, there was a sadness he was incapable of hiding.

"Where were you?" I whispered. I had no idea why I'd spoken so softly, but I felt strange asking him. I didn't want him to know I actually cared what he'd been doing.

"With someone who needs me," he said, and I knew from his way of speaking that it wasn't just another one of his girls. "Why, did you miss me?"

I felt him coming closer to me, but I didn't move away. Something about him being here made me want to smile and had taken away that sorrow, that pressure in my chest, that I had felt the entire day.

"I don't like being all alone somewhere so big," I admitted.

His hand stretched across the back of the couch and made me feel like I was suffocating when it tenderly stroked my hair and then my earlobe. Time seemed to stop. I didn't hear the movie or anything but his respiration and the mad beats of my heart.

"Good thing I'm here then," he said, and bent over, pressing his lips into mine. It was a warm kiss and full of expectation. I closed my eyes and let the moment take me away, lifting my hands to his face to feel his stubble against the palms of my hands and then his hair. His lips were insistent, and I opened mine and let his tongue inside. I got goose bumps when he reached down past my shoulders, touched my ribs, came to a stop at my waist.

This was nothing like the other night. His touch was warm, soft, as if he were afraid of breaking me. I heard myself moan almost inaudibly as his hand moved from my waist to my back, which I arched almost involuntarily to let him closer to me. Then I acted without thinking at all.

I sat up, stretched a leg across his lap, and rested on top of him. He looked hypnotized and sat up to squeeze me in his arms. Our kissing was deeper now, more eager, and his hands were all over me. But just as I thought I would melt, I stopped, opening my eyes, my mind a blank. That was what he did to me—made me forget everything—and that was exactly what I needed.

I saw he was looking at my lips, and I needed him to kiss them again, but instead he pulled away, turning serious and telling me, "This isn't right. Don't let me do this again. You're my stepsister, and you're seventeen years old. This can't happen again."

He got up and left me on the sofa.

I was angry and hurt. *First he kisses me, and then he says these things?* And what did my age matter? I wanted him back, wanted him to make me feel good again. I needed him more than ever because this day had been horrible. I'd felt like shit, with no one to talk to, no one I could even call. Everyone I loved either was busy or had betrayed me.

"If you don't want this to happen," I said, "stop trying to make it happen. You were the one who started it all three times."

I shoved past him, shouted, "Come on, Thor," and went upstairs to my room. I slammed the door and got into bed. But I, too, saw that he was right: it couldn't happen again.

———————

The next morning, a familiar voice woke me, cradling my ribs and rocking me back and forth.

"Get up! It's after twelve!" my mother said. I opened my still-sleepy eyes and saw her sitting beside me looking radiant. "Did you miss me?" she asked with a big smile. I smiled back and sat up to hug her. Finally she was home! Of course I'd missed her. She was the one normal thing in my life.

"How was New York?" I asked, stretching out and rubbing my eyes.

"Incredible! It's the best place ever for shopping. I brought you a ton of presents."

As I walked to the bathroom, I remarked sarcastically, "Great, Mom! Like I don't have enough clothes I don't wear already."

While I washed my hair and brushed my teeth, she sat on the toilet lid and talked to me about all the amazing places she'd been.

"I'm happy you had such a good time," I said, walking off to my closet and looking through everything hanging there, uncertain what to put on. It was easier when you didn't have so many clothes, and that was why I kept going back to my suitcase, which was half-open on the floor. A part of me refused to unpack it because that would mean that all this was real, that I was staying here and there was no turning back.

"We've got plans today, Noah, that's why I came to wake you

up." When I heard the tone in her voice, I was sure I wouldn't like what she was proposing.

"What plans?" I asked, one hand on my hip.

Walking past me, my mother started looking slowly through the dresses in my closet.

"We've got an interview at St. Marie's."

"An interview where?"

"At your new school, Noah. I told you, it's one of the best in the country. Not just anyone can go there, but thanks to William's contacts and the fact that Nick is an alum, they've agreed to meet you," she said patiently. "It's just a formality, but you'll want to see the school, it's something else."

I wanted to puke.

"Dammit, Mom! Couldn't you have just stuck me in some regular school?" I shouted, jerking the hangers back and forth. I was completely freaking out. "I don't want to go to some stuck-up school, I told you that. Plus, why do I need an interview? It's not a job, for God's sake."

"Noah, don't start. This is a big opportunity. People who go to that school end up at the best colleges, and they're willing to let you in as a senior, which isn't something they usually do."

"So I'm gonna be the weirdo who got in because I've got a hookup? Great, Mom."

She crossed her arms. That was the gesture she always made when her mind was made up, so I knew there wouldn't be any more arguing about the subject.

"You'll thank me in the future. Anyway, your friend Jenna goes to St. Marie's, so you won't be on you own." At least that was one thing I was happy to hear. It was consoling to know that I'd have someone to be with at lunchtime. "Now get dressed. We need to be there in less than two hours."

I sighed and looked around until I found a pair of black skinny jeans and a sky-blue shirt. I wasn't about to put on a gown or anything like that. Just the thought of how the girls at that school must dress gave me the creeps.

The one good thing about the outing to visit the school was that afterward, my mother took me to get a new car. I'd had my license for a year, and it broke my heart to have to leave my pickup in Canada, so I had taken all my savings, and with the help of my mother, I was going to get a secondhand car to drive around town. William insisted he would happily buy me a brand-new one, but I had to put my foot down. One thing was him buying my mother stuff or paying for my school and clothes, but the car—that was a different story. I was also thinking of finding a job to cover my expenses. I didn't like the idea of that man paying for all my stuff like I was a twelve-year-old. I was old enough and capable enough to find a job and take care of myself.

My mother didn't oppose my decision. She approved of me working. I'd done it since I was fifteen, and I liked not having to beg for money anytime I needed it. She helped me apply for a job waitressing at a well-known spot twenty minutes from our home by car. It was called Bar 48 and served food and drinks; obviously I wasn't allowed to serve liquor, but they would let me wait on guests. I'd done that before, and I was pretty good at it. I'd start the following week on the night shift.

It didn't take us long to find a car. I didn't care much about the details as long as it ran. We chose a vintage Beetle in decent condition. I didn't know much about cars even though I was good at driving them, but it was cute, and I loved the red paint job. I paid and signed and felt truly free when I could drive myself home.

It was funny parking that little thing between Will's Mercedes and Nick's SUV. It was kind of a metaphor for how I fit into the family. I got out in a good mood at the very moment when Nick emerged from the house spinning the keys to his Range Rover on one finger. He took off his sunglasses to look at my new acquisition.

His face was both amused and horrified. I squared off, ready to listen to his comments.

"Please tell me you haven't brought that car here," he said, walking over and shaking his head as he looked condescendingly from me to the Beetle and back.

I wasn't going to let him mess up my good mood, so I bit my tongue and kept the insults to myself.

"It's *my* car, I like it, and I'd appreciate you not looking at it like that," I said, trying to restrain my nerves at seeing him for the first time since we'd made out on the couch.

He looked baffled. Without even asking, he went to the back and opened the trunk to look at the engine.

"What are you doing?" I asked, walking up beside him. I reached up to shut the trunk, but he grabbed it and held it up, ignoring my vain attempts to overcome his strength.

"Did you have it checked out?" he said, manipulating different internal parts I wouldn't even know the names of. "This hunk of junk will leave you stranded in the middle of the road. It's dangerous to even look at. I can't believe your mom let you buy it."

"Well, it wouldn't be the first time I got stuck in the middle of the road, thanks to you. So don't worry, I'll work it out," I said, peeling off one of his fingers. When he finally gave in, I slammed the trunk shut.

"If you'd had your phone on you like a normal person, you wouldn't have had to get in the car with some weirdo. Anyway, isn't it time for you to get over it?" He was hissing at me, but I thought I saw a little regret in his eyes.

"You threw me out without checking whether my phone had any juice," I said. "Anyway, who cares? Just forget you know me." I hoped he would finally walk off.

He looked at me as if he could hardly stand me. *Great, welcome to the club*, I thought.

When I turned to walk away, he grabbed my arm and pulled me till I was face-to-face with him.

His brain must have been in conflict, as if he didn't know what to do or say. Only after a few seconds, when I'd already yielded to his deep-blue eyes and my heart was throbbing, did he speak.

"I'll take you wherever you want to go," he said, knitting his brows, as if not even he could believe what he was saying.

I stalled and then finally responded, "No need."

Was Nicholas Leister actually being nice to me? *Wake yourself up—this can't be happening.*

How could having that boy close do this to me? Where was that hatred I'd felt for him just a few moments ago? Why was it that the only thing I now felt was a dark, irrepressible desire to kiss him and let him wrap me in his arms as he had that night at the party, when he was too drunk to realize what he was doing?

The hand he'd grabbed now moved toward him almost imperceptibly. We were close enough that something could happen. My God...those lips! Just thinking about him holding me and his tongue stroking mine...

Just as I thought we'd kiss, the sound of a horn made me jump out of my skin. Nicholas, calm, turned to see who it was, while I struggled to catch my breath.

"Hey, Noah," Jenna said from the passenger window of Lion's car. He waved to us in turn. "Nick, you don't care if I invite Noah, do you?" she asked. Nick's hands were on his head in a gesture of something—it was impossible to tell whether it was frustration, anger, or disgust.

He looked at me for what felt like ages before finally asking, "You feel up to it?"

I don't know why, but I responded automatically.

"Hell yeah. Where to?"

Nick gave Lion a mysterious look.

"I don't know if she can handle it," Lion said, laughing as he peeked out the window.

Nick smiled irresistibly. "This could be fun."

Twenty minutes later, we were getting out of Lion's car near what looked like an abandoned industrial bay. There were tons of people milling around and cars with their trunks open playing music at full blast. It reminded me of the day of the races, but the ambience was different. Nick's and Lion's friends came over and said some very loud hellos. Jenna threw an arm over my shoulders. She was in a tight black dress that left her shoulders and part of her back exposed. Her hair fell over her face in waves and looked spectacular. I felt like a slob in the jeans and shirt I'd put on for the high school interview, but there was nothing I could do about it now.

"You'll enjoy seeing my man in action," Jenna said with a smile, eyes glowing. "And Nick, too." She pulled me through the group of guys talking to Nick and Lion, and when we were inside the circle, I could hear what they were talking about.

"Ronnie's not here, and no one in his gang is, either," one of the guys I'd seen during the races said. Nicholas was leaning against his car with a cigarette in his hand, and when Ronnie's name came up, he looked over at me. Not with rancor this time, but with apparent disappointment at not being able to teach his worst enemy another lesson. From my point of view, Nick was out of his mind if he wanted to get into it with a guy with a gun, but knowing my new stepbrother as I did, I wasn't surprised to learn he was up for it.

"Greg and A.J. are there, and the stakes are high," Lion said. Nick grinned, walked away from the car, tossed his cigarette to the ground, and clapped him on the back.

"What are we waiting for then?"

The crowd around us shouted in jubilation. I had no idea what was going on, but I thought I could sense where this was headed, and I didn't like it one bit.

Everyone walked off toward the warehouse, the doors of which were open. Inside it was crowded, and the music and noise were deafening. Did these people ever do anything on a small scale? Like get a coffee or go to the movies? Immediately I knew the answer was no: Nicholas wasn't the type to date a girl, invite her out for a romantic meal. Nicholas was all about danger, and he liked being surrounded by people who were the same way. But if that was so, what the hell was I doing with him?

Lion leaned in toward Nick, and I heard him say, "Leave A.J. to me. After what happened, you know I want his ass." Nicholas nodded and glanced over. I didn't say a word. I didn't know what I was doing there.

"I'll go first, same as always," he said, and then pushed me away from our group. His fingers gave me chills.

"What are you going to do?" I asked him.

He looked excited.

"I'm going to fight, Freckles. I'm good. People like watching Lion and me fight. But I'm warning you, it's going to get packed, so stick close to Lion until I'm done and I can take care of you and Jenna."

He was going to fight. He was going to exchange blows with another guy just for fun. I mean, there was money on the line, but Nicholas didn't need money—he was a millionaire—so why the hell did he get into these kinds of situations?

"Why are you doing this?" I asked, frightened. I didn't see any sense in this at all.

"I gotta relax somehow," he said. He left me there, terrified at what I was about to see.

18

Nick

I WAS LIGHT-HEADED AS I LEFT HER THERE. I DIDN'T THINK ANY girl had ever affected me as much as Noah. That was nice, but it also irked me. I'd always liked having control over everything, especially the women around me. I always knew how they'd react. I always knew they'd want me. Noah was different. All you had to do was look at her to see she was the opposite of the people I'd grown up with and those I surrounded myself with now. I still couldn't understand how, with the chance to blow my father's money, she kept insisting on wearing simple clothes or driving that dangerous piece of junk. She was even looking for a job. I couldn't stop trying to figure her out. Beyond that, there was the physical attraction I felt for her. Every time she was in front of me, I wanted to kiss and caress her. I had done it when I was drunk, not knowing what I was doing, and now all I could think about was repeating the experience. That was why she was here with me that night. I had been about to kiss her when Jenna and Lion had shown up. I'd planned on spending the whole night with her. What the hell did a fight matter when I could be kissing those soft lips?

It was funny to see how she reacted when I touched her. I almost lost control that first night, hearing those soft moans come from her as we kissed. And there we were again, and I was asking myself why the hell I'd invited her to watch me going to town on one of the biggest idiots I'd ever met. Her face had been horrified when she'd found out what we were up to. Still, it was nice to see her there. And funny because she didn't fit in one bit.

I walked off into the abandoned building we used for those events. Fights had been a part of my life ever since I met Lion. He was talented, and I'd learned almost everything he knew. My fury might have been more intense than his, though, and that was why almost no one ever beat me. I had an easy time finishing most of my opponents. When I was fighting, all my senses were focused on winning—nothing else mattered—and that helped me center myself, get rid of all the shit I was carrying around inside. Today, I needed it especially: I was torn up after that last visit with my sister, even more so when I found out she'd be on her own a whole week while her parents took off for Barbados. I couldn't understand how a parent could just abandon her first child without any sort of remorse and then do the same thing all over again with her young daughter... It drove me crazy.

It could get dangerous here if you didn't watch out, so I usually just showed up, won my fight, got the money, and left. Most people hung around for the afterparty, which was full of drugs and alcohol. I wasn't into that, and I kept a cool head as I took off my shirt and entered the ring.

Greg was a big guy, a gym rat, and we'd never gotten along. Before I showed up, everyone had him up on a pedestal, and when he fought me, he gave it his all. His weak point was his technique; he was all brute strength, and I'd never had much trouble slipping his punches. A.J. was a whole different story. He and Lion had history. Once A.J. had tried to rape Jenna at a club. Thank God I had been there with her and gotten rid of him before things could go south. Lion hadn't known Jenna then, but when they'd started going out and she had told him, he had nearly beaten A.J. to death.

Everybody was gathered around the ring. Bets were live, and that would only make the crowd shout and whistle louder. I started jumping in place, trying to warm up, while Greg entered from the opposite end. He gave me a hateful, bloodthirsty look, and I had to try not to smile, knowing in ten minutes I'd be done with him.

The guy in charge of the money shouted my name and Greg's, and a minute later, the fun started. Greg had a bad habit: he threw haymakers right from the bell, and he always got tired early. You just needed to know how to wait to attack. The first time I lurched forward, I landed a body blow. Everyone shouted wildly afterward when he bent over and I kneed him in the nose. The adrenaline had kicked in, and I felt capable of anything. Greg recovered and tried to hit me again, this time in the face. I smiled as I dodged it and got him in the right eye.

It was a stiff one, and he fell to the floor, which gave me the opportunity to kick him again, but what was the fun in kicking a man when he was down? Greg got back up, danced around, shoved me, grazed my right cheek. But I fired back with a punch that left him flat on his back, and this time, he couldn't get up.

The euphoria of victory did me good. I was glad to know I had the strength to get the finish.

Everyone was shouting my name, and people pressed in around the ring trying to reach me. But I jumped out and went straight to get my prize money. The purse was five grand, and once I'd stuffed it into my jeans, I went to look for Lion. He was in the last row with Jenna and a group of friends, getting ready for his grand entrance. It was more relaxed there than in the front. Nobody there was pushing or shoving.

My heart sped up involuntarily when I reached them and saw Noah was gone. I looked around and couldn't see her anywhere.

"Where is she?" I asked Lion, my body tensing up again.

He grinned.

"It was too much for her. When she saw you get hit, she went outside," Jenna said.

"I'm going to go find her. Jenna, you stay with the guys."

Noah was sitting against the wall by the door hugging her knees. I didn't like the expression on her face. I threw on my T-shirt as I got closer. Her eyes focused first on my torso and then on the small cut on my face.

"What the hell are you doing here?" I said, a little disappointed that she hadn't seen me finish my opponent.

She stood up, glowering.

"What you're doing in there... It's not for me."

I guessed she was scared. I hadn't thought it would affect her so much. Any other girl would have seen what I'd done and thrown herself straight into my arms, but Noah...

"Fights aren't your thing, I get it," I said, and tried to be gentle as I put my arm around her neck. Noah was like someone from another planet: there were times when she was hard as a rock, not hesitating to punch me square in the face, but then she could be so small and fragile that I couldn't resist the urge to take her into my arms.

I tickled the back of her neck, and she looked up, about to say something, I thought, but before she could, I bent over to kiss her and pull her into me.

She melted in my arms, just as I wished. I liked feeling how her body reacted when I touched her. Her fingers sank into my damp hair, and I had to struggle to keep from touching her all over.

When I pulled away a moment later, she looked at my cut and ran her fingers over the swelling. That soft but significant caress made me feel something strange inside.

"I hated every second you were up there," she said. I knew she was telling the truth. Noah cared about me, and that was something so strange and so new that it took me aback.

"This is who I am, Noah," I said, letting her go.

"Why do you do it, though? I don't understand. You've got more than enough money, you don't need it—"

"Lion does though," I cut her off, on the defensive now.

She seemed to grasp that, but still, I felt I needed to add something.

"I don't do it just for the money. I like to fight. I like to know I can stop the person in front of me. That I have control of the situation. I can tell what you're getting at, but if you think I'm going to stop doing these things just because you and I—"

"Because you and I what?" she interrupted me. "What's the end of that sentence?"

I couldn't answer. I didn't even know what was happening. I just knew it was a mistake. Noah was a simple girl, the kind you'd give flowers to and candies in a heart-shaped box, and that just wasn't me. The mere thought of it was ridiculous. But the problem was all my misgivings vanished when I had her close. I knew I shouldn't kiss her, touch her…but I couldn't help it. She was right: I was the one who was looking for her.

"It's fine, Nicholas, don't say anything. I know who you are. I'm not going to expect anything more from you than what we have right now."

I turned around and went back inside to watch Lion's fight.

What did she mean, she knew who I was? I didn't like the sound of it. I felt gripped by anger, but I couldn't say exactly why.

19

Noah

IT WAS A MISTAKE, COMING HERE TONIGHT WITH NICHOLAS. YEAH, he was attractive, and, yeah, I couldn't even think straight when he touched me or kissed me, but I didn't like who he was. Nicholas Leister moved in a circle I had avoided my whole life: fights, out-of-control parties, drugs, alcohol… Those were all things I didn't want to be a part of. I was still trying to get used to my life here. I'd only left home two weeks ago, and literally everything had changed. I was still messed up over Dan, and starting a relationship with Nicholas made matters worse because I was perfectly aware of what a guy like him would want from a girl like me. Maybe I was old-fashioned or weird or whatever, but I liked to do things the traditional way. I wanted a guy to *want* to be with me and show me that every day. I liked sweet words, kind gestures, and that just wasn't Nick. I wasn't ready for my heart to be broken again before it had begun to heal. I wasn't even sure I had a heart anymore, just thousands of little pieces I kept trying to glue back together.

I told myself I would have to try to have a normal relationship with Nick. We couldn't be together, but that didn't mean we had to hate each other. The fights with him, the push and pull since we'd met, all that was exhausting. We lived together, so we should try to be friends, if it even was possible to be friends with someone who stirred you up in that way.

I stayed by the door waiting for Lion's fight to be over. I couldn't watch. I hated physical confrontation. It was upsetting that people could enjoy it; they were even making money betting against the fighters. It was gross and humiliating.

Nicholas had walked past me to go stand with Jenna and their friends. There must have been two hundred people in the crowd. Lion won his fight after fifteen minutes, but unlike Nick, he had bruises from blows to the chest and an ugly cut under his left eye. Jenna threw herself in his arms when she saw him and kissed him while everyone cheered. Was that what Nick had wanted? For me to throw myself at him just because he'd left some guy laid out on the ground? Ridiculous.

Nick came over to me, took my hand, and walked me out. It was strange to feel his fingers intertwined with mine but somehow distant, as if this were just something practical—a way to keep me from getting lost—and there was no affection in it. Something had changed since our last conversation. He seemed mad at me, as if he didn't even want me there. It hurt, but what could I expect?

I looked at his wounded knuckles. There was dried blood on them where he'd struck his opponent. I felt nauseated, and I needed air. What the hell was I doing here?

When we were close to his car, he left me to talk to his group of friends. Jenna was gone, and I felt lonely and scared. I decided to get an Uber and started to pull up the app. But Nicholas hurried over and tore it out of my hand.

"What are you doing?"

"Getting an Uber."

"Are you crazy? This is illegal. You can't give away our location. We could get arrested."

I didn't care. This place felt dangerous, and I wanted to avoid trouble. However good he looked, he wasn't worth it.

"I need to leave," I said.

"Why?"

"Because I don't like your world, Nicholas."

He didn't seem offended. If anything, he seemed indifferent.

"You're not built for this. I shouldn't have brought you."

I wasn't built for this? His response didn't bother me per se; it was the tone he said it in.

"I'm the one who decided to come here. And now I'm the one who's deciding to go."

He laughed.

"I don't know what I expected, but this definitely wasn't it. I thought you were tougher, Freckles. You didn't flinch when you and Ronnie got into it. I sure didn't think a couple of guys punching each other would do this to you."

What he couldn't see, as we stood there looking at each other, was the cold sweat coating my body, the soft tremors in my hands...

"I guess my bravery comes and goes," I said, opening my palm so he'd hand me back my phone. But he kept toying with it, and his mind seemed elsewhere.

"I wanted to ask you. Where'd you learn to race like that?"

"Beginner's luck. Phone, please."

He grinned.

"You've got more secrets than I would have imagined, Freckles." He stepped toward me, and I stepped away until my back touched the door of his car.

"We've all got secrets," I said, quieter now.

"I should warn you, I'm a pretty good detective," he said, leaning in for a kiss. I stopped him as best I could.

I woke from the spell he cast on me. My pulse started racing.

"Stay away from me, Nicholas," I said, more serious than ever.

Discovering my past—that was the last thing I wanted. The mere thought of it made me panic. I'd always kept my demons in check—no one knew anything—but with just a wall between him and me, there were things that I wasn't going to be able to hide. I hardly knew him, and already, he was unearthing things I never let anyone see.

"You want me to stay away from you? That's not what your body seems to be saying..."

Damn him. Nobody had ever gotten to me like this before. Seeing him there before me, so big, so masculine, I felt like a cornered animal someone was getting ready to slaughter at any minute. And I didn't like that, that sensation of feeling so small and vulnerable.

He placed a hand on either side of my head, almost like a cage.

"What are you so scared of?" he asked, his mouth close to mine, his breath heating up my face. His eyes were so blue, with bits of aquamarine in the pupils.

"I'm scared of you," I whispered.

Nick grinned. Maybe he liked my answer. It was as if someone had tossed a jar of ice water over my head. I shoved him and got away from his grasp.

"Asshole," I said. I couldn't believe I'd been sincere with him.

"Why? Because I think it's funny that you're scared? That's normal, Freckles. If you weren't, it would have worried me."

"I'm scared you'll get me into trouble," I lied, hoping he'd forget what I'd just said. I didn't want him having that much power over me.

"I've got a talent for wriggling out of it. You don't need to worry there."

"That's exactly it. I don't want to worry. Now give me my phone so I can get out of here."

Nicholas sighed, but his expression didn't change.

"It's too bad you're so stiff. I thought you and I could have fun together."

"There is no you and I... and there never will be."

Twenty minutes later, Jenna had dropped me at home. I was breathing easy again, and I promised myself I wouldn't fall into any more traps. Nicholas and I needed to keep our distance from each other.

I spent the next day washing my car. Nicholas stayed inside doing God knows what, and we barely crossed paths. My Beetle had been on the sales lot for a long time, so no one had taken care of it, and it was covered in dirt and grime. It was funny to me that all my new neighbors with their Chanel clothes and their stuck-up attitudes were gawking at me as I washed my own car in shorts and a T-shirt with some company's logo on it and with my hair pulled back in a bun. I looked like hell, but why should I care what my bleach-blond neighbor and her husband who ran some TV network or another thought of me?

As I blew a strand of hair out of my face and leaned over the hood with a sponge, trying to get out a particularly stubborn spot, I heard the last voice I would have expected to hear at that moment.

"I see you still hate the drive-through car wash." I froze. It couldn't be true.

I turned around and looked at him. He was standing next to Nicholas's car looking no different from when we'd said our goodbyes three weeks ago. His blond hair was disheveled, his chocolate eyes projected a self-assurance I'd always admired, and he had the build of a hockey player. I had to catch my breath.

Dan, who'd cheated on me with my best friend, was now standing in front of me.

I stopped what I was doing, holding on to the dripping sponge and letting my other hand flop to my side. I couldn't move. Just having him in front of me hurt, and all the memories I'd shared with him flooded into my mind like a slideshow: when we'd met; after I'd gone to one of his games and he'd won and he'd come over to tell me he couldn't concentrate once he'd seen me in the stands; our first date, when he'd taken me to an Indian restaurant where the food was so spicy we had been sick for three days; our first kiss, so soft and special that until recently, it had been on the list of my most treasured memories; the first time he'd ever called me his girlfriend…

Then I remembered the image of him and Beth hooking up, and everything else vanished.

I struggled to find a voice that wouldn't let him know how much his being there affected me.

"What the hell are you doing here?" I asked, dropping the sponge in the bucket. Water droplets splashed my bare feet.

"I miss you," he said.

I laughed mirthlessly.

"You don't miss me. You've had company, haven't you?" I replied, turning around.

"Noah…I'm sorry," he told me in that same velvety voice that had told me so many times he loved me above all else.

I shook my head, wishing this wasn't happening. I wasn't ready to confront Dan. There was a part of me that still wished everything was as it had been before, that wanted to turn around and let him hug me, kiss me, tell me how much he loved and missed me. I desperately wanted to be with someone from my previous life. Even for just a few seconds, I wanted to be the Noah Morgan I had been before getting into a car and heading off to a new city to live a life I didn't want.

"Noah…I love you," he said, coming up behind me.

My heart had already broken into a million pieces. Was he going to stomp on them now, crush them into dust?

"Don't tell me that," I said. But then I turned, and I saw him there, so close…saw those spots of gold in his brown eyes, the scar on his cheek where he'd been hit with a hockey stick—I was there when he'd gotten the stitches, I had been hysterical because I couldn't stand the sight of blood. Everything about Dan brought back so many memories—memories that now stung unbearably.

He looked nervous. I knew him well enough to know this was harder for him than it was for me.

"I'm saying it because it's the truth, Noah." He took my face in his hands and stroked my cheeks with his fingers. "Please forgive me. When you left, my whole world fell apart. I didn't know what to do, where to turn. You have to forgive me. Noah, please, say you forgive me."

His hands slid down to my shoulders. There was desperation in his voice. I closed my eyes. This shouldn't be happening. Why? And why was his presence making me so sad? I should have gotten over him already. He shouldn't have come here, asking forgiveness, but still…seeing him again, having that piece of my old life back, was comforting somehow.

Just then, I felt his lips on mine. It was unexpected but at the same time felt normal. That had been something I was used to, something pleasant, even necessary, something I'd wanted from the moment I got into that car to leave and never come back.

He cupped the back of my neck and pulled me toward him. I was so shocked, so overwhelmed by the thousands of contradictory feelings I was having that all I could do was hold still.

"Noah, kiss me, please, don't be like that." He tried to press himself into me and managed to get me to open my mouth, looking for my tongue with his just as he had the first time we'd done it. There was a kind of warmth there but also something different. Something had changed. My body seemed to be expecting something more powerful. I didn't want warmth; I wanted fire.

I heard someone make a noise, trying to get our attention. I stepped back, and Dan looked at me with joy on his face. Then we turned to see who had interrupted us.

My mother and William had just appeared. I'd been so wrapped up in my thoughts and feelings that I hadn't even heard them pull up in their car. She looked at us with a big smile on her lips and turned to William, who had a bright-eyed, satisfied expression on his face.

"You like our present?" he asked.

I didn't understand.

"Your mother sent me a ticket to surprise you," Dan said with a shrug, but I could see a look of guilt on his face, too. Now I got it. My mother thought she was giving me the best gift ever, bringing my boyfriend for a visit. She'd just missed one tiny detail: he was no longer my boyfriend.

"You were just so sad, Noah," Mom said, coming over and giving me a hug. "I knew Dan was the one person who could make you smile, so what was the harm in inviting him to spend a few days with us?"

Oh, Mom. You've screwed up now.

I forced myself to smile, hard as it was, while William shook Dan's hand firmly. My mother gave him a hug in turn, and they both stood back to look at us.

"We'll give you all a little privacy. You must want some time alone," Mom said. "Dan, I'm having them prepare the guest room. Anything you need, don't hesitate to ask."

Dan nodded politely, and my mother and William vanished through the front door.

When they were gone, I looked at Dan, enraged.

"I can't believe you had the balls to come here," I shouted, picking up the bucket and soap I'd brought out for my car. I wouldn't be able to finish now. I had much more important things to do.

This was wrong. Dan couldn't stay in my home. I didn't want him there, and I sure as hell didn't want him kissing me again.

"It was the perfect opportunity to say I'm sorry in person."

"You can't stay here, Dan."

"I know you're still mad, and I know you'll need lots of time before you can forgive me, but just let me be with you these days, Noah. Whatever the problem is, we'll solve it together, please. You're mine and I'm yours, remember?"

That phrase struck home.

"I stopped being yours the moment you hooked up with my best friend." I said that knowing that having to break up with him definitively in the coming days would leave me feeling worse than I already did. "You can stay here because I'm not going to upset William or my mother, and I don't want them to have to know what you did to me. But when that time's up, I never want to hear from you again."

"I know I hurt you, Noah. But I love you, I have always loved you, and without you, my life's a disaster. Since I saw you just now, everything makes sense again. When you told me you were leaving, I tried to make a plan in my head to be able to deal with it, but it didn't work. Noah, the thing with Beth meant nothing to me. I just leaned on her because she reminded me of you. You two were always together. You were so much alike. I know I've been an asshole, but I can't let what we have end this way."

I looked down, trying to suppress the tears that wanted out. I wasn't going to cry. I didn't cry anymore. I wouldn't cry.

"So this is where we are now," he said. "You can't even look me in the eyes."

He grabbed my face again.

"Please, just tell me you forgive me," he whispered, his lips nearly pressed to mine.

I don't even know what I said, but he kissed me again, hard, with feeling, and I let him do it, *again*. I couldn't control it. It was something I needed. But I knew it wasn't right. I had a strange feeling as I went along with him; I felt guilty, guilty because I was deceiving someone very important: myself.

At last, I managed to get out the words "I need some space." And it was true; I needed to think, needed to not have him in front of me.

"Fine," he agreed. "Can I at least leave my things in the guest room?"

I agreed and led him up there. I couldn't spend another minute with him, so I walked off to my room, thinking I would just climb into bed and sleep until the next day. I didn't care how early it was. I needed to think and get my feelings in perspective, but then my body made me stop at a room that wasn't mine, and before I could stop myself, I was knocking at Nicholas's door.

I don't know whether he answered. All I know was I heard a noise and went inside.

He was sitting in front of his laptop at a desk in the corner. When he saw me come in, he closed it. He spun his chair around to look at me, and I observed every inch of his anatomy as if it were a work of art. He was shirtless in gray sweatpants. I could tell he wasn't expecting a visitor, especially not me. It was the first time I'd ever knocked at his door since I'd lived there, but something in me told me my stepbrother would be able to console me, even as I was trying to grasp why I'd chosen to torture myself by being in his presence.

He must have seen something in my face because he immediately asked what was going on and approached me cautiously, not sure what to do. Just as with every other time we'd been alone together, an irresistible attraction crackled in the air. In a way, I was happy to realize Dan couldn't make me react that way—happy but at the same time confused.

Those eyes of Nick's only promised darkness. But without thinking twice, I grabbed the back of his neck, pulled him close, and kissed him desperately.

At first, he didn't react. He was surprised, I guessed, but his body clearly knew what it wanted. He grabbed my waist, and his mouth and tongue took over. He made me forget why I'd even come there, forget everything but him. I had to pull away a second to catch my breath. When I did, he asked me what I was doing, and then his teeth bit into my earlobe before his mouth traveled down to my cheek, my neck... Any notion of pain, loss, or nostalgia vanished from my mind. But then he pushed me away.

"What happened?" he asked.

Why did he have to ask that? Why couldn't he just kiss me and let me enjoy his undoubted abilities? Since when had Nick cared why someone wanted to hook up with him?

Now I found myself thinking about Dan again. That wound of being betrayed by someone I had loved so much—and I had loved them both, him and Beth—reopened again. That, and the wound of knowing I'd lost them both forever because I would never be able to forgive them because they didn't deserve it. And the worst thing was the fear—the fear that I wasn't strong enough to keep away from him.

I rested my head on Nick's bare shoulder, and he held me. This was the first time we'd ever shared a moment like this. His smell was entrancing—it must have been one of those fancy colognes models advertised on TV—and his chest was warm and comforting, and even though I felt frozen, somewhere deep inside me, a small fire had started to burn.

"It's not like I don't love holding you, Freckles, but if you don't tell me what happened, I might draw the wrong conclusions, and I'll wind up pounding the shit out of the wrong guy."

Despite my mood, those words got a smile out of me.

I started to pull away, but he walked me backward and sat down at his desk with me in his lap.

"Please God tell me you didn't fuck my other car up, too, and now you've come to me because you feel bad about it because I swear, all the kisses in the world won't help that..."

I didn't know this side of the normally cold and standoffish Nicholas Leister—the side that cracked jokes, that tried to get people to laugh—and I admitted that I liked it. A lot.

So I decided to tell him why I'd come to his room. Because, believe it or not, I hadn't planned to hook up with him or anything like that.

"Dan's here," I said. He took a second to absorb what I'd said. Then his body tensed.

"That motherfucker who cheated on you is here? Where, in Los Angeles?"

"Uh...he's here. In this house." I knew as I said it how pathetic and ridiculous the situation was. Nick seemed to be waiting for the punch line. I tried to explain.

"My mother invited him. She doesn't know anything about what he did, has no idea we've broken up...but he's here, Nicholas, and I feel like I'm completely losing it..."

I got up and started pacing around the room. I had no idea why I was telling my stepbrother this, but Nick was good at getting you to think about other things.

He took a cigarette from his desk and put it in his mouth. I didn't know if he was angry or disappointed.

"Why are you telling me this?" he said, taking a curt drag. That old coldness in his eyes was back, the one I'd seen many times before, the same one that made us hate and insult each other.

Trying to put aside my feelings for him, things that I myself didn't understand, and I told him what I really needed.

"As soon as he sees you, Dan will know who you are," I said, trying to hide behind that armor I always used to defend myself, even if it seemed to have disappeared since Dan arrived. "He'll recognize you from the photo of us, from when we...kissed."

Who'd have thought a simple photo would bring me so many headaches? If I'd known that kissing Nick would mean that the desire to do it again would invade my body and mind, I would have avoided it from the beginning.

Nicholas laid his cigarette in an ashtray and looked at me with contempt.

"What do you want, Noah?"

"I just want him to be gone and to never have to see him again." It was true; that was what I wanted, no matter how much it hurt. I didn't want to be around someone who had deceived me.

That seemed to relax Nicholas, and I continued:

"But I don't know how to make it happen." I wiped my forehead with my hand. "He came here for the sole purpose of getting me to forgive him...and there's a part of me that wants to, but I know I can't, I shouldn't..."

"So this is where I come in?" he asked.

I nodded.

"It's just a couple of days. If he sees that I've moved on, that I'm not interested in him, maybe he'll leave me alone."

He nodded, picking his cigarette back up. I didn't like people smoking, but when Nicholas did it, it was sexy.

"So we've got to make out in front of him," Nicholas concluded.

I was ashamed of what I was asking for, but he had already offered to do the same thing, basically, when he took that photo of us kissing. What made it strange was that we'd now hooked up a couple of times recently for very different reasons.

"You want him to think we're together." He got up out of his chair. "Wouldn't it be easier if I just broke his face and got it over with?" There was anger in his eyes, and something else, something dark, that I couldn't quite place.

"My mother can't know," I murmured. I felt trapped by the hand he'd suddenly reached out to grab my chin. One of his fingers softly stroked my lower lip.

"You owe me big-time," he said, and even though his voice was sour, he kissed me. His kiss was powerful, not sweet, and I couldn't help comparing him with Dan. My ex-boyfriend was delicate and caring—even if deep down, he was a jerk—whereas Nicholas was cold and dominating. I never knew what he was thinking. His hands weren't even touching me then. Just his lips.

"I hope you're not stupid enough to let that asshole put his hands on you."

He turned around, grabbed a T-shirt and the car keys on his desk, and left me there, trying to figure out if I would pull myself together.

20

Nick

I WAS PISSED. NOT JUST PISSED. SOMETHING ELSE. SOMETHING I'D never felt in my life. I didn't even understand how I'd let Noah tell me what I should do. The only thing was, now I could be with her as I liked. Every cell in my body lit up, but that wasn't reason enough for me to accept that ridiculous idea she had for getting rid of her boyfriend. I'd gotten over all that high school bullshit a long time ago, and to be honest, there was a faster, better way to deal with it: breaking his legs and kicking him out of my house, for example. Noah would get what she wanted, and I'd be able to blow off some steam.

I got in my car, slammed the door, and didn't stop to think how I was leaving Noah at home with that jerk. After seeing him, I doubted anything would happen between them. But at the mere thought of them together, I had to stomp the gas and get far away from something that could easily turn into a prison, a torture for me.

Since we'd first hooked up, everything had changed. Our irritation with each other was now an unquenchable longing, and it put me in an awkward situation. I didn't know what I wanted, but I was sure being in an actual relationship with Noah was no good for a guy like me. Noah seemed like the girlfriend type, and I'd never had a monogamous relationship. I liked variety, and I ran away from commitment with all my might. No woman deserved more attention than I felt like giving, and I'd never let anyone control me or my decisions. I did what I wanted with whomever I wanted. Noah Morgan attracted me more than any other girl—that much I had to admit—I wanted her so bad, it hurt even to be away. I had so many fantasies about her that when she was nearby, my mind got away from me, and my body moved on its own. Everything was different with Noah. That's why I had to be careful.

I parked outside Anna's house, grabbed my phone, and called her.

"I'm outside," I said when I heard her on the line. Two minutes later, she came out of her house and walked toward my car with a very alluring smile.

I lowered the window when I saw she didn't open the door to get in.

"My parents are away. Want to come inside?" she asked with a hot, sexy smile.

I didn't hesitate, and she came around to my side of the car when I got out. Before I could even speak, she was all over me. She had on the same lipstick as always; it had an odd flavor, but it had never bothered me until today. I pushed her away, and we walked inside.

"It's been a while," she said.

"I've been busy," I replied brusquely. I wasn't thinking about her—I was thinking about how Noah was sleeping just down the hall from her ex.

I walked to the living room. For some reason, I didn't feel like going to her bedroom.

"I miss you, Nick," Anna said, sitting down next to me.

Her cheeks were pink, her lips gleaming. She looked good, and I edged over, putting a hand on her bare knee and stroking it the way she liked.

"You shouldn't miss me, Anna," I said. "We're not anything."

Her eyes looked tense, but she didn't let me throw her off. We both knew the score. Anna did get special treatment, that was true, but she knew we'd never be anything more than we were. I'd never belong to a woman. I'd never let a woman hurt me again.

She kissed me, and I kissed her back, more from habit than desire. That irked me. Anna was hot; I'd always had chemistry with her, more than with any other girl, but now, there was nothing—and that got to me.

I grabbed the back of her neck and pulled her face closer to mine. She went along with it—she knew what I liked and how I wanted her to behave. She grabbed onto my T-shirt, we felt each other's warmth, but...it didn't matter. It wasn't what I was looking for.

I gave up. She looked at me full of fire, ready for more.

"Why don't we go up to my bedroom?" she asked. I grabbed her hands, pushed them away, and stared at the TV.

"I don't feel like it," I said.

She picked up her purse off the table.

"Want some of this?" she said, pulling out a joint.

I pulled out a lighter as she brought it to her lips.

"This will put you in a better mood," she said, passing it over.

That night, I let my problems disappear.

I got home at three in the morning. I was sore, almost as if I'd gotten a beating. When I passed by Noah's room and saw her light on, I felt furious. She must be awake; she probably had company. I opened the door, ready to knock out that dickhead who'd invaded my home.

I stopped short when I saw Noah relaxed and asleep, curled up under a thin sheet, her blond curls spread over the pillow, her eyes closed, at peace. The lamp on the nightstand cast a faint light over everything...and there was no trace of Dan.

I tried to calm the waves of anger that had crashed over me as I'd imagined Noah lying in bed with her ex-boyfriend, doing anything but sleeping. I remembered that she was scared of the dark, and that awakened something tender inside me.

Her breathing was soft and regular. I'd never just watched a girl sleep. It was fascinating. I walked over close, wanting to confirm a theory. The closer I came, the harder my heart started beating. I felt relieved...strange but relieved. My hand twitched, I wanted to touch those lips so badly; they were succulent, the color of cherries. Every inch of me wanted to touch every inch of her, and I knew then that everything had changed. It didn't matter if I hooked up with Anna or anyone else. Nothing would be as intense as the feelings I had for that girl now sleeping in my home.

21

Noah

I GOT UP LATER THAN NORMAL THAT MORNING. I DIDN'T KNOW IF it was all the contradictory thoughts I'd gone to bed with or the knowledge that I had a hard day ahead of me, but when I saw the clouds in the sky, I knew I'd made a mistake asking for a favor from Nicholas and that nothing good would come of my ex staying at my home. I put on a swimsuit and a sundress, telling myself I'd just have to hang on till seven, when I could go to my new job and avoid whatever problems Dan had in store for me.

I'd thought it over a long time before falling asleep, and the only feelings I still had for the guy who'd been everything for me were rage and resentment. I was angry. I didn't want to see him. I felt stupid for ever letting him kiss me. Maybe that was just because he wasn't in front of me to stir up old memories. But I hoped it stayed that way that morning. I didn't even want to see his face.

When I went to the kitchen and saw Dan sitting at the table with a cup of coffee staring at his phone, I couldn't keep myself from scowling at him. I walked straight past him to the fridge and got out the orange juice.

"I was waiting for you to come down," he said, standing up

and leaning on the counter. I ignored him as I sliced the bread and put it in the toaster. "Your parents are gone."

"My mother's gone," I corrected him. "William is not my parent."

Dan sighed, and finally I looked over at him. His hair was well combed, and he'd put on jeans and a T-shirt with a stupid phrase on it.

"You don't want to talk to me?" he asked. "I want you back, Noah. I didn't come here from another country just for a vacation. I came here to get you to forgive me."

"I can't forgive you, Dan. You cheated on me, and not just once. I've got photos, I don't know who sent them, but I'd assume it's one of your little girlfriends. They never liked you and me going out, and I guess they don't like you going out with my best friend, either."

Before Dan could respond, Nick came in with no shirt on, wearing pajama pants that hung low on his hips. His hair was scruffy, his feet bare...and he made my heart start pounding. Dan looked over at the young man who had immediately entranced me.

Nick stopped in the doorway and analyzed the situation. I bit my lip. What would he do now?

"Hi, we haven't been introduced," Nick said, stretching out his hand. Dan reacted a second late. I could see the veins in my stepbrother's arm tense as he squeezed Dan's hand. Dan visibly tried as hard as possible to pretend it didn't hurt while I stood there fidgeting. "I'm Nicholas."

"Dan," my ex said.

The next thing that happened must have shaken him to the core: Nick walked over and bent down to kiss me lovingly on the lips.

"Morning, Precious," he said, eyes glimmering in a way I couldn't quite decipher. Then he poured himself a coffee and walked out into the yard.

Wow, Nick. Thanks for putting me on the spot.

"What's this all about, Noah?" Dan asked, seething.

I shrugged, trying to ignore him.

"It means that I've moved on," I said, sitting down and taking a sip of my juice.

"You didn't even need two weeks to find that meathead to replace me?"

"You didn't even need twenty-four hours."

Dan walked over and grabbed the back of my chair.

"I know what you're doing. I get it. You're trying to give me a taste of my own medicine. But that doesn't change anything, Noah. You and I have a relationship."

"*Had*. We *had* a relationship," I said, getting up and raising my voice.

"What else do I have to do for you to forgive me?"

I laughed. "What else? What the hell have you done? Let my mom buy you a plane ticket? My God, you're pathetic."

I walked out the door into the yard. Nick was lying on a deck chair. I sat down beside him. He took off his sunglasses and looked at me impassively.

"Can I break his face now?" he asked.

"I don't think we've fooled anyone," I replied.

"I called you *Precious*. For me, Freckles, that's tantamount to asking for your hand in marriage." He slid a lock of hair back behind my ear. "Your ex is looking out the window, by the way."

"What should I do then?"

"Just do whatever I tell you," he said, bending over to whisper in my ear. "Like now—touch me."

What?

"Come on, do it."

I reached up and did as he asked. His skin was warm, almost feverish beneath my cold hands. He tensed up as my fingers followed the lines of his abs, and he buried his face in my neck, nibbling softly.

"Now you lean in and do exactly what I'm doing now." My hand had already reached the soft hair around his belly button, but he had grabbed me, stopping me from going farther.

"You mean I should kiss your neck?"

"That's right, Freckles."

I put my hand on the nape of his neck and planted my lips in the hollow between his shoulder and collarbone. He reached under my shirt and stroked my back. I bit his ear, tugging softly at the lobe. I was enjoying this too much for it to just be playacting.

The next thing I knew, Nick was pulling on my ponytail, and when my head jerked back, he pressed his lips into mine. I arched my back until our bellies touched, desperate for contact, and when his tongue pushed into my mouth, I thought I would melt on the spot.

He held my head firmly, immobilizing me while his tongue moved tirelessly in circles around mine. I needed to touch him again—not because he'd ordered me to, not to make Dan jealous; I just needed it, the same way I needed oxygen to breathe. I felt Nick's arms, his hard pecs, and when he pulled me on top of him in the deck chair, his erection pressed into my stomach.

Nick opened his eyes. His pupils were dilated. A savagery filled his blue eyes that seemed to hint at danger.

"Is he still watching?" I asked with labored breathing.

Nick smiled.

"Who said he was watching?"

I looked over at the kitchen window. There was no one there.

"You said he was looking out the window!"

"Did I?" he replied in a mock-naive tone.

I stood up, pissed.

"That's enough!" I shouted.

"Not for me it isn't, Precious."

"You can stop faking, Nicholas. No one's here to see us."

"Who said I was faking?"

That surprised me, threw me off-kilter.

Fuck. What was I getting into?

I didn't know what to do. The house was big, but I couldn't just forget Dan and Nicholas were there. I needed to escape, kill time until work started, so I put on a pair of shorts, a tank top, and my Nikes and walked out in the hall, ready for a run on the beach.

Just then, the guest bedroom door opened, and Dan came to join me. I ignored him, heading for the stairs.

"Dammit, Noah, just wait," he said as he reached me on the landing.

"What do you want, Dan?" I asked, exasperated.

"If you're not even going to talk to me, I don't know what the hell I'm doing here."

"Maybe you should have thought of that before you showed up here and put me in this awkward position," I said, turning around and walking the rest of the way downstairs. He followed me, obviously.

"So what should I do then?"

"Honestly? You should leave."

"I guess I thought after nine months together, we could at least try to fix things," he said.

Was he really trying to pretend I'd hurt him? *Him?*

"I'm not that kind of girl, Dan. And I don't want to be."

"What kind of girl?"

"The kind of girl who lets her boyfriend cheat on her and then just because he says 'I'm sorry' a couple of times decides to act like nothing ever happened. I thought you knew me well enough to realize that, but I guess I was wrong."

"What the hell did you think would happen?" he screamed. "That things would just go on like before? You fucking left!"

My lip started trembling. I knew I'd left. I didn't need him to shout and remind me of it.

"Right, I left. So the question is, what the hell are you doing here?"

"I didn't want things to turn out this way. You hooking up with the first dude who came along just to hurt me. But I see you've done that. I can take the hint."

I laughed scornfully.

"Is it really so hard for you to believe that I'm actually with Nick because I want to be with him?"

Dan's expression was condescending.

"Come on, Noah. I'm not an idiot. That whole act you're putting on, the kiss in the kitchen—you don't think I know what you're up to?"

I felt myself blushing, and that only made me angrier.

"You want to know what I'm up to?" I said, stepping toward him. "All the stuff you and I never did—that's what I'm up to with him."

I knew I was on shaky ground. Dan was very jealous, and I was sure the only reason he'd come here was to make sure I was still eating out of his hand. He couldn't stand the thought that I'd turned the page that quickly; it was a blow to his fragile masculine ego.

By his expression, I could tell I'd hit him where it hurt.

He must have wanted to strike back, but before he could, Nick appeared in the entryway, walked over, and stood between us.

"How about you fuck off?" he asked Dan icily.

"You sleeping with my girlfriend?" Dan asked, squaring off. His muscles were tense, and the vein in his neck twitched.

"Whatever I do with Noah is none of your business."

Dan seemed to be thinking over what to do next. I understood his hesitation. Nick was scary, especially when he talked calmly and coolly, as he was doing just then. Plus he was older, bigger, stronger. I even felt a little bad for Dan...but not much.

"Dan, you should go," I said, walking around to Nick's side.

There was nothing else to talk about. The situation was ridiculous and uncomfortable for both of us. Not just because I was pretending Nicholas and I had something that we didn't but also because Dan and I had passed the point of no return. He'd told me that himself when he'd admitted he'd cheated on me after I left. So what more was there to say?

"I'm sorry for all this, Noah," he said, ignoring my stepbrother's presence.

I bit my lip. I never thought things could end up like this between us.

"I guess we're just a perfect example of how long-distance relationships don't work."

Dan nodded and walked up the stairs, to get his things, I assumed.

"I'll make sure he gets on the plane," Nick said. I had forgotten he was there, observing me. I tried to pull myself together. I didn't want him to see me this way, feeling sorry for someone who didn't deserve it.

"I've got to run," I said.

I needed that just then—to get away from him, from Dan, from that house, from everything.

As I turned around, he grabbed my arm.

"You okay?" he asked.

Was Nick actually worried about me?

"I will be," I said, walking off.

I spent the next hour and a half walking on the beach, thinking—or, rather, trying not to think. I couldn't deny how much it hurt that I'd probably never see Dan or Beth again or anyone else from my old life. I had no reason to go back to my old city, and that shattered me inside. My boyfriend, my friends, they would have been a reason to, but now...

I ran and ran until my body forced me to throw myself on the sand, exhausted. I looked at the clouded-over sky and asked myself how everything could change so fast. One minute you were one person, the next minute you were a different one.

Without even meaning to, I thought back to the kiss Nick and I had shared that morning. I could almost feel his lips against mine still. It had been so intense. I was scared of what I was getting into, and I had to be careful: I didn't want to fall into anyone's trap, and especially not into Nicholas Leister's.

I had to protect my heart, and the best way to do that was to stay away from anything that made me feel so much when he'd given me so little.

I couldn't give that power to Nicholas. If I did, he'd be the one person who could destroy me.

On my way home, I got in the water to cool down. My body was burning from the exercise. As I walked along the shore drying off, I ran into Mario, the bartender from Nick's gang who had taken me to the races.

"Hey, Nick's little sister," he said with a perfect smile, pulling on a leash until his dog, a beautiful German shepherd, walked up by his side.

"Hey!" I said, actually happy to see him, and bent over to scratch his dog behind the ears.

"You over the Leister family yet?" he asked. He had a contagious smile and very white teeth.

"More like over everything in general, but I'm still trying to get used to it all." I tried to hold something back. I didn't want to weigh the poor guy down with my problems.

We started walking together.

"If you ever want me to show you the town, just say the word. There are places I think you'd love."

I was thankful for the offer but a little worried Mario might have had other plans for me. I liked him, sure, but I wasn't trying to get wrapped up in anything. I had enough problems with guys as things were.

"I mean, I haven't had much time to see the sights, and I don't know that I will now that I need to start my job."

"You got a job! Cool! Where?"

"At Bar 48, by the boardwalk. Today's my first day."

Mario seemed to be searching for something in the back of his mind, but then he said, "Yeah, I know people there. It's a nice spot." But he seemed not to be telling me something.

Just then, we reached the cliffside and the stone steps that led straight up to my yard.

"Come see me when you want. I can't buy you a drink, but I don't think they'll mind if I throw a free Coke your way," I said.

He laughed.

"I'll be there. And remember—if you feel like hanging out, my offer still stands."

I nodded, but without committing myself to anything, and waved goodbye.

When I climbed the stairs to my room, I couldn't help but peek into the guest room. There wasn't a trace of Dan or of his things.

Was I an idiot for feeling sad at the absence of a person who'd hurt me so badly? Whatever. I didn't want to think about it anymore, so I went to my room, showered, and dressed for work.

When I got to Bar 48, I parked in the lot out front and walked inside. It was a nice place; there were pictures of rock singers on the wall and a stage in the corner where they sometimes had live music. All around were tables with black chairs and a huge bar with all the bottles behind it. When I walked in, the manager, a round woman, told me what my duties would be.

"We all change here. I'll give you a T-shirt in a sec," she said, showing me a door in the back that led to dry storage, which doubled as a changing room. "You punch in when you get here and punch out when you leave. If anyone orders alcohol, just ask me or one of your coworkers."

I nodded eagerly. The job was very similar to the one I'd had before in Canada. I introduced myself to the other three waitresses working my shift, which ran from seven to ten at night. It wasn't many hours, but with my tips, it would be enough to get by.

The time passed quickly, and I was glad to have something to distract me for a few hours. I got to work right away, taking orders and waiting on customers. Before I realized it, it was ten to ten. That was when Mario walked through the door.

I smiled, surprised he'd decided to show up.

"You look good," he said, referring to my uniform: a black shirt with the bar's logo and a white apron tied around my waist.

"Thanks. You want something?" I asked.

"I'll take a Coke."

"Something funny?" I asked when I opened the bottle and poured it into a glass for him. His smile was almost awkwardly wide.

"I'm just asking myself why you're waiting tables when we both know perfectly well you don't need to."

"I don't like other people paying for my shit. I'd rather do it myself," I said, glancing around to see if anyone needed me. But we weren't busy, and I could stand there for a while and talk.

I liked this Mario.

"When do you finish?" he asked after a few minutes' joking around.

I looked at the clock.

"Now," I said, picking up his glass and setting it on the bar.

"How about I invite you to the movies?"

All I really wanted to do was go home and get into bed. But Mario was handsome and nice, and it would be fun to go out with someone who wouldn't be a pain. Not my ex, not my stepbrother...

"Today's not a great day for it, but I could do the weekend if you're into it?"

Getting down from his stool, he replied, "I'm going to hold you to it."

We walked out together. I was holding my keys; he had his motorcycle helmet in his hand. I looked up to see the last person I ever expected to find leaning on the hood of my car: Nick.

I stopped and noticed how his eyes went from me to the guy next to me. His whole body seemed to stiffen, and in his eyes I could see a growing rage that I knew he had no problem unleashing. But he forced a smile and walked over. Before I could say anything, he wrapped an arm over my shoulders and pulled me in, so tight I couldn't move.

"Hey, Precious," he said. I couldn't help but roll my eyes.

"Nick," Mario greeted him, but without looking over.

I tried to say this wasn't what it looked like, not by a long shot, but Nick pulled me off toward his car, waving a curt goodbye to Mario.

"Sorry, big guy, but d *my girl* and I have plans."

"What the hell are you doing?" I asked, wriggling away only to find that Mario was already walking off. "Are you crazy?"

"Crazy about you, Precious," he said, lighting a cigarette as if nothing were out of the ordinary.

"You can drop the *Precious*. It doesn't suit you," I said, crossing my arms.

"It doesn't, right?" He laughed. "*Babe,* that's more my style, I think."

"Why'd you do that?"

"Didn't you want that? For me to pretend to be your boyfriend?"

"I meant in front of Dan, Nicholas."

"Ah!" He clicked his tongue. "Help me out, Freckles, you're confusing me."

"Now he's gonna think there's something going on that isn't," I said, unable to ignore the electricity that crackled every time we were together.

"By which you mean…"

"By which I mean us being together."

"What do you care what that idiot thinks?"

His voice turned gravelly, harsh. We both noticed.

"I don't want anyone to think you and I are hooking up. With Dan, it was necessary. But now that he's gone…"

"He's not gone yet," Nick replied, throwing his cigarette to the ground. "I bought him a plane ticket, but he doesn't leave for thirteen more hours. It's going to be the longest trip in history!"

I felt bad for Dan. Thirteen hours in the airport and another five in the air…

"You think I shouldn't have done that? I can go pick him up if you want. We can all go get dinner together."

I had to admit, I liked his sarcasm.

"Thanks for helping get him off my back," I said, still struggling to believe Nicholas had gone out of his way on my behalf. "You didn't have to."

"I'm keeping track," he responded. "At this rate, you'll be my indentured servant before my twenty-second birthday."

I didn't exactly like what he'd just said, but it did remind me of what it felt like to have his lips against mine, and I thought, *You can make me pay you back for as many favors as you like.*

Damn his attractiveness…

"So you're saying you can't just do something from the goodness of your heart?" I was getting nervous. He was so close to me, I had to lean back to look him in the eyes.

"I don't do anything out of the goodness of my heart, love."

That last word almost made my heart stop, but it was even worse when he bent over, grabbed my neck, and kissed me hard. I couldn't speak, couldn't think, couldn't do anything...

I saw myself reach up and pull him in. There I was again, trapped between him and the car. He reached for my waist with his other hand, and his muscles felt so hard against the softness of my body. Our breathing grew labored. I wanted more, needed more. Nick awakened sensations in me that had been asleep my whole life.

His knee pressed between my legs, and an exquisite heat suffused my body.

Just when I thought I'd been teleported to another world, Nick's phone rang, waking us from the trance that simple kiss had become.

He stood back a bit and brought it up to his ear. Looking away, I realized how easily he could seduce me with just a single touch—and right there in public, in the middle of a parking lot!

"I'll be there in a minute," he said in a tone of voice as distinct as possible from the one he'd used with me just before.

He hung up and told me, "I've got to go. I've got something to do."

I nodded.

"I'll see you at home," he added.

What had happened to make him seem so distant?

"See you, Nicholas," I said, climbing into my car.

What I couldn't understand, after all that had happened that day, was that his attitude was the only thing that had pissed me off.

22

Nick

My intention hadn't been to hook up with her in the bar parking lot. Quite the opposite: the conversation in my car with that dumbass Dan on the way to the airport had affected me more deeply than I cared to admit. It kept replaying in my mind.

"You've got no idea what you're getting into," he'd said after an intense silence in which I couldn't stop thinking about pulverizing him. "Noah's hot for sure, but she's more fucked-up than you and me put together."

I watched my breathing, tried to stay calm and not enter into his game, but I wanted to know what he was getting at. I wasn't trying to be in a relationship with Noah, but there was no denying my attraction to her.

I gripped the wheel without responding.

"I'm telling you from experience. That chick's got a lot more hidden secrets than you'd think at first glance, and—"

"That's why you decided to come out here, right?" I said, turning onto a side street.

"I guess it's hard to resist a girl who keeps so much to herself. There's always another layer you're trying to peel back."

I tried to guess at what he meant by that: *a girl who keeps so much to herself*... I hadn't met many of those.

"I'm not trying to ruin things for you, but I don't think you're the type of guy who's willing to wait. I don't know if I'm explaining myself."

"I can be patient," I said, staring at the line of cars in front of me, "but I can be impatient, too. Like right now, I'm impatient to pop you in the nose."

Dan smiled, and it took everything I had not to turn around and give it to him then and there. That dickhead was talking about his ex-girlfriend with no kind of respect whatsoever.

I get it, I was no knight in shining armor, but at least I didn't try to pretend. I was straight-up about who I was. This dude was a liar and a cheat.

"I'm just warning you, bro. When you let her in, it's hard to let her go. Just like you said, I'm here, right? If you don't watch out, you'll find yourself eating out of her hand, and you won't know how or why you got there."

I stopped at the gate at the airport.

"Disappear," I ordered him with a clenched jaw.

Dan grabbed his bag and got out, but not without a few last words:

"I wanted to fix it. Beth is nothing compared to her."

And then he turned around and walked off.

———

I'd spent the rest of the day on the beach. I couldn't stop thinking about what Dan had said, and despite his warning, all I wanted was to see Noah and be sure she was okay. I had no idea how to deal with my feelings for her.

I grabbed my surfboard and paddled out into the ocean. I didn't know what else to do. Having her in my home was torture. I lusted after her like crazy, and whenever I saw her, my imagination went wild. If my father knew what was happening, he'd kill me. I couldn't forget, Noah was five years younger than me.

Even so, I went to find her at the bar she'd been stubborn enough to get a job at. I couldn't understand why the hell she'd do that, especially as a waitress. Bar 48 was a place a lot of bands played. My friends and I went there pretty often. The drinks were cheap, and all kinds of people went there. I wasn't at all pleased to have Noah working there, and it was even worse when I saw her come out with Mario.

He and I shared a past—one I didn't want Noah ever to know about. The things I'd done when I'd left home, the way I'd acted after my mother had run off... Mario had been there through every stage of it and knew about all I'd had to get through to end up where I was now. I didn't want those secrets coming to light— certainly not with someone I shared my house with.

Noah's hair was down. She looked tired. She was clearly stressed out by my presence. She was brusque with me, and her answers made me want to dig at her further. That push and pull between us amused me. I was having fun seeing her grow irate.

I should have stayed away, but I couldn't. My legs kept pushing me toward her until there was practically no space between us. Either I kissed her or I went crazy—there was no other alternative. I wasn't even conscious of what we were talking about. Something about doing favors or making her my servant... I don't know.

Just the thought of having her at my mercy turned me on unbearably. I needed it, even if I knew it was wrong. I needed her the way I needed oxygen to breathe.

I buried my hands in her long hair and pulled her close. I was on the verge of desperation. Noah's hands wrapped around my neck, and our bodies collided. I tasted the sweet flavor of her mouth, savored her with my tongue, and I thought I would die.

There was nothing like kissing those lips. I wanted to feel her shiver in my arms, make her feel things nobody, and certainly not her asshole ex-boyfriend, had ever made her feel before. That was my number one priority: her pleasure. I came closer, pushed her into the car door, pressed my knee between her legs.

The sigh that came from deep inside her made me quiver all over until my phone rang and we couldn't continue what we'd started there in the middle of the parking lot.

I took one more look at her and knew I was lost.

If you don't watch out, you'll find yourself eating out of her hand, and you won't know how or why you got there.

I tried to turn away from her pink cheeks and her swollen lips and concentrate on whatever I was hearing. I needed to go, needed to put distance between us. I couldn't let Noah take over my thoughts, my life.

"I've got to go. I've got something to do," I said, hoping she wouldn't notice my consternation. "I'll see you at home."

Noah pursed her lips and got into her car.

I had an unpleasant feeling as I watched her go.

Was it already too late?

23

Noah

A WHOLE WEEK HAD PASSED SINCE THE LAST TIME I TALKED WITH Nicholas. A whole week of work, a whole week without a single message from Dan. For that, I was grateful. After what had happened in the parking lot, Nick was avoiding me. It was almost insulting. When I got up, he was already gone, and when I came home from work around ten, Mom would tell me he'd left just a little while before. It was like all of a sudden he didn't want to see me anymore, and the worst part was the distance hurt me in a way I could never have imagined. My body was demanding I kiss him again, crawl into his arms, and I was tormenting myself wondering what I could have done wrong, why he was being so cold to me after we had shared such moments of arousal.

I knew he was spending time at home because Mom saw him almost every day, but he only came home when I was gone or late at night after doing God knows what. And so one Saturday evening, which my boss told me to take off because they were closing the bar for three days, I thought I would finally catch up with Nick. I didn't know for sure he would be home. For that matter, I wasn't sure I really wanted to have him in front of me.

Escaping from my own mental conflicts, I went to the kitchen.

Mom and I had talked about having dinner that night and watching a couple of movies. When we were in Canada, we had done that almost every night, but since we'd moved, we hardly spent time together. Mom was always accompanying William on his work trips or shopping or organizing endless events or parties for Leister Enterprises. That night, though, she was free: William was going to be at the office late, and she and I had coordinated our schedules so we could see each other.

It was a little after eight, and Mom still wasn't home, so I decided to make a roast with potatoes. I liked cooking. I wasn't a fancy chef, but I could hold my own at the stove. I was cutting the potatoes with one of those knives like they sold on QVC when I heard the front door open. I stiffened. I didn't know it was him, but my heart began to pound as I heard those heavy footsteps getting closer.

When we met eyes, we both froze, him in the doorway, me next to the island where I'd just set down my knife. He looked surprised and then indifferent. I tried to be angry, but too soon I was hypnotized by his outfit, a black suit and a white shirt buttoned low and his intentionally mussed hair framing his handsome eyes.

"I thought you were supposed to be working," he said when we—or at least I—had recovered from the impact of not seeing each other for seven long days. He walked inside and around the island, opening the refrigerator with a distant air.

"They let me off," I said, knocked off guard by the incredible attraction I felt for him. My fingertips were itching with the urge to mess up his hair even more and tear off his carefully ironed shirt.

"Good for you," he said.

"Where've you been?" I asked, slamming the knife down a bit harder than necessary, cutting through the potato and leaving a mark across the wooden cutting board with a dull, almost thudding sound.

"Around," he said from behind me. I couldn't turn. If I did, he'd realize how out of sorts I was. I didn't want Nicholas to know about that unbearable obsession that had overtaken me in recent days. It made me nervous to know he was watching me, leaning on the counter. After an intense, uncomfortable silence, he remarked, "Your back's sunburned."

Knowing he was looking at me that way made me even more nervous.

"I fell asleep by the pool," I said, cutting more potatoes, trying to concentrate on my work.

I felt his breath on my neck and stopped moving the knife as he said, "You should be more careful."

I nearly cut myself, he made me so anxious. But Nick's reflexes were fast enough to catch my hand. I dropped the knife and looked back at him.

"Why have you been avoiding me this past week?"

"I haven't been avoiding you."

I exhaled.

"Okay, we live in the same house and I haven't seen you in a week. I'd say that's avoiding me."

Why did I care, though? Hadn't I had enough trouble with Dan? Why was I going to jump into another relationship when it was evident that nothing good could come out of it?

"I don't have to report to you. I was busy."

I felt the blood boiling in my veins.

"Oh yeah? Well, I hope you stay busy for a long time." I acted like I was about to take off, but he stopped me.

"What are you insinuating?"

I knew my reaction was the exact opposite of the one I should have had. There was no reason for me to care if he was out living his life. Sure, we'd hooked up a few times. Sure, I was attracted to him, and sure, I'd missed him, but that didn't detract from all the bad things Nicholas represented.

"Nothing," I replied. Why was I letting him affect me?

"Noah, you should stay away from me," he warned me.

"Is that what you want?"

"Yeah, it's what I want."

I'd be lying if I said his words didn't hurt. Now everything had been said. I turned away, promising myself I wouldn't get caught in his web.

But I wasn't good at keeping promises.

Work was great to keep me out of the house and away from the emotional burden of trying to ignore Nick twenty-four hours a day. One night, Jenna called me and invited me to a late dinner at a Mexican place, and I was dying for ten to come so I could go home and get ready. I took a quick shower and threw on a pair of shorts and a Dodgers shirt someone had given me a long time ago. I was in LA now—where better to wear it? I tied my hair back in a ponytail and didn't even bother with my makeup.

I was trying not to think of how little time was left until school started or how weird it would be to be surrounded by strangers at a school full of unbearable rich kids. So that night, I was going to have fun.

Someone knocked on my bedroom door right when I finished getting dressed.

"Come in!" I shouted, tying my Converse, assuming it was my mother there to ask how my day had been.

How wrong I was. When it opened, I saw Nick on the threshold. I stared up at him, one shoe still in my hand. He was dressed in jeans, a black T-shirt, and sneakers. His black hair had the same bedhead look as always, and his blue eyes were staring at me coldly.

"What?" I asked, trying as hard as possible not to show him how angry I was.

"I heard you're coming out with me tonight?" he said in a distant tone.

I crossed my arms.

"Far as I know, I'm going out with Jenna, not you."

"Funny. I'm going out with Jenna...and Lion...and Anna." He put a certain emphasis on that last name.

Dammit, Jenna. Why didn't she tell me? I felt an explosion of jealousy.

"The plan was just to go out and have fun, so fine by me," I said, tired of arguing with him, tired of kissing and then getting angry with him. It was exhausting. I needed to find a way for us to get along. "Let's just party and have a good time," I said, forcing a completely unconvincing smile. His words hurt me, and the fact that he didn't want to touch me again hurt even more.

He seemed to be thinking over my offer.

"Are you proposing a truce, little sister?" he asked in an odd tone. I couldn't help knitting my brows hearing those words, *little sister.*

"Exactly," I said, putting on my other shoe.

"Great. We can take the same car then." Before I could protest, he continued, "Jenna told me she can't pick you up, and it's dumb to take two cars if we're going to the same place."

"If that's what's convenient," I said, grabbing my purse and walking out the door.

"I would have preferred *thanks*," he said, catching up with me as I jogged down the stairs.

I looked at his T-shirt, which was tight across his upper arms and back. Why did he have to be so hot? Why?

As we walked past the vestibule, I realized I didn't have any cash. I stopped, not sure what to do.

"What are you doing?" he asked me, annoyed.

In desperation, I made up a lie.

"I think I lost my wallet." I pretended to look through my purse. I hated putting on a show, and if I hadn't known he was loaded, I'd have just stayed at home, but at that second, the idea of doing so seemed dreadful.

"Why are you making me waste my time?" he asked.

"What I mean is, I don't have any money," I said, making sure he understood.

He rolled his eyes.

"You already made me lose two hundred thousand dollars. Buying you a taco now won't make any difference. Come on, go get in the car." He jumped into the driver's side and threw it into gear.

For a brief moment, I felt guilty, but as soon as I remembered what a jerk he was, the sensation vanished.

The restaurant was twenty minutes away. I watched him in silence as he shifted gears and fooled with the radio. I hadn't been alone with him since that day in the kitchen, and the feeling was strange.

The station he chose played the worst rap songs in history, but since he seemed to know all the words, I opted not to complain. I looked out the window at all the huge houses we were leaving behind and was surprised when, instead of pulling onto the freeway, he turned north, toward a development next to ours.

"Where are we going?" I asked.

"I've got to pick Anna up," he said without looking over. I tried as hard as I could to ignore the horrible feeling those words inspired.

He could tell that had affected me. The tension and discomfort were palpable, and my thoughts turned to all that had happened between us.

"Look, as far as the way things have been lately," he said in a calm but cool tone. Great. The very thing I didn't want to talk about.

"I propose we try to get along better, like brother and sister, and forget everything else that's happened."

I turned to him, one eyebrow raised.

"You think you're going to treat me like a sister after feeling me up all those times?"

He clenched his jaw, and his veins danced beneath his skin.

"Like a friend, then, goddammit," he said. "You're impossible. I'm just trying for us to get along better."

"By treating me like a sister," I said, getting more and more pissed off with each minute that passed.

He glared at me, and I glared back. That burning emotion in our eyes when they met was too dangerous to express in words.

"I told you: we're friends," he barked, and the contrast between his tone and what he was saying made me laugh. Thankfully he turned back to the road.

"Fine," I agreed after a few seconds. I guessed pretending to be Nicholas's friend was better than us attacking each other twenty-four hours a day, even if I couldn't trust myself not to lust after him every time I laid eyes on him. I didn't think *friends* was the right word, though. *Relatives obliged to tolerate each other.* I said this to him, and I was happy with the term because *friends* implied too many things. To be friends meant being together through thick and thin. I wasn't even there with Jenna yet, and getting to know her had been wonderful.

An impossible-to-interpret smile crossed Nicholas's lips.

"I'm not so sure about *relatives*… How about *distant pseudo-relatives obliged to tolerate each other and hook up once in a while*?" Oh, so he was making fun of me.

I slapped him playfully, and his smile just got bigger. It was strange how comfortable I felt after that, in the few minutes remaining until our arrival. It had even been fun, in some weird, twisted way.

Nicholas stopped the car in front of a big house—not as big as ours, but big enough to make a person like me gawk and stare. Nick picked up his phone and dialed.

"I'm here. Come on out," he said coldly, especially compared with the past few minutes, when he'd been more relaxed than I'd ever seen him.

"You really are a gentleman. You know that, right?"

"I don't go for that bullshit," he said, putting away his phone and shifting into first as he saw the door crack open. "A girl is perfectly capable of leaving her house without an escort."

Nicholas's date wasn't too tall—I had a good five inches on her—and her expression was so stiff and snobby that I'd put her straight on my list of enemies. I could still remember her comment about my ex, and it made me livid.

It was funny how her eyes got bigger as she saw who was in the car. First her lips pursed, then she scowled, and by the time she got here, she was actually ugly.

She stopped in front of my window, clearly intending to say something. Too bad I didn't feel like rolling it down so I could hear her. Nicholas groaned and touched the button on his side, lowering it against my will.

"What is this?" Anna asked, looking at us incredulously.

"A car," I answered, laughing at her.

I felt a pinch on my thigh, and I was about to slap Nick's hand away, but then I saw he'd appreciated my remark. He was trying to look serious, but his eyes were shining as he held back a giggle.

"Get in, Anna," he said, and rolled my window back up.

She stared daggers into me one more time before opening the back door and getting in. She wasn't used to being back there, and it entertained me to watch her in the rearview acting like a spoiled little girl.

Once we left the development, we finally turned onto the interstate. I was starving, and I wanted to get there as soon as possible.

No one said anything; there was just the noise of the motor and the road, and this time I was the one who turned on the radio. Then I leaned back, crossed my arms, and looked out the window. Anna seemed to have run out of her dumb, supposedly witty remarks, and Nicholas was lost in thought, apparently unconcerned with how hard it was for me to sit in the same car with the bimbo he was having sex with. I didn't know anything about their relationship, but it couldn't have been too serious if he'd hooked up with me all those times.

I was grateful when we reached the restaurant on the outskirts of the city on a road full of bars with noisy people milling around. I saw Jenna and Lion by the door, and when Nicholas parked, I ran off toward them.

Jenna hugged me. Lion's response was cooler, but still, he was friendlier than Nick. I was surprised to see Mario was with him. He'd come to see me and talk at the bar where I worked several times, and I'd gotten used to that smile and those pearly-white teeth.

"If it isn't my favorite waitress!" he said. But his smile vanished when he saw Nick and Anna come over.

They exchanged an unmistakably hostile look.

"What are you doing here?" Nicholas asked gruffly. Why did he always have to act like such an asshole?

"We just ran into him, and I told him he should come eat with us," Jenna said, winking at me. She clearly knew nothing about the tension between them.

Before my stepbrother could start a fight right on the spot— knowing him, it wouldn't have surprised me in the least—I shouted "Great!" and forced a smile.

There was a long line to get into the restaurant. Luckily it was nothing fancy, so I fit right in, unlike Anna in her heels and tiny dress. "Mario, you'll be my date tonight," I said. "I wasn't in the mood to play third wheel anyway." Mario seemed pleased and threw an arm over my shoulders, pulling me in close.

"Excellent!" he said and walked over to the host stand. I turned my back on Nicholas. He looked incensed.

A few minutes later, we were seated at a round table in a side room away from all the racket. I guessed the names Nicholas Leister and Jenna Tavish meant something there.

I sat between Mario and Jenna. Since Lion was next to Jenna and Anna next to Mario, that meant Nicholas was right across from me. After everyone ordered their drinks, we sat there in uncomfortable silence. With Nicholas trying to play the tough guy, it was all I could do not to tell him to fuck off. Thankfully, Jenna finally piped up.

"You know what, Anna?" Jenna grinned at me, clearly aware of Anna's irritation as she glanced all around, trying to figure out what was going on. "Noah's going to go to St. Marie's. You should introduce her to Cassie, since we'll probably all be in the same homeroom." Ever since Jenna found out we'd be going to the same school, it was all she could talk about.

"Who's Cassie?" I asked, trying to keep the conversation going even though Anna clearly wasn't in the mood for it.

She looked up from her cell phone with a glimmer in her dark eyes. I felt intimidated. What was she cooking up in that dumb head of hers?

"She's my little sister," she said, glancing over at Nick. When she caught his eye, he leaned over the table and took her hand.

"Little?" I asked, dubious. "How old are you?"

With a look of superiority, she replied, "Twenty. And in a year, I'll be done with college." So she thought she was better than me.

"I'd have never guessed," I responded, provoking her indignation. Nick shook his head vigorously while Jenna tittered.

"Tell me something, Noah, where'd you learn to drive so well?" Mario asked, changing the subject. I knew that subject would irk Nick, reminding him of how he'd lost his car.

"Nowhere. It was just good luck that I won the race," I said, shrugging my shoulders. Then I dug into the chips and salsa and nervously started chewing. I didn't want to get into it. *Let's say some things are better left dead and buried.*

"Get out! It was amazing!" Jenna said. "It had been forever since anyone beat Ronnie, and you left him in the dust, even Nick…" She realized where she was going and seemed to decide to trail off.

"You actually want us to think you just happened to win?" Anna asked with false friendliness.

Nick leaned both forearms on the table and pinned me with his blue eyes.

"Spit it out. How'd you learn to race like that?"

The question was so direct that only the pure and simple truth would do. But I wasn't willing to give him that. There were things in my past I didn't want to talk about. So I lied.

"My uncle was a NASCAR driver. He taught me all I know."

I saw surprise in his face and a little bit of doubt, but just then, the waitress showed up with our order. I had always liked Mexican food, especially tacos, and I used the distraction to chat up Mario. He was always easy to talk to. At some point, I started cracking up at something he'd said that no one else had heard because everyone was wrapped up in their own conversations.

After calming down, I bent over to take a sip of my soda and looked up at Nick, who seemed furious and uninterested in talking with Anna, Jenna, and Lion.

I couldn't imagine what had happened, but I wasn't going to ask, either. Our truce over these past few days seemed as fragile as a thread, and I knew I could break it if I said or did anything that got under his skin.

"The party at your place was great, Nick. We should try to throw an even bigger one and get everyone over to celebrate the end of summer," Jenna said.

The whole table nodded, but all I could think about was what had happened between Nick and me there. It had been the first time we'd really hooked up.

"Noah, you're red as a tomato," Jenna said.

I wanted to die, especially when I looked up at Nick and saw he seemed to be thinking exactly the same thing as I was.

"It's the salsa," I said, taking a sip of my drink.

Soon afterward, we asked for the check. I'd forgotten I needed to borrow money from Nick, and that made it weird when Mario said he wanted to pay for me. Nicholas interrupted him:

"I've got her."

I could tell Mario was going to argue, so I jumped in. Anna was pissed, too, especially since Nick hadn't said a word about paying for her.

"I lost my wallet," I said, trying to sound indifferent.

"Okay, that settles it. I've got her, Nicholas," Mario said.

"Sure you can afford it?" Nicholas asked maliciously. "I wouldn't want you to blow all your tip money on one meal."

I couldn't believe what he was saying. There was an uncomfortable silence, and Mario tensed like a dog under attack. I knew there was about to be a confrontation, and I had no idea how to avoid it.

Before Mario could respond, I grabbed his hand under the table. He was surprised, but he squeezed back a second later.

"Pay it if you feel like it," he said, standing up and pulling me along with him. He dropped a twenty on the table and turned toward me. The fact that we were holding hands was lost on no one.

"How about I treat you to an ice cream?" he said. I liked how he hadn't let his rage get the better of him. Mario wasn't a violent guy, even if he had the muscles to tangle with Nick. I smiled.

"Hell yeah!"

Jenna gawked at me at first and then smiled knowingly.

We said goodbye—I didn't even bother looking at Nick—and left.

24

Nick

I COULDN'T STOP THINKING OF MY FIST CRASHING INTO THAT fool. The whole dinner, I'd been fantasizing about slamming him into the wall and using him as a punching bag. Mario couldn't be with Noah—that was that. I didn't want anyone to be with her, actually, and I didn't care to think about why. I couldn't take my eyes off her the whole meal. The way she laughed—so different from me—how easy she was to talk to, that way she unconsciously rubbed that part of her neck where she was tattooed, all of that drove me crazy the whole night.

After seeing her leave with Mario, I had gotten up and taken Anna home, and I now found myself on the way to a bar. I couldn't stick around Anna's place; it was unbearable. I'd been spending too much time with her these past few weeks. If I didn't want things getting serious, I'd need to find another girl to hang out with. I headed for a club I'd been to a lot in recent years, in a rough part of town where many less than respectable people hung out. The door guys knew me, so I didn't have to wait in line. Inside, the music was deafening, and the blinking lights gave a strange, even eerie glow to the sweaty bodies dancing there. Who knew what they were all high on.

I walked over to the bar and ordered a whiskey while glancing around at the crowd. Since the year I'd lived with Lion in that neighborhood far from my father, his money, and everything the Leister name represented, I'd found my place among these people. They respected me, they accepted me, and they were the perfect escape route from everything I hated about the life I was now being forced to live. I'd run away as soon as I'd turned eighteen. Since Mom had left, my relationship with Dad had dwindled away to nothing, and I didn't think anyone would care if I just up and disappeared and tried to go it alone. But Dad had wound up sending his security chief, Steve, to find me. It had been ironic, seeing a tall guy in a suit showing up at the house I'd been living in then, and even more so when he'd realized that if he wanted to make me go back, he'd need an army.

Steve had worked for my father since I was a kid, and he knew me well enough to recognize there was no way he could force me to go home against my will. But then the thing with my sister had happened, and I'd needed my father's help.

The day after Steve showed up, all my credit cards had been canceled, and my checking account had been blocked. I'd had to get a job at Lion's dad's garage to make a living. But I had never felt freer or more myself.

Life in that neighborhood had been tough. I'd gotten the shit kicked out of me as soon as I'd shown up there, and I'd realized that I would never make it, being a millionaire's son, unless I turned into one of them. I had started training every day without fail: no one was going to put their hands on me again without knowing I'd hit back. Lion had shown me how to defend myself, how to throw a punch, and how to take one. My first real fight had come two months after I'd started training. I'd left Ronnie laid out on the ground covered in blood, and that had gotten me the respect of all present. The races and the gambling had come a while later, and Ronnie and I had made a truce, but that meant people started choosing sides. There were Lion and our guys and I and then Ronnie and his dealers and delinquents. He knew it worked out better for him to be cordial with us, especially after my father got us out of jail when we'd been charged with disturbing the peace.

Everything had changed when I'd come to need my father's help. I couldn't have ignored the fact that I had a sister and wanted to meet her. Dad had said he'd help with the trial and get me visitation rights if I'd move home, go to college, and stay with him for at least three years. I'd had to agree and go back to Leister mansion, and once there, I had realized my father wasn't indifferent to me. Our relationship had improved, but my life had basically stayed the same. I lived with him now, but I spent most of my time with Lion, getting drunk, getting high, and getting into trouble. As long as I slept at home and went to school, Dad didn't get mixed up in my life, and I stayed out of his business, too...and things had continued that way until now.

Fights and races were an everyday thing for me, and Ronnie's and Lion's gangs were getting into more and more confrontations. Things were worse now than before, but I'd always seen the hidden resentment in Ronnie's eyes. We needed that truce: we lived in the same town, and we ran with the same people. But our friendly rivalry had turned into a feud between two gangs, and it was getting dangerous, as last time had shown. Me smashing his face at the last race had been an affront, and there was going to be backlash, I just didn't know when. Noah beating him was the greatest humiliation imaginable, and I knew I'd end up having to deal with it. The problem was, Ronnie wasn't just a street fighter anymore. This was getting ugly. I knew after he shot at us how dangerous he could be, and I couldn't stop thinking he'd come for Noah at some point in the near future.

Damn her. Why'd she have to do that? Damn her for fucking up everything for me. I needed to stop thinking about her, get back to my life, have fun the way I always did, enjoy myself the way I always had...

A blond stuffed into a skimpy halter top and black-leather pants sidled up to me at the bar.

"Hey, Nick," she said, and when I saw the dragon tattoo on her collarbone, I realized I'd hooked up with her before. Her name started with an S: Sophie, Sunny, Susan, something like that.

I nodded to her. I wasn't in the mood to talk, but I *was* in the mood for other things. She was already close to me; it didn't take much to turn that proximity into a kiss.

I grabbed her waist and pulled her into me. Her breath smelled like vodka and something sweet. She was exactly what I needed to relieve the tension from the past few days. I grabbed her hand and dragged her to one of the VIP tables, where we could escape from the lights.

But when I saw how Susan's hair shone in different colors as she passed under the neon, I thought of Noah. Cursing, I pushed her against the wall harder than I needed to, but she sighed with pleasure, so I felt free to keep going. Her body pressed against mine in all the right places, but her lips were too greedy, that wasn't what I wanted. I leaned in and kissed her on the neck. She smelled like liquor and smoke. I pulled aside her hair and looked at the dragon tattoo...but the tattoo I wanted to kiss was another, and that wasn't the neck that drove me wild as soon as I looked at it.

I grabbed her face. There wasn't a single freckle on it. Her blue eyes weren't honey-colored, her lashes weren't long.

I pulled away.

"What is it?" Susan asked, her hands moving down to my crotch and stroking me. I grabbed her wrist and jerked it away.

"Sorry. Gotta go," I said and turned my back. I didn't even bother listening to her complain. I needed to leave.

I walked around a corner toward an alley, trying to ignore the intimation that I was screwing up. Bad. I was so angry, so self-absorbed, that I didn't even realize who was at the end of the street until familiar voices made me look up. Right away, I was on edge.

Ronnie and three of his drug dealer friends were leaning on a car, a Ferrari…*my* Ferrari. I stopped, clenching my firsts, struggling to restrain a fury that was crying to get out.

"Look who we have here!" Ronnie shouted, stepping away from the hood and toward me. "Daddy's little rich boy." He laughed, and his goons laughed along. I recognized all three of them: two tattooed guys who were high as a kite and Cruz, Ronnie's right-hand man.

"You here to beg for your car back?" Ronnie asked. I'd have happily knocked that smile right off of his face.

"You mean the car you cheated your way into getting?" I asked. "Whatever. Maybe with a real car, you'll actually learn how to drive. I mean, you don't want to lose to a seventeen-year-old girl again, do you?"

It was deeply pleasing to see how the remark affected him. He wasn't smiling now. No, the veins were swelling in his neck.

"You'll regret that," he threatened me, trying to act calm. "Get him!" he shouted.

I had known that was going to happen. I knew it as soon as I saw them, and I was ready. I punched the first guy who came over and grinned when I felt his nose break. Someone grabbed me from behind, and I fired back with an elbow, striking something hard, probably someone's mouth. Cruz came over to help the two others, but before he got there, I'd already hit goon number one again in the face. Now it was my turn to suffer. Someone punched me in the right eye, hard enough to knock me aside, but still, I managed to kick whoever was trying to grab my arms. I held out awhile longer, but three against one was too much even for me, especially with Cruz in the picture. He was every bit as tough as Lion. One-on-one, I might have taken him, but with the other guys restraining me, there wasn't much I could do.

Cruz started pounding me in the ribs, and I tried not to scream as I thought how much I'd like to kill him with my bare hands. Ronnie came over. The look on his face told me this wasn't going to be the end of it.

"Tell your little sister I haven't forgotten what happened on the track," he said. Noah's innocent face appeared in my mind. Ronnie grabbed me by my hair and pulled my face close. He stank like cheap beer and weed. "And tell her when I see her, I'm going to make her pay, and I'm not just talking about cash or a car." I saw red all over. I was trembling with violence. I was going to kill that motherfucker.

"I'm gonna bust her wide open, Nick," he said. If I could have moved, I'd have headbutted him and knocked his nose bone up into his brain. "And when I do, I'm gonna wreck that pussy so bad you won't even want to go near it."

"I'll kill you," I said. Three words, one promise.

He laughed and punched me in the stomach. Every ounce of air in me came out, and I had to bend over to cough and spit up blood.

"Don't come around here no more or I'll be the one to kill you. Don't think I won't," he said, turning around. The guys holding me let go after one final punch in the face.

Those sons of bitches.

I stumbled off to my car. I barely made it home. Everyone was asleep; it was after one in the morning. Strangely, there was no light coming from Noah's room. No way she was still out. I opened the door. Her bed was made.

I cursed, walked into my room, and pulled off my clothes, trying to grit my teeth through the pain. I was in bad shape; it had been a long time—four years to be exact—since I'd received a beating like that. It had been dumb of me to wander down that alley by myself. I'd made it easy for the bastard.

I got into the shower and let the water wash away the blood and sweat. They'd mostly stuck to my stomach and ribs, so I could cover up my bruises with a T-shirt. The black eye and busted lip were a different story. I'd need to come up with a good explanation for Dad or avoid him until the swelling went down. I had some practice. I didn't get hit in the face often, but when we had our fights and money was on the line, sometimes there was nothing I could do about it.

I couldn't stop thinking about how Ronnie had threatened Noah. He must have wanted to strangle her after that public humiliation at the races. The mere thought of that scumbag touching her made me so mad I could hardly keep from punching the mirror in front of me.

I dried off and threw on some sweatpants. I stayed shirtless, since some of my wounds were still bleeding. I rinsed out my mouth and made sure I hadn't cracked any teeth, but I was good. My lip had even stopped bleeding, but it was red and purple, just like my eye. And both would be that way for some time.

I grabbed my phone and walked out into the hallway, thinking I'd try to find out where the hell Noah was and get some ice for my wounds.

Five minutes later, as I was walking out of the kitchen with my phone to my ear, I heard the key turning in the front door, and the main reason for my bad mood appeared.

Her phone was buzzing. It stopped when I hung up. She looked up at me. Her eyes were surprised and then horrified.

"Where the hell have you been?" I asked.

25

Noah

THE LAST THING I EXPECTED WHEN I OPENED THE DOOR WAS TO
see Nick standing there with the shit kicked out of him. I was
surprised, as I walked up the stairs, to see that he was calling me.
When I looked up at him, that feeling changed to terror.

"Where the hell were you?" he shouted. As always, he was
intimidating. The question was unsettling, but his appearance was
truly awful. His left eye was purple, his lip split, but that wasn't
the worst: his torso was covered in bruises still spreading under
that tanned skin, over those shapely abs. Seeing those wounds
paralyzed me. In a panic, I started to feel faint. I hated the sight
of blood, and my ears started ringing. I had to hold on to the
doorframe to stay standing.

"What happened to you?" I asked quietly.

He was angry. I could see it in his every gesture. It was almost
as if his wounds were my fault.

"I asked you a question," he said.

I shook my head and shut the door soundlessly. My mother and
Will were in bed, and I didn't want to wake them. Nick didn't seem
to care, though, to judge by his voice, which was nearly shouting.

"I was with Mario," I said, walking closer to him. I wanted to run away from those horrible wounds, but I couldn't ignore the state he was in. "Lion and Jenna met up with us to have ice cream. What do you care, anyway? Have you seen yourself?" I reached out without realizing it to touch a bruise on his ribs.

He reached out to brush me aside but seemed to change his mind and grasped my hand tightly until it hurt. I looked up and saw the rage and fear in his eyes.

"Come to the kitchen. I need to talk to you." He pulled me away, and I couldn't help looking at his bare back. My God, you could see every single muscle in it as he walked! That awakened in me a desire to touch his firm body. Another bruise was starting to form on his side. I hated whoever had done that to him so much, my vision started clouding.

Nick turned on a table lamp, so the light was dim as we sat down on a bench next to the island. He never let go of my hand. It was killing me to see him like this; his eyes were squinting from the pain, and all I could think about was what I could do to make him feel better.

"Did you notice anything weird while you were out?" he asked, worry clouding his face. "Anyone following you or something like that?"

I hadn't expected the question. Looking him straight in the eye, unable to believe what I was hearing, I said, "No, of course not. Why?"

He let me go and turned aside, frustrated. I wished he had gone on holding me, but I just sat there, still.

"Ronnie hasn't forgotten about the race." Now I could guess what this was all about. "He wants revenge, and if he sees you, he won't hesitate to hurt you."

"Is he the one who beat you up?" I asked, cursing the bastard in my mind.

"Him and his three friends," he admitted.

"My God, Nick!" I said, feeling a strange pressure in my chest. I brought my hands up to his face, feeling his wounds. "Four against one?"

He stiffened and then relaxed. Skirting over his wounds, my fingers traveled down his cheeks, feeling the raspy touch of his stubble, which made him so frightening and sexy at the same time.

"You worried about me, Freckles?" he asked. He was trying to be funny, but I couldn't laugh as I felt his bruises and he grimaced. He reached up and pulled my hands away. "I'm fine," he said.

"You have to go to the police," I said, walking off toward the fridge. I grabbed a bag of frozen peas and returned to him, placing it over his eye.

"With guys like that, you don't go to the cops, but anyway, we've got other problems." He grabbed the bag and pulled it away from his face so he could look directly at me. "Noah, until things calm down, I don't want you going anywhere by yourself, hear me?" His voice sounded like that of a big brother. "These people are dangerous, and they've got their eyes on you. Me, too, but I don't care if I have to take a beating. I can defend myself. You, though… If they find you out on your own, they'll eat you alive."

"Nicholas, they won't do anything to me. They don't want problems just because I wounded some dickhead's ego," I said, ignoring the look of warning in his eyes.

"Until this is over, I'm not going to take my eyes off of you. I don't care how you feel about it."

Were we never going to get along?

"You're unbearable, you know it?" I hissed.

"I've been called worse." He shrugged.

"Put a warm cloth on your bruises and keep something cold on your eye and lip," I said, feeling bad for him. "You'll feel like shit tomorrow, but if you take an aspirin and stay in bed, you'll be fine in two or three days."

His forehead furrowed, but a smile spread across his lips.

"You an expert in helping people recover from beatings?"

I didn't bother responding.

That night I went straight to bed... and I had nightmares.

The next morning, I got up in a bad mood. I hadn't slept well, and the one thing I wanted was to stay there lying around my room. Only one thing made me slide out of the bed and walk toward the bathroom. Whether I admitted it or not, I wanted to know how Nick was. I don't know when or how or why, but I felt suddenly worried about him. Things seemed to be going smoother with us. He hadn't tried anything with me since he'd touched me in the kitchen that time I had almost cut my finger, and a part of me was bitter over it. The only time my life felt good in LA was when I was in his arms. He made me forget everything else. But I knew it was better for us to get along than to be constantly shifting between making out and hating each other to death, which was the way things had been before.

I took a quick shower and thought about the night before. I'd been angry at Nick for how he talked to Mario at dinner, but my fury had disappeared as soon as I'd seen him looking like hell in the vestibule of our home.

Mario had been a gentleman the night before. He'd invited me out again, and I'd said yes. I wanted to forget my ex and my ridiculous obsession with Nicholas.

I got dressed quickly and walked down to the kitchen barefoot to have breakfast. There wasn't a trace of Nick, but Will and my mother were sitting at the table talking loudly about something.

"Good morning," I said, going to the fridge and serving myself a glass of orange juice. Prett, our cook, was making something that smelled wonderful. I walked over and looked down into the pot, where she was stirring bubbling chocolate.

"That looks delicious! What are you making?" I asked.

Prett smiled.

"Mr. Leister's birthday cake," she said cheerfully. I turned to Will.

"Wow, happy birthday, I didn't realize," I said, looking sheepish. He laughed.

"It's not my birthday, it's Nick's," he said, amused. My mother smiled, too.

Wow. Nick's birthday… I didn't know why, but it made me mad that I hadn't known.

"He's outside. Go congratulate him," my mother said. "Yesterday he got in a fight with some thug who tried to rob him, so don't get scared when you see his face."

I nodded, impressed at my stepbrother's skill at lying. I grabbed a pastry from the table and walked out to the yard. He was lying on a deck chair in the shade, wearing sunglasses, a T-shirt, and a swimsuit. He looked asleep. I imagined he hadn't slept any better than I had.

I crept up beside him.

"*Happy birthday!*" I shouted as loudly as I could, laughing as I saw how I'd startled him.

"Goddammit!" he shouted, taking off his glasses to reveal his eye, which was now an iridescent mix of green, purple, and blue.

I couldn't help cracking up. He tried to act tough, but when he saw I couldn't stop laughing, his anger dissolved into a smile.

"You think this is funny?" he asked, putting aside his glasses and standing up. I started walking backward. "I'm sorry!" I shouted, raising my hands, still unable to stifle my giggles.

"Oh, you'll be sorry, all right," he said, and charged after me. I ran, but it was pointless. A second later, I had him behind me, and soon he'd lifted me up over his shoulder. He groaned; he must have been aching all over, but I could barely hear it over my laughter.

"No, Nick, please!" I shouted, shaking all over. He ignored me and jumped straight into the pool, both of us fully dressed.

I struggled away from him as soon as we plunged into the water. It was warm on that late-summer day. When I got to the surface, I splashed water in his face. He was dying laughing. My white dress was clinging to me. I was glad I'd put on black underwear. Otherwise, it could have been really embarrassing.

He shook his hair with a Justin Bieber–like movement and paddled over to me, trapping me in a corner of the pool.

"You can apologize now for nearly giving me a heart attack on my twenty-second birthday," he said, wading over until our bodies were just inches apart.

I tried to push him away, but no luck.

"In your dreams," I said, playing along. Adrenaline was rushing through my veins, and butterflies were flapping in my stomach. The feeling was like racing at two hundred miles an hour over the desert sands.

With a calculating look, he wrapped his hands around my waist.

"What are you doing?" I asked in a muffled voice when he was so close his chest was touching mine.

"Tell me what you feel right now," he said in a hoarse voice. There was nothing funny about his expression now—it was 100 percent desire. I felt a wave of pleasure and fear all at once. What if they saw us?

I shook my head as his hands moved down to my thighs. His fingers pushed aside the wet fabric of the dress and slid between my legs. I opened them and wrapped them around his hips.

"I'm not going to stop until you tell me to," he said, pushing me against the wall of the pool. The water reached up to his shoulders and my neck. I was practically at his mercy. I knew with a word I could get him to let me go—he'd said that, hadn't he? But what was it I really wanted?

"They're going to see us," I mumbled. My cheeks were burning, my body burning; the water did nothing to quench them.

"I'll worry about that," he said, pushing my dress farther up and rolling it under my breasts. He looked down at me. His gaze and his fingers, which were stroking my back now, excited me. I could feel him throbbing against my hips, and all I could think about was our lips joining one more time.

"You want me to stop?" he asked, his mouth millimeters away from mine.

In his eyes, I could see every single shade of blue. I was drunk on him, on the way he looked at me, as if he wished to devour me.

I shook my head and came close so he would kiss me. My hands were already wrapped around his neck. I couldn't even remember how they'd gotten there, and I pulled him toward me, but he resisted, moving in the opposite direction.

"Tell me what you feel and I'll give you what you want," he ordered me.

"What makes you think I want something you can give me?" I asked, burning with desire.

He grinned. "Because you're shaking and you can't stop looking at my lips."

"I'm not going to tell you what I feel," I said.

I heard a grunt come from the back of his throat.

"You're impossible," he said, and then he did press his lips into mine. The euphoria of winning that game soon turned to something more. I felt a million sensations, none of them ones I could speak aloud. His tongue slid into my mouth, and he kissed me ferociously. We were soaked, our bodies joined like two halves of a whole. I tugged at his hair, he bit my lower lip, and I thought I was going to die from pleasure.

I heard the sliding door open, jerked away, tugging my dress down, and grabbed the side of the pool to keep from sinking into the deep end.

"Hey guys, we're going!" my mother shouted. Nicholas waved, looking completely relaxed. I had to take a few deep breaths before looking up. "Did you tell her, Nick?"

"Not yet!" he called back to her, clearly amused.

"Okay. Well, we'll talk later. Have fun!" she said.

I turned to Nick as she walked back inside.

"Tell me what?"

He pulled me back toward him. I didn't struggle: I didn't have the strength to, and I didn't want to miss out on that feast for the eyes.

"They gave me four tickets to the Bahamas for my birthday. They made it pretty clear they want you to come along, you know, to help us develop our relationship as siblings." He grinned maliciously. "I've invited Jenna and Lion, and I want you to come, too."

I could hardly believe it, especially after our previous conversations. Going on vacation with Nick… I could tell he was observing my reaction.

"What happened to us just being friends?" I asked. I wanted to know what had made him change his mind.

"That's still on the table…especially now, when you're in danger and it's my fault."

"That's why you want to take me? To keep me safe from Ronnie?" If that was the real motive, I was disappointed.

He pursed his lips.

"That's *one* reason, but not the primary one, Freckles."

He leaned his forehead into mine.

"Nicholas, what are we doing?"

"Don't flip out, okay?" He grabbed my waist as I started to sink. "I don't want you here when I'm not around. I said that yesterday, and I meant it. You could wind up hurt."

"Nicholas..." That stung, and I tried to turn away from him, but he wouldn't let me.

"Come! We'll have fun," he said, kissing me again on the lips. The sweetness of that gesture made me shudder.

"What about us, though?" I replied. I couldn't help but think what might happen if our parents found out. "I can't do this with you. It's absurd, we don't even get along, we're just letting our physical attraction get the better of us—"

"All I know is when I see you, the only thing I can think about is touching you and kissing you all over," he said, planting his lips just below my earlobe.

"I can't be with anyone right now," I said, pushing him away. He looked mad.

"Who said anything about *being* with anybody? Stop analyzing everything and just enjoy it. This is going to be fun."

I could tell he wasn't being straight with me—he had to want something more—but then again, this was Nick; he used girls and threw him aside. He had to just want me for my body. What else could it be? And if I wanted him for the same reason, why should I forgo the pleasure?

"Fine, but there are conditions," I said. "No tying anyone down, no arguments. I just got out of a relationship, and the last thing I want is to relive what happened with Dan."

"Are you saying you want an open relationship?" he asked. "I think you're the first woman I've ever known who's asked for that, but whatever. Just sex then?"

His eyes were cold. I didn't like that remark one bit.

"Jerkoff!" I insulted him. "What do you mean, just sex? Who

do you think I am? I'm seventeen, not twenty-seven. I'm not going to just up and sleep with you!"

Baffled, he responded, "You just told me you want an open relationship. What the hell do you think that means?"

I was lost. In my world, an open relationship meant you made out sometimes and that was basically what we were doing. But then again, Nick had been around the block multiple times. Compared to him, I was just a girl; I couldn't play in his league. Nicholas wasn't going to be happy with a little bit; he'd want to go all the way. I'd have known that if I'd thought over the past three weeks clearly. In that brief time, I'd gone way further with him than I had with Dan.

"Forget about it," I said, feeling I was playing at a disadvantage. He was fire, and I didn't want to get burned. "I like this new relationship we have. I even feel like we can start to get along. Why would I want to mess that up?"

He looked at me as if he didn't understand a word of what I was saying. I didn't really know what I wanted, either, but casual sex wasn't something I was into.

"Noah...we won't do anything you don't want to do," he said in a tone that made me melt. He seemed to understand every single thing going through my head. It almost scared me how easily he could read my thoughts.

Blushing, I wished the earth would just open and swallow me up.

"I'd rather we just be friends," I said, not especially convinced.

"Are you sure? Just friends?"

I nodded, looking down into the water.

"Fine," he said in what sounded to me like a condescending voice. "But you're coming to celebrate my birthday with me. If you're my friend, then you can act like one."

He swam off and then reached up and lifted himself out of the pool. To me, his words sounded like *You're scared and I know it, so I'll wait till you're ready.*

But if that was so, what was it about me that would make Nick wait?

I spent the rest of the day in my room reading and writing a short story I'd begun working on a long time before. I liked writing as much as I did reading, and one of my dreams was being a great writer in the future. Sometimes I imagined myself being known all over the world, selling millions of copies, and traveling to promote my books and tell stories people would remember forever.

My mother had never done anything with her life because she had gotten pregnant with me when she was sixteen. My father had been only nineteen then, and he hadn't had any education. His one shot had been racing in NASCAR. Mom still remembered how hard it had been to raise me when she was just a girl herself, and she wanted to give me all the things she had wanted when I was her age, a good college. Those had always been her dreams, and she was going to make them come true. To please her, I'd always tried to get good grades, had played on the hockey team, and had written from the time I was a girl. A part of me always wanted to make her proud.

As I got lost in thought, looking out the huge window in my room, someone knocked at my door and came in. My mother was there with a bag with the St. Marie logo. I knew whatever was in there would ruin what was left of my day.

"Your uniform arrived. Try it on, and then go downstairs so Prett can make any adjustments to it you need. Also, we're going to give Nick his cake in a little bit. They don't blow out candles or anything the way you and I do on our birthdays, but I think that's terrible, and I'm going to do whatever I can to change their habits."

"Mom, I don't think Nick's going to be into it," I said, trying to imagine him sitting at a table making wishes.

"Whatever," she said, closing the door behind her.

I got up and took out my uniform. It was as horrible as I'd imagined. The skirt was pleated green plaid with some kind of clip on the side to close it. It hung down below my knees. The shirt was white and baggy, and to my horror, there was even a green-and-red tie that matched the gray, red, and green sweater. The socks were green, too, and reached my knees. When I put them all on and looked in the mirror, I made the nastiest frown in history. I took everything off but the skirt and shirt—the two things Prett could fix—and went downstairs.

On the landing, I found Nick with his phone pressed to his ears. When he saw me, his eyes bulged, and a smile crossed his face. I scowled at him, resting my fists on my waist.

"Sorry, I gotta go. I need to make fun of someone," he said, chuckling and putting his phone in his pocket.

"You think you're funny?" I asked, dying from shame.

"This must be the best birthday present you could have ever given me, Freckles," he said, laughing at my expense.

"Yeah? How about I give you this, too?" I said, flipping him off and moving past him to the living room, where my mother and the maid were waiting on me.

"If you come to dinner with me tonight, I promise I won't send around the photos I just took of you," he said. I turned back, furious. He was taking the jokes too far.

"I'm having dinner with Mario tonight, so no thanks," I replied, knowing it would make him mad.

In the living room, there was a footstool ready for me to stand on so Prett could take my measurements. As I got up on it, Nick flopped down on the sofa, observing me with a cold and pensive look.

"Lift your arms up, Noah," my mother said, helping Prett with the pins. I tried to ignore Nicholas's presence, but it was hard, especially when I remembered that kiss we'd shared in the pool and everything else that had come along with it. I wasn't sure if I'd be able to resist him, but one thing was for sure: I wasn't going to let him just use me. That's why I was going out with Mario that night. I wanted to have fun during what was left of the summer, enjoy the company of different guys, not be tied down by anyone, and forget that asshole Dan.

"Ow!" I said when a pin pricked my thigh. Stupid Nick started laughing on the sofa.

"Be still, okay?" my mother said. There wasn't much left to do. They'd taken in the skirt above my knees, and after their alterations, the shirt would look almost feminine.

Five minutes later, I was ready to take the clothes off and give them to Prett so she could work on them.

Nick stood, about to follow me upstairs, but my mother took us both by the arm and pulled us toward the kitchen.

"Today's your birthday, Nick, so you're going to blow out candles just like Noah and I do and everyone else does," she said with a smile.

I grinned when I saw the unbelieving look on Nick's face. He looked so old next to me, so mature…

"Really, there's no need," he started to object.

William was in the kitchen wearing his glasses and looking at his laptop. He must have been working. He smiled when he saw us come in.

"You look lovely, Noah," he said, looking at my uniform full of pins. I had to be careful not to stick myself when I walked.

"Yeah, right," I said.

My mother pushed Nicholas into a chair and brought over the chocolate cake Prett had made. Nicholas looked so out of place that I couldn't help but be amused, just as he'd been amused at my dilemma minutes before.

On the cake, there were two candles shaped like the number 22. My mother lit them and began to sing, shoving Will to try to get him to participate. The whole thing was so funny that I joined in as Nick glared at all of us with his sky-blue eyes.

"Don't forget to make a wish," I reminded him before he blew the candles out.

As he did so, looking up at me, I had to ask myself: What could a person who had it all wish for?

26

Nick

I STILL WASN'T SURE WHY I'D INVITED HER TO SPEND THE WEEKEND with me in the Bahamas. Her face had just popped into my head when I'd seen the tickets. I didn't even need to listen to my father as he told me I should take Noah along—the same idea had already occurred to me.

Since she'd chilled out and become easier to get along with, I'd found myself thinking about her more and more. I couldn't imagine leaving her alone ever since Ronnie had threatened her, and I freaked out anytime I thought of some other guy getting close to her. Even remembering that she used to be with Dan put me in a bad mood. I wanted to crush him for hurting her. For hurting her and because he'd had nine months to relish her, touch her, kiss her, God forbid, maybe even take off her clothes...

The idea of Noah giving herself to someone besides me tormented me all night and all day. I'd never thought of myself as the jealous type, probably because I'd never considered any girl mine, but now it was killing me. The way she smiled, innocent, almost... She was naturally sexy, which was what I liked about her most. It didn't matter how she dressed, didn't matter if she had on makeup. She could be a wreck, but still, every time my eyes settled on her, I imagined a thousand different ways I could make her moan with pleasure. Maybe what had happened in the pool hadn't been exactly right, but I'd promised myself I'd stay away from her after that. She made it hard, though. I'd wanted to kill her the night before after what had happened with Ronnie—that beating had been her fault—not to mention for going out with Mario, but as soon as I'd seen the look of fear in her eyes as she'd seen my wounds, as soon as her warm fingers had touched my bare skin, I'd had to draw on all my self-control not to jump her right by the kitchen counter.

Worst of all, she was getting more confident. She was less defensive; she wasn't even scared to shout at me while I was asleep. She hadn't pulled away when I'd lost control of my hands and caressed her under the water. Her legs were so long, her curves so damn sexy...

And tonight she was going out again with that moron Mario. He was always quick to feel a girl up, take her to bed if he got the chance. Same as me, but I couldn't let him do that to Noah. She was too innocent, just a kid—a kid who would drive any man with eyes wild.

It especially bothered me that she was leaving on my birthday. I wanted her to myself; I wanted to show her the fun things to do in town. I wanted her view of me to change. I couldn't bear her thinking I didn't deserve to have her.

Someone knocked on the door. I was still getting dressed, so I shouted for them to come in. As I buttoned the shirt I'd be wearing that night, a pair of honey-colored eyes stared at me in the mirror.

"Back from dinner already?" I asked sarcastically, trying not to turn around and trap her, make her stay with me in my bedroom all night.

"You're having a birthday party?" she asked, ignoring my question. I tried to feign indifference.

"What did you think, little sister, that I was going to stick around here watching a movie?"

"You should have told me. Jenna and Lion thought I was invited. They're downstairs waiting." She crossed her arms over her black dress. It was tight and hung just four or five inches from the bottom of her ass. I was furious as I asked myself whether Mario had managed to get his hand under that dress.

"I don't have time for this. You want to come along? Then do it. You're on the list. But your little friend isn't, so figure it out." I walked closer to her. If I couldn't have her, at least I could smell that perfume that turned me on so much.

"You're looking at me like I'm a movie villain, but it's not my fault. I didn't know it was your birthday till a couple of hours ago. Mario had already asked me out. I couldn't just ditch him."

"And you think he didn't know?" I asked, annoyed. I knew Mario had set the whole thing up on purpose.

Surprised, angry, even a little guilty, she looked adorable. She felt bad for nearly missing a party she hadn't even known about.

I couldn't help but wrap an arm around her waist and pull her close. Her eyes were skeptical but expectant.

"Come on, Freckles, come to my birthday party," I said, pushing her hair off her shoulder and kissing her there. I smiled as I saw her goose bumps. At least I could be sure she liked me and I still had some influence over her—or over her body, to be more precise.

"You want me to go?" she asked as my lips climbed her neck.

Did I want her to come? Obviously I wouldn't be able to touch her at that party; no one could know what was happening between us, and we couldn't kiss. It was going to be complicated.

"Of course I do." I didn't know what I was getting into, but it was better to have her there than not know what she was up to.

She turned and kissed me on the lips, too quickly for me to enjoy it.

"I'll be there when dinner's over," she said.

"*What?*" I shouted, much louder than necessary, holding her so she couldn't walk out.

"Nicholas, I'm not going to leave him hanging. I'll be a little late, that's all. Anyway, I feel like hanging out with him. He's cool."

This girl was going to kill me.

"Do what you want," I said, picking my keys up off the desk and walking past her to the steps.

If she wouldn't put me before an idiot like Mario, I wasn't going to let her waste my time. I was going to have fun that night, and I'd finally get her out of my head.

But not even I believed that.

———————

The party was at the home of Mike, one of my friends from the neighborhood. He was a good guy; I knew him from college, and he almost always let us use his lake house when we needed to go big. Anna had taken care of the décor, including black and red helium balloons and all sorts of other stupid shit. The important stuff was in Lion's and the guys' hands: alcohol, food, and more alcohol. When I walked through the door, people shouted *Happy birthday* in unison. I greeted everyone, and five minutes later, they were all dancing, acting silly, taking off for the lake, and drinking anything they could get their hands on.

The good thing about these parties was there were always plenty of girls for me. I grabbed a drink and sidled up to the two dancers they'd hired for me. A part of me kept thinking about when Noah would get there, but another part said it was time to cut loose.

One of the dancers—I forgot her name—wouldn't keep her hands off me. The other, a pretty young redhead, vanished as soon as she was done with her number. Nobody with a Y chromosome would have been indifferent to the chick who kept trying to drag me off to the bathroom. But one of my unbreakable rules was no sleeping with strippers or prostitutes or anyone similar, so I ditched her as politely as I could and walked to the back of the house. From there, I could see Toluca Lake and the reflection of the full moon in the water. My friends were all fooling around, splashing each other and dragging girls down to the shoreline.

Just then, Lion came over, leaned on the wooden railing, and looked at me. I remembered the first time I'd ever seen him. He had been way bigger and scarier, but at least I had been tall enough to look him in the eye before he'd split my face open. I hadn't even known what he was pissed off about—I think I'd hooked up with his girl or something at this party I'd been taken to—but the funny thing was, thanks to my reflexes, I had been able to get away, and he'd wound up hitting the wall behind me.

It had been so ridiculous, I'd burst into laughter while he'd clutched his fist in pain and started sweating. I guess he'd thought it was funny, too, though, and we'd been best friends ever since.

"Thanks for inviting me on the trip, dude. I can never go anywhere with Jenna, and finally we'll be able to get that alone time we've been needing." He was beaming. I took a sip of my beer. That trip... I couldn't think of it without thinking of Noah.

"I know she's your stepsister and all, man, but why'd you invite her?" he asked a second later, intrigued, and I felt like he was reading my thoughts.

I weighed my response before answering. I wasn't sure myself, but I just knew the idea of spending two whole days without her made me unbearably anxious.

"I don't want her to stay here while Ronnie's still mad about the race. He threatened her. I can't let anything happen to her." I left out the detail that if he even looked at her wrong, I'd kill him with my bare hands.

Lion turned his back to the lake and looked at me sternly.

"I don't know what you're really about, bro, but I've seen how you look at her. You can't hook up with her. She's your stepsister. I've been talking with Jenna, and Nicholas, Noah isn't like other girls. You're going to scare her."

I tried to calm down, to keep from telling him to go to hell. He wasn't wrong. Noah was different: you could see it in her eyes, in the way she was, in how she didn't even understand the effect she had on people. She was naive and innocent, and I could corrupt her so easily.

"I know what you mean, but nothing's up," I said, while my mind shouted back to me *LIAR* in capital letters. "We're just friends. We need to be—we live together, our parents are married. It would be impossible if we hated each other, so I've decided to try to get along."

Lion seemed to buy the story.

"You know what you're doing," he said, and then stripped off his shirt and ran over to where everyone was swimming.

I wouldn't have minded going with him, but I couldn't help keeping my eyes on the door, waiting for Noah to return from her stupid date. That was when I saw her come in with Jenna. Their arms were locked, and Noah smiled when she saw me. She was radiant when she smiled that way, and I wanted to grab her and kiss that dimple that had appeared in her left cheek.

"Happy birthday again!" she shouted. Jenna observed us for a moment before turning to the lake, where Lion was shouting for her to come in.

"What about you guys?" he asked, and Noah looked down at her black dress.

"I didn't bring a swimsuit," she said, shrugging.

"Don't be a prude. Just wear your underwear. It's the same thing," Jenna said, dragging her off.

Just imagining her in her underwear made me nervous, not to mention the idea of her stripping in front of all those drunk assholes at my party.

I could tell she was uncomfortable.

"No way," I said, pulling her back toward me until she almost fell into my side.

"Damn, Nicholas!" she complained. But then she smiled back at Jenna. "I'm not in the mood. You go, though, and we'll see each other afterward." Jenna took off.

I couldn't help but smile. Jenna was crazy, but I cared about her too much to be mad at her for trying to convince Noah to strip in front of God and everyone else. I looked down at those freckles I could barely see in the shadows.

"Enjoy your date?" I asked, unable to suppress my sarcasm.

"It was great, but who cares. I brought you a present."

I leaned against the railing and looked at her—at those lips I wished I could bite—and a good mood immediately overtook me.

"For real?" I asked, wanting to know what was lurking under that cheerfulness, so unlike Noah's usual attitude. "I'm scared to ask."

Her expression changed. Was she getting nervous? Now I was even more curious.

"It's dumb, but with everything that's happened, and especially with last night…here. I bought it in a little shop. It was just a spur-of-the-moment thing, but it's my way of saying sorry."

Saying sorry?

I grabbed the box and tore off the cream-colored wrapping. It was a tiny black Ferrari, exactly like mine.

"There's a note," she said, pointing to the car's chassis.

In teeny letters, I read:

I'm sorry about your car, for real. Someday, I'll buy you a new one. Happy birthday. Noah.

It was so silly, I couldn't help but laugh. Standing there next to me, she did the same.

"I did owe you one, right?" she said.

"I ought to throw you in the lake for this," I threatened, picking her up and swinging her around.

"No, Nick!" she screamed. "I'm sorry, I swear!"

"You're sorry?" I said, lowering her slowly and squeezing her tightly, just as I'd wanted to do ever since she'd left with Mario.

I looked around. There was nobody there. Everyone was either in the lake or inside the house. I pushed her over to a tree and trapped her with my body.

"You could have caused me big, big problems. Luckily I've been wanting to kiss you ever since you walked through my front door."

I remembered then what Lion had told me: Noah wasn't like the others.

I rested a hand on her cheek and caressed those freckles I liked so much. Her skin was tense, alabaster, and it was impossible not to lean down and kiss it, feel its smooth texture on my lips. I kissed her cheek, then the place where her dimple showed up when she smiled, then her throat, coming in close and savoring her sweet skin. She moaned almost inaudibly, and I couldn't take it anymore. Our lips joined, and a thousand different feelings took hold of me: uncertainty, heat, a deep, dark desire. Between my body and the tree, I felt her melting into me.

Her tongue looked for mine, and when they met, I almost died from pleasure. She pulled me down, and I couldn't control my hands, which went crazy feeling her all over.

My hands climbed her thighs and touched the fringe of her

panties. My God, I wanted to touch her there, make her shout with pleasure, hear her say my name over and over!

"Nick," she panted.

"Tell me to stop and I will," I said, looking her in those eyes that seemed to have come up from hell to torture me and drive me insane.

She said nothing, so I kept going. My fingers pushed aside her underwear, and she groaned into my shoulder. She was shaking, and I held her up with one hand as I pleasured her with the other. I watched her the whole time, bewitched.

A minute later, I had to cover her mouth with mine—I was worried someone would hear her.

She was perfect...and I was falling in love like an idiot.

27

Noah

I WAS SHAKING SO HARD—SHAKING FROM PLEASURE—THAT I HAD to let him hold me up. I couldn't believe what had just happened; I hadn't seen it coming, and it had been so fast. I had been giving him his present and laughing, and all of a sudden, he had me pushed against a tree and his caresses had been making me tremble. I'd wanted to stop him. My God, I should have, but feeling those hands all over me... It had been incredible.

"You're precious," he whispered in my ear after kissing me to keep me from shouting and getting us both caught.

I could still remember all the times Dan had tried to touch me that way. I'd immediately said no, and he hadn't even gotten close. Nick, though... I must have been losing my mind.

"I think...we should go back," I said, adjusting my dress. Why did I feel so bad all the sudden?

"Hey," Nick said, grabbing my chin and making me look up. "Are you okay?"

"Yeah, it's just... I didn't see that coming," I said, trying not to look at him. "We let ourselves lose control, or I let myself lose control, and I'm sorry about it... Go back to Anna or whoever.

You don't have to stay here with me." I was trying not to let him see how stirred up I was.

I wanted him to hold me. Deep down I wanted him to stay with me. I wanted us to be in love or at least to know each other better. Nick was a total mystery to me, and I was to him, too. I couldn't let him know that a part of me wanted him to tell me he loved me or to take me somewhere we could really be alone instead of leaning against a tree at a party.

"You want me to go be with Anna?" he asked, suddenly pissed. Maybe he was mad I didn't want to keep going. Maybe he thought I wanted to do the same to him. But just thinking about sex with him in the middle of the woods made me sick.

"Yeah, go be with her," I said, looking down at my toes. "You don't have to stay with me. I told you—this was a mistake, we're going too far, it's not right."

Nicholas turned around and kicked a rock. I heard him curse under his breath. Then he turned around in fury, his eyes looking like ice.

"Fine," he said. He reached back with one arm and pulled off his shirt. Before I knew what he was doing, he'd turned around, pulled off his jeans, and taken off running for the lake. The people swimming there saw him and chanted his name.

My good mood and my self-esteem sank like his body sinking into that cold water.

For the next hour and a half, I avoided him as much as possible. I didn't want to see him; the mere thought of it made me nervous. When five in the morning struck and most of the people had gone, the only ones left were Anna, Lion, Jenna, Mike, who owned the place, someone named Sophie, a friend of Nick's named Sam, Nick, and me. We were in a living room full of big white sofas and armchairs, sitting in a circle. Sophie and Jenna were on one side of me; Sophie was a bleach-blond dummy. Mike was to my right, and Nicholas was next to him. I was glad because that meant I didn't have to look him in the face.

He hadn't said a word to me since we'd been standing by the tree. Maybe he was mad, or maybe he was glad he could wash his hands of me. I felt an ache each time our eyes accidentally crossed and he looked away, but part of me felt relieved. I'd rather he ignore me than have to talk about what happened.

"Why don't we play that game we used to play when we were kids?" Sophie said.

"Truth or Dare?" Jenna said, grinning. "Grow up, Soph."

"No, come on, let's play," Mike said, looking mischievous. That put me on alert. I hated that game. I'd said *dare* one time, and they'd made me drink a glass of cooking oil. It was disgusting.

"Grab the bottle on the table there," Mike asked his friend.

He placed the beer bottle in the center of the circle and spun it, and it pointed to Anna.

"Truth or dare?" he asked. Nick shifted uneasily.

"Uh...truth," she said, glancing over at him. I looked down. If it hadn't been ridiculous, I'd have covered my ears to not hear them.

"What's the last time you hooked up with someone?" Mike asked. *For real?*

Anna smirked. I hated the way she looked over at me as she described sleeping with Nick.

"It was in the back seat of a car," she said, laughing. "I'd have preferred a bed, but you know..."

Why did it hurt me so much to hear that? Why did the simple thought of Nick's hands roving her body make me want to get up and pull her hair out?

I spun the bottle myself. I didn't care if her story was over or not. I wasn't interested in the details.

Shit, now the bottle was pointing at Nick.

"Truth or dare?" I asked him, a little brusquely.

"Dare, obviously."

I tried to think of something that would really irritate him, but before I could, Sophie butted in.

"Take off your shirt," she ordered him, and I huffed as I watched her devour him with her eyes.

"That's not an actual dare," I said.

"You should learn to be faster, little sister," Nick said, stripping it off. All the other girls in the room must have been as entranced by his physique as I was. He was still to die for, even with the bumps and bruises Ronnie and his guys had dealt out to him.

"Thanks for the view, Nick. My turn," Jenna said, reaching out and spinning the bottle.

Dammit. I was up. I almost shivered wondering what she'd ask me.

"Truth or dare?"

"Truth," I shrugged.

"Tell us the worst thing you've ever done in your life," Jenna said. She thought I was a good little girl who never did anything out of the ordinary. If only she knew...

Seeing the mocking looks on everyone's faces, I felt the urge to open their eyes, but did I really want to tell them about the thing that had been eating me up inside since I was eleven? No. Honestly, I didn't.

"I stole a pack of gummy candy from a store in my town when I was nine. They caught me, and I tried to run off, and I ended up pulling down two shelves full of stuff. I was grounded for a month. I've never stolen anything since then," I said, remembering that day affectionately. The chase had been the most fun part.

Everyone laughed.

Some friend of Nick's whose name I'd forgotten had to spin

the bottle this time. He'd had his eye on me all night. To my great displeasure, it slowed down and came to a stop on me again.

"Truth or dare?" he asked with a twisted smile.

"Dare," I decided, since I'd picked *truth* last time, but I had the feeling I might have made the wrong choice.

"Take off your dress," he said, and the blood rushed into my face.

No. I couldn't do that. The lights were too bright; everyone would be able to see every inch of my body.

Nicholas didn't seem to like the idea, either. All I wanted was for him to come up with something that would get me out of it.

"Can I change back?" I asked.

Anna, clearly amused, asked me whether I had some kind of hang-up about my body. "It's just a game," she said.

"You can change," Nick grunted. Everyone protested, but there was no changing his mind, and they had to give in.

"Fine. Since you didn't want to go along the first time, your dare is going to be a little more complicated," Anna said. I could tell she was enjoying making me suffer. I had the urge to get up and smack her in the head with the bottle. Triumphantly, she continued, "So you've got to go into that closet and make out with Sam."

What the hell? No way I was getting in some dark closet. This night was going from bad to worse.

"Great!" Sam said.

"I'll do it," I said, "but here. I'm not getting in any closet."

"Why?" Anna asked.

"She's afraid of the dark," Nicholas said. I couldn't believe he'd just blurted that out without any consideration for me. Everyone cracked up.

"What are you, like, four years old?" Sophie said.

I could feel myself blushing. That subject was off-limits. Only a few people knew the truth about that fear. I hadn't even told my stepbrother the reason behind it.

"Same difference as far as I'm concerned. I'm going to need that kiss, though," Sam said, edging over to me with no sense of shame. Whatever, it was just a kiss. Why should I care? I stood up, ignoring everyone around me.

Sam was blond with brown eyes. Jenna had told me he went to our school. When he reached me, he put a hand around my waist. Everyone else was jeering. I'm sure they could tell I was embarrassed, but my only thought was getting it over with.

I'd meant to just give him a quick peck, but he was too quick for me, and he forced my lips open and slipped his tongue inside. I froze, and a second later, I shoved him away.

"That'll do," I said and sat back down. I was angry, even if I didn't exactly know why.

"You kiss like an angel, Noah," Sam said, returning to his place.

Nick got up. He seemed worried, as if he had something on his mind, and both his hands were clenched into fists.

"It's late," he said, looking at me. "We need to go. This game's stupid anyway."

I got up, and the rest followed suit. Everyone was tired—the party had dragged on too long. Nick threw on his T-shirt, and Sophie observed him with what seemed like sadness.

We said goodbye and walked to our cars. Thank God Anna had come in her convertible and we didn't have to take her home. Jenna promised to call me the next day so we could plan what we were packing together. I was a bit distant—that trip seemed like the least appropriate idea ever.

Nick said goodbye to Anna, and we hopped in the car and took off. I didn't want to talk about what had happened, so I turned on the radio. As soon as we were on the road, though, he reached out and turned it off.

"I didn't like you kissing Sam one fucking bit," he said, drumming his fingers nervously on the wheel.

"It was just a dumb game. What was I supposed to do?" I said, remembering Anna's confession. I didn't care to hear that, either.

"You should have said no."

"I already said no once. I don't ask you to explain what you're doing or not doing with Anna or the hundreds of chicks you rub up on right in front of my face," I said, raising my voice.

"I haven't done that," he said, and I raised my eyes. "Hundreds of girls is too many, even for me, Freckles."

"What about Anna, though?"

"My thing with Anna... It's different, but if it makes you feel better, it's been weeks since we've done anything," he responded. I could tell he was trying to keep calm.

"Well, I don't believe you, but even if it is true, you don't owe me any explanation. I'm not jealous." I crossed my arms and looked outside into the darkness. Of course I was, but I would never admit that aloud.

"I am," he said, turning to look at me. "I'm jealous, I'm super-jealous, and I don't even know why. I've never been jealous of anyone in my life, Noah, and certainly not of some jerkoff like Sam."

I was confused.

"You shouldn't feel that way over a dumb game—"

"You think I don't know that?" he interrupted me.

Just then, we arrived home. Nick opened the car door in silence. Before I could get out, he grabbed my wrist, and I looked over at him.

"I'm sorry what happened in the woods wasn't what you expected. I didn't want to scare you or make you uncomfortable."

I felt the wall I'd built up around myself start to crumble.

"You gave me the option to stop you, Nick, and I didn't," I replied. And I felt his hand stroke my wrist.

"I'd do it all with you, Noah, you know that...but I won't do anything until the fear disappears from your eyes."

Dammit.

He got out. It took a long time before my heart felt normal again.

The next day, Jenna picked me up at three in the afternoon to go shopping. According to her, this trip to the Bahamas was the perfect excuse to spruce up our wardrobes. My mother, overjoyed that Nicholas had invited me along, gave me her credit card and begged me to buy something. It was weird to see my mother so happy just because her stepson and I were getting along, especially since from her point of view the whole farce was just him trying to treat me as his sister. I couldn't even imagine the look on her and Will's faces if they found out what we'd been doing the past few weeks.

Still wavering about whether I should even go on the trip, I waited for Jenna as she walked in and out of the dressing room with a thousand different designer outfits. She was so thin, so svelte... I was envious. Her dark skin looked beautiful in every single thing she tried on. I still hadn't picked anything, and I wasn't even particularly into the idea. I already had way too many clothes I hadn't even worn.

My phone rang, and I grabbed it out of my back pocket.

"Hello?" I said. No answer. I looked at the screen. Unknown number. "Hello?" I said again, louder. I could hear someone breathing on the other line, and my whole body shivered. I hung up just as Jenna walked out of the dressing room again.

"Who was it?" she asked as I slipped my phone back in my pocket.

"Dunno. Unknown number," I said, picking up my bag and heading for the door.

"Weird! I got this call from an unknown number once, and it

turned out to be this weirdo who was obsessed with me. He called me, like, a million times. I had to change my number and everything. Lion was losing his mind."

Honestly, though, who was going to stalk me? But then I remembered Nick telling me about Ronnie's threats and how I needed to take them more seriously. I wasn't going to let a stupid phone call freak me out, though. I pushed my worries aside and walked with Jenna to the register.

Ten minutes later, we were sitting at a table outside a Starbucks, where I picked apart a blueberry muffin while she drank a strawberry Frappuccino.

"Can I ask you something?" she asked.

I nodded, putting a piece of muffin into my mouth.

"Do you have feelings for Nick?"

I almost choked. I didn't see that coming. Was it so obvious? I tried to swallow and stop coughing, taking a sip of my OJ and asking myself how the hell I was going to respond.

"Why do you ask?"

"Yesterday at the birthday party... I don't know... I thought I saw something. Like Nick... He's never been so happy to see someone, but when you showed up, he was like a completely different guy. I could be imagining things, but your reaction when Anna talked and then his when you kissed Sam, they were almost exactly the same."

Hmm. Nothing got past her. It was true we'd let ourselves go that night, not stopping to think that people around us might pick up on what was happening between us. But then what was happening between us?

"Jenna, he's my stepbrother," I said, trying to change the subject.

She rolled her eyes.

"Yeah, which means he's not your real brother or anything

like it, so you can cut the bullshit," she said. "I know Nick, and he's changed... There's something there... Maybe it's true you're trying to be friends now...or maybe you actually have feelings for him?" I felt as if I were being placed behind an X-ray machine.

What were my feelings for Nick? I certainly felt something, I had to admit that, at least to myself, but what was it exactly? I had no idea, I only knew that he was managing to drive me completely insane.

"We're trying to be friends for our parents' sake," I said, knowing it was a lie. "And I don't dislike him, especially now that we're actually trying to get to know each other."

Jenna sucked on her straw. "Fine. But don't tell me it wouldn't be amazing if y'all hooked up. That doesn't count as incest, does it?"

Once again, I found myself choking on my muffin.

28

Nick

The Hotel Atlantis in the Bahamas was considered one of the best. I'd been twice, and it really was incredible. There was a huge aquarium where you could see sharks, rare fish, and all kinds of sea creatures as you walked down the hall toward the dining room or the casino. Noah was freaking out, and I was happy to know I'd helped her have this experience. We'd reserved two rooms: one for the guys and one for the girls.

We got to the hotel at five in the afternoon. The girls wanted to go straight to the beach. I was dying to see Noah in her bikini, so in thirty minutes, I made sure we were off. The sun was warm, but I wasn't one to lie down on a towel and soak up rays. I liked to surf, but even if that wasn't in the cards, I was content to know I'd have something pretty to look at.

Hence my disappointment when we got to our beach chairs and Noah took off her dress. Unlike Jenna, who was wearing a provocative bikini, Noah was wearing a black one-piece. It was hot, sure, but I wanted to see a little more skin, a little more of that soft, flat stomach, that waist…

Jenna and Lion went straight to the water. She jumped on his back, and he threatened to throw her in. I turned to Noah, who was busy putting on sunscreen.

"Are we back in the nineteen fifties, or did you just forget your bikini at home?"

"If you don't like it, you don't have to look," she said, turning away.

I grimaced. It seemed like whatever I did pissed her off.

She lay down and took a book out of her bag. She read all the time at home. I wondered what it was she liked about Thomas Hardy, but I let it go. My literary tastes and hers had nothing in common, that much was obvious. What was it about her that completely changed who I was, how I acted? Was it those sweet, honey-colored eyes that concealed an indomitable character that would cause anyone to buckle and give in? Was it those freckles, which made her look so innocent and sexy at the same time? I didn't know, but when she looked up from her book, I knew if I didn't watch out, I'd go as gaga for her as Lion had for Jenna.

"Come into the water with me," I said, stretching out a hand and snatching away her book.

"Why?"

"I can think of several reasons. We could swim, look for seashells... Why, Freckles, what did you think I was talking about?"

The flushed pink of her face now turned deep red.

"You're an idiot, and I'm not getting into the water with you. Now give me back my book." She reached out, and I grabbed her hand and pulled her close.

"You can read when you're old. Come on."

She resisted at first, but then I picked her up and carried her down to the water.

"Let me go!" she shouted, kicking and screaming.

I obeyed, throwing her into the water and laughing when she

surfaced, gaping like a fish. She came after me, and I spent the next
ten minutes dunking her, running off, and cracking up.

The afternoon was uneventful. I realized that if I kept my hands
off Noah, she was capable of relaxing and having fun. On the
beach, we drank margaritas and enjoyed the crystal-clear water.
I fell asleep in my chair, Lion and Jenna disappeared to do who
knew what, and an hour later, when I opened my eyes, Noah was
gone. I looked all over for her. Then I heard her laugh. I turned
to my left, where a group of college guys was playing volleyball.
There was Noah in her swimsuit and skimpy shorts jumping and
smacking the ball like a pro while all the guys gawked at her.
Most of them were tall and in good shape. One of them hugged
her and spun her in the air when she scored, and I fumed with
jealousy.

Dammit! I stomped over to them. I didn't know what was
going on, but I was pissed. When she saw me and smiled, I froze.
She was happy. Blissed out.

"Nick, come play!" she shouted, passing the ball to one of her new
friends and running over to me. The sun had darkened her cheeks, and
her eyes gleamed. "Did you see me score?" she asked proudly.

I nodded, unsure what to do with the rage that was eating
me inside.

"I didn't know you played volleyball," I said, realizing as I did
so how gruff my voice sounded.

But she ignored it and replied, "I started when I was ten. I told
you, I was the captain of my team in Toronto."

I got a grip on myself and smiled back at her.

"Well, I'm very proud of you, and it's great that you were
so good and all, but we need to go," I said. I didn't like all those
dudes staring at us, almost salivating over her.

"Come on, Noah," one of them, the guy who had just hugged her, shouted. I gave him a look that froze him.

"Sorry," she said, "I didn't realize how late it was. Let me say goodbye real quick." I was uncomfortable watching them all talk to her. One even groaned when she said she had to leave. I would have pressed his face into the sand if I didn't think I'd get in trouble with Noah for it.

When she was back beside me, she said, "That was amazing. It's been three months since I've played. I felt like I was back home, seriously." I understood then how hard it must have been for her to leave absolutely everything behind to move with her mother: her friends, her school, her boyfriend. "The guys invited us to meet them in the club at the hotel. Supposedly it's great. We should go."

I wanted to say absolutely not, that those guys just wanted one thing from her and that I wasn't about to stand around all night watching them try to get in her pants, but when I saw the happiness on her face, a happiness I hadn't ever seen before, I couldn't say no.

"Sure, but we need to grab a shower and have dinner first," I said. "Jenna and Lion already went back. I talked to them."

"Cool," she said.

But cool was the last thing you could call this situation.

———————————

When Lion and I met the girls in front of the elevator, it was all I could do not to shove Noah back into her room. Who told her to dress like that? She was bursting out of a white dress with thin straps that crisscrossed in the back. The sight of all that exposed skin couldn't be good for my health. I had to restrain myself to keep from rubbing her down and taking her to my room where I could stare at her for hours. Her legs, long and graceful, looked even more so in those aquamarine heels.

Who had convinced her to ditch the Converse and jeans? The answer, of course, was right beside her: that goddamn Jenna.

29

Noah

I HAD NO IDEA HOW I'D LET HER CONVINCE ME TO PUT THE DRESS on. It was anything but appropriate. My whole entire back was exposed. I'd needed to put on a special bra. I felt completely naked. But when Jenna got something in her head, she couldn't be more annoying, and there *was* a little part of me deep down that wanted to see how Nick would react. All day, he'd acted like he really was my friend—he'd kept his hands off me, and weird as it seems, I didn't like it.

I understood his expression of distaste when we met in front of the elevators. He looked me up and down. For a second, I thought he actually didn't like what he saw.

"Is something up?" I asked, disappointed. That wasn't the reaction I'd expected.

"Aren't you going to be cold?" he asked with a strange glimmer in his eye.

"I'm fine," I said, and got into the elevator as soon as the doors slid open. Next to me, Jenna was wearing black hot pants and a provocative pink top. She was showing way more flesh than I was, and Lion seemed unsure whether he liked it.

The boys walked behind us. When we reached the restaurant, I couldn't believe the décor and ambience. It was at an elegant spot right next to the pool. It was a privilege to be able to enjoy that place with Nicholas and our friends. I guessed that was how it was when your mother married a millionaire.

We were seated at a nice table next to a trail leading through the gardens. The views were spectacular. Our plates were served quickly, and the food was exquisite and the conversation entertaining.

My phone buzzed, interrupting us. I kept getting calls from an unknown number with someone listening to me silently on the other line.

"Hello?" I said automatically, and a familiar voice responded. It was one of the guys I'd played volleyball with on the beach. Jess, I think his name was. He told me the name of the club and said we should go there as soon as dinner was over.

I communicated his message to Jenna, and she started hopping up and down while Nick gave me a weird look. What the hell was up with him?

I sent him a text. It was ridiculous, but if I didn't put him in check, he'd ruin our night.

What the hell's up with you? You've been giving me nasty looks since I came out of my room.

It was funny to see his eyes when his phone buzzed and he read my text. He looked back at me as my own phone vibrated.

I think I like it better when you pick your outfits. You shouldn't wear something you're not comfortable in.

How did he know Jenna had picked my outfit? Was it so

obvious how ridiculous I felt? Jenna was so hot. I must have looked like a stupid doll next to her.

I could have teared up. I'd wanted to make Nick's jaw drop, and I'd gotten the opposite effect.

I put my phone aside, deciding I wouldn't answer anymore. I'd never been a girl who dressed up much, but I'd also never really cared what anyone else thought of me, especially guys. Doing that for Nick, and in vain, made me feel stupid.

My phone buzzed again, noisier than before against the surface of the table.

I felt a tingle when I saw the message.

You look precious, Noah.

Our eyes met, and I felt the heat inside me. If he was being serious, he sure had a weird way of showing it.

I was angry with myself for letting those four little words have that effect on me. I shouldn't have done all that for him. I should have just worn what I had been planning to wear.

"Hey!" Lion nearly shouted. "What's up with you guys?"

"Nothing," Nick said, taking a sip from his fine-crystal glass.

"We should go. I told Jess we'd be there in fifteen minutes, and I don't want to leave him hanging," I said. If Nick expected me to thank him for that message, he had another thing coming.

As we walked out and toward the club, a blond-haired, blue-eyed guy stopped me: Jess.

"Jeez, Noah...you look...incredible!"

I smiled. See, Nick? That was the attitude I was looking for.

I introduced him to everyone. Nick took a few seconds before shaking his hand, and when he did, I could tell he was squeezing it tightly.

"The club's right over there. The scene is lit." Outside, there were two bouncers and a long line of people. "They're with me," Jess told one of the bouncers, and after eyeing us up, he let us through. The dance floor was packed with people moving to the rhythm of the music. The lights were distracting, but otherwise, it was the perfect place for a fun evening.

"We've got a booth over there," he said, pointing to an area just off the dance floor in the nicest part of the club. "Follow me." I tried not to fall over as we cut between all the people. These shoes were deadly, and my feet were already killing me. There were four guys in the booth. I'd already met them on the beach. Now they shouted my name and said a boisterous hello to the rest. The whole situation was funny. Most of the guys had girls with them, and their warm welcome made me like them even better than before. I didn't fail to notice Jess jockeying to sit next to me or Nick settling in right beside me.

"So, Noah, how long have you been playing volleyball? You were ten times better than any of these losers!" Jess said, passing me a drink. I was nervous as I brought it to my lips. After what had happened the night I met Nick, I didn't trust anyone who handed me a glass if I didn't know what was in it.

"It's fine. I watched them pour it," Nick whispered. I wanted to thank him, but when I turned, a super-tall, super-hot chick had already come over and sat beside him. Nick turned around and started talking to her, and immediately, rage began eating away at me.

"You want to dance, Jess?" I asked just as Jenna dragged Lion onto the dance floor.

"Hell yeah," he said. I didn't even look back at Nicholas before grabbing Jess's hand and letting him lead me off toward the frenzied dancers.

I'd always loved dancing, and I wasn't bad at it. I had to thank my mother and her adolescent soul—she used to do all her chores at home with the music at full blast, so I'd never been ashamed to swing my hips. Dancing was fun. But Jess wasn't the guy I wanted to do it with just then. When I saw Nick appear with that other girl, my heart sank.

He was so sexy when he danced. I'd never seen him do it, and watching him with that blond made me angry and jealous in a way I'd never felt before. His hands went directly to her ass, and I had to turn around and take a deep breath to keep from running off back to my room. I knew we weren't anything, but I hated seeing him touch another girl, especially right there in front of me. Jess grabbed me around the waist, and I pressed my back into his chest. Nick could see me, and I could tell he was staring.

I wanted to push Jess away. I didn't feel comfortable, but Nicholas's every gesture was daring me not to buckle. His cheek touched the blond's cheek, and she turned her head and whispered something in his ear while I felt the air grow thin...

Even if I was dying inside, that also made me want to respond in kind, so I let Jess wrap his arms around me, grinding my hips into him, feeling his hard body. I was playing with fire, and I knew it.

Nick scowled at me as he nibbled the girl's earlobe. Watching it, I knew exactly what she was feeling.

That was enough.

I jerked away from Jess and told him to wait for me in the VIP. I said I'd be right back. He nodded, just asking if everything was all right. I eased his mind and walked over to one of the railings around the dance floor. There were still dancers there, but at least I had a little space to try to compose myself.

That was when Nick showed up in front of me. His eyes looked for mine, and he grabbed my hands and pulled me into him. My heart started pounding when I felt his palm on the bare flesh of my back.

"Why do you make me do things I don't want to?" he asked.

I didn't respond. I had nothing to say. I was angry at myself for trying to be something I wasn't and mad at him for calling me out on it.

"You drive me crazy, Noah," he confessed, his lips grazing my ear.

I looked up at him. I could see he was suffering—from jealousy, from longing, from lust. He wanted me... I drove him crazy. A smile blossomed on my lips.

"You know how to dance," I said, reaching my arms up over his neck. I touched his hair and stroked his neck slowly, trying to provoke him.

"Don't do that," he said, but I didn't stop. "You're going to make me do something I can't do here," he warned me, jutting his head to the right. I looked over and saw Jenna and Lion watching us as they danced. I wanted to tell Jenna what was really going on, but then I told myself that was insane. No one would just accept such a relationship.

"I should go back," I said, disillusioned.

"Screw that," he said, pulling me into him. He bit my ear, stroked my back, made me close my eyes and try to keep from sighing from pleasure.

"You should stop," I said, and I heard him curse, and then his lips were on top of mine. I hadn't expected that kiss. We were being watched, we were giving ourselves away, but even more than that, his kiss was passionate, immediate, and tremendously arousing.

"Nick," I said, hyperventilating, "Nick, stop." By now his hands were all over me. If I went on like that, he'd soon have me stripped naked in the middle of the dance floor.

He put his hands on my shoulders and pushed me back, looking me in the eye.

"Let's go to my room," he said. I froze. "I can't take seeing you here in the midst of all these people who want to do exactly the same thing to you that I do. Please, Noah, come with me. I want to be alone with you."

He seemed upset, or else he was barely holding on to his sanity. I felt bad seeing him suffering like that. And after that kiss, I didn't really want to be there with all those people, either...plus my shoes were killing me.

"Fine, let's go," I said, taking his hand. He smiled and led me over to where Lion and Jenna were gawking at us. She grabbed me and glared at me.

"You lying little bitch!" Then she died laughing. "Are y'all out of your minds?" I guessed Lion was speechless, but the way he looked at Nick seemed to say he didn't entirely approve.

"We're leaving," Nick said, ignoring them both.

"So soon?" Jenna complained. I was sure she'd interrogate me till dawn once she was back in the room, but at that moment, I didn't care.

"My feet are in agony. These shoes are a torture device." At least I wasn't lying about that. As Nick led me away, I shouted, "Say goodbye to everyone for me," trying to get Jenna to hear me over the decibels. She nodded, still clearly unable to process what she'd just seen.

The soundproof walls muffled the music outside. It was late, but people were still lined up trying to get in.

"Your feet hurt, huh?" Nick asked.

I nodded and sat down on a bench. Nicholas knelt in front of me and started unbuckling them.

"What are you doing?" I giggled.

"I don't know how you put up with these. Just looking at them is painful," he said, taking off first one shoe and then the other.

"Thanks. That's a relief." I didn't just mean the shoes, though.

Ten minutes later, we were in his room. The only light came in through the windows, but it was enough to see by. He pushed me into the wall, dropped my shoes on the floor, and kissed me again, deeper, with more desire.

I didn't know why, but anytime he had me in his arms, all I could think of was our bodies joining as one and my hands rubbing him all over. And now I was doing it. I grabbed a handful of his hair and pulled him close. He gripped my hands and held them over my head.

"Don't move," he said, kissing my neck, biting me where my pulse was pounding, sucking my collarbone. I moaned with pleasure when he started stroking my thigh, pushing up the bottom of my dress. Now I thought the light, faint as it was, was too much. If I let him keep going, he'd see me naked.

"Stop, please," I asked him, but he didn't care. "Stop," I repeated, and he moved back, but I caught his right hand in mine, where it was resting, on my thigh.

"Why?" he asked, and his eyes were begging me to let him keep going. Never in my life had something tempted me that way. All I wanted was to give in to his wishes, to tell him to take me to bed and do what he wished to me, but no... I couldn't yet.

"I'm not ready," I said, and I knew that was true, in a way.

He pressed his forehead into mine until our breathing returned to normal.

"Okay," he said after a minute. "But don't go."

I wondered what was going through his mind.

"You said before that we didn't know each other well enough, and you were right. And I want to know you, Noah, I really do. I've never wanted anything so bad before. And I want you to stay with me tonight."

Seeing him open up to me, Nicholas, the hard-ass who hooked

up with hundreds of girls without an ounce of remorse…it touched me deep inside.

"Fine… Let's talk," I said.

I wanted to know him better, too.

I was in the bathroom in Nick's hotel room. I'd taken off my white dress and was looking at myself in the mirror in my underwear. He'd lent me one of his T-shirts so I could be comfortable as I talked with him, but I couldn't take my eyes off the scar on my stomach. My scar had always been a problem. It was why I never wore bikinis and never let anyone see my stomach. Just the thought of it horrified me.

But I tried to forget it, splashing water on my face and throwing the T-shirt over my head. It hung off me like a dress, so I didn't need to feel too exposed. I washed my feet in cold water, too, and enjoyed feeling my muscles relax after the torture of those high heels.

When I came out, I saw Nicholas sitting on the balcony. He'd taken off his jeans and button-down and put on pajama pants and a gray T-shirt. I tried not to look at his body when I went out to see him.

As I set foot outside, he turned and said, "You look good in my clothes."

"I'm lucky you're tall. Otherwise this could be embarrassing." Just then, his phone started to ring. I saw the name before he answered and walked off to be able to talk without me eavesdropping. It was someone named Madison.

I felt my jealousy flare up as he moved past me, and I tried to pick up any snippet of their conversation I could.

"How are you, Princess?" he said in a sweet voice. Since when had Nicholas called anyone *Princess*? I wanted to run away just then. "Yeah, I'm great, I got lots of birthday presents. I'm still waiting on one from you. Hopefully it's a big hug and a kiss?"

This was getting worse and worse. I needed to go. Now. I couldn't bear to have him here in front of me flirting. But there was nothing I could do. I was the one who had insisted that he didn't need to explain anything to me. I was the one who'd said I didn't want to be exclusive. So what excuse did I have?

"You know I do, honey, but I have to go right now. I'll call you tomorrow, okay?" he continued. There was too much affection in that conversation. It was like I was listening to a completely different Nicholas. "I love you, too, Princess. Goodbye." And he hung up.

I crossed my arms and turned toward the ocean. I didn't want him to know that his call had bothered me. It would set a bad precedent.

"Sorry. I had to take that one," he said, kissing me on the neck by my tattoo.

"You said we needed to talk," I responded, turning around. He let me go and sat in one of the chairs.

"Great, let's talk," he said, a tranquil look on his face. He didn't have any remorse! I could feel my anger mounting. "How about we each ask ten questions? But you have to answer honestly, and we've both got a right to one veto."

I nodded. He was almost having fun.

"You wanna start?" he asked.

I took a deep breath.

"Who the hell is Madison?" I asked.

He didn't seem surprised, but still, he grimaced and ran a hand through his hair, as if it wasn't tousled enough.

"If I tell you this, you have to accept my answer and not ask me any more questions about it," he warned me, and I nodded, trying to imagine why. He exhaled a long breath. "She's my little sister, she's five years old, and she's my mom's daughter from her other husband."

Okay, that wasn't what I'd expected.

"You have a sister?" I asked incredulously.

"Yeah, and with that, you've wasted another question, so now you've only got eight left."

I shook my head. Did my mother know? Did Will?

"How did I not know? I mean, no one ever mentioned it. You've got a five-year-old sister!" I exclaimed, sitting on the edge of the table in front of him.

He rested his elbows on his knees and leaned in toward me.

"You didn't know because almost no one knows, and I want it to stay that way."

It obviously had to do with his mother. I didn't know much about her, just that she had walked out on him and his father, that they'd divorced when he was just a kid. That was about it.

"Do you have a good relationship with her?" I asked, trying to imagine him playing with a five-year-old girl and getting teary-eyed holding her. I just couldn't imagine it.

"Great. I adore her, but I don't see her enough," he replied, and I could see the sorrow in his eyes. It was clearly hard for him to talk about...but still, he was doing it, for me.

I climbed off the table and curled up in his lap. It surprised him, but instead of pushing me away, he wrapped his arms around me.

"I'm sorry," I said, not just because of his sister but also for the way things had gone with his mother.

"Sometimes I imagine bringing her out to LA, but by law, I can't see her very often. My sister doesn't get all the attention she needs; she's diabetic, and that only makes matters worse," he said, squeezing me into his chest.

What could I say? I felt like a complete idiot now. Not only had I misjudged him, I'd always just assumed his life was perfect, without problems of any kind. How stupid.

"Do you have a photo of her?" I asked. I couldn't imagine what she looked like.

He took out his iPhone and swiped through his photos until he came upon a picture of a very small, very pretty blond girl. I smiled.

"She's got your eyes," I said. She had his mischievous expression, too, but I kept that to myself.

"Yeah, that's the only thing, though. Everything else is exactly like my mom."

I turned to look at him. I knew he was hiding things from me; I knew something had happened with his mother, but I didn't dare ask. I decided to change the subject.

"Your turn," I said.

He seemed to be thinking it over and then asked, "What's your favorite color?"

I laughed.

"Out of all the questions in the world, you ask that one?"

He grinned as he waited for a response.

"Yellow."

"Your favorite food?"

"Macaroni and cheese."

"We've got something in common then," he said, resting his hand on my forearm. Being with him like that...was wonderful. Wonderful and so, so new.

"Why do you like Thomas Hardy?" he asked. That one surprised me. It meant he'd been watching me and knew what I was reading.

"I guess...I guess I like books that don't necessarily have a happy ending. They're more real, more like the way life is. Happiness is something you have to look for, you don't just find it so easily."

"You don't believe people can be happy?" he asked. Now the questions were getting personal, and my body began to stiffen.

"I think you can be less unhappy. Let's put it that way."

He scrutinized me, as if trying to grasp what was passing through my mind. It made me uncomfortable, being looked at in that way.

"Are you unhappy?" he said, stroking my cheek with one of his fingers.

"Not right now," I said, and he smiled back at me sadly.

"Me neither."

Was I just imagining it, or were we crossing an invisible line to reach our real feelings?

"What do you want to study when you're done with high school?"

Okay, that was easy.

"English literature. In Canada. But I want to be a writer," I said. Just then I realized maybe Canada was no longer such a good idea.

"A writer..." He seemed to be thinking it over. "Have you already written anything?"

I nodded. "I've written some stuff, but I've never let anyone read anything."

"Would you let me read something you wrote?"

I shook my head. I'd die from shame. Plus, the things I'd written were more like diaries than stuff you could just share with people.

"Next question," I said before he could push me on that point.

He looked at me attentively, hesitant at first but then resolute, choosing every one of his words carefully.

"Why are you afraid of the dark?"

That I didn't want to answer. Not just did I not want to—I couldn't. Thousands of memories bunched together in my mind.

"Pass," I said with a trembling voice.

30

Nick

I OBSERVED HER REACTION. SINCE I'D SEEN HER TURN WHITE AS A sheet when we were playing Truth or Dare and she was supposed to go into a dark closet, I couldn't stop asking myself what the hell had happened to make her so scared. Even mentioning it just now had terrified her, as if the memory of something were tormenting her inside.

"Relax, Noah," I said, hugging her. I'd dreamed of holding her like this, but now I'd screwed up everything by asking her that damn question.

"I just don't want to talk about it," she said, and I could feel her shivering. What the hell was going on?

"It's fine. Everything's fine," I said, rubbing her back. Tonight I hadn't been able to resist kissing her; it had been too long since the last time, I couldn't keep my hands off her. Noah had put a spell on me, and I was starting to realize a new Nicholas existed, one that couldn't stop thinking about her if he tried.

"I should probably go," she said. I cursed myself for provoking that reaction. I didn't like how she ran away from me every time things turned serious or we got closer to each other.

"No, stay," I said, burying my face in her neck, smelling her magnificent, captivating aroma, sweet but also tremendously sexy.

"I'm tired. Today was a long day," she said, standing up. I grabbed her hands to get her to stay.

"Sleep here with me," I asked, realizing immediately what she'd think when she heard those words.

From her expression, I saw I was just making matters worse. I needed to tread lightly with Noah.

"I said sleep. I'm not implying anything else," I begged her.

She looked like she was thinking it over.

"I'd rather sleep in my bed," she said, breaking free of my hands. She seemed to want to tell me something else, even to regret not saying it, but I understood that I had shaken up bad memories and she didn't want to be in this room anymore.

"It's okay. I'll walk you back," I said, standing up.

She giggled, and my heart filled with happiness. That was the Noah I liked.

"Nicholas, my room is right across from yours. You don't need to come with me," she reminded me, going inside and gathering her things. It was hot to me, seeing her in one of my T-shirts. It hung just below her butt, and I had to struggle to keep myself from lifting it up to get a better view.

"I don't care," I said.

"Thanks."

I grabbed her shoes and opened the door to let her through. I didn't know why, but she made me want to act like a gentleman.

We crossed the hall to her room, and I watched her take out her key card and slide it into the slot. A green light glowed, and the door opened with a click.

She turned around. She looked nervous or frightened. I didn't really understand what I'd done by asking her that question, but she felt so much further away than before. I grabbed her around the waist and pulled her close before she could go inside, kissing her deeply, in a way that left me yearning for more. She kissed me back but broke off abruptly and grabbed her shoes out of my hand.

"Good night, Nick," she said with a timid smile.

"Good night, Noah."

I didn't know what to expect the next morning, but when we all met in front of the elevator, Jenna and Lion were staring at us. I didn't care. I walked straight over to Noah and kissed her on the lips. She wasn't expecting it, but she didn't try to stop me. She was wearing jean shorts, a T-shirt, and sneakers. Those informal clothes were completely different from her outfit the night before and from the way the girls I usually went out with dressed. On the outside, she was simple, but inside, she was like a thousand-piece puzzle, and I still didn't know where I fit in.

"Get a room," Jenna said, laughing.

"Shut up, Jenna," I said. "You look good," I told Noah. I thought I'd hurt her feelings the night before when I'd sent her that message, and I didn't want to risk it again.

"You, too," she said blithely.

We got into the elevator and went to breakfast, conversing about what had happened the night before. Jenna thought we were out of our minds. Noah barely uttered a word, so I was the one who had to defend us.

We were supposed to go around the city that day, visit the shops, and eat out. The next day, we had to go home, and I was scared that everything that had happened between us would mean nothing once we'd passed through the front door. We couldn't deny that our personalities were constantly clashing. Most of the memories I had of Noah were either arguments or stolen kisses, and that worried me. I didn't want to lose her; I wanted to go further with whatever was happening between us.

The afternoon flew by. The restaurant we ate at was nice; I treated her to whatever she wanted, and it didn't matter, it was nothing compared to Jenna, who couldn't let a single shop slip by without going in.

I stopped next to Noah, who was looking at colored gemstone necklaces. They were cheap trinkets, but they were the first thing she'd seemed interested in since we'd left the hotel. She'd loved the city and its surroundings, but she didn't seem to care about having more things.

"Give me that one, please," I said to the shopkeeper. Noah was startled to hear my voice and looked over.

"You don't have to get me that. I was just looking at it."

"I want to," I said as I grabbed the necklace with its little amber pendant. "It matches your eyes," I said, wrapping it around her neck.

"Thanks," she said, grabbing the pendant.

"No problem," I said with a grin. I liked her wearing it and knowing that I'd been the one to put it on her.

After that, we had ice cream together on the shore and then returned to the hotel. The girls were hungry, and dinner service started soon. Jenna told us she had passes to a club in the city if we wanted to end the trip on a high note.

We said our goodbyes, and Lion and I went into our room.

"I don't know what you're up to, but you better be careful," he said. "I've had my eye on you, Nick, and that chick's got you sprung."

"We're just having fun, Lion. Don't screw it up," I replied, taking off my T-shirt and turning around.

"Nicholas, I know the types of girls you go for, and I don't see this ending well. I've never seen two people more different than you and Noah."

I looked straight at him. He was pissing me off now.

"Lion, mind your business. You want me to believe you and Jenna had anything in common when you two met?"

"I'm just saying." With that, he walked out, leaving me alone in the room with a head full of anxious thoughts. It was true; Noah wasn't anything like me, but maybe that was exactly what I needed. I'd never even wanted to get to know anyone before. Noah was like a riddle I had to find the answer to.

I showered and put on a black T-shirt and jeans. When I was ready, I went to the elevator. Lion was there with Jenna and Noah, who was wearing tight black pants and a blue top. She took my breath away.

Our relationship had changed completely since we'd arrived. We'd barely argued—that was already something—but I still disliked that distance it seemed we could never break through. Every time one of us took two steps forward, the other took five back.

When we left the hotel, the weather was pleasant. The sun had already gone down. We walked to the club. Only when we reached the door did I realize this wasn't going to go well. The volleyball players were all outside waiting for us. It had been stupid of me not to realize they must have given Jenna the passes the day before after Noah and I had left.

Noah stepped away from my side to greet them. I had to use all my self-control not to pound Jess into the pavement when he hugged her and picked her up off the ground just as he'd done the day before.

"You left yesterday without saying goodbye!" he reproached her. I stepped forward. Thank God he let her go. Noah seemed excited; her cheeks were flushed. Did she like that idiot? If so, I couldn't be responsible for my actions.

The other players greeted her in turn, and some of them were clearly captivated with her. In those tight pants and those high-heeled sandals, she looked like a runway model. Her hair was pulled back loosely with a couple of locks falling down and framing her angelic face.

When we walked in, I could see the place was more crowded than the club had been the night before. Apparently it was singles' night. At the door, they gave you a green bracelet if you were single; if you didn't want to say, they gave you yellow, and if you were with someone, you got red. I kept my mouth shut when I saw Noah pick a green one, even though I wanted to tear it off her. Two could play at that game.

We sat in a small booth close to the bar. Jenna dragged Noah off to get drinks. Lion was already on his way back with one drink for him and one for me. We clinked glasses, and he smiled at me. It was strong stuff.

"Happy twenty-second birthday, my man!" he shouted over the music. The girls returned a second later.

"We're getting drunk tonight!" Jenna shrieked. Noah giggled. I wasn't into the idea, but I didn't say anything.

As the night passed, I felt more and more on edge. Those fucking bracelets were an invitation to any guy who felt like it to rub up on the girls with the green or yellow ones. Sitting in the booth, I could see Noah dancing with a much older guy. She was damn sexy when she moved her hips that way, and it was pissing me off that she seemed perfectly happy to dance with any dude who wasn't me.

I downed my fourth drink and walked over to her just as the guy she was with pulled her in close and planted a kiss on her lips.

Right away, I saw red.

I pushed Noah away and grabbed the fuckhead's shirt. Next thing I knew, I was on the ground exchanging punches with him. I didn't care—seeing his body that close to Noah's had driven me insane.

"Nicholas, stop!" shouted a voice too familiar to ignore. Lion's arms grabbed me from behind, and I heard him cursing as he pushed me outside. I'd gotten hit in the eye—the same eye that wasn't yet healed from my last fight.

"What the fuck are you doing, man?"

"Where's Noah?" I asked, looking around. There were people everywhere, and I couldn't see her. When she did appear, she stared daggers at me.

"Are you out of your mind?" she shouted, incensed, hurrying over and shoving me. What did she have to be pissed off about? I yelled at her:

"You like that, when some guy feels you up in front of me?"

"I was dancing!" she shouted. "Dancing!"

I tried to suppress my desire to shake her as I walked close and asked, "And you let him kiss you, too?" I couldn't control myself anymore, and I was too drunk to think about the consequences of my words as I continued, "If you're going to let any jerkoff who comes along put his hands all over you, then you should drop the good girl act, walking around with a stick up your ass like you're some kind of nun—"

She slapped me so fast, it didn't even start hurting for a few seconds.

In a reflex, I grabbed her by the shoulders.

"Do that again and see what happens."

Only once I'd spoken did I realize what I'd done. The look of horror on her face made me take a step back. She hyperventilated, and her eyes started watering.

"Noah."

She stepped back.

"I can't be with you, Nicholas." Those words cut like a knife. "You represent everything I've spent my whole life running from."

I tried to hold on to her, but she ducked under me, fire shooting from her honey-colored eyes.

"Don't you dare put your hands on me!" she screamed. "If you want to solve everything with your fists, that's your problem, but don't do it in front of me!"

I wanted to say something, but she turned around and headed for the hotel.

"You're an idiot, Nick," Jenna said, hurrying after her.

A hand came to rest on my shoulder. I wanted to shove it away, but I didn't.

"You fucked up, dude," Lion said.

"Leave me alone."

31

Noah

I STILL COULDN'T BELIEVE THINGS HAD GOTTEN SO OUT OF HAND. One minute you were dancing with a guy, the next you were almost falling over while the guy you wished would ask you out onto the dance floor was pounding the hell out of the dumbass who kissed you without asking. I'd have gotten rid of him on my own if I'd had time, but Nicholas had gone berserk before I'd gotten the chance.

I hated violence above all else. I'd seen too much of it, and I knew it was always the problem, never the answer. I didn't want to be with a guy who was violent. Nicholas had already shown me he was quick to use his fists when things got ugly, but like a fool, I'd overlooked that detail because what I felt for Nick was stronger than anything I'd felt for anyone. The past few days with him had been amazing. I'd even started to open up to him, but after tonight, it was over. He was revealing he was just a jealous tough guy trying to mark his territory, and I didn't like that one bit. I'd been terrified when he'd grabbed my shoulders, and I'd seen how furious he was. I couldn't be with anyone who scared me; that was a deal breaker.

When Jenna and I got to our hotel room, she was still raging about Nick's behavior at the same time as she begged me to forgive him, but I didn't care, I just wanted to get into bed. The day hadn't ended the way I'd planned, and all I could think about was getting back home and looking at things from a clearer perspective.

An hour later, I heard a noise in the hallway. I knew Nick had stayed out late, and I was worried about him. I got up and went to the door, cracking it to glance out into the hall. What I saw made me freeze.

Nick wasn't alone. He had a girl pinned between him and the door. They were making out. He was feeling her up.

I didn't know if I made a noise, but Nick seemed to realize I was there. He turned and looked at me. Letting the girl go, he turned toward me, covered his eyes with his hands, and started walking over to me.

"Dammit, Noah," he said, the girl's lipstick still on his lips.

I turned around and shut the door in his face.

I didn't sleep all night.

The next morning, I was so tired I felt sick, and my head hurt. I didn't even bother caring about my appearance. Since arriving, I'd tried to look pretty for Nick, but what was the point? In the end, the obvious thing had happened. Nicholas was violent and a womanizer. He'd been deceiving me, and like an idiot, I'd fallen for it. I didn't even want to see his face.

I didn't know what had happened afterward, but I couldn't get out of my head that image of her touching his body, her mouth on his... He'd freaked out when that guy had kissed me in the club, and I hadn't even wanted it...and what he'd done was way worse.

Jenna noticed how quiet I was, and as she was getting ready, she tried to distract me with jokes and comments about the weather and air traffic. I didn't know how I'd manage to avoid Nicholas the whole trip back, but I was determined to do so.

When we dragged our suitcases out of the hotel room and reached the elevator, I saw him. His hair looked like he'd been pulling on it, and he was sitting in a chair with his elbows propped on his knees, staring into his hands. When he heard us, he looked up.

"Noah," he said, and just hearing my name in his voice made me want to cry.

"Stay away from me," I ordered him. Jenna was aghast, with no idea what to say or do.

He came over, and I could see the bags under his eyes.

"Noah, please, I'm sorry about last night. I was drunk and didn't know what I was doing." He tried to grab my hand, but I pulled it away. Even in this state, he was stunning, and I hated myself for still feeling something for him. I'd need to work on that.

"I don't want you near me ever again. Whatever there was between us, it's done. We should never have started this. It's been a mistake since the beginning."

In his eyes, I saw thousands of feelings: anger, remorse, pain, shame…

"I was drunk, Noah… I didn't know what I was doing."

I observed him without reacting.

"Fine, but I do know what I'm doing now. I want us to be stepbrother and stepsister again. That's all you are for me. My mother's new husband's kid. Nothing more."

The elevator arrived, and I got inside. Jenna did, too, while Nick turned around and walked off. I didn't know what was in store for us, but all I wanted was for that weekend to be over. For the first time in ages, I wanted to be with my mother. I wanted her to surround me with her arms and tell me everything would be all right.

The flight seemed to last forever. I didn't know if my impatience was evident from my face, but all three of them left me alone the whole time. When we dropped off Jenna and Lion, a silence fell over the car. I looked out the window. I didn't want to be there. I wanted him as far as possible from me; I felt betrayed in a way I never had been before. For a moment, I'd thought happiness was possible, thought I'd touched it with my fingertips. I could almost see a future with Nick, but that had fallen apart as quickly as it had arisen. My eyes were burning from the urge to cry. I could still see Nick hitting that guy; it was almost like a clip from a horror film. And then there was him with the girl. I'd known since that moment that what I felt for him was much stronger than I'd realized. That had been even worse than seeing Dan with my best friend.

I felt a tear slip down my cheek, and before I could wipe it away, his fingers were on my skin, stealing something that wasn't his. I slapped him away.

"Don't touch me, Nicholas!" I ordered him, grateful that I hadn't burst completely into tears.

He looked as if my rejection had hurt him, but that must have been a lie: Nicholas didn't feel anything for me. He'd proven that.

Just then, he stopped the car. I looked outside and saw we were still far from home.

"What are you doing?" I asked, disoriented, angry, stunned. I felt vulnerable, and I needed to be away from him.

He turned.

"You have to forgive me," he begged.

I shook my head. I wasn't going to go on listening to him. I didn't even want to be in the same car as him. I unbuckled my seat belt and got out. I didn't care if we were in the middle of the road.

I heard him running after me as fast as he could. I tried to get away, but soon he'd gotten hold of me and was jerking me around to face him.

"I'm sorry, Noah," he said. "I didn't want to do it. I'm not used to this. Don't you get it? I've never felt this for anyone, and yesterday when I saw... I almost lost it. That idiot kissing you, I mean."

"So what do you think I felt when I saw you split his face open?!" I shouted, trying to avoid his grasp. "Admiration? Gratitude? No! I was scared! I already told you, I don't like violence! And then, to top it off, you hook up with someone right outside my door!"

When he heard me, Nick let me go, almost as if he'd been electrocuted.

"Are you scared of me?" he asked.

I knew I was on the verge of falling apart, but I nodded anyway.

"I would never lay a finger on you," he said. "I don't know what happened to you in the past, Noah, but whatever it was, I promise—I will never hurt you."

I shook my head.

"You already did, Nicholas."

He tried to say something, but I interrupted him.

"Please just take me home."

We didn't talk the rest of the way, and once we got there, I took my suitcases straight to my room after saying hello to my mother and William. Nicholas didn't even stay behind. Once he'd taken out our bags, he got back into his car. I didn't care, not anymore; I never did, or at least I kept trying to tell myself that.

The next morning, a letter came for me. I was supposed to hang out with Jenna, Lion, and Mario, and I left it in the passenger seat as I drove to the place we were meeting. There was no return address, and I opened it after I got out of the car to wait.

I'd never imagined what I'd find in it. When I started to read, my heart sped up, and I felt the blood drain from my face.

I'm writing you this letter because I hate you more than anyone in the world. Watch your back, Noah.

A.

Those words burned into my mind like fire. No one had ever said anything like that to me before, and I felt my hands start to shake. Somebody must have dropped the letter in our mailbox because there was no stamp. A? Who the hell was A? The first person to come into my head was Anna, but it couldn't be her. She was a bitch, but I didn't think she was capable of something like that. Then I thought of Ronnie and the threat he'd made to Nicholas, but why would he write A? I didn't know anyone whose name started with that letter... This was insane. I was scared, but I decided to consider it a joke. No one was going to hurt me, not in that city, not at my home.

"What's up?" a familiar voice asked. It was Mario. I'd invited him because he hadn't stopped sending me messages since I left for the Bahamas. Mario and I had had a *moment*, so to speak—we had kissed, but it had seemed to mean more to him than it did to me. I'd been planning on putting the brakes on anything romantic with him, but after what had happened with Nicholas, I wasn't so sure. Mario was nice, gentle, caring; he respected me, and he seemed genuinely interested in me. I knew I was lying to myself, but I wanted to be with someone normal for once in my life, find a person who could make me happy and who respected me as a person, and Mario seemed perfect.

I smiled at him. I doubt I looked very convincing, especially because I still had that letter in my head. I stuffed it into my pants pocket and tried to put on a happy face.

"Nothing. I'm good," I responded, giving him a hug. We were going to a bowling alley. I wasn't a pro at bowling, but I was going to try to have fun, distract myself, and forget about Nick.

Jenna and Lion arrived just then. She hugged me; she knew I wasn't doing well and wouldn't want to talk about what was happening. Lion didn't seem to know how to act.

I smiled at him anyway, and the four of us walked inside. The place was huge, with people playing and eating snacks all around. The noise of balls striking the pins echoed regularly through the room. I felt good with all those people around yelling when someone got a strike.

While we were waiting for our shoes, Mario asked whether I really didn't know how to play.

"Don't laugh at me," I said. "Anyway, throwing a ball on the ground can't be that hard."

"Well, I'm glad you came," he said. His brown eyes were so different from Nick's. "I know something happened with you and Nicholas," he continued, and I had to look away. I didn't want to talk about Nick, and certainly not with Mario. "I don't care, though, Noah. I just want you to give me a chance. Nick's no good for you. I'm not saying that because I want a shot, I'm just telling you the truth. He's not a one-woman guy, and you deserve someone better than him."

He was right, I thought, but at the same time, part of me wanted to defend Nick, tell Mario he was wrong, say that Nick could change, that I could make him change.

How naive.

"I can't be with anyone right now," I declared. "I don't want to hurt you, but I need you to understand." I cursed myself just then for not being able to love the right people for me.

He came close and ran a finger over my cheek, leaving behind a warm feeling.

"I'd be happy just to be your friend. *For now.*" He grabbed his shoes. I did the same, not really grasping what he'd just said to me.

————————

Bowling turned out to be far more difficult than I'd imagined. I started off watching until I finally dared to go myself. I didn't manage to knock even one pin over. Everyone laughed at me and it got to me. I couldn't help it—I was very competitive.

When I started to get the hang of it, I got a little too motivated. I rolled the ball too hard, it slipped, and I fell on my back on the lane. But that wasn't all—my fingers were stuck in the ball, and it wound up on my stomach.

It went without saying that it hurt, and I was terribly embarrassed to boot. I almost threw up, and when I stood, I was seeing stars. At first people laughed at me, but then they came over to see if I was okay. I wasn't going to die, but the side of my hip was hurting so badly I could nearly cry.

"Let's go to the hospital," Mario said.

"Noah, when you fell, you hit your head. You need to see a doctor," Jenna urged me.

"I'm fine!" I shouted. Actually I was aching, but in less than an hour, I had to go to work at the bar. I'd already missed a day for the Bahamas, so there was no getting out of it.

Seeing how angry I was getting, everyone laid off me.

"Are you sure you don't want me to take you?" Mario asked for the eighth time in a minute. When he saw my scowl, he threw his hands up to let me know he'd given up.

"Okay, okay!" he said, laughing. "But put some ice on it, and if you get sick or anything happens, call me. I'll take you to the hospital."

Ugh… I had to get out of there now.

"Thanks, Mario," I said, kissing him on the cheek and getting into my car.

A half hour later, I was walking through the door to Bar 48. I didn't love working, but on that day in particular, it was the last place I wanted to be. I'd lied to everyone—actually I wasn't fine at all. My side was hurting, and my head felt like it was going to explode.

"Hey, girl," said Jenni, one of the waitresses working that shift. She was nice, even if we didn't have much in common. "You're in a good mood, bitch," she said, smacking her gum.

See what I mean?

I changed into my work shirt and got started. It was a Thursday, but the place was packed. I got off at ten, and I couldn't wait to get back home.

"Hey, Noah," my boss said. He was breaking his back serving drinks. "Any way you can stay late tonight? You can make back your hours from the other day."

No, please! I wanted to shout, but there was nothing I could do. I scuttled off briefly to the break room, made myself a little ice pack, and pressed it against my forehead. That jabbing pain wouldn't go away, and I was feeling worse by the second.

I kept on working even though I had to step off the floor twice to vomit in the staff bathroom. Something was evidently wrong, and I started to wonder if I really should go to the hospital. I washed my mouth out. When I emerged, I nearly had a heart attack: Ronnie was there. He was standing in the corner with a group of guys. I was terrified. That letter in my pocket felt like it was burning, and I had the urge to take off running. I could still remember his face as he was shooting at me.

"Take care of those guys," my boss ordered me, passing me a tray of shots. Shit. I wasn't even supposed to serve alcohol, but we were so busy they didn't care about breaking the rules. I tried to ask Jenni for help, but she was even busier than I was.

I grabbed the tray and set the shots down quickly, hoping against hope they wouldn't notice me.

"I can't believe it," Ronnie said, grabbing my arm.

"Let me go." I tried to keep a cool head.

"Oh, come on, stick around a while." I could feel his hatred for me, his contempt. I'd humiliated him, and a person like him couldn't let that go.

His friends were cracking up. I didn't know what to do. With all those people there, my boss couldn't even see me.

"What do you want, Ronnie?" I asked between clenched teeth.

"I'd like to fuck you every which way, how about that?" His friends started laughing.

"You better let me go if you don't want me to have the door guy toss you out on your ass," I threatened.

"How's your boyfriend?" he continued. "Last time I saw him, he was crying like a baby asking for us to leave him alone."

I remembered the beating Nick had received—the beating that had been my fault—and the nausea I'd felt that whole afternoon returned.

"Let me go—you're hurting me," I said, twisting my wrist in his iron grip.

"You listen to me real close," he said, pulling me closer so I could see his repulsive mouth moving. "You tell Nicholas that—"

Just then, an arm wrapped around my waist, a dull thud knocked Ronnie away, and all at once, Nicholas was in front of me, blocking me with his body.

"What should she tell me?" he asked calmly.

Ronnie smiled and stood up, face-to-face with him.

My heart started pounding. *Not again, please.*

"Hey, we missed you, bruh," he said with a dark smile that horrified me. "You don't come around no more... It's like you've gone soft."

"Leave Noah alone," Nick said, the muscles in his body all tense.

"Or what?" Ronnie stepped forward until their noses were touching.

I grabbed Nicholas's hand.

"Nicholas, don't do it," I whispered. I knew he'd heard me. Ronnie, too. Nick pressed his fist into Ronnie's chest and pushed him away.

"Stay out of my life, Ronnie. You don't want problems with me. There are too many witnesses here for you to risk going back to jail."

Ronnie clenched his teeth and forced a grin.

Just then, the manager walked over with the door guy.

"You two," he said to Ronnie and Nick, "out of here, now."

I was trembling all over.

I followed them outside. Nicholas went to his car and Ronnie to his—or, rather, to Nick's Ferrari. He shot past Nick and vanished down the street. I walked over to Nick with a strange feeling in my chest.

"Are you okay?" he asked me, looking at my face with worry.

"Yeah, I'm fine, I just…" Suddenly a strange feeling overtook me. I couldn't see Nick clearly anymore, and everything went dark.

32

Nick

I GRABBED HER AS SHE WAS ABOUT TO HIT THE GROUND, CURSED, dragged her around to the other side of the car, and laid her in the passenger seat.

She'd fainted. I shouted to the security guy to bring me a bottle of water. Slowly, Noah came to.

"Hey, Noah," I said, bringing the bottle to her lips. "Here, take a drink."

She opened her eyes and grabbed it, taking little sips.

"What happened?" she asked, looking all around. "Where's Ronnie?"

I breathed a sigh of relief, knowing she was all right.

"He left," I said, leaning on the headrest. "Dammit, Noah, you scared the hell out of me."

Pale as a ghost, she said, "I'm all right."

"No, you're not," I said. "Lion told me you fell when you were bowling and hit your head, but you refused to go to the hospital."

"I didn't go to the hospital because I already know what they're going to tell me. That I need to rest."

I was starting to lose patience.

"You could have a blood clot."

"That's not it."

By then, I'd stopped listening. I got in the car and took off toward the highway.

"What are you doing?"

"I'm taking you to the emergency room. You hit your head and passed out. Maybe you're okay playing with your life like that, but I'm not."

When we got there, Noah got out and walked into the emergency room on her own. She filled out the papers and waited for them to call her.

"I don't want you going in with me. Wait here."

"Come on, Noah."

"I'm serious."

I was angry at having to stay in the waiting room. I knew I'd screwed up with Noah, but it was killing me to think she was hurt and I couldn't be there to make her feel better. Ronnie wouldn't stop until he got what he wanted, and I was afraid things were only going to get worse.

I thought about calling Steve, my dad's security chief, and explaining the situation, but that would require me revealing too much. My father would learn what was going on and would want to call the police. If Ronnie heard the law was after him, he'd be three times as dangerous as he was now. Gang beefs had to be solved in the streets, but I couldn't do that if it meant losing Noah in the process. It had taken everything I'd had not to split his face open then and there, but I knew if I did, Noah would never forgive me.

To get her back, I'd need to rethink my relationship with violence. Noah had finally opened up to me, and we'd gotten closer. I had told her about my sister. I'd come to understand what it meant to love someone. I knew it, I knew I loved her now, I needed her to breathe... How could I have been so stupid?

Noah was the last person I wanted to see cry, the last person I wanted to hurt. I didn't know when things had changed so much or when I'd passed from hating her to feeling what I felt now, but all I knew was I didn't want to lose her.

She emerged from the exam room and walked toward me. I stood up, anxious.

"It's a minor concussion," she said.

Dammit. I knew it.

"It's not a big deal. They told me to come back if I feel light-headed or pass out, but as long as I get some rest, I'll be okay. I got a note to stay home from work and some pain pills for the headache."

I was so relieved, I reached out to touch her, but she jerked away before I could.

"Can you take me back to work? I want to get my car."

I was pissed, but I decided it was best to keep my mouth shut. I took her to the bar and followed her home to be sure she'd made it okay. I realized she wasn't going to let me close to her, especially not after this, so I went to Anna's.

Anna had reached out to me several times since my trip, and I knew I had to be honest with her: I'd let my hatred for my mother get the better of me, and I'd treated all women the same even when there were some who were incredible—in my case, one in particular I had to make mine no matter what.

When I stopped in front of Anna's house, she came out and walked over, looking unsettled.

She bent over to kiss me on the lips, but I pulled away automatically. My lips would only kiss one person from now on, and that person wasn't Anna.

"What's up, Nick?" she asked, wounded by my rejection. I

didn't want to hurt Anna; we'd known each other a long time. I wasn't as big a jerk as I acted like.

"We can't keep seeing each other, Anna," I said. The color drained from her cheeks, and her face looked shattered.

After a pause, she replied, "It's her, isn't it?" Her eyes started watering. Was this what I wanted—to make all the women around me cry?

"I'm in love with her." Confessing it aloud wasn't as hard as I'd thought. It was freeing, gratifying, the truth.

She swiftly wiped away her tears and said, "You're incapable of love, Nicholas." She was angry now. "I've spent years waiting for you to fall in love with me, doing everything I can to try to get you to open up just a little bit and make space for me, and all you've done is blow me off, use me...and now you're telling me you're in love with that high schooler?"

This wasn't going to be easy.

"I never wanted to hurt you, Anna," I said, but she shook her head.

"You know what?" she replied furiously. "I hope you never get what you want. You don't deserve to be loved, Nicholas. If Noah's smart, she'll stay away from you. You think you can live a life like yours, with a past like yours, and get a girl like that to fall in love with you?"

I balled up my fists. I wasn't in the mood for this shit, but part of me knew Anna was absolutely right. Trying to control myself, I told Anna goodbye. I could see the fury in her eyes as I started my car back up and pulled off.

———

I knew I'd have to work to get Noah to forgive me, but I had no idea how. When I got home that night, all I wanted was to see her, but she wasn't in her room. I ended up finding her in the living room asleep, with her head in her mother's lap. Raffaella was watching a movie and stroking Noah's long hair. She looked relaxed, and I felt a tightness in my chest when I saw her that I hadn't felt for ten years because of the fight, because I'd kissed that girl and she'd seen me, because I'd hurt her...and it also made me sad to see that relationship between her and her mother. It awakened memories I'd kept locked up in the back of my mind. My mother used to do the same thing. When I was just eight, she used to calm me down after I'd had a nightmare—her hand on my hair had been the perfect remedy to make me feel safe and relaxed. I still remembered all those nights when I'd fallen asleep crying, scared, waiting for her to come back, open the door to my room, calm me down the way she used to. I felt a pain deep in my chest, a pain that only ever went away when I was with Noah. I loved her. I needed her next to me to be a better person, to forget those bad memories. I needed her so I could feel loved.

Raffaella looked over and smiled.

"It's just like when she was a little girl," she whispered.

I nodded and wished I was the one doing it.

"I've never told you this, Ella, but I'm glad you're here, that you're both here," I said, not really aware of what I was doing. The words just came out of my mouth. But they were true. Noah had changed my life, had made it more interesting, had made me want to fight for something and not just give up—for her. I wanted her.

I was going to change, I was going to be a better person, and I was going to treat her the way she deserved, no matter the cost. I wasn't going to stop till I had her.

The next morning, I went downstairs for breakfast and saw Noah as always, with a bowl of cereal and a book. But she wasn't reading. She wasn't even eating. She just spun her spoon around in her bowl, her mind clearly elsewhere. When she heard me, she looked over and then turned to the pages of her book. Raffaella was there in her reading glasses looking at the paper.

"Good morning," she said. I poured myself a coffee and sat down across from Noah. I wanted her to look at me, wanted to see her react somehow to my presence. Even anger would have been fine, as long as she didn't ignore me—that was worse than a shout or an insult.

"Noah, aren't you going to eat?" her mother asked, a little louder than normal. Noah looked up, pushed away her bowl, and stood.

"I'm not hungry."

"Forget that, Miss. You didn't even have dinner yesterday. You better finish your breakfast," Ella ordered her.

Shit. Now Noah wasn't eating, and it was all my fault.

"Leave me alone, Mom," she said and walked out of the kitchen.

"What happened, Nicholas?" Ella asked me, taking off her glasses. I ignored her and got up.

"Nothing, don't worry." I caught up with Noah in the hallway.

"Hey, you!" I called her, hurrying to get in front of her.

"Move," she said.

"So you're not eating now?" I asked her. She didn't look right. She was haggard. "How are you, Noah? Don't lie. If you don't feel good, we need to go to the hospital."

"I'm just tired. I didn't sleep much."

I walked with her up to her bedroom.

"How long are you going to go without talking to me?" I asked.

"I'm talking to you now, right?" she replied, waiting for me to move away from her door.

"I mean talk to me, not bark at me, which is what you've been doing ever since we got home from the Bahamas," I said, trying my best to reach her the way I'd been able to before.

"I told you, Nicholas, this is over. Now move so I can get to my room."

Dammit.

33

Noah

I KNEW I'D BEEN AN IDIOT FOR NOT TAKING BETTER CARE OF myself. Things had piled up, and I'd let them get out of control. Nick, the letter, the fall, everything had gotten the better of me. Being with Nicholas had brought problems and suffering, more suffering that I knew, and I realized that I needed to let it all go. Not doing so was bad for me, and it was bad for him, too. It was painful to admit I wouldn't be able to hold on to him, but I realized it was right, even necessary, if I wanted to build a new life here, find a place for myself in this city, and put back together the shattered fragments of my heart.

So I got out of bed ready to leave all the bad things behind. I was supposed to go shopping with Jenna that afternoon. There was only one day left before class started, and even though I was nervous and scared, I was happy to leave the summer behind, start over, do better, get the old me back.

Thank God, Jenna was the type who sucked you in when you were with her, so I got distracted between her and the thoughts of what my first day at St. Marie's would be like. Jenna said it was an elitist school, and even if there were lots of different kinds of people there, they all had one thing in common: they were loaded. I didn't know how I'd fit in there, but before I could even blink, it was seven in the morning, the alarm was going off, and it was time for my first day of class.

My uniform, now properly tailored, was waiting for me on the chair by my desk, and when I emerged from the bathroom, I started dressing, unable to avoid feeling weird. The skirt was now about five inches above my knee, and the shirt fit snugly in all the right places. I put on my black shoes and looked at myself in the mirror. My lord, why did it have to be green—moss-green at that? Even worse, I had no idea how to tie a tie. Leaving it off for now, I grabbed my bag and walked out with the typical apprehension of the first day of school: typical for a six-year-old anyway, if not for a seventeen-year-old.

Mom was in the kitchen, dressed but looking sleepy, with a cup of coffee in her hand. Nicholas was sitting in front of her at the island. I'd hardly seen him since I'd come back from the hospital. One time he'd checked in on me, and even then, I'd pretended to be asleep. That was three days without talking. My mother said he hadn't even slept at home. I couldn't help but pause in the doorway to look at him briefly. His hair was disheveled, and he looked good in his jeans and his loose black shirt. I had to remind myself of everything that had happened.

"I have no idea how to put this stupid thing on. I need help," I said.

"Oh, Noah, you're so cute," my mom said, laughing. I frowned at her.

"Don't laugh. I look like an elf." I took a seat across from Nicholas, who was sitting there reading the paper with a slight, almost imperceptible smile on his face.

"I'll make your breakfast, and you can ask Nick to help you with the tie." I looked up, uncomfortable, as Nick laid down his paper and raised his eyebrows.

My mother put on music, so I alone could hear my pounding heartbeat. I didn't want Nick to touch me, but I didn't know how to tie that damned thing, and I didn't want to spend half an hour on YouTube watching tutorials about it. I stood up and walked over, eyes looking elsewhere.

Without getting up, he grabbed my waist and pulled me between his legs.

"Your uniform looks good," he said, trying to catch my eye.

"It's ridiculous, and I don't want you to talk to me," I hissed as his long fingers grazed my neck, trying to lift up the collar of my white shirt.

My mother, cooking and humming, had no idea what was happening ten feet away.

"I won't stop talking to you, and I will get you to change your mind about me," he said, bring his face closer to mine than was appropriate. "I want you for myself, Noah, and I won't stop until I have you."

What the hell? Had he lost his mind? This was Nicholas Leister—Mr. I Don't Belong to Anybody.

His fingers touched my neck, this time on purpose. It was so sensual, I had to close my eyes to concentrate on what I was really thinking, what I really wanted. And what I wanted was not to be hurt again by Nicholas—or any other guy, for that matter.

"You done?" I asked. He stopped and observed me. Then he quickly adjusted the knot and gave it an expert look.

"Yeah. Good luck on your first day." He got up and unexpectedly gave me a quick kiss on the cheek. I almost wanted to shout for him to hug me, hold me, take me to that stupid school in his car, kiss me until I passed out. But instead I stood there waiting to hear him go out the front door.

"Noah," my mother said from the other end of the kitchen. I'd gotten lost in thought and hadn't been listening to her. I turned as she set a cup of coffee in front of me along with a letter with no return address.

"This arrived this morning," she told me, drinking the last sip of her coffee. "It must be from someone around here. It doesn't even have a stamp on it or a return address. Do you have any idea who it could be from?"

I shook my head, took it with trembling hands, and opened it. My mother returned to her newspaper. I was glad she did because it meant she didn't notice how I turned completely white just then.

The handwriting was the same as the other day:

I'm watching you. You shouldn't be here. You shouldn't have ever come. PS. Good luck at your new school.

P.A.

I dropped it on the table in terror. This was really getting frightening. Who could be cruel enough to threaten me like that? Whoever it was had to know me pretty well because they knew I was starting school that day. Ronnie was the only person I could think of, and if that was true, then I only had one person to turn to, as much as I hated it.

I put the letter in my sweater pocket and stood up.

"Aren't you going to finish your breakfast?" my mother asked.

"I'm too nervous. I'll have something later," I said, running up to my room. I grabbed the letter from before that I'd hidden in my nightstand and placed it next to this one. I was right—the handwriting was the same, the length was almost the same, too, there was just one difference: the signature. *P.A.* Did that mean more than one person was writing me? How could I already have enemies here? I hid the letters in a drawer and tried not to think about them. I didn't want to be worried about something like this on my first day. If more came, I decided I'd say something to Nicholas. I didn't want to, but I knew he'd help.

I went downstairs again, and Mom and I got into her car and headed for school. She'd insisted on taking me. Now I regretted it. I'd have rather gone in my own car. Driving would have taken my mind off everything.

The front door of the main building was packed with students dressed in green. Some were sitting on the benches outside, others filing in. A few outside were finishing their last cigarette or just dragging the minutes on until the routine of school began. I remembered it had been the same at my school. People were already gathered into cliques and seemed happy to see their friends again after summer.

"Have a good day, honey," my mother said. I could tell she was stirred up.

"What the hell, Mom?" I asked, laughing.

She tried to act normal but failed dramatically.

"Hush. I'm just happy you get to go here, that's all." She wiped away a tear.

I shook my head and kissed her on the cheek.

"You're nuts, but I love you," I said, chuckling as I got out of the car.

She waved goodbye and left. As I walked toward the door, crossing the lawn and passing all the students still on the benches, someone appeared beside me, startling me.

"Oh my God, you look terrible!" Jenna said, shoving me. Seeing her in that uniform, glamorous as she normally was, cracked me up. Still, she was hot even in that god-awful green sweater and tie. Her legs were uncovered, her socks cute, her skirt very short. Mine wasn't long, either, but it was modest compared to hers and the other girls'.

"Shut up!" I said.

"Come on, I'll introduce you to my friends," she said, dragging me off to one of the benches. There were two girls and three guys there, among them Sophie and Sam, whom I'd met at the party.

"What's up, Noah?" Sam said. I remembered having to kiss him during that stupid game of Truth or Dare. He was blond and had attractive brown eyes, but at the same time, he had a mirthful air that made him look like a little boy to me. He stared me up and down. "You look good in that uniform."

I rolled my eyes. No one but Jenna looked good in this horrible get-up, thought the boys were sexy in their button-down shirts and black slacks. Sophie, the girl who'd been eyeing Nick at the party, stared at me, and I wondered what was passing through her mind. Next to her, a brown-haired girl with bright eyes glared at me. I almost felt like I recognized her.

"Noah, this is Sam, who you already know," Jenna said. I ignored her sarcastic tone. "This is Sophie, and this is Cassie, Anna's sister. I mentioned her that time at dinner." Now I realized why she looked familiar. She didn't seem to like me any more than her older sister did. I tried to avoid her stare, turning to the other two guys. One was brown-haired with glasses and very handsome, and the other was the usual blond-haired quarterback type. "This is Jackson and Mark."

"Hi," I said, smiling.

"So you're Nicholas Leister's new stepsister?" Jackson, the guy with the glasses, asked.

"The one and only," I said.

"You can't imagine how I envy you," Sophie said. She was evidently hung up on Nick, and I chastised myself for wanting to tell her he'd never be hers.

As Jenna and the guys finished their cigarettes, the bell rang.

"Torture time," Mark said, stubbing out his and throwing his backpack smoothly over his shoulder. "See you inside, Noah," he said with a smile.

As everyone else walked in, I went to the secretary's office to find out my class schedule and get the papers I needed. That was in another building, and as I made my way over, I looked all around. I couldn't help but feel someone was watching me, and I had a strange feeling in my chest as I went inside.

———————

The day sped by without incident. Jenna was popular and introduced me to tons of people as the hours passed. I wound up having her in almost all my classes except math and Spanish. Mark, the hot guy, and Sophie were in those two. Cassie was in most of my classes, too, and I realized she couldn't stand me over the course of the day. She tried to make me look stupid whenever she got the chance. She had a lot of friends; apparently her sister had been a legend in this school for millionaires, just like Nick. Everyone asked me about him, what he was doing, what it was like living with him, and so on. Some of them had been there for the race and had seen the fight I'd caused, and they felt that was reason enough to look down on me. Damn you, Nicholas Leister, was there anywhere you wouldn't screw my life up? Everyone was also talking about the party that Friday to celebrate the start of school and welcome the new kids. I didn't know what it would be like, really, but whenever it came up, everyone gave me weird looks.

When it was time to go home, my mother was outside waiting. She asked me about everyone and everything, but I was exhausted, and I didn't say much on the way home. All I could do was rest, and I was happy I didn't have to work that night at the bar. I lay down when I got home, but soon a familiar voice nearly made me jump out of bed.

"Wake up, sleepyhead!" it said. It had to be Jenna.

"What do you want?" I asked, opening my eyes from a deep sleep.

"Jackson and Mark have invited us over. Almost all the seniors will be there... You've got to come." Her smile was radiant.

"Jenna, it's a Monday. There's school tomorrow," I protested, knowing there was no point.

"So? The parties at the beginning of the year are always the best... Seriously, Noah, do you know how hard it's going to be to make you popular?"

I shook my head, sitting up.

"You're like a Martian sometimes," she complained. "Come on, take a shower and I'll choose your outfit."

She pulled me out of bed. As I took my hot shower, I tried to ignore her as best I could.

"What are you doing in there?" she shouted from the other side of the door.

I came out wrapped in a towel with my hair dripping. Jenna could be a pain when she felt like it. As I dried my hair sitting at my dressing table, I opened a drawer to take out my makeup and saw those envelopes again. Those dumb letters were ruining everything for me; I couldn't get them out of my head. I wanted to tell someone about them, but I worried that would only make things worse. I was mad at Nick, but I didn't want him getting into another fight, especially over me, and I knew that was exactly what would happen if I told him about the letters. I slammed the drawer shut and told myself again it was just a sick joke. Ronnie wasn't stupid enough to threaten me in a letter, and there were thousands of girls who hated me for the simple reason that I was Nick's new stepsister.

Looking at myself in the mirror, I told myself I did need a distraction, that there was no point staying there and ruminating on a problem it was best to forget. I put on my makeup, and Jenna left to do the same at her place. I focused on what I saw in the mirror. I didn't want to leave a second free for my worries. Once my makeup was on, I spent another half hour fooling with my hair and then tried on almost all the dresses Mom had bought me, most of them still on hangers with the price tags attached. I finally chose a swing skirt and a tight black top.

Just when I was about to call Jenna to ask what time she was picking me up, I heard screaming outside my door. Still barefoot, high heels in my hand, I looked out to see what was going on.

The shouts came from my mother and William's room. I walked out into the hall to hear better. They were arguing.

"What did you want me to do?" my mother shouted. She never shouted unless she was furious. I asked myself what William must have done to put her in such a mood.

"You should have told me!" William roared, even angrier than she. "You're my wife, for the love of God! After all this time... how could you hide a thing like that from me?"

There were many things my mother might have hidden, but only one that would drive a person crazy that way.

"I couldn't!" she replied.

As I was listening in, someone squeezed my hips, and I jumped in the air and dropped my shoes. Turning around scared, I screamed:

"What are you doing?"

Nick looked at me with curiosity.

"I should be asking you the same thing," he replied, not subtle as he looked at my clothing. I couldn't help checking out his torso, either, in that white shirt that fit him so snugly... What a contrast it made with that jet-black hair!

"Do you know why they're fighting?" I asked apprehensively.

He looked back and said a simple *no,* pressing his hands in the wall on either side of my face and imprisoning me against the wall. "So are you talking to me again?" he said, and I watched every movement of his lips.

I wanted to push him away, but I refused to touch him. If I put a single finger on his body, my resolve would shatter.

"How long are you planning on continuing like this?" he asked, frustrated.

"Until you understand I don't want you around me."

He grinned, but his eyes were still desperate.

"You're dying to kiss me."

I felt sick. I hated being this nervous, hated that what had started between us had ended up this way.

"I'm dying to kick you," I said.

He smiled, and I crossed my arms with indignation.

"You going out?" he added.

"Yeah."

"With Jenna?"

"No, with your dad," I replied sarcastically. "Do I even know anyone else?"

His hand slid from the wall to the side of my face, and he looked at me differently, so intensely I could hardly stand it.

"Don't make this harder than it is," I told him. As much as the distance hurt me, I wanted him to keep away from me. I couldn't forget what had happened as much as I wanted to, and I could no longer trust him.

His pain burned itself into my retinas. I didn't know what I was doing, denying my feelings for him, but I was scared to get close, scared to open my heart again, especially to someone like him. It was better to be alone so no one could control me or tell me what to say, or make me suffer.

That night I was going to forget everything, the letter, my stalker, and Nicholas. That night I was going to get drunk and let alcohol wash away all my grief.

34

Nick

I WAS DEAD ASLEEP WHEN MY PHONE BUZZED, WAKING ME UP. I rubbed my face and got a move on when I saw it was Jenna.

"You better have a good reason for waking me up at three a.m.," I grunted, closing my eyes and falling back into my mattress.

"Nick, I need you to come…Noah's in bad shape," she said. I got up, suddenly tense, and turned on the light.

"What is it? Is she hurt?" I said, crossing the room, already looking for something to wear.

"She's been throwing up for like half an hour. She's totally shit-faced."

I cursed and grabbed my keys.

"Tell me the address."

It took me fifteen minutes to get there. The place was packed, and I had to shove my way in. I looked in the living room and kitchen, and just as I was about to grab my phone and call Jenna back to ask where she was, I saw her walking downstairs.

"Where the hell is she?" I asked.

It wasn't Jenna's fault, but weren't they supposed to take care of each other? Not only was Jenna fine, she was 100 percent sober.

"We took her to the upstairs bedroom," she said, and I went up there, taking the steps two at a time. "I knew she was going too far, but she didn't want to listen to me, Nick." I ignored her as I passed through the doorway. Once inside, I kneeled down next to Noah. She was pale and sweaty, probably because she'd been vomiting so much.

"How long has she been like this?" I asked. No one responded, so I turned and yelled at Jenna. "How long?"

"She was throwing up for more than half an hour, and five minutes ago, she passed out…or maybe she's just asleep… I don't know, Nicholas, I'm sorry, I tried to get her to stop, but—"

"Drop it, Jenna," I said, noticing Lion walking in from the corner of my eye.

The girl next to Jenna gave me a serious look.

"I'm a med student. Relax. Her pulse is stable. She just overdid it. She needs to sleep, Tomorrow she'll have one hell of a hangover, but she's fine."

"How can you say she's fine?" I almost shouted, holding Noah's unconscious face in my hands, feeling like a nervous wreck.

"She just is. Take her home and keep an eye on her," the girl said.

"I'm sorry, Nick. I never thought this could happen," Jenna confessed.

"Honestly, I don't care what you have to say right now," I replied coldly, bending over and lifting Noah up. I was scared when she barely made a sound, but her breathing was normal. Her head leaned on my shoulder. I blamed myself once more for failing to protect her. It was my fault she was this way, but something didn't add up. As I walked down the stairs, I kept asking myself what the hell had happened to make her get drunk like that.

When I parked at home and turned to look at Noah, I couldn't help but feel an awful sense of déjà vu. The same night I'd met Noah, she'd ended up like this, but that was because someone had put drugs in her drink. That had been my fault, too, and remembering how I'd left her in the middle of the road made me realize what an asshole I'd been to her from the moment I laid eyes on her. I didn't deserve her, but it was too late now; I was caught in her trap.

I got out of the car and lifted her from the passenger side carefully. She was still out of it, and I had to hurry inside and get her upstairs. It was late, and I didn't want Raffaella to see her in that miserable state. Without thinking, I went straight to my room. I wouldn't take my eyes off her until she awakened. When I laid her on my bed, I couldn't help but think how I'd wished to have her here ever since the first time I'd seen her in her gorgeous dress. But instead, it had to be like this. I took off her shoes and turned on the small lamp on my nightstand. She hadn't even noticed the complete darkness that had surrounded us, and that made me nearly panic. What if she was worse than she looked? Should I take her to the hospital to have her examined? I decided not to because she was a minor and she could get in trouble for drinking, especially that much.

Her clothing was stained with vomit, and her skin had goose bumps. My mind frozen, I took off her skirt and her tights. I grabbed one of my T-shirts, but before I could put it on her, I noticed something: Noah had a long scar up one side of her stomach. I stared at it in shock... How could that have happened to her? It wasn't just an everyday scar; it was huge, and it must have needed dozens of stitches. I ran a finger over the smooth surface of that tear in the most beautiful body I'd ever seen. Sleeping, Noah pushed my hand away. Was that why she hadn't wanted to wear a bikini? Because of the scar? Finally, lots of little moments that were piled up in my head started to make sense:

the way she always wore a one-piece, the way she freaked out if anyone said something about her getting undressed, the way she'd been so uncomfortable during that game of Truth or Dare...

I saw Noah was a thousand miles away from me. There was so much I didn't know about her and so much I needed to protect her from. I pulled the T-shirt over her head and covered her with blankets.

What had happened to her? Who was the real Noah Morgan?

With those thoughts in my head, I lay down next to her, pulling her into my chest, wanting to protect her from everyone and everything. Something had happened to her. I was going to find out what.

35

Noah

IT WAS HELLISHLY HOT. I COULDN'T SEE A THING, AND I FELT LIKE I was choking. In an instant, I realized why it felt like it was a hundred degrees. A pair of arms was wrapped around me, pulling me into a warm, burly body. When I opened my eyes, I was shocked to see Nicholas, deep in sleep.

How had I gotten there? What was I doing in bed with him?

I looked down and saw I was dressed in a T-shirt that wasn't mine and that was every bit as big as a nightshirt.

I could hardly breathe. Someone had taken off my clothes.

Panic overtook me. I sat up as best I could, leaning into the headboard. Nicholas opened his eyes when he felt me move, getting up and looking at me cautiously.

"Are you okay?" he asked.

"What the fuck am I doing here?" I asked, hoping I'd been so drunk I couldn't remember changing in some bathroom.

"Jenna called me to pick you up. You were completely passed out." He looked bedraggled and had fallen asleep in his clothes.

"Then what happened?"

He seemed to be weighing his words. My heart was racing.

"I took off your clothes—they had vomit all over them—and I put you in bed."

I got up and walked to the other end of the room. I couldn't believe what he'd done.

"How could you?" I shouted. He couldn't know about my scar—he couldn't! That would open the door to a past I couldn't and wouldn't ever go back to.

He stood and walked over warily.

"Why are you being this way?" He was clearly angry and in pain. "Whatever it is that's bothering you, I don't care, and I'll never tell anyone. Noah, don't look at me like that. I'm worried about you."

"No!" I shrieked. "You can't be worried about something you don't know and never will know!"

I needed out, needed to be alone; things weren't going the way I wanted, nothing was. My stomach was in knots, and I wanted to burst into tears.

As I turned around, I saw him, looking at once confused and yet somehow decided.

"Don't make me tell you again," I said. "Stay away from me."

In a rage, he came close and grabbed me. I stood still, trying to control my breathing and my fear.

"You better get this through your head. I'm not going anywhere. I'm here for you, and when you're ready to tell me what the hell happened to you, you'll realize you were making a serious mistake trying to push me away."

I shoved my way past him. Thankfully he didn't resist.

"You're wrong. I don't need you," I said, grabbing my things off the ground.

I slammed the door on my way out.

———————

I wanted to cry, cry without stopping, let out all the anguish that was building up inside me. Nicholas had seen my scar. Now he knew something had happened to me, something I didn't want anyone to know, something I was ashamed of and had decided to bury deep down.

With trembling hands, I took off the T-shirt and got into the hot shower until my body warmed up because I felt frozen, ice-cold, inside and out. When I emerged from the bathroom and saw a white envelope on my bed, I thought I'd faint. Not again, not another letter, please, not today.

I grabbed the envelope. This was harassment; I needed to tell someone. I took out the paper inside and, getting hold of myself, started to read:

Remember what you did to me? I'll never forget that moment when you ruined everything. Absolutely everything. I hate you. I hate you and I hate your mother. You think you're important just because you've shacked up with a millionaire? You're just a couple of whores who have sold themselves for money, but that won't last. I'll make sure of that, and when I do, your days of fancy schools with uniforms will go bye-bye.

A.P.A.

This was getting worse and worse. I needed to tell my mother. But I stopped myself. Will was giving my mother enough to deal with. Yesterday they'd argued. The last thing I wanted was to worry her and tell her I already had enemies in this new city. No, I couldn't tell her about Ronnie, not without getting Nicholas into trouble. Those races were illegal, and if we went to the police, we'd have to tell them everything. Nicholas was twenty-two; that was old enough for prison, and if Ronnie got picked up, he wouldn't hesitate to spill the beans about Nicholas and my friends.

If I wasn't careful, things could go south.

I was scared to leave. I felt overwhelmed and sad, and all I wanted was to forget it all, just as I had the night before. Drinking until you passed out was bad, and I'd woken up with the worst hangover of my life, but it had been worth it. I'd done it because I couldn't handle all my problems, all the demons inside me. Nothing made any sense, everything was threatening to destroy me, and I just needed an easy way out.

I sat down and looked at the clock. In forty-five minutes, I was supposed to show up for my second day of class. Nothing could sound more preposterous just then. As if under a spell, I put on my uniform, feeling bad or guilty. The words of whoever had written that letter wormed their way inside me. It was true—I didn't deserve this life. It wasn't rightfully mine.

When I went downstairs, Nicholas was in the kitchen with his father, immersed in a conversation. They stopped talking when I came in.

"Where's Mom?" I asked, walking over to the refrigerator and taking out the milk.

"She's resting still. I'll take you to school today if it's all right," William said with a tense smile. The day before, my car had been making strange noises, and we had taken it to a garage. William looked more serious than normal. Whatever happened yesterday must have left my mother in bad shape if she didn't want to get out of bed. I nodded, making a mental note to find out what the hell had happened between them.

Thankfully, Nicholas hardly looked at me. I didn't want to see his face. Not knowing what he knew about me.

William took another sip of his coffee and turned to me.

"You ready, Noah?" he asked.

"As soon as you knot my tie, I will be." He smiled. It was the first time I'd ever asked him for anything directly. It was strange. Without realizing it, I'd come to trust him, and I felt comfortable enough that I wasn't afraid to ride alone with him.

The day passed mercifully quickly: Jenna couldn't stop apologizing for letting me drink so much, even if she shouldn't have. It was my fault, my fault alone. More girls who didn't even know me came up to ask me what it was like to live with Nicholas Leister. I guess I'd turned into the talk of the school, and everyone either wanted to criticize me or be my friend. Jenna told me that was the price of popularity and I'd better get used to it, but I just wanted to crawl under a rock and hide. Especially because of the haters who couldn't stand that I got to hang out with him whenever I wanted, and one of those was Cassie, Anna's sister. I didn't know what she was up to, but every time we looked at each other, she'd start whispering to whoever was next to her and laughing. It was childish, and I wasn't in the mood for childish nonsense. I ignored her and her groupies and spent the day with Jenna and her friends. Surprisingly, I liked them. They were making plans for parties and all kinds of other stuff.

On the way out, I didn't see my mother's car waiting for me, but as more people left, I did see someone crouching behind a tree and leering.

Ronnie.

Adrenaline flooded my body. If he was the one writing the letters, I was screwed. He smiled when he realized I'd seen him and motioned for me to come over. He was some ways off, but if he tried anything, he'd easily be seen. There were still enough students around that I didn't feel completely vulnerable. But where the hell was Mom?

I told myself I should just try to get it over with, and I walked over as resolutely as I could. When I was close enough, I looked at his nearly shaved head and the dozens of tattoos on his arms and neck.

"What?" I asked, cutting to the chase and trying to convince him he hadn't gotten to me.

He laughed.

"Not so fast, sugar. You know you look sexy in that naughty schoolgirl uniform. You're a bad little rich girl, I'd love to take it off and spank you," he said, coming out from behind the tree and standing up straight.

"You're gross, and if that's all you have to say…" I turned around to walk off, but he held me back.

"You think you can just humiliate me the way you did and come out smelling like roses?" he whispered into my ear. I tried to get away from him but couldn't, and a part of me wanted to listen anyway to figure out if he was the one sending the letters.

With all the self-control I could muster, I told him, "You're a sore loser, and if I were you, I'd find a new hobby."

"You're a frisky one," he replied. "I could use a girl like you, but if you open your mouth to spit some more of that bullshit, I promise you, I'll—"

"You'll what?" I asked, motioning behind me to be sure he knew doing anything to me there would be a stupid idea.

Thinking it over, he responded pensively, "I'll do it all, baby, you can believe that. Just give me a little time. Anyway, I got something for you, something I'll bet you didn't expect."

Then I saw it: the letter. It was him. Ronnie was the one threatening me.

"Your sick joke isn't as scary as it was before," I said, trying to keep a cool head. "What's to keep me from reporting you for stalking?"

He seemed to find that funny.

"I'm just the messenger, sugar," he said, stroking my face with the envelope. "Seems I'm not the only one who wants to get his hands on you."

I didn't get it. If he wasn't writing the letters, who the hell was?

Just as I reached out to grab it, a car pulled up.

"Get away from her!" Nicholas shouted. He jumped out and ran in front of me.

Ronnie didn't seem to care. Actually he smiled, as if this was what he'd wanted all along. I put the letter into my bag before Nicholas could see it.

"What the fuck are you doing here?" he shouted. He was clearly on edge.

Ronnie stared at us.

"I see I was right... You're trying to get between those legs too, aren't you, Nick?"

Nick stepped forward while I grabbed his arm, trying to hold him back.

"Don't do it," I said. Nick fighting that dirtbag again was the last thing I wanted.

"Listen to your little sister, Nick. You don't want to get into it with me. Not here."

But Nick wasn't scared. He stepped forward again, telling him, "Make sure I don't see you near her again or I swear to God it'll be the last time you ever see the light of day."

Ronnie smiled, winked at me, and got into his car. Once he'd disappeared, I broke down, shaking all over.

Nick clutched my face.

"Please tell me he didn't do anything to you."

I shook my head, trying to keep my emotions inside. I couldn't appear weak, not in front of him.

"I'm fine," I said. "Just take me home."

In the car, I managed to relax. I tucked my hands under my thighs to conceal my tremors. But still, I couldn't stop thinking about opening that letter. I told myself I wouldn't read it, that whatever was written there could only make things worse.

"What did he say, Noah?" Nick asked after a moment's silence. I didn't really know what to say.

"He threatened me," I replied. Vague but sincere.

He gripped the wheel tighter.

"How, exactly?"

I shook my head.

"It doesn't matter. What does matter is he wants revenge for the race."

"He won't lay a finger on you."

I was thankful for his preoccupation, but it wasn't necessary. I knew how to take care of myself.

"Of course he won't," I agreed...but was that the truth?

Back at home, William was in the living room with a group of lawyers, and when he saw me enter, he shut the door without even greeting me. It was strange, but I was more concerned with my mother then.

She looked tired and had bags under her eyes. She hugged me when she saw me. Whatever they were fighting about, it was clearly worse than I imagined.

"Are you okay, Mom?" I asked when she let me go.

"Of course," she replied, hardly convincing.

"Is everything all right between you and Will? You can tell me," I said, trying to get something out of her. She shook her head and gave me the fakest smile I'd seen in a long time.

"Everything is absolutely super, honey. Don't worry."

I nodded, but I couldn't stay there trying to get information out of her. I needed to read the letter Ronnie had given me.

I went to my room and took it out of my bag with my nerves feeling raw.

The letter contained just one sentence.

You stole everything from me and now you'll face the consequences.

P.A.P.A.

The letter fell out of my hand. And the memories returned.

The school bus had just dropped me off in front of my door. I was only eight. I had a drawing in my hand. I'd won a prize. My first prize. I wanted to tell my parents. I was running with a smile on my face, and then I saw.

My mother was on the floor surrounded by broken glass. He'd broken the table in the living room again. Blood was pouring out of her left cheek, her lip was split, and she had a black eye. But she got up as best she could when she saw me.

"Hey, honey!" she said in tears.

"Were you bad again, Mom?" I asked, stepping nervously toward her.

She nodded, and then a big strong man walked through the door.

"Go get washed up. I'll take care of her," my father said. My mother looked at us for a moment and then vanished behind her bedroom door.

I turned to him, still holding my picture.

"What did my precious little girl do?"

I was hyperventilating as the memories flooded in. I sat by the bed and hugged my knees. This couldn't be happening.

I was helping Mom cook, but she was anxious. Things weren't going well that day. She'd burned the bread; the pasta had gotten stuck to the pot. She knew what was going to happen, she knew, and she could feel the fear in her body. I was just a kid, but I understood that if you messed up the way my mom was messing up, you'd get in trouble.

"What the hell is this shit?" he said and got up, overturning the table brusquely. The plates and glasses crashed to the floor. I took off running and covered my ears with my hands and hummed a song, the same way I always did when that happened. That was what Mom told me I should do, and I didn't want to disobey her.

But even then, I could still hear the screams and the kicks and punches.

I felt the tears stream down my face. I had gone so long without remembering.

Papa smelled bad. That day was going to be an awful one. Whenever Papa smelled bad like that, it was always a bad sign. The shouting started soon afterward, and I heard something break. I ran to my room and locked the door. I got under the blankets and turned off the light. The darkness would protect me. The darkness was my friend...

Suddenly I came back to reality. This couldn't be happening again. I felt a sudden urge to vomit, ran to the bathroom, and expelled everything I'd eaten that day. I leaned against the sink and tucked my hands between my knees. I had to regain my composure somehow. My father was in jail. My father was in jail... He couldn't hurt me, he was locked up, in another country, thousands of miles away. But if so, who could be doing this?

No one knew my past, absolutely no one, just my mother, the social worker, and the court that had put my father away. I needed a distraction. One, at least.

I picked up the phone.

"Jenna?" I said a second later. "I need your help."

36

Nick

SOMETHING WAS GOING ON. NOAH WAS ACTING DIFFERENT, strange. Since we'd returned from her school, she hadn't come down from her room. I knew she wasn't well, and I wanted to see her. Since I'd seen that scar, alarms had started going off. Something had happened to her a long time ago, and something was happening now to make her act like this. Getting drunk until she passed out… That wasn't Noah, not the Noah I knew, not the one I'd fallen in love with.

She hardly spoke to me. I'd hurt her, and I deserved to be pushed away, but I couldn't let anything bad happen to her. I needed to protect her from that son of a bitch Ronnie, even if that meant following her around or watching her in secret.

My phone rang. I picked up and talked to my sister. I couldn't be there for her first day of school, and that broke my heart, but I also couldn't leave Noah alone. I felt guilty, but something told me I needed to be there with her. I told my sister I would visit as soon as I could and wished her a great day at school. I imagined her in her little uniform and her *Cars* backpack, and I was filled with remorse.

The days passed, and on Thursday, something knocked me back: I went up to my room after an exhausting day at college and heard laughter and noise coming from Noah's room. I threw the door open and found her with two guys and three girls. The room was smoky, and the dense odor was unmistakably marijuana. Jenna was there with that dumbass friend of hers Noah had kissed when they'd played spin the bottle. Sophie was there, too, in her uniform skirt and a red bra.

"What the hell is going on here?" I shouted when I saw the spectacle. At least Noah was fully dressed, but she had a little white joint smoking right between her fingers.

"Nicholas, get out!" she shouted, standing up.

I wanted to shake her and kick every single one of them out of there, but instead, I just stepped forward and took the joint out of her hand.

"What are you doing smoking this shit?"

She stood still for a moment and then shrugged indifferently. Her eyes were red, her pupils dilated. She was blazed.

"Everybody out!" I shouted.

The girls jumped and ran, while the two guys tried to bow up.

"What's with you, dude? We're just having fun," one of them said, trying to get in my face. With one look, he turned meek and said, "Okay, take it easy, bro," before gathering his things.

Noah rested her hands on her hips, defiant.

"Leave me alone!" she said, trying to get around me and through the door. I grabbed her by the arms and forced her to look at me.

"You want to tell me what the hell's going on with you?" I asked, furious.

She looked back, and I could see her eyes were hiding something dark, and yet she smiled at me joylessly.

"This is your world, Nicholas," she replied calmly. "I'm living your life, hanging out with your friends, and feeling like I don't have a care in the world. That's how you are, and that's how I'm supposed to be, too," she said and stepped back, pulling away from me.

I couldn't believe what I was hearing.

"You're out of control," I hissed at her. I didn't like what my eyes were seeing; I didn't like who the girl I was in love with was turning into. But when I thought about it, what she was doing and *how* she was doing it were the same things I had done before I met her. I was the one who'd gotten her into all this. It was my fault. It was my fault she was destroying herself.

In a way, we'd switched roles. She had shown up and dragged me out of the black hole I'd fallen into, but in doing so, she'd wound up taking my place.

"For the first time in my life, I feel like I'm in control, and I like it, so leave me be," she said, shoving me and walking out the door.

I stayed where I was. What could I do? Noah was hiding something, and she wasn't going to tell me what. I'd lost her trust a long time ago, and to get it back, I was going to have to play her game. I wanted to protect her, wanted to keep her away from where she was going, but how could I if she barely wanted to be in the same room as me?

Loving that girl was going to put an end to the last bit of patience I had.

That night, my father and Raffaella left for a meeting and spent the night in the Hilton downtown. I stayed home keeping my eye on Noah and making sure she didn't get into any more trouble. I didn't really know when I'd turned into her bodyguard, but something about her kept me from leaving her alone. I could hardly be under the same roof as her without wanting to get close to her and wrap her in my arms.

I was worried about the change in her behavior and especially about the possibility that she might start acting like the people around me. Her freshness, her natural innocence, had made me realize that outside the world I lived in, there was much that I didn't know, and seeing Noah transform into someone like me killed me inside.

It was after midnight when I heard the front door open. Noah had gone out with Jenna. I didn't know where, and by the time I'd asked her, she had already been peeling out in Lion's girlfriend's convertible. Now I walked to the door to see her. She was drunk again. She didn't even notice I was there. She was barefoot, shoes in one hand, purse in the other.

"Where are you coming from?" I asked. She was startled and scowled at me.

"What are you doing there? You scared me!" she responded, trying to keep her balance. After watching her nearly fall over, I picked her up, despite her protests, and took her to the bathroom, resting her on the counter while I turned on the shower.

"You've got a really weird way of trying to get me into bed, you know?" she said. But at least she wasn't screaming or trying to get away. Her eyes were glassy as I took off her coat. Her hair was messy, her cheeks were pink, and her lips looked fleshier than normal. Even drunk, she attracted me, and I had to keep a cool head to avoid taking her off to the bedroom the way I had the last time she was like this. I was angry, though, and her attitude worried me.

"When I finally do sleep with you, weird is the last thing it will be," I sat cuttingly as I took off her blouse and stared a second at her black-lace bra.

"Now I don't care what you do. You saw my scar, and it didn't gross you out, didn't even seem to scare you like it does me. It brings up a lot of bad memories, you know?" I stopped undressing her. I couldn't stand to see her naked; her body had too strong an effect on me. I hated that I couldn't stop obsessing over how good she looked even when she was talking about something so serious. When people were drunk, they told the truth. I needed to take advantage of the situation.

"Noah, what are you scared of?" I asked.

After a few seconds, she replied, her voice wavering:

"Right now, I'm scared of you."

I stood very still and tried not to make a sound. She was trembling, and I knew it was because I was touching her. She wanted me, I wasn't too stupid to see that, but I also knew she had feelings for me, however much she refused to accept them.

Her lips were an inch away from mine, and that lower lip of hers was begging for someone to kiss it, to nibble it. But I wouldn't. Not when she was in this state.

I lifted her up and set her directly under the cold water of the shower. She screamed when the water hit her skin, but she was too drunk to even put up a fight. She stayed there, freezing, silent under the water as it cascaded over her nearly naked body.

"This is what you get for acting like an idiot," I said. I wanted to get in, too. I could use it...

Once she was more or less clearheaded, I wrapped her in a towel and accompanied her to the bedroom. I could tell she was embarrassed about her behavior. Or, at least, I hoped she was.

"You a little better?" I asked when she leaned back against the pillows and looked up at me.

"Why are you doing this? Why are you making it so hard for me to hate you?"

"Why do you want to hate me?"

"Because if I let someone hurt me again, I don't think I'll be able to get over it," she said.

"I won't hurt you," I told her, and knew I was promising myself that as well.

Before turning over and falling asleep, she made a remark that cut me like a knife:

"You already have."

37

Noah

NO MORE LETTERS CAME, BUT THAT LAST ONE WAS SEARED INDELIBLY in my mind. The word *Papa* had caused those childhood memories I'd tried to hide from to reemerge. He'd been out of my life for six years; I hadn't even heard his name. As the days, weeks, months, and years had passed, my mind had grown a kind of shell that had protected me from the pain of remembering feelings or situations from that stage of my life. And I didn't want to go back there. There were a before and an after. For my mother, too. But now everything was back.

Just remembering what had happened in those days frightened me so deeply that I couldn't ignore it, and that was why I stayed out partying, drinking, doing anything I could to escape. I couldn't deal with it just then. I wasn't strong enough, not yet. I was still a girl; not enough time had passed. I needed to keep that darkness buried in my mind, and if that meant acting like an idiot, so be it. I knew what I was doing, and the numbing effects of alcohol were the only things that could still my heart and mind.

Anyway, my new friends didn't see anything strange about getting drunk almost every day, so I could do what I wanted without much effort. The only obstacle was Nick.

Since we'd come back from that stupid trip, he'd been acting like a real older brother. He chewed me out if I drank too much, he took care of me when I was drunk, he even put me in the shower to help me sober up. It was ridiculous and also confusing. I didn't want him to worry about me. I needed to face things on my own and in my way. When we were finally free of my father, I'd seen my mom get drunk that way. If it had helped her, why should I abstain?

All this was in my head that day as I went to school. I barely paid attention to my teachers. I hadn't even eaten since the night before. My stomach refused all nourishment, my mind was dead, and all this was the only way to keep my demons at bay.

Jenna took me home that day. My mother was gone with William again and wouldn't be home for a couple of days. I didn't know where they had gone, and I didn't care. A couple of times, I remembered my father's threats, and I got so scared I could hardly breathe. But he was far away, in jail, and couldn't get his hands on us. Still, though...how was Ronnie getting the letters?

I dropped my bag on the sofa and went to the kitchen. Nicholas was there with Lion. They looked up as soon as I entered.

"Hey, Noah," Lion said with a tense smile. Nick watched me but didn't move.

"Hey, your girlfriend just left," I said, walking over to the refrigerator and taking out a handful of grapes. On the table were the crusts of what I supposed were grilled cheese sandwiches. Thor hurried over, wagging his tail.

"Beat it, Thor," Nick said.

"Don't be a jerk, Nicholas. He's not bothering me," I responded. Glowering, he grabbed the dog by his collar and dragged him away.

"He's bothering me."

Lion laughed.

"You could cut the tension in here with a knife," he said, standing up. I put a grape in my mouth. "I should warn you, Noah, today is initiation day... Watch out."

"What's that?" I asked distractedly.

Nick seemed irritated at his remark, but Lion went on: "Today's the Friday of the first week of class. It's when they welcome in the newbies. And you're one of them. Jenna would kill me for telling you, but I feel bad for you."

"She's not going to that bullshit, so there's nothing to worry about," Nicholas said.

"I don't really follow, but if there's a party tonight, then, yeah, Nick, I am going," I said.

He shook his head. "Your mother told me you can't go out tonight. She says she doesn't want you away when she's not here. So I'm just following orders."

I laughed sarcastically.

"Since when do I pay attention to what you say?" I asked, eating another grape. They were delicious.

"Since I started staying here to keep my eye on you. You're not going anywhere, so don't bother arguing." This was surreal. Since when did I have to do what Nicholas Leister said?

"Listen up, Nicholas. I do what I want when I want, so you can drop the bodyguard act because there's no way I'm staying in on a Friday night."

I got up to leave. Lion was chuckling.

"This is like watching a tennis match," he said, but he turned meek when Nicholas gave him a piercing stare.

I walked past them to my room. I needed to decide what to wear.

Jenna called me around seven. The initiation party was a tradition at St. Marie's, and funny enough, it took place on campus. We had to sneak in. It was supposed to be the wildest party ever. The freshmen took care of the food and drinks and then cleaned up afterward, and they did such a good job, no one had ever been caught. Since I was a new senior, I was just there for the fun part. Jenna told me I should wear something comfortable, so I chose black jeans, a sleeveless T-shirt, and sandals, and I left my hair down. I needed almost no time to get ready, so I still had a half hour left before she'd pick me up.

I was about to head downstairs to grab dinner, but I ran into Nick even before I hit the steps. He seemed to be lurking outside my bedroom.

"Going somewhere?" he asked. I wanted to hate him, hate him and make his life impossible, and I was determined to try to do it even as another part of me wanted to drop everything and kiss him then and there.

"Are you planning on stalking me all night?" I asked. He hurried ahead of me and turned and faced me on the bottom stair.

"Nicholas, forget me, please."

I started to make a sandwich in the kitchen. I'd be drinking that night, and I needed something solid in my stomach. But as I was cutting the bread, a pair of hands grabbed me from behind, and a body pushed me into the counter. Feeling him that way after so long made me drop the knife I was holding. Despite my best efforts, I shivered when I felt his lips on my bare shoulder.

"Let me go, Nicholas." My body wanted that contact, but my mind shouted *Danger! Danger!*

But he kept kissing me, my ear, my neck. He pushed my hair aside, and that simple touch made me close my eyes with pleasure.

"I'm tired of playing this stupid game," he said, one hand against my stomach. "I wasn't lying when I said that what happened in the Bahamas would never happen again. I'm here for you if and when you need me, Noah... You want me, and I want you..."

As he attacked my neck again, I lost the thread of my thoughts. I did want him, and as he kissed me, all those thoughts about my father, about my past, dissolved. Nicholas Leister was at least as distracting as alcohol, probably more so.

I stretched my arm back and ran my hand through his hair, pulling his head toward my throat. He put his hands around my waist and turned me around swiftly.

"You want me to kiss you?" he asked.

What kind of stupid question was that?

"Stay home and we'll do more than that, I promise," he said, his lips approaching mine.

"Are you bribing me?" I asked him, baffled and maybe a little resentful. He had been kind with me recently, and he'd resisted fighting with Ronnie when he'd given me the last letter. But I still didn't know if I was ready to forgive him.

"That's an ugly word. I prefer the term 'seduction.'"

I let him kiss me. The feeling was marvelous but dizzying. Every time we touched each other, I felt a million different sensations, and this time was no different. But something had changed. He was kissing me with desperation. That frightened me, but when I felt the pressure of his tongue, I couldn't help but respond the same way.

"You staying?" he asked then, standing back.

We were both struggling to breathe normally.

I pressed my hands into his chest.

"I'm going, Nicholas. But thanks for distracting me."

And I left.

When we reached the school, we had to turn off the radio in Jenna's convertible and sneak in. The party was in the back, in the fitness complex, where the pool was. From there, no one would hear the music. It was thrilling to scurry under the fence with the other kids who were arriving at the same time. The darkness wasn't total—there were lampposts spread around—so we didn't worry about tripping or falling as we crossed the green. When we entered, we saw the pool itself, a weight room, the risers. Most of the kids from the high school were there, and everyone had a plastic cup in hand. Lots of them were swimming. The music was deafening. I turned to Jenna and laughed.

"Now this is a party."

———————

As the night went on, weird things started happening that I didn't like at all. The initiations for the new arrivals were really cruel. They tied one girl's hands and feet and threw her into the pool. The poor thing thrashed around and tried to stay afloat for ages until some kid finally dove in and saved her from drowning. As I saw her crying, I realized this party was different from what I'd imagined. There were many more *pranks* of this kind. They stripped this kid with a face full of zits down to his underwear and laughed at him. They made someone else eat this gross plate of mashed-up something or other and he ran off and threw up.

What the hell was up with these people?

The scene didn't seem to be getting any more pleasant, so I decided to go. Unlike me, Jenna was having a blast, but then, she didn't even know what was going on; Lion had taken her off somewhere to make out. So that meant I was alone and surrounded by idiots. I grabbed my phone and sent Nick a text.

You said before you'd be here if I needed you... Can you come pick me up?

A minute later, I had my answer:

I'll be waiting for you in the back parking lot.

He must have already known where the party was, and I told myself that if I found out Nicholas had pulled those same kinds of pranks in the past, I really would need to stay away from him. I didn't like the vibe there at all, and I wanted to go.

At the door to the gym, four dickheads plus Cassie and her little girlfriends kept me from going outside. I wondered what the hell they wanted.

"Let me through," I said.

Cassie smiled.

"You're a newbie, too," she said.

Oh no.

"You've got to pass your initiation, Noah, just like everyone else," one of the big guys said.

"Don't you dare put one finger on me," I said, feeling the panic invade me. By then, the other guys had already surrounded me, blocking my path.

"A little bird told us someone's scared of the dark," Cassie said in a voice that reminded me too much of her sister. Had she been the one to come up with this idea? "You're a big girl now, though, so it's high time you got over your fears."

My heart stopped. Was she suggesting…

My nightmares came true when two guys three times bigger than me grabbed me from behind.

"Let me go!" I shrieked as panic flooded my body. "Let me go!" I repeated as they carried me off to a closet where they kept swimming equipment.

"It'll just be for a bit," one of the guys said as I shook all over trying to get free.

"*Please. No!*" I screeched. Everyone behind me laughed and laughed.

Mom had left. Papa and I would be alone that night. I knew things would turn out bad. He stank; he smelled like that bottle I spilled that time without meaning to. I was scared Mom was gone because if Mom wasn't there, he'd get mad at me. He never hurt me, but he'd threatened to many times.

When he got home, dinner was on the table. Mom had made it, and I had to heat it up... When he brought his fork to his mouth, I knew something was wrong. His face transformed, his eyes narrowed, and he overturned the table, scattering all the plates and glasses on the floor and making a huge mess. I crawled to a corner and curled up in a ball. I was scared; now was when the shouting and beating and blood came... But Mom wasn't there, so what would happen this time?

"Ella!" he shouted. "What is this shit?"

I curled up more, remembering suddenly that I hadn't put the sauce on the meat and potatoes. I must have left it in the refrigerator... I'd forgotten, and now Papa was mad.

"Where the fuck are you?" he shouted as fear gripped my entire body. When he started breaking things and shouting, I was supposed to go to my room. I ran toward it, and before I could stop myself, I slammed the door shut. I crept under the covers.

Papa kept shouting. He was angrier with every second that passed. I guess he didn't remember Mom was away that night; she'd gone in at her job, and he was supposed to take care of me till she got back. As I heard the doors slam in succession, I knew he was getting closer to my room. I curled up even tighter as I heard the creak of the door opening.

"Here you are... You're playing in the dark today, huh?"

38

Nick

WHEN I GOT TO THE SCHOOL, I COULD SENSE SOMETHING WAS UP. I don't know if it was instinct or the little voice in my head, but I got out and walked straight for the fences. There were lots of kids standing around outside the fitness complex, so I headed in that direction. People's eyes were wide as they saw me show up. Some people were elbowing each other and pointing. Jenna and Lion were walking down the stands around the track headed toward the pool.

"What are you doing here?" Lion asked me.

"Have you seen Noah?" I asked. I had a bad feeling.

Jenna shrugged.

"I left her inside fifteen minutes ago."

I turned around and walked off with the two of them close behind.

Despite the surprise of those who saw me inside, the only things that penetrated my awareness were the screams coming from the back of the room. They were bloodcurdling. I was so terrified, I lost control of myself.

"Where is she?" I shouted, following her voice to the door of a closet. She was inside. They'd locked her in, and she was crying and pounding on the door trying to get out.

"*Let me out of here!*"

Trying to keep calm, I pulled on the door, but it wouldn't give, and I turned around, angrier than I'd ever been in my life.

"Who the fuck has the fucking key?"

Everyone around me looked clueless as Noah went on shrieking.

Terrified, Cassie suddenly showed up and reached her hand out with the key. I snatched it away so quickly, it almost cut her fingers.

"It was just a—"

"Shut up," I said, unlocking the door.

I only managed to see Noah for a second before she threw her arms around me and buried her face in my collarbone, sobbing and twitching from terror.

Noah was crying...*crying*. Since I met her, I'd never seen her shed a single tear, not when her boyfriend had cheated on her, not when we'd fought in the Bahamas, not when she'd gotten angry at her mother, not even when I had left her on the side of the road. I'd never seen her cry for real, but now she was completely broken down.

The circle of people standing around us had fallen silent.

"Go away!" Noah shouted at them. But no one moved. "I said go away!"

Those fucking brats had locked her up in a closet in total darkness.

"Nick, I..." Jenna said, looking at Noah with worry.

"Go, I'll take care of her," I said, holding Noah tightly.

When the room had cleared out, I sat on a riser with Noah on my lap. She was pale and couldn't stop moaning. This wasn't the Noah I knew. This Noah was completely destroyed.

"Nick…" she bawled.

"Shh…relax," I said, hugging her. I was terrified, too. All my fears had come true, and I could hardly keep a grip on myself. I just wanted to hold her, to keep her there in my arms so I'd know she was safe. I'd been so scared when I had gotten her message. I'd even thought Ronnie might have found her and was hurting her or worse.

"Make them go away," she said, shaking like a leaf.

"Who, babe?" I asked, stroking her hair.

"The nightmares," she said.

"Noah, you're awake," I said, wiping away her tears.

"No." She shook her head. "I need to forget… I need to forget what happened… Make me forget, Nick, make…" Then she leaned into me and kissed me. Her lips were damp from the tears and twitching from sorrow and terror.

"Noah, what's going on?" I asked.

"I just can't take it anymore," she said.

When she was done crying, I walked her to the car. She was melancholy, lost in thought, in thoughts probably no less intense than the memories that had assailed her when she was locked in that closet.

I kept my arm over her shoulder on the way home, driving with my left hand. She curled up as close to me as she could, as if I were her life raft. I wanted to teach a lesson to each one of those snot-noses at that stupid party, but first, I needed to make sure Noah was okay.

At home, I took her straight to my room. She didn't put up a fight. Once I closed the door, I turned on the light.

"You really scared me today," I said.

"I'm sorry," she said, tearing up again.

"Don't be, Noah. But you do need to tell me what happened. Not knowing is killing me, and I want to be able to protect you from all the things you're scared of."

She shook her head.

"I don't want to talk about that."

"Okay. Let me get you a T-shirt, though. You're sleeping with me tonight."

She didn't complain, not even when I took her old T-shirt off and slipped a fresh one over her head. She pulled down her pants and walked over to my bed and lay down after I pulled back the cover. I got in and pulled her into my chest, as I'd wanted to for so long. I'd fought against my feelings. I'd even deceived myself, trying to ignore what I felt for her through one-night stands and just pretending she didn't exist. I was afraid of what was happening to me; I had no defenses if it didn't turn out well. But I couldn't help it; I was in love with her. I felt what I felt, and there was no denying it. I couldn't swim against the current anymore. So I decided to tell her, take the risk, open my heart after twelve long years.

"Can you tell?" I asked her, seeing that she had her eyes open and was staring at me. "My heart never beats that way. Only when you're nearby."

She closed her eyes and remained still.

"Every time I see you, I'm dying to kiss you. Every time I touch you, the only thing I know is that I wish I could keep doing it the whole night long. Noah...I'm in love with you. Please stop pushing me away. You're just hurting both of us."

She opened her eyes again. There were tears in them; they seemed to be pleading.

"I'm scared of you hurting me, Nicholas." Her voice rent my heart.

I grabbed her face tightly.

"I won't. Never again. I promise," I said, and kissed her. I kissed her the way I'd always wanted to, with all the passion and feelings I had. I kissed her the way every man should be able to kiss a woman at least once in his life. I kissed her until we were both shivering. I only pulled away to plant my lips on her neck, to taste her the way I wanted to, the way I'd been longing to for what felt like forever.

"You drive me crazy, Noah," I confessed, kissing her all over, biting her earlobe, licking her tattoo.

She did something then that I'd never expected: she cupped my face and pressed her forehead into mine.

"If you love me, you have to hear the whole story," she said. Her honey-colored eyes glowed between her eyelashes, and her freckles looked adorable on her cheeks and her small nose.

"Tell me. Whatever it is, we'll get through it together."

She seemed to be deciding whether to continue. She took a deep breath, let it out, and began:

"When I was eleven years old, my father tried to kill me."

3 9

Noah

I KNEW THE TIME HAD COME TO BE SINCERE, BUT I WAS SCARED TO unearth those memories. Just the thought of breaking down again as I had in that closet filled me with despair. But Nicholas had told me he was in love with me, so how could I resist?

"My father was an alcoholic. I barely remember him any other way. He was a NASCAR driver. I lied when I said it was my uncle. When he broke his leg, he had to give up racing. He changed, he stopped eating, stopped smiling, and the rage and pain just ate him up inside. I was eight the first time he hit my mother. I remember it because I was there. Wrong place at the wrong time, I guess. I fell off my chair when he was doing it and ended up having to go to the hospital. But he never actually touched me until I was eleven. My mother he beat almost every single day. It was so routine I thought it was normal… She couldn't leave him, she didn't have anywhere else to go, and she didn't make enough money to take care of me. My father had a retirement account from racing, and we could get by on that, but like I said, he was a drunk. When he came home after a night at the bars, he took all his frustrations out on Mom. He almost beat her to death twice, but no one helped her, no one had anything to offer her, and she was scared that if she called the cops, she'd end up losing custody of me. I learned to live with it, and anytime I heard that thudding sound or my mother screaming, I'd go to my room and hide under the covers. I'd turn off all the lights and wait for it to end. But this one time, that wasn't enough... My mother had to be gone two days for work, and she left me with him, thinking since he'd never turned on me, I'd be safe..."

It was as if I were reliving it just then. "He showed up drunk, overturned the table... I hid, but he finally found me..."

When I heard those words, I knew Papa was going to hurt me. I wanted to tell him it was me, not Mom, but Noah, but he was so drunk he didn't even care or didn't notice. Everything was dark; I couldn't even see the least glimmer of light.

"You want to play hide-and-seek?" he shouted, and I pulled the sheets tightly around me. "Since when have you been hiding from me, you little slut?"

The first blow came right afterward, then the second, then the third. I didn't know how, but I ended up on the ground, screaming and crying as he hit me. Papa wasn't used to that, and it made him even madder. Where was Mom? Was this what she felt every time he got angry with her?

He hit me in the stomach, and I couldn't breathe...

"You're going to learn what you get if you don't treat the man of the house the way he deserves," he said as he took off his belt. He'd often threatened to hit me with it, but he'd never actually done it. Now he did, and it hurt. I stood up, trying to get away, and he struck the window in my room. The shattered glass fell all over; I could feel the shards cutting my knees and the palms of my hands as I tried to crawl away...

He just kept getting madder. He didn't seem to even recognize me. It was like he had no idea that the person he was beating was an eleven-year-old girl...

"He didn't kill me, but he came close. I slipped past him and jumped out the window. The scar on my stomach is where I cut myself on the windowpane." I teared up again, but this time, I kept talking through it. "The neighbors heard me screaming, and the cops showed up right afterward. For two months, I was a ward of the state, living in a group home, because after what happened, they didn't think my mother was fit to look after me. The funny thing is I got hit more in those two months than I ever did living with my dad. Finally they let me go back to Mom's and they put Papa in jail. The last time I saw him was when I had to testify against him. There was so much hate in his eyes... I never saw him again."

I stopped talking, waiting for an answer...that didn't come.

"Say something," I said.

He looked down, as if trying to hide something.

"So that's why you're afraid of the dark."

"The darkness brings back those memories, and I panic... If you hadn't shown up when you did, it would have probably gotten a lot worse... I had a bad panic attack like that when I was in the group home. It was horrible." I tried to smile, but his face remained tense as he reached out and touched me.

I exhaled all the air I'd been holding in. I still remembered when I had been about to tell Dan about all that. But he'd frozen, and I'd made it no further than when my father was beating my mom.

"I sent my own father to prison. That must make you rethink your feelings about me, no?"

"Noah," he said, shocked, "you did the right thing. All I want is to be there for you and protect you with my life if I have to. That's what I'm feeling right now, and I swear to you, those fuckers who stuck you in the closet, I'll kill them with my bare hands."

"Nicholas, I'm damaged goods."

"Don't ever say that again," he ordered me, angry that I'd even said it.

I felt a cascade over my cheeks and lips as I started crying again.

"Nick... I might not be able to have kids." That was my biggest secret, the one that hurt the most. The worst consequence of that night. "Because of how hard he hit me... The doctors said they don't think I'll be able to get pregnant...*ever.*"

He pulled me into him.

"You're the bravest, most amazing woman I've ever met," he said, kissing me on top of the head. "You'll be able to have kids. I know you will...and if not, you can adopt one. There's no one who would make a better mother than you...hear me?" He got on top of me and stared me straight in the eyes.

"I love you, Noah," he said then, and I froze. "I love you more than my own life, and when the time comes, I'm going to give you the most precious children the world has ever seen because you're beautiful and I know you'll make it through all this shit...and I'll be right beside you to make sure of it."

"You don't know what you're saying," I responded, at once frightened and relieved.

"I know exactly what I'm saying. I'm saying I want to be with you, I want to kiss you whenever I feel like it, I want to protect you from anyone who tries to hurt you, and I want you to need me in your life..."

I couldn't believe what I was hearing.

"I love you, Nick," I declared. I'd had no idea I would say it. But it was the truth, the absolute truth. "I've tried to ignore my feelings for you, to hide from them…but I love you… I love you like crazy, and I want all the things you just said, I want you to be with me, and I want you to love me because I need you, I need you more than the air I breathe…"

"I need to kiss you," he said.

"Then do it," I replied.

"You don't understand. I need to kiss you all over…touch you, feel your skin… I want you to be mine, Noah…in every sense of the word. I've never felt that for anyone…and it scares me… It scares me because I feel like I'm going crazy."

I pulled him into me. He was lost, I could see it in his eyes. Nicholas had never in his life been with a woman for more than a few hours. He didn't know what commitment was, but since he'd confessed his love to me, he seemed like a totally different person. I loved him, too; I could feel it in my heart, in the way my body reacted when he touched me, when he was near. I was in love, and I was scared, just like him, and this had nothing to do with what it felt like when I was with Dan. This was so much more, so much better, so intense.

He pulled my hips toward him, squeezing me so tightly it hurt, but I didn't care once his lips touched mine and kissed me passionately. I felt him all over; his arms were strong and clutching me, but at the same time, he was gentle, as if he knew I was fragile and didn't want to break me.

I didn't resist. I wanted him to know I was ready. His smile made me breathless, but soon it was replaced by a look of desire so intense I was almost frightened. He tugged off my shirt and kissed my belly button and my abdomen. I thought I would lose my mind. His hands stroked my back, and his mouth and his fingers then touched my scar. I jerked suddenly and pushed him away.

"No," he said, looking up at me. "Don't be ashamed, Noah. All this means is that you're braver than anyone, that you're strong."

I nodded.

"You're perfect," he added, covering me in hot kisses.

My hands climbed his back, where I could feel the muscles under his hot skin. I wanted to touch him all over. I was tingling and panting as he moved his hand up my left leg and kissed me softly one, two, three times before forcing his tongue in and tasting me as if doing so were his destiny. As his fingers reached my midsection, I knew I had to tell him something: I'd never done it with anyone before. Not even with Dan. Maybe it could have waited—we were only at second base—but I thought it was better to get it out of the way. He had a lot of experience, and soon I'd be feeling scared.

"Nick," I said, trying to meet eyes with him. "Before we keep going…"

"Tell me you've never done it before, at least not with your stupid ex," he interrupted, and I couldn't help but giggle nervously.

"Well, actually…" I was enjoying the chance to make fun of him. He got tense all over. "I'm kidding, Nicholas! I'm a virgin." I turned red as a tomato when I admitted it.

He smiled and kissed me on the corner of my lips.

"I knew it the first time I laid eyes on you," he said, laughing. I punched him on the shoulder, but I knew he'd been well meaning, that he'd wanted to clear away some of the tension. Then, more seriously, he continued:

"We can drop it if you're not ready." I could tell he was sincere, but it was hard for him to say.

"I'm ready," I said. "I want to…but promise me one thing first."

"You name it."

I couldn't help but grin.

"Promise me it'll be unforgettable."

An endless supply of love and affection flooded his eyes.

"Don't you worry about that."

As he began working his way down my neck, I felt a jolt that reached all the way between my legs. He was still dressed, but my hands went to work tearing off his shirt. When I had it partway off, he sat up, grabbed it with one hand, pulled it the rest of the way, and threw it sexily to the floor. I wrapped my legs around him. All I wanted was to have him as close to me as possible, with no room even for air between us.

Just feeling his hips against mine gave me a kind of stinging pleasure that made me close my eyes and arch my back.

"You're gorgeous," he said, bringing his fingers down and pushing my underwear delicately aside. "If you want me to stop, Freckles, just tell me because even if I'm dying to be inside you, I don't want to do it until you're ready."

But there was no turning back for me; this was what I wanted, what I needed. I needed him with me, I needed to relieve that pressure inside me, that pressure that I'd been feeling for months and that flared up when we kissed, when we touched, even when we argued.

"You were made to be my personal torture," he said, pressing into me in places that had never burned as they did just then. His heart, his breathing were racing. My fingers wrapped around his waist, and he went stiff as I tried to unbutton his pants.

Then everything turned intense, and those slow, tentative touches were suddenly a whirlwind of sensations. Nick turned me over and put me on top of him. I pulled off his jeans. I could see something hard concealed in his boxers, but I didn't have much time before he grabbed my hips and moved me on top of his erection. Still in our underwear, we pressed our bodies together and started to moan. I ran my hands over his shoulders and stomach, caressing his abs. My mouth followed them; all I wanted just then was to lick his body, nibble it, savor it with my tongue, and I didn't hold back. All the while, he pushed his hips upward, grinding into me and giving me pleasure.

"Jesus, Noah," he said, rolling back on top of me. His hands pushed my legs up until I wrapped them around him.

"Touch me, Nick... I need it," I said, asking him for something I still didn't know or comprehend.

His fingers worked their way inside my underwear, and I arched my back, pushed to desire's edge as he started to move them in little circles right in the spot where I was aching with pleasure.

"Noah, you know I don't want to hurt you, right?" he said, and I could see through the fog of ecstasy that he was worried. "But I'm going to have to, my love."

"I know," I responded, feeling one of his fingers pushing inside me. "Oh my God, Nick!" I shouted as he began to explore me, opening me up for what was to come.

"The sounds you're making are driving me wild," he said as I felt another finger push in beside the first one. He pushed his mouth atop mine to silence the scream emerging from it. His other hand climbed my back and unfastened my bra. Oh God—he was going to see my breasts! No one had ever seen them, but I was so rapt, I barely had time to think about it. He squeezed the left one and sucked on my nipple, circling it with his tongue...

"Jesus, you're perfect, it's like you were made just for me, Noah," he said and took off his boxers. When he pulled out the two fingers, I felt suddenly empty and frustrated. I opened my eyes and saw him naked in front of me. My jaw fell open.

"Dammit, don't look at me like that!" he said in a gruff voice as he opened the nightstand and took out what I assumed was a condom. I couldn't believe what my eyes were seeing, but everything he did, the way he moved, the way his chest rose and fell as he breathed, all of it turned me on. I wanted him, wanted him inside me. There was nothing I wanted more.

When he opened my legs and he got on top of me, my body seemed on the verge of explosion. We were both so tense, it hurt.

"I love you, Noah," he said, his mouth just inches from mine. His blue eyes looked at me in a way I'd never seen before. His words made me swell with happiness, and I knew he was only doing what he had to do, that this had to happen, that Nicholas loved me. Despite all we'd been through together, despite the hatred we'd felt for each other, us being with each other was always in the cards.

"Keep going," I said.

He arranged himself over me carefully, and slowly, I felt him enter me. The muscles inside me tensed, and I moaned wildly when he pushed farther in. He was trying not to hurt me; the sweat was dripping down his back, and every inch of him was straining.

"Go fast, Nick," I said, pulling him in with my legs.

"Are you sure?" he whispered.

I nodded, and he kissed me behind the ear. His arms were on either side of my head, and he was panting uncontrollably.

He broke through the final barrier that lay between us. I felt a sharp pain, intense and fiery, and at last, he was all the way inside me. We were one person, connected in the most powerful way imaginable, and a tear welled in my eye when he tried to get me to look at him.

"Noah...Noah," he said, almost frightened, reaching up and caressing my face. "I'm sorry... I'm sorry, babe."

"No," I interrupted him, wrapping my arms around his neck and drawing him in. "I'm fine. Don't stop."

The pain was still there, but just seeing the pleasure on Nick's face helped me forget it. I wanted to give this to him. I wanted him to remember it forever.

"Jesus, Noah...you can't imagine how good this is making me feel." Pulling out and pushing back in a little harder than before. When I closed my eyes, he said, "No, Noah, look at me, oh my God, I'm dying..." As he kept thrusting, the pain went away entirely; I wanted him there, and when he grunted from pleasure, I felt like I was losing my mind… He liked it, liked being with me; I was the one who gave him this pleasure now, me and no one else.

I pulled his hair.

"Faster," I said, and he did it, and I utterly lost control, and a wave of something magnificent rose up inside me and threatened to crash and take absolutely everything away with it.

"Now you're mine," he said, groaning with pleasure and pain at the same time. "You're all mine… Say it, Noah… Say it."

"I'm yours," I said, scratching his back.

Everything seemed to stop then. My senses burst apart; nothing seemed to matter, just the person on top of me, just him, just Nick. I shouted when we orgasmed at the same time. We were exhausted and sweaty and could hardly catch our breath. He rested his head on my shoulder, and my fingers loosened their grip. I relaxed, enjoying the final flickers of pleasure, caressing him softly.

He kissed me on the shoulder, on the face, and then pulled back to look me in my eyes.

"You're incredible," he said, "I love you. I loved you from the very first time you told me you hated me."

I laughed, feeling a little regretful. "I just hated not having you to myself."

"From now on, you will. I'm completely yours, body and soul…completely."

40

Nick

SLEEPING WITH NOAH HAD BEEN THE MOST AMAZING EXPERIENCE of my life. I couldn't believe it had happened. It still seemed like a dream. I'd been thinking about doing it since I saw her in her tight dress for the first time and realized how gorgeous she was. But making love to her? I was in heaven. Feeling her under me and caressing her to my heart's content had given me more pleasure than I'd known in years of sex with other women. Now she was mine, mine forever, because there was no way I was letting her go.

With all that had happened and with all she had told me, I didn't know how we'd made it that far, but we'd finally knocked down the wall that had separated us from the beginning. Noah's childhood had been horrible, so traumatic that even years later, it still had consequences for her daily life, and it was all I could do not to hunt down her father and kill him for what he'd done. I was angry at her mother, too. What kind of fool left an eleven-year-old girl with an abuser? I didn't want Noah to know it, but I blamed Raffaella as well as her father, and I'd make that clear when the time was right. And yet, even with all she'd told me, I still had the feeling she was hiding something. I wasn't sure what, but I saw a trace of worry in her eyes, and I wanted to know what it was about.

She was asleep in my arms. I thought back to what we had done, and I almost woke her up to pick up where we'd left off. There was a little light on, and in the reflection I could admire her beauty. She was stunning; she took my breath away. And her body... Touching it and pleasuring it had been one of the most pleasurable things in my life.

I heard my phone vibrating. I didn't want Noah to wake up, so I took it off the nightstand and placed it where she wouldn't hear it. Whoever it was, they could wait...

When I pulled her in tight, she opened her eyes, a little groggy.

"Hey," she said in that soft, pleasant tone she'd been using with me for exactly one day.

"Have I told you how incredibly sexy you are?" I asked, getting on top of her, happy to see her awake. I'd been wanting to kiss her for at least an hour.

She kissed me back as only she knew how and hugged me close.

"You all right?" I asked. I'd been as careful as possible; I'd never worried so much about hurting someone, but after what I'd heard about Noah's past, I didn't want her to feel even a scratch.

"I'm hungry," she said, laughing.

Her cheeks were pink, almost feverish-looking, but that was normal, since I hadn't let go of her all night while she slept next to me.

"Me, too," I said, kissing her cheek and her throat on that special spot that drove her wild.

She laughed and tugged at my hair so she could look in my eyes.

"Hungry for food," she clarified. Why could that smile of hers drive me so crazy?

"Fine, let's eat," I said, pulling her toward the shower. We got in together, and after we were done, I gave her a T-shirt and put on a pair of track pants. I couldn't be more thankful my father and her mother were out of town for the weekend.

"What are you in the mood for?" I asked as we went downstairs and she sat at the island.

"You know how to cook?" she asked incredulously.

"Of course I do. What do you think?" I said, smiling and grabbing her hair into a bunch to pull her head back and kiss her.

"I meant something edible," she said. That was the best sound in the world: the perfect tone for a perfect morning.

"I'll make pancakes so you won't complain," I said, letting her go.

"I'll help you," she said, jumping up and walking to the fridge. We cooked together: I made the batter, and she made a strawberry smoothie for both of us. Then we sat at the island and ate side by side. It was exquisite when I poured syrup on her and then licked it off. I'd never done anything like that with anyone, and it made my breakfast much more appetizing. Things were finally the way they should be: Noah was mine, she was happy, and I was, too. After years without trusting a woman, I had chosen one who was complex but perfect, one who could give me back all the love and trust that I had lost at such an early age. I started to see that Noah and I had a lot in common. She'd lost her father at eleven, and I'd lost my mother at twelve. We'd both suffered at an early age, and now we'd met to help each other get over it.

"We need to do something," she said as she ate her last bite of pancakes. "Give me your phone."

I didn't know what she wanted, but I didn't hesitate a second in handing it to her.

"Since you're my boyfriend now," she said, observing me warily, and I smiled. I liked that term. Yeah, I was her boyfriend and she was my girlfriend: *mine.* "I'm going to erase all the girls in your phone except for me and Jenna."

When I started laughing, she said, "I'm serious," unlocking my phone and entering my contacts.

"Do what you like. I don't care," I said, "but don't erase Anne or Madison. I've got permission to keep talking to my sister, right?" I asked, getting up and taking the dishes to the sink.

"Who's Anne?" she asked, wrinkling her nose. It sounded too much like Anna. I hurried to explain:

"Anne is the social worker who brings Madison when I go to visit her. She keeps me informed about what's going on with her, and she calls if anything comes up."

"You've got a missed call from her, from an hour ago," she said. And then, as if she knew we were talking about her, the screen lit up and Anne's name appeared. "Here she is again." I grabbed the phone from her hand, worried. It was too early for Anne to be calling.

"Nicholas?" she said when I picked up.

"What's going on?" I asked, feeling the terror in my stomach.

"It's Madison." Her voice was calm, but I could sense the alarm in her voice. "She's in the hospital. It looks like they forgot her insulin over the past twenty-four hours, and she's had an attack... I think you should come."

I was squeezing the phone so tightly it almost shattered in my hand.

"Is she all right?" I'd never been so scared in my entire life.

"I don't know anything about her condition," she said. I nodded and hung up.

Noah's face was pale. She stood up and walked over to me, asking in a nervous voice what was wrong.

"It's my sister. She's in the hospital. I don't know what the deal is exactly. Apparently she hasn't gotten her insulin... I need to go." I took off running for my room. Noah followed, but the only thing that mattered to me was my five-year-old sister and the fact that the people taking care of her were too stupid to give her the medicine that kept her alive.

"I'm coming with you," she said.

I looked at her for a few seconds and nodded. Yes, I wanted her with me. My mother would be there...and I hadn't seen her in three long years.

41

Noah

I'd never seen him so worried—or just one time, if I counted the night he'd found me screaming in the closet. He looked the same now, sad and frustrated. We were in his car. He was driving with his left hand and holding my hand with the right, just over the gear shift. I had no idea his worries could affect me so deeply. I wanted to wipe away that sorrow and make him smile the way I had those past few hours, but I knew it was impossible. Not many people could make Nicholas Leister break down and give everything, but I knew his sister was one of them. What little he'd told me about his mother was enough for me to know that he hated her or at least preferred never to think about her again. Not giving his diabetic sister her insulin was the perfect reason to hate her even more.

We drove in silence. It saddened me that, after being so happy, so together, everything had suddenly crashed and burned, but at least he kept kissing my hand once in a while or stroking my cheek. He was gentle, and each of those caresses stung even as they consoled me. Sleeping with him had meant something, and it was the only thing I could think of when I felt his skin touch mine.

We didn't even stop to eat. When we reached Vegas six hours later, we went directly to the hospital.

Madison Grason was on the fourth floor of the pediatric wing. As soon as we found out, we took off running. In the waiting room, we saw three people: a couple and a portly woman. The latter walked over to the door when she saw Nick looking at the woman behind her.

"Nicholas, I don't want you starting a scene," she said, glancing from him to me and back.

"Where is she?" he asked. In the meantime, the woman in the back of the room had gotten up and was looking at Nick with preoccupation.

"She's asleep. They've administered insulin. She's fine, Nicholas, she's going to make a full recovery."

I squeezed his hand. I wished he would calm down, but he was completely beside himself. He walked past Anne and straight toward the other women. She was blond, and when I saw her up close, there was no doubt in my mind: this was his mother.

"Where the fuck were you? How could you let this happen?" he shouted. The bald man next to her tried to get between them, but she stopped him.

"Nicholas, it was an accident," she said, calm but with eyes full of grief.

"Leave my wife in peace. We were already sick with worry before you showed up—"

"Fuck you!" Nick was squeezing my hand so tightly it hurt, but there was no way I would try to break free just then—he needed me. "She's got to have her insulin three times a day. It isn't rocket science, but what do you expect when you don't think twice about leaving her in the hands of a bunch of dumb babysitters?"

"Madison knows she's supposed to take her injections, and

she didn't say anything. Rose just assumed she'd done it—" the bald guy explained before Nick cut him off again:

"She's five fucking years old! She needs a mother!"

This wasn't just an argument about Nick's sister. That much was clear. He was shouting at his mother because of Maddie but also because of himself. I hadn't realized how much she'd hurt him until then, but it must have been hard, losing your mother at such a young age. I had lost my father, too, but in a certain sense, I'd saved myself from him, and my mother had always been there for me. Nicholas hadn't had a father who loved him, just one who gave him money. I hated that woman for hurting him, and I hated William for not caring for his son enough.

I stepped back when a doctor appeared.

"Are you the family of Madison Grason?"

Everyone turned to him.

"She's responding to treatment. She'll get better, but she needs to spend the night here. I want to keep an eye on her glucose levels and her condition in general."

"What's going on with her, exactly?" Nick asked.

"You are...?"

"Her brother."

The doctor nodded.

"Your sister's suffering from diabetic ketoacidosis. That happens when the body doesn't have enough insulin and it starts burning fat as a source of energy. When this happens, the liver produces ketones, which are a type of acid that is toxic when it builds up in the bloodstream."

"What do you have to do when that happens?"

"Your sister's glucose is up above three hundred. Her liver is cranking out glucose, but her cells can't absorb it without insulin. With the doses we're giving her, we'll get that under control. We'll run more tests, but there's nothing to worry about. What bothered me when she got here was the dehydration because she'd been vomiting so much, but that's behind us now. We're through the worst of this. Kids are tough."

"Can I see her?" Nicholas asked.

"Yes. She woke up, and if you're Nick, she's been asking about you." Even knowing this didn't seem to improve Nick's mood. The thought that things could have been worse for his sister and that it was her parents' fault must have been killing him inside.

"Come, I want you to meet her," he said, pulling me behind him. I'd supposed he'd go in alone, but knowing he wanted me there for something so important filled me with joy.

When we entered Madison's room, I saw her, a tiny little girl, prettier than any I'd ever seen. She was sitting up on her bed. When she saw Nick, she reached up and smiled.

"Nick!" She frowned from pain just as she said it. She had an IV in her arm; it must have hurt.

Nick let go of me for the first time in hours and ran over to her. It was funny to see him hugging her, sitting there in that giant bed.

"How are you, Princess?" he asked. I wasn't sure what I felt just then, after seeing him so upset and then so relieved.

The girl was gorgeous but very petite for a five-year-old. She was pale and had big purple bags under her eyes. She made such a sad impression that I was reassured to see her smile.

"You came."

"Of course I did. What did you think?" he replied, picking her up and putting her carefully on his lap as he leaned against the wall. She reached up and started playing with his hair.

The image warmed my heart. I'd never have guessed Nicholas could treat a child the way he was treating Madison. Honestly, I'd never have been able to imagine him with a child, period. Nick was the kind of guy who made you think of hot girls, drugs, and rock 'n' roll.

"Look, Maddie, I want to introduce you to someone really special. That's Noah." Only then did she seem to notice me. She only had eyes for her big brother. That was normal, right? But now those eyes, blue just like Nick's, settled on me.

"Who is she?" she asked with a frown.

Before I could say I was a friend, Nicholas interrupted me: "She's my girlfriend."

"You don't have girlfriends," she said.

I walked over to them.

"That's true, Maddie, but I think I've made him change his mind," I said with a grin. She was funny.

"I like your name," she said. "It's a boy's name." Nicholas burst out laughing, and I couldn't help but join in.

"Uh, thanks. I'm not sure what to say." *Like brother, like sister,* I thought, remembering what Nick had said about my name when we'd met.

"With a name like that, I'll bet the boys let you play soccer," she said.

"You like soccer?" I asked, disbelieving. Nicholas always called her *Princess,* and she looked more like one of those than a soccer fan.

"I love it. Nick gave me a ball. It's so cool. It's pink," she replied, still tugging and slapping at Nick's hair. I understood. I wanted to touch it, too.

We spent a good while with her, and there was no denying it: she was adorable. She was bright for her age and very funny, but she looked exhausted, so we decided to let her rest.

On the way out, we ran into Nick's mom. You'd think a mother would be worried about her daughter, but she seemed to be on a different planet. She feigned indifference in front of her son, but certain barely perceptible nervous gestures showed me that his presence did affect her.

"Nicholas, I want to talk to you," she said, looking back and forth between the two of us.

"I'll leave you alone," I said, but he held me close.

"I have nothing to say to you," he hissed.

"Please, Nicholas. I'm your mother... You can't spend your whole life avoiding me." She didn't seem to care that I was there listening. Nicholas was tense as a guitar string.

"You stopped being my mother the moment you abandoned me for that idiot husband of yours." It was frightening to see him like that, so serious.

"I made a mistake," she said, as if abandoning your child were something anyone might accidentally do. "But you're not a child anymore. It's time for you to forgive me for what I did."

"That wasn't a mistake. You disappeared for six years. You didn't even call to ask how I was. You just left me!" he shouted. "I wish I never had to see you again, and if I could, I would take that precious little girl from you. You don't deserve her. You don't deserve to have her as a daughter."

We walked away. He pulled me down the hallway, then turned, and then turned again until we reached an area that was empty. He pulled open the door of a small closet, and we stepped inside. The only light came from a window near the ceiling.

His face looked lost, his breathing was out of control, and his eyes were gleaming with fury or maybe sorrow, I wasn't sure. I was scared to see him like that, and I didn't realize what was happening when he pushed me against the wall and his lips pressed into mine.

"Nicholas," I said in a trembling voice, caressing his face. But he was elsewhere, incapable of controlling his emotions. He kissed me again. I didn't manage to say a word.

"Thank you for being here," he whispered, and when I heard the desperation in his voice, I held him steady and tried to look him in the eye. "I don't think I'll ever get over her just leaving me like that. But now you're here, I have you, and I know what it feels like to be in love. I don't care what she did to me anymore, Noah. You've closed a wound that was still raw, and that makes me love you even more."

We were so close, his tears streamed into my eyes and I felt a smile cross his lips.

"Come here," he murmured and kissed me.

That was the second time we made love…and it was tarnished by memories from the past.

───────────

We went to eat afterward. We wouldn't be able to visit Maddie again for a few hours, so we decided to see the sights in Las Vegas. I had never been, and it was as impressive as it looked in the movies. Wherever I looked, there were huge buildings, luxurious hotels, and spectacles. I couldn't even imagine what it must look like at night—unfortunately I wouldn't be able to stay there too late.

"Tomorrow we'll release her. That's better than we expected. We could probably just let her go now, but I'd prefer to keep her under observation a little longer," the doctor said.

It was five in the evening, and if we wanted to be in LA before midnight, we needed to head back. Nicholas seemed not to want to go, but his mother was there, and I knew how hard that was for him.

"I'll be back this week," he told Maddie, who got teary-eyed. "I'll come Wednesday, and I'll bring you a present, and we can play together." He hugged her carefully but lovingly.

"In two days?" she said, pouting.

"Just two days," Nick said, kissing her on her blond hair.

───────────

He looked destroyed, exhausted, as we left the hospital, and he had good reason to. It had been a day full of emotion, and the day before had been, too. We both needed a few hours to sleep it off.

"You want me to drive?" I asked. He grinned as he pinned me against the driver's side door.

"I seem to remember I ended up losing the last car you drove."

"You'll never let that go, will you?" I asked, rolling my eyes.

I turned around and got into the passenger side. We stopped several times on the way for coffee, and when we were on the road, we kept the music blasting to help us stay awake.

Once home, we didn't even stop to think that our parents might have arrived. Nicholas had an arm around my shoulder and I had mine around his waist as we climbed the porch.

Seeing my mother was like returning to reality. We were startled and pulled quickly away from each other.

"Finally, you're back. We were starting to get worried," Mom said, coming over and hugging me tightly. I hadn't seen her for two days, and with all that had happened, the memories of my father, the things with Nick, I squeezed her harder than I should have.

"Did you miss me?" she laughed.

She greeted Nick as well, and we went inside and were interrogated about the condition of Nick's sister. I guess he had called them so they'd know where we were, and William was worried about Maddie's health.

"I'm glad she's all right," he said, getting up from the sofa.

Nick was on one side of the room, I on the other. It was strange not to be touching each other, and I felt an odd emptiness in my chest. I'd gotten so used to having him close these past forty-eight hours that I needed him near me at all times. I looked into his eyes just then. I saw promise.

"I'm tired," I said. "If you don't mind, I'm going to go on upstairs. I've got class in the morning…"

My mother was watching a movie with Will, and they still had a good bit of it left before bedtime.

"You staying with us, Nick?" my mother asked him, and I had to suppress a scowl. Fortunately, I don't think she noticed.

Nicholas grinned.

"I should go up, too. I've got class myself. Good night," he said, walking around the sofa and joining me.

I didn't know if it was the feeling of doing something bad or just knowing our parents were down there and would lose it if they caught us, but when Nick pushed me against the wall in my room and stuck his hand under my shirt, it was the most exciting thing I could imagine.

"Come to my bed. Sleep with me," he whispered in my ear. The whole time he spoke, he was kissing, nibbling, licking my neck.

"I can't," I moaned.

"You can't make those noises and then tell me not to take you to bed," he said, pressing his hips into me sexily.

I giggled and closed my eyes.

"My mother could come up at any time, Nicholas," I said as he skillfully squeezed my left thigh. "I don't want her to have a heart attack."

"You're coming with me anyway," he said, dragging me off.

"No!" I shouted, digging my heels into the floor. I had no idea what we were going to do now that we were together and living under the same roof with my mother and his father, but I knew there had to be some kind of rules or self-control in place.

He stopped, noticed the noises downstairs, and realized I was right.

"I love you," he said, giving me a quick peck on the lips. "If anything happens, you know where I am."

"I do. Second door on the left."

I closed the door. I needed to analyze everything that had happened. I needed...to catch my breath.

Everything that had happened those past few days had sunk me in a cloud of contrary thoughts and feelings. I was happy when I was with Nick: I didn't know if it would last a long time, since we had a tendency to clash, or at least it had seemed that way over the past few months. Either way, I was crazy about him. I had hidden it, even from myself, but now it was out, and I couldn't stop thinking about it, especially knowing he was just a few feet away. It was hard not to go looking for him when I had trouble sleeping, but I forced myself. I had to learn to keep my distance from him. But when I wasn't with him, my every thought turned to my father and his threatening letters. I still didn't know if I should tell anyone...why? He was in jail, and I wasn't even sure if he was the one sending them. Maybe Ronnie had just found out about my dad and was using all that against me. So I decided to say nothing, at least until another letter came, and my guess was that was never going to happen.

The next morning, I got up in a rush, knowing I was at risk of being late for school. I was nervous because I'd have to deal with the fallout from the party. Everyone had heard me shout like a madwoman, and nobody had come to my aid.

I put on my uniform and ran downstairs. William was already gone, same as most mornings, and Nick and my mother were having breakfast at the island in the kitchen. When Nick looked up at me, I had to struggle not to run over and kiss him. Mom got up and started making my breakfast. With the excuse of getting help with my tie (which I knew perfectly well how to tie by now), I walked over to Nick and gave him a quick kiss while my mother wasn't looking.

He whispered to me: "Right now I have all these images of my head of you in that uniform in a room upstairs." As he said this, he knotted my tie, kissed me softly, and stroked my neck.

I turned to make sure no one was watching. But my mother was busy scrambling eggs, and her music was blaring from the speakers.

It was a dangerous game we were playing but a very exciting one, too.

He reached down and felt under my skirt, stroking my legs and my ass.

"You're pushing it," I said.

"I know," he agreed, pulling away just as my mother turned and served my dish.

For the first time, I had my breakfast sitting next to Nick, and all I could think about was that morning when we'd had pancakes and smoothies together. That was a sweet memory, especially the part that had come just before we ate...

My mother didn't say much to us. She seemed immersed in her thoughts, and I reproached myself for not taking more interest in her marriage and whether she was happy we were living there.

"Are you okay, Mom?" I asked with a worried look. That lost look, that distraction I noticed in her was becoming all too common.

She came back from wherever she had wandered off to in her mind and feigned a smile.

"Yeah, sure... I'm great," she said, picking her plate up and dropping it into the sink. "Nick told me that he doesn't mind taking you to school today. I'm sorry, hon, but my head hurts a little... I think I'm going to lie down." She gave me a kiss on the head and squeezed Nick's shoulder affectionately.

"She's being kind of weird, right?" I said as he finished his juice. He pulled my chair over to his.

"A little, but I don't think it's a big deal." He put his hands on my knees and leaned in. "You ready to go?" His voice was seductive. His hands tickled me. I nodded. I guessed my car being in the shop wasn't as bad as I'd thought at first.

Five minutes later, we were leaving, but he did stop on a corner where no one could see us, cup my face, and kiss me intensely.

"What's that all about?" I asked as he grinned and put the car back in gear.

"It's been seven hours and twenty-five minutes since we've kissed," he said calmly.

"You're counting?" I said, laughing. That put me in a really good mood.

"I get bored when I'm not with you. I need to keep my mind busy."

Fifteen minutes later, I was at the door of St. Marie's. I couldn't help but feel nervous. Nick was looking serious, too, and clutching the steering wheel tightly.

"You going to pick me up?" I asked.

"Of course. I don't have a choice—I'm your boyfriend, right?" he said almost presumptuously.

I laughed.

"That's not necessarily a boyfriend's duty. You've never even had a girlfriend, have you?" It cracked me up to know I was right and that I was his first.

"I was waiting for you," he said, planting a hot kiss on my lips. I liked those words so much, I held him close. Kissing him reminded me of the two times it had gone further than that. I wanted to do it again.

"You'd better go if you don't want me to kidnap you for the rest of the day," he warned me. His hand around my waist told me he wanted to keep me there.

"I'll see you at four," I said with a smile and opened the door. This was addictive.

"Love you," I said.

"Love you, too! See you, Precious." He shook his head and drove off.

Before I reached the door, many eyes turned to me, but before I could let it get to me, Jenna jumped into my arms and hugged me.

"Noah! I'm so, so sorry." She squeezed me tightly. "I didn't know they were going to do that. I should have been there to help you. They're just a bunch of immature babies. They should be over stupid pranks like that, but you know..."

"It's fine, Jenna. It wasn't your fault," I said.

"Are you sure?" she continued. "You looked like you were freaking out. I didn't know the darkness affected you like that."

"It's a trauma from when I was a kid, but it's over. It doesn't matter anymore." Just then, the bell rang and we walked to our lockers.

It wasn't over, though. Rumors had spread, and anywhere I turned, people were staring at me. I felt like a Martian or worse, like people were *pitying* me. I didn't realize how angry I was until I went to the dining hall and saw Cassie there with the guys who'd stuffed me in the closet. I was so enraged that I didn't even realize what I was doing until I was right beside her throwing my strawberry shake in her hair.

Everyone around froze, and before I knew what I'd done, I heard the principal's voice behind me.

"Miss Morgan, my office, please."

Shit.

42

Nick

I DIDN'T THINK ALL THOSE DARK FEELINGS WOULD CATCH UP TO me when I left the school, but they did. I couldn't stop thinking about how that girl I loved so much had been tortured, almost killed. For that reason, I went straight to my father's office. I wanted to know his thoughts about all this, but especially what could be done after finding out the woman I loved had been beaten and mistreated for years.

I reached Leister Enterprises and headed straight for the top floor. Janine, my father's secretary, had known me her whole life; it had been her job to buy me birthday presents and take me to my friends' parties. She'd gone to my soccer games when my father was too busy working. She'd even chewed me out when I'd had bad grades on my report card. Janine was a kind of mother to me, but I'd never opened my heart to her. I'd never opened my heart to any woman until Noah showed up. But still, Janine and I were close.

"Nicholas, what are you doing here?" she asked with a smile. She was a thin woman over sixty. My father held on to her because she was as hardworking and loyal as they came, and it wasn't easy dealing with my father at work. I knew—I was interning at his practice.

"Hey, Janine, I need to talk to Dad. Is he in a meeting?" I asked, trying to keep myself from bursting in.

"No, you can go ahead. He's looking over this afternoon's case." I headed straight back and opened the door without knocking. My father's dark-blue eyes looked up from his documents and straight at me.

"What are you doing here?" he asked me sternly. He never said hello; that was a habit of his.

"I'm here to talk to you about Noah. And about Raffaella, to be precise." I stood there in front of his luxurious desk, hoping he'd be sincere with me for once in his life. "Do you know about what her bastard ex-husband did?"

After staring at me a moment, my father pushed aside his documents, stood, walked to the bar, and poured himself a glass of cognac.

"How'd you find out?" he asked.

So he knew. That didn't particularly surprise me. That wasn't the kind of thing you could keep hidden too long.

"Noah freaks out if she's in a room with the lights off. The other day she almost had a panic attack. When she calmed down, she told me." The memory of what those fuckers had done to her enraged me, but I kept calm. "Dad, do you know what that son of a bitch did? Noah almost died... A piece of glass stabbed her in the stomach. She might not even be able to have kids."

"I know," he said, sitting down with an expression of grief on his face.

"You do?" I started pacing angrily through the room. "Her own mother left her alone with an abuser! Raffaella's as much to blame as he is," I shouted in impotent rage.

"Nicholas, I'm not going to let you talk about my wife that

way. You have no idea what she's been through or how much she regrets leaving her daughter there… She didn't have a life like ours. She didn't have money or anyone to help her fight for her child. She suffered that man's abuse for years. Her body is a map of scars… So I won't let you—"

"Noah was a little girl, Dad!" I interrupted him. "For God's sake! She had to jump out a window! He should be dead, that son of a bitch!"

"Nicholas, sit down. There's something you need to know." He motioned at the chair in front of him.

Instead of sitting down, I stood behind it. As he brought his drink to his lips, I wished he'd poured one for me.

"A month ago, he got paroled," he said. My body tensed as my brain tried to assimilate those words. "It's been six years since they sentenced him. If Raffaella had pressed charges for abuse earlier, he might have gotten more time, but he was only sentenced for his crimes against Noah… She was hurt, but the worst of it was when she jumped out the window and a shard of glass injured her. He wasn't blamed for that. It seems he had friends in high places and got his sentence reduced. What I'm trying to tell you is, he's out, and Raffaella's scared he'll try to get in touch with her. I found out not long ago, and I was angry. She should have told me before. We need to keep our eyes open for anything strange… I don't think he'll try anything, but I'm worried still. Raffaella's terrified. She's been having nightmares every night, and she doesn't want Noah to know he's gotten out. You need to keep the secret."

"How can he be out? You can't do anything?" I asked, feeling deeply unsettled. That madman could be trying to hunt down his wife and daughter that very moment, and I didn't know how Noah would react if she saw the man from her nightmares again.

"I tried to get a judge to file a restraining order, but since we don't have any evidence of him trying anything, it's been impossible. Probably we're overthinking it. He's in another country. I doubt he would come all the way to America. Still, we should keep on our toes, especially for Ella's sake..."

"Agreed. You take care of your wife, and I'll take care of Noah," I said, serving myself a drink from the bar.

I could feel him staring into me from behind.

"Son...please tell me you haven't hooked up with your stepsister," he said, closing his eyes.

Shit...was it that obvious?

"I just want to take care of her, Dad," I said, downing my drink in one go.

"Look, I don't know what you two have got going on, and I don't want to know, but please, I beg you, don't do anything idiotic. It's hard enough to keep Raffaella from losing her mind with what's going on. The last thing I need is to learn you're hot for your stepsister."

I hated him treating our relationship so blithely.

"I'm not *hot for her*, Dad... I love her. And I promise you, I won't let anyone lay a finger on her."

He nodded.

"Be careful, Nicholas."

I left the office, and just as I did, my phone rang: Noah.

"What's up?" I asked. She was supposed to be in class. What the hell was she doing calling me?

"Nick...you've got to come get me," she said in a strange voice.

"Why? Are you okay?" I asked, getting in the elevator and going down.

"It's just... They suspended me for the rest of the day."

I smiled as I picked her up out front of the school. She ran over to my car, so adorable I couldn't help but kiss her even before she told me anything about what had happened.

"You threw a strawberry shake at her head?" I asked, cackling. "For real?"

"I don't know what happened," she admitted. "But I don't care, either. She deserved it. Don't judge me. I had something inside me I had to let out." She put on her seat belt, and I pulled out, laughing.

"You think anyone will be home?" I asked a minute later.

"Probably. Why?"

"Because I want to make love to you so bad right now, I think I'm going to explode." I wanted her with an intensity that frightened me. I put a hand on her thigh and started pushing up her skirt. Her skin was soft.

"Two can play at that game, right?" she said, and it took all the self-control I had not to crash into the car in front of me. Noah undid her seat belt and came close. Her hand rested on my knee while she planted her lips on my neck.

"Come on, now, Freckles," I said when I felt her tongue on my ear. "I can't drive and do this at the same time."

"You started it." Her hand glided up my leg while she nibbled at my neck and jaw.

I stopped her hand when it got to what it was looking for.

"Get out," I ordered her, eyes burning with desire.

"I think I'll pass. The last time you told me that, you left me standing in the middle of the road."

"Get out or I'll do you right here," I threatened her.

She returned to her seat. When I saw she wasn't listening, I got out myself, walked around to her door, and pulled her out.

"You're not thinking of doing it here?" she asked, looking at the cliff and the seaside behind us.

I ignored her and pushed her into the door of the car, forcing her to wrap her legs around me.

She arched her back and closed her eyes. I kissed her ear, her jaw, anywhere there was bare skin. I wanted to see her, and with one hand I unbuttoned her shirt completely.

"Did I tell you how much this uniform turns me on?" I said as I kissed her breasts.

"You and every other guy on earth," she sighed.

Noah and her sarcastic sense of humor. I squeezed her tighter, and she sighed louder now. Fortunately, we were alone.

"Now I'm going to make you mine again," I said, looking her in the eye.

"You are mine, and I'm yours," she said, returning my stare. "I love you, Nick."

"And I love you, Precious," I said, sinking into her and enjoying how she responded to me. "I love you like crazy," I said, as I clutched her tightly and we attained the most profound pleasure known.

We spent the rest of the day at the beach, lying on the sand and getting to know each other better.

"Who gave you your first kiss?" she asked, lying on her belly with her head resting on her hands. She was young; she was beautiful. I had to struggle not to touch her every second.

"You, obviously," I responded, watching the wind tousle her hair and the sun redden her cheeks, making her freckles more visible.

She rolled her eyes.

"I'm serious," she said, ignoring a lock of hair that kept blowing into her eyes. I stretched my hand out and tucked it behind her ear.

"You really want to know?" I asked. "Fine, but you're going to laugh... It was Jenna."

"No!" Her eyes widened like saucers. "No way! Are you serious?"

"We were kids, she was my neighbor and only friend, and we just wanted to see what it felt like... I thought it was weird, she thought it was gross, and she said she'd never do it again."

Noah cracked up. I was happy to know it hadn't bothered her. That kiss had meant nothing to me: Jenna was my friend, one of my only true friends.

"What about you?" I asked her, uncomfortable, not wanting to imagine Noah in any other guy's arms.

"Well, when I did it I wasn't that little, so I didn't swear I'd never do it again... Actually, I liked it."

"So who was it with then?" My attitude was a little more serious than I would have liked, but she either ignored or didn't notice my tone.

"It was with the lifeguard from the public pool... He was super hot, and we hooked up in the emergency room."

I grabbed her and pulled her on top of me.

"So you liked it, huh?" I said, trapping her so she couldn't move.

"I loved it," she admitted, and I realized she was making fun of me.

"You like torturing me?"

"Honestly, I think it's hilarious, yeah," she admitted, smiling and making me kiss her until we were both out of breath.

"I'm going to have to teach you what it means to actually torture someone," I said, bringing my lips close to hers but without touching. I slipped my hand down her leg, watching the desire grow inside her. When my fingers were in the pit of her knee, I stopped and then brought them back up her thigh while my other hand unbuttoned her shirt and I kissed the soft skin of her stomach.

Then I stood up, leaving her there with her cheeks flushed, dying from unfulfilled longings. It took her a few seconds to realize what I was doing. She looked at me like an abandoned dog.

"What the hell?" she asked, exasperated.

"Like this, you'll think twice before you try to make me jealous again." It was almost impossible not to finish what we'd started, but I wouldn't; I was having too much fun.

Slack-jawed, she started buttoning her shirt again.

"You're the same dickhead you always were," she grumbled, getting up, grabbing he blanket, and walking off to the car. I chuckled as I admired her long legs and her hair flapping in the wind.

Before she could make it there, I brought her back and kissed her deeply. I couldn't stay apart from her any longer; a few minutes was my maximum. I rubbed my lips against hers, but she kept her mouth closed, hesitant, not letting me slip my tongue in until I'd licked and venerated her. When she gave in, I responded with the best kiss ever...a kiss worthy of remembering, not like that kiss from that idiot lifeguard.

43

Noah

I WAS SCARED OF HOW FAST THINGS WERE MOVING. AFTER ALL that had happened with Dan, falling in love again hadn't entered into my plans. But there I was, wild about my stepbrother, the last guy I could ever have imagined having a relationship with. Maybe it would have been easier if I'd fallen in love with someone like Mario, but I knew that wouldn't have worked. Ever since I'd told him we could just be friends, he'd completely ditched me. Obviously I wasn't interesting enough for him. With Nick, everything was excitement. He made me feel happy; I had no complaints. It scared me how badly I wanted to be with him; even when we were just separated for a little bit, I suffered from his absence, which worried me. I couldn't keep my legs from trembling when I saw him, let alone when he kissed me or we made love. I was on a cloud, and if it hadn't been for the threatening letters, I would have been the happiest person on the globe.

I knew I couldn't keep them a secret forever, but I didn't want to mention my father's name in front of my mother. She'd suffered from that man's abuse as much as or more than I had, and now that she was happily married, I didn't want to stir up those memories, but what else could I do? My father was in jail, for a long time, and it was practically impossible that he would do anything to me. That meant Ronnie had to be behind all this. He'd found out about my dark past somehow and had brought all this up to scare me and hit me where it hurt. And the only person capable of dealing with that situation was Nicholas.

That night, after a party we were going to as a couple—the first time we'd done so—I was going to tell him. He'd be climbing up the walls and would upbraid me for not telling him before, but I'd been scared of his reaction and scared of what that gangster Ronnie might do.

I tried to conceal my mood when we arrived at Nick's fraternity party and smiled widely when he came around to open my door. Since our relationship had begun, he'd transformed: the Nicholas who'd used to say girls could open their own door had disappeared, and a true gentleman had taken his place. I didn't need all those old-fashioned gestures, but I liked knowing I was the only person who received them.

"Have I told you how hard it's going to be to keep my hands off you tonight?" he asked me, not letting me out for a moment. It was chilly out, and the tight black dress I was wearing hadn't been the most practical choice.

I looked up at him, admiring those bright eyes and their long black lashes. I got lost in them and the warmth and desire they concealed. Nicholas Leister was the spitting image of a Calvin Klein model, and now he was all mine.

"Well, you're going to have to," I said, wrapping my hands around his neck and playing with his hair. It was hard to keep my hands off that splendid body, too. "You know everyone's going to be staring at us, right?"

"Then they'll know you're mine," he said, bending over and kissing me. Every time he did it, I lost the thread of my thoughts.

Nicholas was the one who always took the initiative, and for me, nothing could be hotter. There in the darkness, just his fingers on my waist made everything inside me quake. Slowly, his tongue made its way through my lips, avid to caress mine with slow, sensual movements, nothing like the frantic way we'd been kissing lately. I felt like I was melting.

"Let's go home," he said, pulling away for a second. When I saw how bad he wanted me, any worries about the cold vanished. I smiled.

"Our parents are home," I told him. We'd barely managed to be together that past week. My mother hadn't left me in peace— she was constantly talking to me, trying to get me to hang out with her—and William had needed Nick to be at his office almost full-time. They seemed to be plotting to keep us apart.

Nick grunted, "I'm going to have to find a place of my own." I froze.

What?

"I've been looking for a few weeks. Now that we're together, I think it's a good idea. I'm an adult, and my stipend at the firm is enough to pay for something decent. That way, we won't have to worry about our parents."

Theoretically, Nicholas moving would be for the best. Living with your boyfriend and your parents in the same house was weird, uncomfortable, but the mere thought of not having him there every morning, not seeing him before I went to bed, not knowing that he was at the other end of the hall, made me bitter and afraid. I felt safer knowing he was just a room away, especially after Ronnie had been threatening me...

"I don't want you to go," I said. I was being irrational but sincere.

"You want us to keep having to hide, not even able to touch each other?" he said, rubbing his hand in a circle on my back.

"You know, my father knows about us. He won't put up a fight about me going, and then we could have all the time we wanted together. We could stop the whole brother-sister act if we weren't sleeping next door to each other. Your mother could even deal with it, I think, if she knew it wasn't happening a few feet from her room."

"I know," I said, pulling him close, "but...don't do it yet. I don't want you to go." I knew it sounded desperate, but I didn't care.

Consternated, he asked, "What's going on, Noah?" He seemed to know I was hiding something.

I shook my head and forced a smile.

"Nothing, nothing... I'm fine, I just like having you at home, that's all." Which was kind of true.

Kissing me on top of the head, he said, "Me, too. Don't worry. We've got time to talk this over. We should go inside. You must be freezing."

I nodded, and we walked inside. This party was packed, just like all the ones we'd been to. There were soft flickering lights and people dancing and drinking in the near-darkness. We soon found Jenna and Lion. Nick dragged me off to the kitchen, where it was a little calmer. Some guys were playing beer pong. Nick and Lion jumped in.

Jenna was happy to see us together, and for the first time in ages, I felt like a part of their scene. I knew almost everyone there, and even if some people were giving me dirty looks because of what had happened at the races, most of them seemed happy I was there.

We had a great night. I didn't drink much. I was over that—I didn't need to—with Nick, I felt calm and secure. Plus, I hadn't received any letters for more than a week. But I got nervous when I went to check the time and realized I had no idea where my phone was.

Shit.

I looked through my bag and inspected the living room, where I'd spent most of the night. Jenna was in the bathroom; Nick was completely immersed in his game of beer pong.

Probably it had fallen out of my bag when I was getting out of the car. That was the last thing I needed—losing my phone and having to spend what little money I had on a new one.

I walked outside and turned the corner to where Nick's car was parked. The music from the party died down as I continued down the street. It was freezing out, the sky was blanketed in clouds, and I realized I was probably going to see rain in Los Angeles for the first time. I missed that. I loved the sun, but I'd grown up in a place where rain and cold were the order of the day.

I looked around the grass next to the car but didn't find anything. I was about to go back to the house and ask Nick for the keys so I could see if I'd dropped my phone inside the car, but I heard someone behind me.

Irrational fear overtook me. I had the sense I was being watched. I turned around but saw nothing other than the evening shadows. Heart pounding, breathing hard, I started to walk back, but then the person emerged from his hiding place. It was Ronnie.

"What's the rush, bae?" he asked, a smile on his grotesque lips.

I stopped. I was ready to scream if I had to, or so I thought, but the fear that had overtaken me was so powerful that I wasn't sure if any sound would come out if I tried.

"I don't know what you want, Ronnie, but if you take one step toward me, I'll start shrieking like a banshee," I said, unable to conceal the panic behind my words.

"There's someone who wants to see you, Noah. You're not just going to leave him hanging, are you? You got his letters, right?"

I tried to turn around and felt hands grabbing me from behind, covering my lips before I could make a sound.

"If I were you, I'd try to behave," Ronnie said, coming close as two men immobilized me. "Your papa's waiting for you...and we both know he ain't a patient man." He gestured to the two men behind me.

They lifted me up while I thrashed around and tried uselessly to escape. They stuffed a damp, stinking rag in my mouth and covered it with duct tape. The last thing I remember seeing was the face of my father, the same man who'd almost killed me.

44

Nick

I HADN'T SEEN NOAH IN TWENTY MINUTES, AND ALREADY, I WAS missing her. I looked around and couldn't find her anywhere.

"Jenna, you seen Noah?" I asked, walking to a corner where she was drinking and dancing. She stopped to look at me.

"I went to the bathroom, and when I came back, she wasn't here. Sophie said she was asking if anyone had seen her phone."

I decided to go outside to look for her. It was freezing, and there was no one around. I looked left and right, even toward the woods behind us, but there wasn't a trace of her. I went back in and checked the bedroom with an uncomfortable pressure in my chest; she was nowhere to be found. Finally I checked every room one by one, shouting her name and dialing her phone. Nothing. Not a single sign.

I ran downstairs and found Jenna and Lion by the front door.

"I don't know where she is," Jenna said, now worried.

A horrible fear overtook me, and I ran around the corner, with Jenna and Lion close behind me. Turning the corner on the way to my car, I saw footprints on the grass. I followed them, my heart in a knot, and when I reached the place where they ended, I found her high heels lying there as if they'd been thrown down.

"*Noah!*" I shouted desperately, looking from side to side. "*Noah!*" Jenna and Lion shouted, too. No response.

I remembered Ronnie's threat. Had that son of a bitch taken her somewhere?

"Call the cops," I told Lion when I got over my panic.

Lion looked surprised, but he took out his phone. As he dialed, we went back inside. I walked into the DJ booth and made him cut the music. Everyone hissed and jeered, but I didn't give a shit. "Has anyone seen Noah?" I shouted. I got up on a chair and stared out at the crowd, wishing I would see her there and hating myself for leaving her alone.

Everyone jeered and shook their head. I got down and clutched my head in my hands. *Dammit... Dammit...*

"Nicholas, calm down," Jenna said.

"You don't understand!" I screamed, not caring if anyone heard. "Ronnie's been threatening her." Just then, Lion grabbed me.

"Nick, the cops," he said, handing me the phone. "They want to talk to someone from her family."

I grabbed it and put it to my ear.

"My girlfriend's disappeared. I need you to come right away," I said, knowing I should control my tone better but unable to.

"Sir, calm down and explain to me what happened," the voice on the other line responded. The person was calm, as if we were talking about the weather and not the entire purpose of my life suddenly vanishing.

"What happened is my girlfriend disappeared, that's what's happened!"

"Calm down, sir, we've already sent a patrol car, and when they arrive, they'll search the area, but for now, I need to you to tell me exactly where you saw her for the last time."

I told the operator what happened, but it was as if I were in a bubble and none of what was happening were real.

Soon a cop car pulled up and everyone in attendance rushed out. I didn't care; I already knew who had done this.

"You are…?" the officer asked after taking my statement. I couldn't believe he was dragging his feet like this; something needed to be done, and now.

"I'm Nicholas Leister," I said for the second time that night. All these questions were absurd; what we needed to do was go find Ronnie wherever he was and rescue Noah.

"So you're her boyfriend?" I nodded, impatient, while Jenna and Lion talked with two other cops. "Noah Morgan…is she a minor?" the officer interviewing me asked. Shit. I hadn't thought of that.

"She's seventeen. Look, she's my stepsister, our parents got married a few months ago, and I already told you, I know who's behind this. Please, we're wasting time and they could be hurting her."

The cop frowned at me.

"To start with, you're not immediate family, so we don't need to tell you anything. What I'm going to ask of you is that you call her parents or legal guardian and inform them of what happened. The law says we can't file a missing person report for twenty-four hours, so—"

"Are you not listening to me?" I shouted, losing my nerve. "She's been kidnapped. Now stop fucking around and do something!"

I didn't realize how close I'd gotten to him until he grabbed me and slammed me against his car.

"Calm down or I'm going to have to arrest you," he said.

I cursed between my teeth until he let me go.

"Now call your parents or I'll do it myself," he said, puffing out his chest and trying to intimidate me.

I turned around, took out my phone, and dialed. Dad picked up on the fourth ring.

"Dad...I need you to come. Something's happened."

Four hours later, we were back at home. Nobody knew where Noah was, but there were people milling all around and plugging in machines to trace our calls in case her captors tried to get in touch with us. William Leister wasn't a nobody, and when his stepdaughter disappeared, the first thing people thought was that it was a kidnapping for ransom. I'd already told ten different cops two hundred times about Ronnie's threats, but what I didn't know was that they'd found the threatening letters in Noah's desk drawer. When I realized her father was the one who'd kidnapped her, I nearly lost control.

I was a disaster; I couldn't believe what was happening. They'd had to give Raffaella a tranquilizer when she'd found out, and now she was in one of the bedrooms with a friend trying to calm her down. My father was on the phone the whole time, talking to cops and officials. All I could do was smoke one cigarette after another and try to ignore the hundreds of horrible images flashing through my head.

Lion and Jenna had come over, Jenna's parents, too, but I had no idea what they were up to. It was past five in the morning, and no one had heard anything.

"If something happens, I'll never forgive myself," I said, almost hyperventilating. "All this is my fault... Dammit! Why didn't she tell me?"

"Nick, if Noah decided to cover this up, she had her reasons," Jenna said. "I've been her friend for a month, and I had no idea her father was in jail, let alone that he was an abuser."

"If he lays a hand on her..." I said, hearing my own voice

crack. I couldn't just sit there doing nothing. I wanted to beat my head against the wall, anything, just to get my life to go back to where it had been earlier that week. I'd been happy for the first time in years, and all of it was thanks to that incredible girl who for some reason had chosen me… Just imagining Ronnie touching her turned my stomach. I knew Ronnie was in on this. I'd bet my life on it.

Just then, the phone started to ring. Everyone was running around like crazy. I went to Dad's office, where everyone fell silent while he picked up the phone when the police motioned for him to do so. The speaker was on, so every word of the conversation was audible.

"Leister," he answered.

"Mr. Leister…it's an honor speaking with you," said a voice I'd never heard before. It was deep, cheerful, as if all this were amusing. "The man who took my wife and daughter to the other end of the continent so I couldn't find them. You're an intelligent man, yes siree. Otherwise, you wouldn't have your business empire and my wife would have never spared a thought for you."

I looked to the left and saw Raffaella covering her mouth with her hand, repressing her tears, and shaking her head.

"Where's Noah?" my father asked in a tense voice.

"We'll get to that. But honestly, the location of my daughter isn't your concern, Mr. Leister. All you need to worry about is how much money you can come up with to get back a person who honestly isn't even part of your family."

My father looked over at me.

"I'll pay whatever it takes, you bastard, but don't you dare lay a finger on her." That was exactly what I would have said, and I felt grateful to him.

"A million dollars in used bills in two backpacks, to be handed over by you in person at midday," Noah's father said. "If you screw this up, I'll leave the consequences to your imagination. And come alone, Mr. Leister—that's an order."

"I want to talk to her," my father said tensely. "I need to know she's all right."

"Of course, Mr. Leister."

I heard her a second later.

"Nicholas…" That was all she said. She sounded horrible. I couldn't help taking a step forward when I heard her on the other line.

But right then, it went dead.

45

Noah

I woke up dizzy and with a terrible headache. All I could see when I looked around was a soft red light. In the room where they were keeping me was nothing but the bed I was lying on and a simple chair in the corner. The smell was awful, like rat piss. Music coming from outside, as in a dance club, made it impossible to hear anything but my accelerated breathing and the rapid pounding of my heart.

When I realized what had happened, I started panicking. A familiar whistling sound rang in my ears, and I'd swear I could hear the blood pumping through my body. There was a bitter taste in my mouth, and I was desperate for a glass of cold water. Whatever they'd drugged me with was still affecting me. I sat up and heard the clinking of chains: one of my hands was cuffed to the wall. I tried to get out, but in vain. Struggling to calm down, I thought of how I might escape. I'd never found my phone, so I couldn't communicate with anyone. What scared me the most was the knowledge that my father was behind all this.

This couldn't be happening. My father was in jail, and even if he'd gotten out, it was ridiculous to imagine the first thing he'd do is come looking for my mother and me and kidnap me. But that was what he'd done. I jerked and jerked against the chain, making a racket, hating the tears that clouded my eyes. How had I been so stupid? Why didn't I take those threats seriously? Why hadn't I told Nicholas?

Nick.

He must have been going crazy just then and blaming himself for everything. I'd have given anything to go back in time to stay by his side instead of leaving that house alone.

When people were in extreme situations, we always thought about the things we wished we'd said to the people we love or how stupid we'd been for worrying about idiotic little things now that we knew how dangerous life could actually be. I'd been kidnapped. That was something to really be worried about.

I heard someone open the door, and Ronnie appeared, causing me to shiver from head to toe.

"Good. You're awake," he said, closing the door behind him. The scant light was still bright enough to see his dark eyes, his lips, his shaved scalp. I could even see the new tattoo under his right eye: a horrifying snake. He walked over slowly and sat beside me on the bed. I pulled away from him as much as I could in the tiny space available to me.

"I gotta tell you, it sure turns me on seeing you chained up in this bed and completely at my mercy," he said, eyeing me up lustily. I cursed the hour when I'd decided to put on that tight dress, but now all I could do was try to control my breathing and my fear. "I don't know if you know this, but you got a bangin' body." He rested a hand on my bare ankle. I tried to push it away, but he pressed me into the mattress.

He could do anything he wanted to me.

"You know what? When I decided to race against you, it never crossed my mind you might be the daughter of a NASCAR driver.

I was pissed when you beat me. If I remember right, you told me I was a dumbass and I should learn how to drive."

His hand climbed up my leg.

"Don't touch me," I ordered him, unable to get away. I wished this was all just a nightmare and I would wake up in Nick's arms.

"Well, this dumbass is about to get his revenge for that night, bae," he said. By now, his hand was on my thigh. I shifted aside, but he got on top of me, and I struggled under his hips. Tears were running down my cheeks. "I'll bet your little boyfriend won't even take one look at you once I'm done. I'm gonna tear that thing up so bad he won't want it back."

"*Help!*" I shouted desperately, trying to get him off me. He laughed, holding me down with one hand while he took off his belt with another.

"Can't no one hear you, stupid. No one who cares, anyway," he said, leaning down and running his tongue over my breasts.

I turned my head away in desperation.

"*Don't touch me!*" I shrieked.

He grabbed me around the neck and pushed me down into the mattress with one hand, and with the other, he pulled up my dress.

"*No!*" I shrieked, nearly tearing my vocal cords. "*Let me go!*"

The hand around my neck squeezed tighter, and I could hardly breathe.

"I'm gonna put it in you every which way, and you're gonna stay nice and quiet," he hissed, bringing his face close to mine. When he did so, his grip softened just enough for me to scream:

"*Get me out of here!*"

Then the door opened. The flickering red light from outside filled the room, and what I saw then scared me even more than my would-be rapist: my father was there, looking terrifying.

"That's enough. Scram," said that voice that had petrified me as a little girl, the voice that had threatened my mother thousands of times and that still pursued me in my dreams—the only voice I'd heard that night I was beaten nearly to death, the voice that haunted me as I had escaped through the window...

Ronnie cursed, and before getting up, he slapped me across the face. It was so quick I didn't see it coming, and it stung.

"Nah, now it's enough," he said, getting in my father's face and then walking out.

My father didn't say a word, just stood there in the doorway watching. Only after a moment did I dare look up. He'd changed... His hair used to be blond like mine. Now it was white and cut very short. His arms were twice as big as before and covered in tattoos. Whatever he'd been doing those past few years had changed his appearance entirely. He was now even scarier than Ronnie.

My father shut the door behind him, grabbing the chair in the corner and turning it around, sitting with his arms propped on the backrest.

"You sure have grown, Noah. It's...incredible how much of your mother I see in you."

All the fear and pressure I'd felt when he was near had returned after six years.

"The night they arrested me," he said, staring me straight in the eye, "I lost absolutely everything...and it was all your fault. What I still can't figure out is how a little girl managed to do that to me. Not even your mother could stop me when I took my frustrations out on her... But with you, it was always different. You were my little girl. I loved you. I promised myself I'd never hurt you. You weren't like your mother. You were a fighter. You'd make sure your voice was heard."

"What do you want?" I asked, trying to control the sobs rising in my throat.

"What every man in this world wants most, Noah," he responded with a horrible smile on his lips. "You took everything

I had…your mother, my home, my freedom… I want money, the same money that's supporting my family right now. I thought it would be hard to find you all, but the only thing it took was looking that bastard up on the internet, and there you were, all standing there like a happy family. When I got here, I figured out your new brother didn't run with the highest class of people. I was following him, and I saw him and Ronnie get into a fight in a bar. After that, all I had to do was tell the kid my plan and he was in."

I couldn't believe what I was hearing. My father was crazy. Prison had damaged him.

"I'm going to get everything I can out of that scumbag who stole my wife, not to mention that little shit who's been feeling you up all week."

So he had been following me… I'd thought it was my imagination, but now I knew I was right. They'd been planning this for some time, and my father had tortured me with those letters, knowing he scared me more than anything in the world.

I looked at the face of the man who had given me life but nothing more. I hated him, I hated him with every fiber of my being… If I ever had loved him, that love had vanished the moment he'd laid hands on me.

"William Leister's a thousand times the man you are. You're worthless, You think you're special because you can beat up a woman? I hate you! And you're so stupid, I'll bet the only thing you'll get out of this is another trip to jail, where you should spend the rest of your miserable life."

I didn't even stop to breathe. I didn't care what he did to me. For a moment, he just sat there and listened, and his face showed a succession of feelings that finally ended in rage.

He got up and slapped me across the face. It stung, but I wasn't going to let him know that. I never thought he'd touch me again, but even now that six years had passed and I'd gone to another country, he'd found me and was punishing me again.

The second blow came right afterward, splitting my lip. I could feel the blood drain down my chin.

"Don't open your damn mouth again," he said, turning around and walking out. My nerves were frayed, and now, the tears started to flow.

———

I don't know how much time passed, but the physical and mental exhaustion of the previous few hours made me fall asleep. Then I was shaken awake and something was stuck to my ear.

"Talk," my father said in a rage.

There was only one person I would have given everything to be with just then. I'd dreamed of him, and the mere thought that he might be listening made me want to cry until I had no strength left. I needed him. I wanted him to save me, to break through that door and wrap me in his strong arms. I wanted him, him and no one else.

"Nicholas," I whispered. A second later, they took the phone away and left me alone.

46

Nick

I WAS DESPERATE. I COULDN'T TAKE THE PRESSURE A MINUTE MORE. That fear burning me inside was so intense that I wanted to tear my own heart out to keep it from aching. There had to be something I could do; we couldn't just let that bastard take the money and maybe not even give us Noah back. Surely there was something I wasn't thinking of, some detail, but I couldn't imagine what. Dawn was an hour away, and I didn't know if I could hold out without going to look for her in town myself. My house was full of people, and not one of them seemed to know what to do next. Some said my father should go hand over the money on his own with the police following close behind. But what if Noah's bastard father caught on and decided to do something to her? He was sick in the head; he'd crossed a continent just to kidnap his daughter and ask for a ransom. There was probably nothing he wasn't capable of.

I got up from the chair in my father's office and went upstairs. I needed to be close to something Noah had touched, smell her clothes, be in her room. I was so scared, I would have given my own life to know she was all right.

When I opened the door, I saw her mother. Her eyes were swollen from so much crying, and she was hugging one of the sweatshirts

Noah had put on a million times. It had the Dodgers' logo on it. I didn't know why the hell she had it, she wasn't even from here, but that was just Noah: strange, perfect. And dammit, I loved her. If anything happened to her, I wasn't sure how I could go on living.

Raffaella looked over from the window where she was standing, and for a second, her eyes lit up.

"I know what you've been hiding from me," she said without any feeling whatsoever. I stopped, unsure how to reply. "I don't know what your feelings for her are, Nicholas, but Noah is my life. She's suffered a lot. She doesn't deserve what's happening." She brought a hand to her mouth to silence her sobs. "It's been years since I've seen her as happy as she's been these past few days. And now…all I know is you had something to do with that, and I want to thank you for it."

I shook my head, sitting on the foot of the bed in despair. I couldn't hear those words, I couldn't, not knowing it had all been my fault… I had taken her to the races; it was my fault she'd met Ronnie, but what I couldn't understand was how her father and that asshole had gotten together and plotted to kidnap the love of my life.

"Noah was always very mature, ever since she was a little girl. She saw things a person should never see, and she never backed down from anybody. With you, she seemed like a different person."

Emotions began flooding over me. Fear, sorrow, desolation. I'd never felt so miserable in my whole life. My eyes grew moist, and all I could do was let the tears flow down my cheeks.

Raffaella helped me up and wrapped her arms around me. Her hug felt strong—the hug of a mother. Raffaella might have made mistakes in the past, but she loved her daughter and would never abandon her. For the first time in my life, I felt like I had a family.

She let me go, still holding Noah's sweatshirt, and stepped back. I made a promise to her.

"I swear to you I won't let anything happen to her. I'm going to find her." I said this as calmly as I could.

She nodded as I turned around and walked to my room.

Where are you, Noah?

I paced back and forth while my thoughts assailed me. Not until I saw the miniature car Noah had given me for my birthday did it hit me. I grabbed it and looked at the note.

I'm sorry about your car, for real. Someday, I'll buy you a new one. Happy birthday. Noah.

Buy me a new one... Technically, the car was still mine. It was registered in my name; I still had the title.

When that hit me, I couldn't believe it. I turned and ran down to my father's office. He was in his chair talking to the police and his security chief, Steve.

I couldn't help feeling excited. If I was right, we were going to be able to find out where Noah was.

"Dad," I said as I went in. He and Steve turned to me. They looked tired after a sleepless night, but both where alert and tense, ready for whatever had to happen.

"What is it?" my father said.

"I think I know how we can find her," I said, praying I wasn't wrong. "Around a month and a half ago, I lost my car in a bet. It's a black Ferrari. I bought it two years ago."

My father grimaced.

"Nicholas, I don't have time for your bullshit right now," he replied, but I ignored him.

"Ronnie took the car," I continued, looking now at Steve. "The car's got a tracking chip the insurance company installed when I bought it. If we can find the car..."

It was silent for a few seconds.

"Then we find Noah," Steve said, finishing my sentence.

47

Noah

MY ENTIRE BODY HURT AFTER NOT BEING ABLE TO MOVE FOR SO many hours. I'd nodded off a few times, but never for more than a few minutes. I didn't know what was going on, but I knew I needed to get out. The incessant pounding of the music in the background was exhausting me, not to mention that claustrophobic room with barely any light.

When light started shining through the window, I started to realize maybe no one would find me. And that made me cry again. Fear flooded my body.

Ronnie was back. He was at the foot of the bed. He'd been tormenting me by turning off the red light outside the room. He'd left me in the dark for long minutes that were the most terrifying of my life, knowing he was there with me in the blackness and could do whatever he wanted with me and I couldn't defend myself, couldn't run. I heard the echo of his giggles in my head as I wept and begged for him to turn on the light.

When he left, I tried to calm down for a long time. The music outside had died down, and all I could her now was my own breathing. Then a noise came from upstairs. It sounded like a crowd of people was stomping overhead. People outside shouted, and I heard gunfire and more voices. My heart skipped a beat, and I went stiff. My father appeared in the doorway, sweating, with a terrifying look on his face.

He hurried over and freed me from the chain. Then I saw something that made me jerk away. He pressed the barrel of his pistol painfully into my ribs and told me as I froze:

"Don't you dare move a muscle."

"Please," I begged between sobs. That man was capable of anything.

"Shut up!" he commanded, pushing me toward the door and down a long hallway. I couldn't see, I was scared, and I struggled just to put one foot in front of the other. I was defenseless and had no idea what to do.

He went on pushing me until we reached another door. I could tell there were people around, but I didn't know how far away. When I heard someone shout *Police!*, my hope was reborn. Thank God, they'd found me!

The light scorched my eyes as my father pushed me outside and into an abandoned parking lot. What he didn't expect was that there would be twenty or more cops stationed there with their weapons pointed straight at us. My father pulled me into him and brought the pistol up to my temple.

"Drop the gun!" someone shouted into a megaphone. Tears rolled down my face, and my eyes roved the scene, trying to find the person who could make all this make sense.

"If they get me, I'm taking you with me, little girl," my father whispered in my ear.

I said nothing. My voice failed me as I laid eyes on him: Nicholas was next to one of the police cars, and when he saw me, he shouted my name. My mother and William were next to him, and all I wanted was to be with the three of them for the rest of my life. They were my family. I knew that now. After seeing what my father was capable of, whatever part of me blamed myself for putting him in jail vanished forever. He wasn't my father, he never would be, and I didn't need him. I had a man in my life who loved me above all else, and it was time for me to love him the way he deserved.

"Drop your weapon and put your hands on your head!" a cop shouted, his voice clear over the commotion.

"Please…let me go," I whispered. I didn't want to die. Not this way. I still had a million things to live for.

Then something happened. It was all very fast. My father said no, his weapon clicked, and it pushed harder into the side of my head. He was going to shoot me, my father was going to kill me, and there was nothing I could do. An explosion made me close my eyes. I waited for the pain to come…but it never did.

The powerful arms that had been holding me let me go, and I felt him fall beside me. I looked right, and all I saw was red… Blood spread across the ground next to the inert body of the man who had given me life.

The first thing I did was turn and take off running.

———————

I didn't know where exactly I was going; my mind was in a trance, completely blank except for one thought: run, run. And I did it, and I didn't stop until my body struck something hard. Arms wrapped around me, and I felt a familiar body and smelled a comforting scent, and all at once, I was calm.

"Oh, God," Nick said, squeezing me into him. He lifted me off the ground, and knowing I was in his arms, I realized I was going to be all right. I would never have to fear for my safety as long as a man like Nicholas was there. I would never have to tremble in fear because he'd raised his voice, I'd never have to worry about what

I did or said. He loved me more than his own life, and he would never be capable of putting a hand on me.

He pushed me away slightly to look at my face, and I couldn't help but grimace from the pain when he touched my cracked lip.

"Noah…" He looked me in the eyes as he said my name. I saw agony in his expression, relief at the awareness I was safe, blind hatred at the knowledge that I'd been hurt. All I needed was to feel him there, and I didn't care that it stung when his lips touched mine.

"There'll be time for that, babe," he said, cupping my face. "I love you, Noah. So, so much."

I felt so many things when I heard that. The tears returned, and a shaking overtook my legs as the adrenaline that had been flooding my body started to drain away. My mother showed up and squeezed me tightly, taking me briefly away from Nick. I hugged her close; again I felt at home, but it hurt me, too, knowing she'd had to suffer when our past had come back this way.

"My baby," she said, her tears wetting my cheek. "I'm sorry, I'm so sorry," she kept repeating.

"It's okay, Mom," I assured her, knowing what she needed me to say.

William was there, too. Our eyes met over my mother's shoulder. I nodded when I saw tears in his eyes. He came over and wrapped his arms comfortingly around both of us.

When we were done with the embraces, I couldn't help but look back at my father. They were carrying him into an ambulance. He'd been hit in the side of the chest. I had no idea if he was alive, but I didn't think about it. Just afterward, I saw the police taking Ronnie out of the house. He was unharmed and in handcuffs. As I was trying to absorb all that was happening before my eyes, Nicholas grabbed my chin softly and turned my face toward his.

"Look at me," he said in the softest voice I'd ever heard. His eyes were red and swollen. He'd suffered as much as I had. I needed him close to me after that experience, to put myself back together, to reassemble all that my father's actions had shattered. "It's okay," he continued. "You're with me now."

His words eased my heart, finally.

"I love you," I said as a strange feeling came over me. I don't know if it was exhaustion or just the stress of all that had happened those past few hours, but I couldn't go on anymore. I grabbed onto his T-shirt as my legs gave out, and I closed my eyes, letting the sweet tranquility of unconsciousness bear me away.

4 8

Nick

WHEN WE CONFIRMED THAT THE CAR STILL HAD THE GPS CHIP active, it was just a matter of time till we found Noah. Or so I hoped. There was always the chance that Ronnie didn't have the car parked wherever they were keeping Noah, but I couldn't let that stop me. I knew he'd hardly been seen without that car lately, so there was a good chance he'd locked her up somewhere in the dingy club the GPS showed the car was parked at.

My father spoke to the cops, who planned what our next step should be. His office was swarming with people. Several agents were looking over the blueprints of the club with Steve. The most likely thing was that they had her in the basement on the west side of the building. If we cornered them, blocking off the main exits, her father could only get out one way, and that was the fire exit in the back. That was where the rest of the unit would wait, and if he came out, there'd be no turning back. That son of a bitch would be back in jail way earlier than he'd anticipated.

"There's always a chance he won't come out, though, that he'll block himself off inside," one cop said, pointing at the room where we assumed Noah was trapped.

"Then knock down the fucking door!" I shouted. I wanted to leave right then; who knew what they were doing to her while we were sitting there chitchatting. She could be wounded or even worse.

"Mr. Leister, leave the work to us," the cop replied with an air of authority.

I hated how they were talking to me, making decisions about Noah's life. But there was nothing I could do.

I walked out and lit what must have been my two hundredth cigarette of the day. All kinds of people were gathered on the porch. Near the gate, beside the fountain, were at least seven squad cars, and dozens of agents stood on the perimeter. The media was there, too, setting up cameras outside the gate. I wanted to puke.

"He could kill her, William!" I heard someone shout.

I ran inside and saw the police rushing out of my father's office and toward their cars. Desperately, I looked at Raffaella, who was crying and clutching my father's arm.

"Easy, now, Ella, he's not going to do that. We know where they are. I promise, he's not going to do anything," my father said, trying to calm her down.

"What's happening? Where are they going?" I asked.

"We were able to access the cameras at the club. They're there, Nicholas. The officers are headed over now."

My entire body froze in panic.

"I'm not sticking around here then," I said and turned toward the door. A hand stopped me.

"You're not going, Nicholas," my father said sternly.

What the hell was he saying?

"I'm not staying!" I shouted, pulling away from him and running down the stairs. Some of the cops were already gone, departing for a mission that might end my girlfriend's life.

"Raffaella!" my father shouted behind me. As I turned, I saw Noah's mother coming toward me.

"Take me with you, Nicholas," she said, crying uncontrollably, but with steely determination on her face.

I looked hesitantly at my father, who came up to us with the expression of a man frightened but completely under control.

"I'm not going to let him hurt anyone else in this family," he roared, grabbing Raffaella's elbow. I knew he was just as scared as we were. Nothing like this had ever happened to us before. The way he was looking at Raffaella was exactly like the way I looked at Noah, and I would have reacted no differently if she had been determined to take off for the scene of a kidnapping.

"I'm going, William Leister, whether you want me to or not. This is my daughter we're talking about!" she shrieked in desperation. Her sobs eventually got the better of him.

I looked back at him.

"I'm going, Dad. Don't try to stop me."

In desperation, he replied, "Fine. But let's go with the cops."

Ten minutes later, we were crossing the city followed by three police cars. Listening to them exchange information over the radio was fraying my nerves. Some officers were already there and casing the exits.

We arrived quickly, and the patrol car went straight to where they were expecting Noah's father to come out. The police fanned out around the door. We could hear the noise inside...and when I heard shots, I got out.

The cop next to me clutched my arm.

"Stay here," he said.

I did as he ordered, staring at the door Noah would come out of, wondering if she would be hurt when she did.

We didn't have to wait long. After ten tense minutes, the door flew open, and Noah and her father appeared, blinking with surprise at the detachment there waiting for them.

Noah was hurt...bleeding.

I felt someone grabbing me from behind. I hadn't even realized I'd tried to take off running.

"*Noah!*" I shouted as loudly as I could. Her teary, terrified eyes turned toward mine. Her father was holding her with one hand while with the other, he aimed a revolver directly at her head.

"Drop the gun!" one of the cops shouted through a megaphone.

I clutched my head in despair. That bastard was saying something, and the terror on Noah's face awakened a killer instinct I never knew I could feel before that moment.

I was going to kill him. I was going to kill him with my bare hands.

"Drop your weapon and put your hands on your head!" someone shouted.

After that, everything happened quickly, though my eyes saw it all in slow motion.

Noah's father took off the safety and pressed the barrel hard into Noah's temple. She closed her eyes, and the sound of a police officer's shot filled the entire space.

Noah's father turned toward us. I knew he was looking at Raffaella when she started to cry desperately. Red blood stained his shirt, and he fell to the ground, badly wounded. Noah looked at him with surprise, then up at me, stunned...and then she started to run.

I pushed aside the cop holding me back and ran to meet her.

Only when I felt her in my arms could I breathe easily again. Only when I felt her body against mine was I sure she was alive.

"God!" I shouted, lifting her off the ground and squeezing her tightly. Her sobs intensified as I did so, trying to cover her with my body, protect her with my life.

I set her down and frantically searched every inch of her body. I looked at her face. They'd beaten her... Dammit! They'd beaten her!

I started to shake all over. I'd let someone hurt her. I'd promised her nothing bad would ever happen to her, and now I saw with my own eyes that I'd failed her.

"Noah" I said, trying to control my voice. I wanted to ask her to forgive me, to apologize for letting that happen. I didn't think I'd ever felt so guilty for something or as profoundly wounded as I did when I saw the girl I loved with bruises and cuts on her face.

She wrapped her hands around my neck and pulled me close enough to press her lips against mine. I wanted to kiss her more than anything in the world, but I worried I would hurt her if I did it too hard.

I pushed her back softly.

"There'll be time for that, babe," I said, cupping her face. "I love you, Noah. So, so much."

Two more tears fell from her eyes, but she smiled. Then Raffaella came over and took her daughter in her arms. I watched them hug desperately. My father looked at me a moment and then joined them, and I knew nothing like this would ever happen again. I could see in my father's face the promise that no one would ever, *ever* touch our family again.

When Noah's mother let her go, she turned to watch them load her father into the ambulance. I didn't know how to describe what I saw on her face then, but I did see the fear return when the police guided a handcuffed Ronnie out the door.

"Look at me," I told her. I didn't want her to be scared again. I wanted to kill that bastard, but more violence was the last thing Noah needed now. "It's okay. You're with me now."

Her hands touched my cheeks and slid down to my shoulders, and I saw her eyes lose focus.

"Noah?" I said, holding her up as she went slack in my arms. "Get a doctor!" I shouted when she didn't come to. I picked her up, and terror invaded me. Had she been shot? Did she have some internal wound no one knew about?

"Wake up, Noah," I said, holding her tightly against me until I reached another ambulance.

"Let me," a paramedic said. Police sirens began to wail, and Raffaella and my father came up behind me.

"What's wrong with her?" I asked. They took her from my arms and laid her on a stretcher, and paramedics gathered around and lifted her into the ambulance.

"We're taking her to the hospital. Are you her mother?" they asked Raffaella, and she nodded, climbing into the ambulance.

"I'm going, too," I said, not leaving room for discussion.

"I'll follow you all in my car," my father said.

The ambulance ride lasted an eternity. Noah was still unconscious, but after looking her over quickly, one of the paramedics said there was nothing to be concerned about.

I leaned over her and carefully ran a hand through her hair.

"I'm sorry, Noah. I'm sorry."

49

Noah

WHEN I OPENED MY EYES, I WAS IN A HOSPITAL BED. MY HEAD and face hurt, but my mind was relaxed once I saw who was there with me.

"At last, you're awake!" Nicholas exclaimed, kissing my hand, which he was holding.

"What happened?" I asked, with no idea how I'd gotten there.

"You fainted," he said, his worried eyes staring at me. "The doctors said it was psychological exhaustion. They gave you some pills. You were worn out."

I nodded, trying to take everything in. I remembered what had happened, the kidnapping, the blows I'd received from my father and Ronnie, the moment when I thought my father had shot me, when he'd fallen to the ground bleeding...

"What happened to him?" I asked.

Nicholas knew immediately what I meant.

He hesitated for a moment and then finally spoke.

"He didn't make it, Noah... The bullet pierced his heart. He died before he got to the hospital."

It was strange. Maybe there was something inside me that

was broken, but I felt nothing, absolutely nothing. Just relief, an infinite relief, and a weight lifted off my chest. A weight I'd borne for almost a decade.

"It's all over," Nick said, getting up from the chair by my bed and bringing his face close to mine. "No one can hurt you anymore. I'm going to take care of you, Noah."

I felt my eyes watering.

"I never thought things would turn out like this. I never thought I'd be thanking the stars for bringing our parents together. Two months ago, everything you represented was hell for me. And now…" I got up on my knees in bed and touched his face, and he wrapped his hands carefully around my waist. "I love you, Nick. I love you like crazy."

His lips kissed mine, gently but with the full force of the love that had grown between us. The kind of love that happened only once in a lifetime, the kind of love that touched your heart and never left you, the kind of love nothing else compared to, a love we sought, a love we may even have hated, but that made us alive, that made us need each other, that turned us into something the other person couldn't live without…the love that I had just found.

EPILOGUE

Nick

"Don't you dare open your eyes," I warned her as I brought her to the middle of the room. Having her there gave me a joy I couldn't express in words. The change she'd made in my life was a new beginning in our relationship, but that was something I needed, and it would wind up being a good thing, enabling us to spend all the time we needed together.

"You know I hate surprises," she reminded me, wriggling around. I smiled to myself.

"You'll like this one," I said, posting myself behind her. "Okay…now!" I took off her blindfold.

She looked astonished as she saw what lay before her. We were in the entryway of the penthouse condo I'd just bought, and she could see the doorways to the bedroom, the kitchen, and the living room. It wasn't big, just enough for one person to live comfortably, but it was a nice apartment. A family friend had decorated it to my taste, and it looked amazing. The brown and white tones gave it a homey, modern feel. I'd had a fireplace built in the center of the living room in front of the chocolate-colored sofa where Noah and I could watch movies and relax by ourselves. The kitchen was compact, but it had everything we needed, including an island perfect for two people to have breakfast together. There were thick rugs on the hardwood floors and a huge window with amazing views of the city. At that moment, the dark night meant the lights were glowing like a carpet of stars.

Noah's mouth was open slightly as she looked around in amazement.

"So...what do you think?"

She shook her head. She needed a moment to find the words.

"Is it yours?" she asked, walking to the sofa and resting a hand on the back of it. When she turned around, she had an expression I would struggle to describe: confused, worried maybe.

"I mean, I'm going to live here, but you're going to spend most of your time here with me. That's why I bought it, so we could be together without anyone coming between us," I said, walking over. I liked seeing her there. Her presence made it feel like a real home.

A second later, a smile crossed her face.

"It's amazing!" she shouted. But I could see in her eyes that she was hiding something.

I stroked her hair, tucked it behind her ears, and took her face in my hands.

"What is it?" I asked. Her expression worried me.

She shook her head and exhaled.

"It's just that I'm going to miss seeing you every day," she said, leaning her head against my chest. I was going to miss her, too: I loved getting up and having breakfast with her, I adored seeing her before she'd fixed her hair, always ready with a smile, and, of course, I loved knowing she was safe and sound behind our locked door. All that would change now that I was moving, but it had to be that way, I knew that. Living with my father and being in love with his stepdaughter was madness. We almost never felt fully comfortable, we were almost never alone with each other, and now that I had my own place, I could see Noah all the time without parental supervision.

"I will, too," I said, "but it's something we need to do. I can't stand seeing you every day and not being able to do this when I feel like it," I said, kissing those perfect lips. "Or this." I kissed her deeper, my tongue wrapping around hers with all the passion she awakened in me. She responded right away, and in a split second, desire had taken over my body. That was the effect she had on me. "Or this." I picked her up, and she wrapped her legs around me, giggling.

"Or this," I said, tugging off my T-shirt with one hand.

I groaned as I felt her hands on my shoulders and neck. I walked to what was now my new bedroom, with its huge bed and incredible views, dropping her on the soft pillows and unbuttoning her white shirt.

"I think you've convinced me. I like your new place." She sighed, letting me kiss every centimeter of her skin.

"I knew you would," I said, reaching her lips.

At that moment, I realized that this woman would be beside me forever. I loved her above all else, and she had rescued me from the black hole my life had been before I'd met her. It had taken us time to understand, but now we were together and would work to make our relationship grow. Our lives hadn't been easy, and that was why we understood each other so well. At a critical moment, in the eye of the storm, we had each been the other's lifesaver, and that was not something easy to find.

A few hours later, when I had her sleeping in my arms, I realized something very important. The lights were out, the shades drawn... and Noah was sleeping with a look of utter relaxation on her face, without a trace of fear. I realized then that I had helped her, too, that I also had caused a radical change in her life. That had been my fault.

Acknowledgments

If someone had told me a year ago that today I'd be writing the acknowledgments for my own book, I'd have told them they were crazy. Since I was fifteen, I've dreamed of this moment, the moment when I could say *I did it*.

First of all, I want to thank Penguin Random House for trusting me. My editor Rosa Samper, who almost gave me a heart attack the day she emailed me. You spoke to me like a friend and gave me the best gift anyone's ever given me. I'll never forget that offer reaching my inbox. Thanks to you and everyone else who made *My Fault* something spectacular.

To my agent Nuria, the first person to tell me the book had potential, thank you for guiding me and helping me with everything I need.

To my mother, for praising absolutely everything I write. I always tell you that you aren't impartial, but I guess you're here to make me feel like I am the best. Thanks for being the very definition of a perfect mother.

To my father, for swelling with pride and telling absolutely everyone his daughter is a writer. Thank you for being my rock and never giving up in the face of any adversity. You taught me that no goal is impossible if you work hard enough.

To my sisters, Flor, Belu, and Ro. We want to kill each other, but we love each other like crazy.

To my cousin Bar, my very first reader. I couldn't have finished this story without your help and enthusiasm.

To my grandparents. Pitu, thanks for helping me whenever I asked you for advice; Abu, thanks for always being there.

To my friends, Ana, Alba, that group that begins with Z. Thanks for making me laugh out loud, for staying together even though you've all taken different paths. I grew up with you and I'll always carry you in my heart.

Eva, Mir. What can I tell you that you don't already know? I never thought I'd find two kindred spirits in the department. Thanks for being by my side since the beginning of this adventure.

To my Yellow Crocodile. Belén, thank you for sharing your passion for reading with me. From the beginning, you believed in this story and supported me unconditionally.

Anita, you taught me that dreaming is an important word. You taught me that believing in dreams makes us who we are. You'll always be my partner on the journey that began with that trip to Los Angeles.

To everyone who was there with me on Wattpad in the beginning. None of this would have happened without you. I've stayed up until the wee hours of the morning reading your comments. I never thought I'd get so much love from you. We're united by what we've achieved together. I wish I could meet all of you and give you a hug.

And last but not least, thank you, the readers of my first novel, my dream in letters, paper, and ink. Enjoy!

About the Author

Mercedes Ron always dreamed of writing. She began by publishing her first stories on Wattpad, where more than 50 million readers were hooked on her books, and made the leap to bookstores in 2017 with Montena's imprint, launching the Culpables saga, a publishing phenomenon that has been translated into more than ten languages and will have its own movie adaptation by Amazon Prime. Her success was followed by the sagas Enfrentados (Ivory and Ebony) and Dímelo (Tell Me Softly, Tell Me Secretly, Tell Me with Kisses), which consolidated the author as a benchmark in youth romantic literature with more than a million copies sold.